About the Author

Sophie Cloud's particular interest lies in the idiosyncrasies of a person's character after studying Psychology at university, which she has channelled into *Orange Lilies of Dallington Place*.

With the light and shade of her characters, it brings a new and never-ending fast-paced story.

Sophie loves the meaning of people's names and places and is always fascinated by the coincidences that have appeared whilst working on the story.

Sophie's other interests are military charitable causes, and the history of Britain, France and America has fuelled her desire to write the book.

Coupled with her poetic skill set, her knowledge of the era has brought exciting experiences and opportunities which are woven into her novel.

Sophie Cloud resides in London with her family.

4th August 2018,

Orange Lilies of Dallington Place

Dear Katia,

Best Wishes

Sophie Cloud
xxx

Sophie Cloud

Orange Lilies of Dallington Place

Olympia Publishers
London

www.olympiapublishers.com
OLYMPIA PAPERBACK EDITION

A CIP catalogue record for this title is
available from the British Library.
ISBN: 978-1-84897-959-8

This is a work of fiction.
Names, characters, places and incidents originate from the writer's
imagination. Any resemblance to actual persons, living or dead, is purely
coincidental.

First Published in 2018

Olympia Publishers
60 Cannon Street
London
EC4N 6NP
Printed in Great Britain

Acknowledgement

I would like to thank my son for his patience and kindness whilst I wrote this book.

Also for Alison, my creative writing teacher who encouraged me at the beginning of my journey, writing the *Orange Lilies of Dallington Place.*

Kindly nurse,
Sacrificing soldier,
I hear the thunder of war
calling me back to the trenches.

Bertram Wright

Dedication

For Barnes

'Ennobled Pilot, you win. Chapfallen we have become.'

By Bertram Wright

Robert, a fictional character representing all those brave men and women that served in the Great War

They cut down a line of lime trees, just where the beginning of
the soil
was turned over to make way for the racecourse railings.
A racecourse as fine as Deauville's, just where the orange lilies
bobbed in the wind.
As if to say yes, this is the future of Dallington Place.

CHAPTER ONE
KATHRYN, THE MAID 1916

This was the time of starchiness, harshness and much needed level-headedness, and Kathryn Beaumont possessed the latter in reams. One did not have time to reflect or waste time. Life was a constant reflex of duty. Duty above all else. Although late into a dusky evening, a little housemaid of Dallington Place lowered her head over a small and liquefying candle to eagerly devour each word of the latest letter and reflect on the news she had received from Bertram, her fiancé in Ypres in France. Kathryn was delighted to be able to spend a few minutes thinking of them and indulge in her lover's words. Kathryn, not yet seventeen and only five feet one inches in stature, seemed to rise to any challenge the Fitch family of Dallington Place set her. As she put down the letter and blew the candle out, walking to her little bed in the servants' quarters, she remembered her first days at the house. How nervous a young girl she had been, almost one year ago, unwitting but not perturbed to the fact that this was her fate and her future. She trusted her mother with all her heart, who wisely had thought Dallington Place to be the best place for her. It would keep Kathryn in good manner and health, her mother had explained. A welcome position as a housemaid in a good household was not easily come by. This was an opportunity for Kathryn as her mother was recently widowed and she was left without a father and an income.

As she pulled the thin eiderdown around her, she took a quick glance at the smouldering candle. It was safely snuffed out. Kathryn shuddered as lying back; she recalled her second day at Dallington Place. She was pleasantly complacent to her new surroundings and the challenges of the house. Whilst cleaning near the hearth of the Great Hall, her lower skirt had caught fire by a cinder that had tumbled out of the hearth. Luckily for her, Mrs Potts the housekeeper, who had been passing by an open window, quickly assessed the situation and, with much haste, came to the aid of the unaware and shocked maid, extinguishing the fire before the flames rose any higher above her hemline. Kathryn had been strongly shaken and for a brief moment had wanted to run back to the safety of her mother's arms. She resisted with the help of a kindly talking to from Mrs Potts and a hot cup of sweet tea.

A greater challenge had now ensued for Kathryn. It was the Battle of the Somme. It was not her own mortality she worried about now but of the young men of England and her beloved Bertram. Her Bertram, young and not yet twenty-one, was doing his duty in France like any other young man worth his salt. How handsome she thought he looked in his uniform of the 35th Battalion of the South Downs. Her own uniform had been reliably replaced with much tutting and disapproving glares from the other young maids at Dallington Place. A jealous throng was set upon her when the Lady Rosalyn Fitch, lady of Dallington Place had taken to Kathryn's pleasing nature and poignantly lent her a pretty lilac dress until her uniform could be repaired and another altered to fit her size. 'Why do the others berate me so Mrs Potts?' Kathryn had asked the housekeeper who was folding some curtains at the time. She put down the heavy brocade and insisted that Kathryn follow her to the kitchen where they could talk privately. 'You do not see what I see my girl,' explained Mrs Potts to the forlorn maid. Kathryn looked up, her tear-stained face revealing too much despair a girl of her age should feel. She watched the bustling housekeeper sit down for once, looking her sharply in the eyes. 'Your Bertram of course, your fancy man has them all stirred up. If I am right, there is not a man that comes close to him in looks in all of Sussex, I should say. They are just jealous, that is all. Young Clara, Rose and Veronica, once they have a fancy man of their own, it will all be forgotten, mark my words,' she continued.

'Yes he is rather beautiful, is he not?' said Kathryn, now smiling with pride and drying her tears with the handkerchief Mrs Potts had given her. Kathryn stood up feeling better and ready to get back to work as she brushed imaginary crumbs from her new uniform. She had tried the cook's new recipe of a jam sponge cake. It was delicious and had given her some renewed energy. This was a hard lesson to swallow for not everyone in the household was glad to see her happy, she thought. 'By the way, your Bertram is a writer, is he not?' Mrs Potts called to Kathryn. 'A journalist,' called Kathryn back as she picked up the dustpan and brush and set to clean under the dining room table. 'Clever lad,' muttered Mrs Potts to herself, 'a journalist and a soldier, what a catch.'

Kathryn thought so too. As she busily swept with long sweeping movements, she pictured Bertram's face. How she loved the way his blond curly hair would fall onto his flashing green eyes and he would sweep the curl away nervously with his right hand when he spoke. Kathryn's own eyes would sparkle and light up when she thought of his face. She hoped Lady Fitch would not ask for the lilac dress back yet, so she could wear it on Sunday when Bertram came to take her out as he always did. She would ask Mrs Potts.

So it was to be. Kathryn was wearing the lilac dress for the last time and at ten o'clock Bertram came to call at the kitchen door. Always diligent in his pursuit of Kathryn and more in love than ever seeing her look so pretty, he strode out that day with his lady-love beside him. Kathryn with a new spring to her step, feeling rather beautiful in her floral dress. She thought of herself as rather middling in beauty but when she was with Bertram, he made her feel very beautiful. They would walk to the village, down the driveway and along the prickly hedgerows. Touching hands and fingers brushing each other with deliberate passion but not yet succumbing to the deliciousness of holding hands. Passers-by on their way to church would wonder who this handsome couple was, a soldier and his pretty maid. They would walk past the church and around the millpond and if the weather was clement, they would take a picnic to the other side of the village across the bridge. This bridge was their favourite place and often they had chased each other across it, acknowledging one day this bridge may just break. Its rickety and unsparing build carried this couple over the other side to where they could see Dallington Place in the distance. If they walked a little farther up a rather steep hill, they could see all the views of the South Downs and if the grass was not damp, they would omit to sit on the wooden seat by the bandstand and lay in the grass and picnic there instead.

Today the grass was dry and Kathryn careful not to mark her dress, had brought a light blanket with her, some left over fruit and some slices of the jam sponge cake. Bertram though, did not seem to be able to relax. He sat down alongside Kathryn and then the next minute he was pacing across the grass, looking at Dallington Place, and then across to the South Downs. His hand shielding his eyes from the wind as his hair was tossed wildly in the ever strengthening blast.

'Do you know it may just rain,' stated Bertram excitedly.

'Only you could look forward to such a change in weather, Bertram, please sit still and have something to eat, said Kathryn trying to convince Bertram to settle down next to her. But the agitated soldier could not. He walked over to the brow of the hill and stood with his back to the bewildered girl. Kathryn watched him carefully as she bit into a sharp apple. He turned to her and for a moment watched her bite into the apple and chew nonchalantly on the fruit.

'I am going to travel and make my fortune from my writings,' he declared. Kathryn put down her apple as he ran over to her and took her arms. 'Look over there, can you see the storm clouds brewing?' he said pointing in the distance over the hill.

'No, Bertram, I cannot,' replied Kathryn. She was not cross with his erratic behaviour but amused by it. Bertram had got his wish that day as just then small droplets of water could be felt on their hands, noses and heads. A crack of thunder in the distance made Bertram grab all the fruit and cake, throw it back into the basket and pull Kathryn to her feet. 'Follow me!' he called out running down the slope of the hill, the basket in one hand and beckoning with the other.

Kathryn did as he instructed and no sooner had they reached the bandstand it started to pour. 'Let us make it to the bridge,' smiled Bertram, as Kathryn caught up with him.

'Have we time?' she asked under her breath.

'Yes we have all the time in the world,' he replied taking her hand and pulling her along, gaining speed on other poor villagers, who had been caught out in the rainstorm.

As they ran alongside each other, Bertram turned to look at her as they dashed over the white, rickety bridge. They stopped abruptly at the end and Bertram decided to seize his moment and pull Kathryn down under the arches of the unstable frame, and careful not to get their feet wet, they stood on large, shiny, grey stepping stones to regain their composure. Wiping the rain out of his eyes and cupping Kathryn's face with his large hands, he stared longingly into her eyes. He held her gaze, which seemed to last an eternity. 'Would you Kathryn, travel with me and see the world?' he asked at last.

These words seem to jolt through Kathryn and shock her. She had never thought of something happening to her like this. 'Leave Sussex and all that I know?' she said, searching into his green eyes for reassurance and trust.

That next moment he knelt down into the muddy water dirtying his knee and asked for her hand in marriage. Kathryn accepted his proposal immediately, knowing this was the man she loved with all her heart, no matter where love took her. Bertram teased Kathryn that once the storm was over, they had better get on their way. He did not quite trust the strength of the little bridge with the barrage of water being pelted upon it. As he helped Kathryn up the slippery slope to the road and eyeing her generous mouth and pretty blue eyes, he probed her soul for the sign he needed. That she would love him forever, no matter what.

Kathryn's eyes grew heavy as she clutched his letter. Her tears had smudged some of the lines and she was cross with herself. She pulled the eiderdown tight around her face. 'What if she had never met him, what would she have to look forward to, she thought to herself. That day at the market was firmly entrenched in her mind. It was her sixteenth birthday, and her mother had sent her to the market to buy some cakes for tea. Her Aunt Silvia was arriving at two o'clock, and her mother reminded her not to take too long. Kathryn acknowledged her mother's words knowing her warning was thinly veiled with the worry. It was a Friday, a market day and the town square full of soldiers on leave for the weekend from the nearby barracks. Kathryn was enjoying her newfound freedom. She walked quietly and slowly past each stall relishing its wares and smiling inwardly that she was a woman now and not a girl anymore. There were many soldiers who noted her radiance that day, but none more than a young soldier called Bertram Wright, who had already noted her beauty a few months back whilst she shopped with her mother. Today on second glance by the town hall, he had fallen deeply in love. Kathryn used to the admiring glances, had long become accustomed to lowering her eyes and adverting her gaze. But today was different. She walked upright and proud and as he approached her, she passed him with a sweet smile and he was hooked. It was not just him that she smiled to, as each orange lapel of a uniform passed her and tipped their caps, she smiled a sweet smile at each and every one of them.

It was Bertram that followed her home that day, and not even her mother's fair possessiveness could keep the keen soldier at bay. He had found his lady-love and knocking on their door that day, a budding romance began to bloom with the invitation to an army ball that Christmas. He followed her to the doors of Dallington Place and every Sunday after that with much diligence to take her out.

Clara knocked on the door to wish Kathryn goodnight. Kathryn not wanting to speak to anyone, turned over pretending to be asleep and let the letter slip out of her hand. Hoping Clara had realised she was asleep; Kathryn was reminded of the knocking on the kitchen door two months previously. It was a cool March night and a night that disturbed her more than ever before. Bertram had not turned up that morning to take her out. She knew something was wrong and had clung to the hope he had been kept in for an extra duty. But in her gut she knew it was not this. Something had changed. The stiffness in the air, the quiet calm of that Sunday did not sit right and there in the barracks that sat below Dallington Place, a call for camaraderie and duty was being declared. Fright took hold of her, when she looked upon his unfamiliar uniform. A cloth heavier and one ready for duty, she knew what this meant. As she held onto the kitchen table gripping it with her fingers, where her own uniform had been repaired, and all the petty musings of wasted cloth spoken by the other maids were remembered. How could they even have those conversations when wastes of life were to be presented to them all, the spoils of war? The Somme was calling and neither lover could speak, their feet seemingly made of lead and their hearts pounding and cold.

Mrs Potts broke the silence, 'Go outside,' she ordered Kathryn, aware that the commotion could have woken others in the house. And this they did, slowly and quietly, just clutching each other's hands until they reached the outhouse behind the stables so Bertram could tell Kathryn his fate.

CHAPTER TWO
BERTRAM, THE SOLDIER

Quietly and stealthily, Bertram made his way back to the barracks late in the evening. He knew that his battalion would still be there getting ready to leave. He hoped that he was not missed, but on the other hand, a small part of him indulged in the fantasy that he had missed his chance to go to war. He would be grounded and sent to work on the home front. Maybe court-martialled or placed in office duties, map reading, general intelligence or whatever and wherever he was needed. But in his heart of hearts he knew as he crossed through the lower woods, he had not missed his chance to go to war. Kathryn would of course be pleased if he had stayed, but he wanted to leave, taste a different life for a while and then commit to married life. He had Kathryn now, his fiancé, and everything was falling into place. As he trod on damp, wet, sticky twigs in the undergrowth, he approached the gates of the barracks, a surge of excitement swelled in him now. Not a fear but of just accustoming himself to whatever fate would bring him. He liked this sense of danger, it suited him. This certain naivety did him justice, as he could not have imagined anything quite like what was going to befall him. As he placed his notepad into his yellow and green rucksack, he had no idea of the extreme and poignant memories he would write down on that parchment.

He had not been missed as he took his place in line late into the evening. His rucksack heavier than before, filled with food, spare boots and outerwear, made his back already ache as he watched his fellow soldiers smoke and chat in line. One army truck after another left for the port, brimming with young, excitable and impressionable men.

'St Omer it is then?' a man of no more than sixteen or seventeen asked an older soldier, Bertram observed. The young man with a cigarette firmly stuck between his lips, which he was chewing more than smoking, looked bleary-eyed and nervous.

'If that is all you have to worry about Weaves, then you are a lucky chap,' the older man replied. 'It is not where we are going but whether we do a good job when we get there. Do not you concern yourself with that right now. Looks like you could do with some kip if you ask me.'

A few older men crowded around the young lad and started laughing. Bertram, now annoyed by their bullish behaviour, asked the young Weaves for a light. The young man fumbled gladly in his jacket pocket, relieved of a friendly request. Bertram beckoned him towards him when two trucks appeared simultaneously, steering him clear of the other men as they boarded the first truck. Bertram nodded to him to get into the next one, aware he would not get any peace from the other men's ribbing if he took the first one.

'Do not take any notice of them, they are just a bit sore. They are leaving their loved ones, that is all,' said Bertram, offering him brotherly assurance.

'Maybe they are afraid of dying, cowards they are,' replied Weaves.

'We are all afraid of dying,' replied Bertram, puffing hard on his cigarette.

'I am not afraid to die for my country,' said Weaves shaking his head and biting the fingertips of his spare hand.

'Well, more fool you,' replied Bertram half smiling at the boy's absurdity. 'We are all afraid of dying!' continued Bertram, 'My name is Bertram Wright, newly fiancéd and writer from Hayward's Heath. And you are?' said Bertram extending his hand.

'Robert Alton Weaves from Bexhill-on-Sea originally, orphaned so I joined the South Battalion,' said young Weaves as if to report to his commanding officer.

Bertram nodded. There were many reasons men had signed up with the South Battalion. Many had stories to tell. 'By the way, none of us know where we are to be billeted. Maybe it is best not to know and see where this adventure takes us,' said Bertram now tired himself and rubbing his eyes as he watched Robert yawn and close his eyes. The truck stumbled over potholes and rough roads towards Dover. Both men fell quickly asleep.

It was early morning before any of the ten men in the truck were awoken by shouts and the noise of other vehicles pulling up close. With whistles being heard, screeching of brakes and slamming doors, Bertram strained his eyes to look at the view of the cliffs. He nudged the now awaking Weaves to pull himself to. For as quickly as they had stopped, they were being asked to board various boats to take them to France. Bertram was the first out and reached in his bag for a cigarette.

It was cold and damp and he shivered, he was unaware this cool discomfort was something he would get used to, and in fact would be so familiar it would become the normality. Pulling on his jacket as he held his cigarette between his teeth, he walked over to the far side of the docking station and eyed the "White Monsters", the cliffs.

Farewell to you, he said to himself as he got himself back in line. He hoped there would be somewhere he could relieve himself as they passed the men checking their personal papers before they set on water. Bertram took out his note pad and jotted a few things down, as he and the other men shuffled their way to the front. Bertram took in the cool air, closed his eyes for a moment, thinking about Kathryn and what she might be doing right now. Probably getting herself dressed and ready for another day. Another day of service, just like him. Which service was more worthwhile than the other, he thought. He thought of her in her uniform, her stockings and her neat shoes with the tiniest of heels. He tried to remember how she wore her hair for service, as he had only come to Dallington Place once whilst she was on duty. He imagined her flustered trying to tidy her unruly hair neatly in place so early in the morning, her face flushed with nerves at the thought of being late. Kathryn hated to be late for anything.

Late was what they were though. A hum of jangled nerves and frenzied activity lurched from one rank to another. Men shouting, and officers doing their best with their clipboards trying to trace names to faces and placing the men in the rank from most in charge to very young fledgling recruits. No one was being as friendly as they could have been. It was all about business and efficiency. With clipboards being held aloft in front of the officers' faces, paper blowing about in the now freezing wind, patience was being tested as men refused to move swiftly. Some had somehow managed to consume beer on the journey down and were being pulled out of line, and being reprimanded and their suitability revoked for the time being. The officer, a man in his fifties with the largest moustache Bertram had ever seen, was taking no prisoners. These men could be replaced in his eyes. There was always another eager soldier to take a place. It made Bertram shudder. He was already aware he was just another number, another body. He hoped his talents as a writer may just set him apart, may make his efforts more worthwhile than flesh and blood being thrown to enemy lines.

As the line moved forward, Bertram looked about for Robert Alton Weaves. He felt responsible for the young lad, having got him in the second truck. Everything about this mission felt as if timing was of the utmost importance. Miss a truck or a particular boat then your life was mapped out there and then. You would take the second boat available and where would that lead you? Would you survive? Bertram rubbed his forehead. Too much thinking, he thought to himself. Peering behind him in the dawn light he could not see the wretched boy. A man in front of Bertram had been pulled out of line and was being questioned. Bertram had the time to note a few more things down of interest. A friendly tap on his shoulder disrupted his writing and turning around noted it was Robert. A huge smile spread across his face. This young man, a face flushed with innocence was relieved to see him and Bertram was glad to find him too. It was unlike Bertram to form such an alliance in such a short space of time. It was apparent to him that any form of association was a comfort, a home from home situation gave him reassurance. He sighed an inward sigh just as they were checked and appointed on a boat together. Whilst they waited to board, Bertram wrote a letter and a poem to Kathryn, holding his pen tightly to the page he silently guarded his words from prying eyes.

March 1916, Dover

Dearest Kathryn, this is you.
My Lily by Bertram Wright

You will not wither whilst I am away.
My Lily,
as lilies of the field do not.
They grow, they do not toil too long and neither do they spin,
so stay upright and proud.
Do not bend in these hard times of ours.
Lilies bring you beauty, colour and fragrance.
My hardy fleur.
We cannot become like a weed and be cut down like her.
So we too need a little care,
to be beautiful and long-lived.
Do not bend in these hard times of ours.

KATHRYN

It was six weeks before Kathryn had heard any news from Bertram. Any news would have been a comfort. Just a short telegram would have sufficed so at least she would have known that he had arrived safely. The letter that had arrived was promptly placed into the envelope of her skirts for safekeeping until she had a free moment to read and slowly imagine where he was and what he was doing. This was six weeks too late in Kathryn's mind. It had been six weeks of turmoil and worry. She desperately wanted to write back and tell him all the things that were going on at the house. Now she could begin, and let the worry lift off on to the pages of her letter. Selfishly returning her fears and love to him. As she sat in the parlour and shutting the back door so the staff smoking outside could not disturb her, she unfolded the creased and rather worn looking letter and began to read.

April 1916, St Omer

My dearest Kathryn,
I can feel your anguish as I write this letter. It has been nearly two months since I have seen your pretty face and I can assure you darling that a day has not gone past that I have not wondered what you are doing and that you must be wondering where I am. I am well but life is far from easy. I fear this is a short letter as we have not been able to write until now, and we have to gather our letters to our loved ones by nine o'clock tonight. I have not had a moment's peace to write apart from scribble things down into my notebook to remind myself of the things I need to tell you, it has been all go. I want at this time to spare you some details, but right now the most important thing to say is that I am alive and fit for duty. Always hungry but that of course is me, and cold of course. We are hoping as May approaches fast, it will warm up here. In a couple of weeks I heard that some men including me from the regiment will be billeted and put out to stay in the local village. Once there I will write as often as I can, as I will be off-duty for two weeks (here is hoping). I need to rest now and give my letter to my commanding officer.

*Please keep safe and you can write to me here, to my regiment.
That is if we will receive them. I have enclosed a poem I wrote for you
'My Lily.'*
   Keep safely.
   Yours truly,
   Bertram

Kathryn stayed sitting as she folded the letter and placed it back
in her skirt. So relieved he was safe and well she wanted to cry, but
she knew she would be serving at dinner. It was nearly nine o'clock in
the evening and she had to keep strong. There was so much more she
wanted to know. Who he was with, were they defending themselves,
where were they sleeping, why was he so cold, she thought. Her
ignorance was childish but understandable, as she had no idea of the
horrors he was witnessing. Content in her thoughts that he was alive,
her palm now unclenched, she smoothed back her hair and went back
to her duties.

'You all right?' whispered Veronica as they shut the main door to
the dining room. Kathryn nodded.

'You received a letter? Cook said you did,' continued Veronica
pushing Kathryn to an inevitable reply.

'Yes thank you I did, and it was from Bertram. He is very well,'
replied Kathryn.

'Well, thank heavens for that, as I have heard they are dropping
like flies over there,' Veronica continued indiscreetly.

Kathryn held onto the doorknob a little longer than was necessary
and steadied herself. The only thing she wanted to do now was to
finish her duties and get to her own pen and paper and tell Bertram all
what was happening to her. Things were changing at Dallington Place
and she had her own selfish worries to write down on paper. If she did
not have a shoulder to cry on here, she would write down her worries.
She went down again to the kitchen to fetch some more bread.
Anything to get out of that dining room tonight. There were raised
voices and she knew what they were about. Fraught nerves and short
tempers were on show for all who would listen. The Fitch family were
not ones to hide their emotions but Kathryn did not want to get
involved. She was well aware of staff being let go. Money was tight
for everyone. She needed to hang onto her post as long as she could.
She was under no illusion now that her position as maid would not last
a lifetime. She had been hoping she would become a lady's maid, but

this seemed impossible now. Brushing her hair over and over again, she wondered who should she ask if she needed employment elsewhere. It was Friday and tomorrow would be busy, but on Sunday she would visit her mother and talk about her future once again. Life was so uncertain. The Fitchs had their own worries, even Lady Alison was causing quite a stir and striking out on her own in a friendship with an American. Kathryn's head began to ache. She wrapped her dressing gown around her, pulled the belt tightly and settled down to write her first letter to Bertram.

May 18ᵗʰ 1916

My Bertram,
What a relief to hear your voice in those tender words of yours. Thank you so much for the beautiful poem too. It made me want to cry. I am a delicate fleur, you are right. Without you I am anyway. I will stand tall for you though, and keep upright. Bertram, I am afraid though. Upright is one thing but I could be out of a job within a year. Who only knows. Some staff have been laid off already at Teddington Grand, you know that stately home in Rye. Veronica's cousin has lost her position there and is now out of work. I am going to enquire about what other work I could possibly do if the worst comes to the worst. I still have my mother to keep so I cannot be idle where these matters are concerned.
On a brighter more interesting note, there is much gossip to feed on and much hilarity for the staff to enjoy. You see, Lady Alison is engaged to a land farmer in Hollimsworth, a man apparently of much wealth and cattle. Their family is only two generations in England, so I use the word American loosely. Stedford is the man's family name. Ned Stedford's grandfather was a cattle farmer in Texas, all very glamorous and foreign. I fear Sir Nicholas does not agree with the match, saying that his daughter is too cultured and delicate to marry such a rough Texan. But one is supposed to not call him American as he was educated at Eton and of course born here. Hardly a rough man I hear you cry!
Anyway, if that was not enough for Sir Nicholas to stomach, I could not help but overhear the heated exchange between Lady Alison and Sir Nicholas. Apparently she has been considering a move to the Americas once the war is over to start a cattle ranch over there. Apparently Lady Fitch fainted! It is not as bad as they make out though.

He is a gentleman through and through. I am sure they will be very happy together.

We have been spring cleaning this week and it has been the hardest week here for me since I arrived. We have been awoken every morning at half past four instead of five and we had to go through all the cupboards in the parlour, clean the inside, dust and put everything back. Today we were in the larder, doing the same, and my back, Bertram, I cannot describe the ache! Worse still we are having to throw away leftover food, what a waste. I asked if we could do something with the leftovers. Cook said she would think this over. I hope we can help the most elderly and poor people in the village. Some of the apples looked just fine to me, well I would have eaten them!

Tomorrow we start on the windows, a mighty task and I find I am already losing weight with all this activity.

I am missing you so much and I miss you taking me out on a Sunday. I am now going to church with my mother and I will do the same this Sunday coming. I have to go to bed now as it is reaching near ten o'clock.

Love always,
Your Kathryn

Kathryn placed the letter in her cherished envelope. Lady Rosalyn had kindly given the staff whose loved ones were fighting in France a set of beautiful cream paper and envelopes. Kathryn cherished hers and hoped that Bertram would be impressed with the quality of the paper and recognise the insignia of Dallington Place at the top. Kathryn had traced her finger over the raised writing, the large letters of D and P were exaggerated to show the importance of the place and on the back of the envelopes the same D and P in blue embossed ink arrogantly stood out. Lady Fitch was right in thinking the more grandiose the envelope the more chance it had in arriving at its destination. Placing the letter by her bed, she sat in quiet contemplation for a few minutes. Now though Kathryn's mind was racing with worrying thoughts. A few things were going through her mind now. What if, Kathryn perused, Lady Fitch had only been this generous because she had felt sorry for Kathryn. What if she were to lose her job? Tucking her now icy feet quickly under the eiderdown, she heard Clara opening the door. Clara glanced down at Kathryn already in her bed and noticed the letter straight away. 'Been writing to Bertram again, have you?' asked Clara.

'Yes I have finished the letter now, I will post it tomorrow,' said Kathryn slightly annoyed of Clara's interference.

Clara got into her bed on the other side of the room and was humming to herself and busily trying to untangle a knot in her dressing gown's cord.

Kathryn sat bolt upright. 'You do not think Lady Fitch gave me beautiful paper and envelopes because she thought that perhaps letters would not get through to Bertram, do you?' she asked almost on the point of tears.

'Do not be daft, you think the Fitchs would waste money like that if that was the case,' replied Clara almost with a grin on her round and plump face.

'Or worse Clara,' exclaimed Kathryn full of anguish.

'Stop it, you will drive yourself insane. Do not say anymore,' said Clara now having untangled herself free and was snuggling down under her covers. 'You have to believe he will come back to you, you know,' she said sweetly, yawning and then pointing to the curtain. 'You could not shut that curtain nearest you, could you?' she asked almost asleep.

Kathryn dutifully got out of bed and almost ran to the window as it was a cold night. It had not started to warm up yet and Dallington was a cold place at the best of times and once the fires had gone out at night it was positively freezing. She could feel a draft around her ankles as she ran back to bed.

She thought of Bertram and wondered if he was warm. He had explained in his letter that he would be staying in the nearest village soon. Maybe he was there already. Hopefully he had somewhere nice to go. Perhaps a kind French family had opened their doors to their simple home and made the Englishman welcome just as the Fitchs at Dallington Place had made her so welcome. That was what she wanted she thought as she turned over feeling less anxious at the thought Bertram was somewhere safe. A simple home that she and Bertram could enjoy, that is what she wanted for the future. Maybe if they had some money, they could have a fireplace in every room. That wish made Kathryn smile and she soon fell asleep more quickly than she had in a long time.

CHAPTER THREE
BERTRAM: THE BATTLEFIELDS

Just another day to go, Bertram thought as he struggled with his left boot in the thick mud. Lifting a sandbag out of his way he continued down the muddy path towards Robert. The trench was thick with mud tonight as it had rained solidly for two days. He and Robert had stuck together since they had arrived and were now desperately trying to repair the damage done to their bunker. The wooden door had been sliced in two and pieces of wood and metal were swimming in the four inch oozing muck covering their boots with the cold water seeping around their toes. They were beginning to get used to their constantly wet feet. Both men had been complaining of a sore throat, but it was not surprising as they never had enough time to change into warm clothing or get enough sleep. There was no point in changing the damp clothes for as soon as you did, you would only get sodden again.

Bertram had been looking forward to getting some sleep that night but they had just heard from the brigadier that the continuous bombardment from shells were unlikely to cease for the next two days. A new battalion was being brought in tomorrow to cover them and by tomorrow night they should be on their way to the village of Mesves-sur-Loire. The men had worked out a good system between them, and if possible would cover each other for half an hour at a time to rest. Tonight though was going to be impossible to get any rest. Their trench was being destroyed. At least twenty of the men they had been with yesterday in the trench had been injured or killed. Between them, Robert and Bertram had removed four or five bodies yesterday, and it would be of no surprise if they came across more hidden in the soggy depths of the stinking and rat-infested water. Their nerves were rattled and Robert could not get the shakes out of his left arm. Bertram kept reminding him to straighten it and tuck his bayonet around it.

Their plan for the night was to start to dig a new crater outside the trench to make a new frontline and wire it. This was to induce the enemy into wasting ammunition, but the problem was their trench was disappearing fast and they had no form of cover. They could either disobey orders and keep sandbagging their own trench to keep themselves safe, or they could be put out on a limb and be running back and forth every fifteen minutes digging the crater and then running back for cover. The soil was so wet a crater could be filled with water and the whole process would have to start again. It was obvious they needed replacements. At night this was easier, as darkness obstructed the enemy, but the weather conditions were so horrendous it was clear it was not going to work. A whole battalion reinforcement would be needed to complete the task and then the trench could be repaired and fully manned again.

Bertram cowered under a stack of sandbags and lit his first cigarette of the night. A habit he had acquired since leaving for France. Never liking cigarettes before but now it was a necessity. 'What do you want to do then?' asked Robert ready to take to any mission if Bertram dictated it.

Inhaling the last few puffs from his lifeline, he shrugged his shoulders in despair. He could see men running up the mud bank and over the edge and into a pit of darkness. There were cries and screams of help and Bertram knew there was nothing they could do to help them once the screams had stopped. 'Let us wait a while and keep working here and then if it goes quiet, we could try and go over the top and dig the crater,' said Bertram.

Self-preservation took hold of both. Robert agreed and both men continued fortifying the trench as another few men beside them fortified the bunker. Men were still going over the top of the trench with their shovels and bayonets weighing them down. None seemed to come back down to the trench again. They worked until their backs ached and for the last few hours enemy fire seemed to have ceased.

Men were being brought back on stretchers, some terribly wounded and some clearly dead. Some were running past the trench now, retreating with the stretchers, back to where they hoped they would be safe. Just as Bertram thought he may try to get to a crater, another bombardment of artillery rained down on them narrowly missing Robert's helmet. Retreating into the bunker, the men realised they just did not have the manpower to sustain this mission.

'Let's hope morning comes quickly,' said a young soldier that Bertram had not met before. 'My name is Rudy,' the young man said holding out his hand to shake Bertram's.

As the young man smiled, Bertram realised all the front row of his teeth had gone and a slow trickle of blood was still flowing from the corner of his mouth. He took a rag out of his pocket and wiped away the offending liquid. 'Bloody stinky hole this is,' he said in a loud Cockney accent.

'Too right there,' Bertram answered. Robert just nodded.

'Damn teeth, if I do not knock them out boxing then I bash them out with my own shovel. I fell on it you see,' said Rudy trying to break into a smile through clenched lips. This for some reason made all the men laugh in the bunker that night, whether it was because they had just survived the worst shelling of their war as yet or they really were going into a state of derangement. Whatever it was, it made the world stop for a moment and lighten everything from the darkness to the aches in their backs and injuries. But before long the moment was lost as a huge shell came down on their bunker and then it went quiet. That was the last time Bertram saw the man with no teeth again. He remembered pulling Robert onto a stretcher with another nameless and faceless man and then they were out of there, for the time being.

There was only so far that Bertram could travel with Robert in the military ambulance. Bertram needed to get to the village of Mesves–sur-Loire, where he and Robert were to be billeted for the next two weeks. Only it was just him this time. Clutching their wages and a few treasured items, which he had managed to grab before Robert was advised to go to the military hospital at Calais to treat his injured leg. Apparently if his leg was badly broken he may be sent back to a hospital in Britain. If not, he would be in Calais for six weeks and then be sent back to the battlefield. Robert was pleased that Bertram had been there for him and travelled some of the way with him. Bertram needed to go and so he tapped on the glass partition of the ambulance to signal to the driver to pull over. The ambulance carried not just Robert but three other not seriously injured soldiers. Bertram, happy that Robert was fairly comfortable and now out of much of his pain, tucked the man's wages into his top jacket pocket, patting down the lumpy pocket affectionately. Bertram jumped off about a mile from Mesves-sur-Loire. 'Thanks mate,' shouted Bertram to the driver as he slammed the door shut. 'Look after young Weaves, will you?' he said to the tall driver suddenly feeling guilty for leaving Weaves alone.

'Sure thing!' the man said, leaving Bertram in no doubt the man was an American. Bertram must have looked rather surprised as the American slapped him on the back and said: 'He'll be just fine, your friend, but do us Americans a favour whilst you're off-duty and visit our boys in the American hospital. You cannot miss it!' the American continued, now jumping back into the ambulance and driving off.

Bertram had not even had time to reply but he knew he would do as the man asked. It was not much to ask.

The ambulance had left a trail of dust in its wake as it sped off. Today was the first day Bertram had not felt cold. It was a warm day; in fact it was the first warm day since he had arrived in France. He stood at a crossroads and looked across the fields where he presumed Mesves-sur-Loire was. He put his hand up to shield his eyes from the noon sun and took out a handkerchief to wipe his now perspiring brow. His throat was dry and he longed for a drink. He sat on the curb for a moment to read the address of his billeting. The now crumpled piece of paper was dirtied and it was hard to read the address. Bertram squinted. It read: Monsieur A. Comte, 15 rue de Vincent, Mesves-sur-Loire. Just as he got up, a few truckloads of soldiers sped past, waving excitedly. Not one stopped for Bertram. The men were in too much of a hurry to enjoy their leave. Bertram figured they were going to the same village where he was heading to so he followed in their tracks.

It was not long before he could see a few houses dotted about and then an old broken sign lying diagonally to the side of the road that read: Mesves-sur-Loire. As he was passing a church on his right, he could see a few soldiers gathering outside a café. Bertram desperately needed a drink and thought he could ask directions whilst he quenched his thirst. Slinging his spare pair of boots over his shoulder and pulling out a cigarette, he asked one of the soldiers talking in the entrance of the café for a light. One of the men was an American and the other had a broad Yorkshire accent. 'Excuse me,' said Bertram politely, 'Do you know where rue de Vincent is?'

The soldier from Yorkshire turned to Bertram and gave his friend a knowing smile. 'You going to Berenice's?' asked the Yorkshire man.

'Sorry? No,' responded Bertram. 'Number 15 rue de Vincent, Monsieur Comte, I believe,' continued Bertram.

'Ay, that is Berenice's husband. But you will not find him there,' continued the Yorkshire man with a wry smile.

'Oh?' said Bertram rather confused.

Both soldiers were now laughing as the Yorkshireman continued: 'See that kid there, the small one with the jet black hair? That is her kid, he will show you where it is,' pointing out to a little boy sitting on a bicycle nearby looking at the men.

'Hey Sebastien, another soldier,' said the American beckoning to the lad. 'Another soldier for your mother here. Come here!' he instructed.

The little boy did as he was told, placing his bicycle down on the dusty road and running across it, narrowly missing an army truck as it sped off down the hill towards the river. The boy could not have been more than seven or eight and promptly snatched a cigarette from the American soldier. He looked Bertram in the eye and beckoned for him to follow. Bertram followed the boy as he rode slowly on his bicycle. Rue de Vincent happened to be the last road out of the village and Bertram was glad of any type of respite by the time they knocked on the door, no matter what state his lodgings were in. Bertram was not disappointed by what he saw, far from it.

CHAPTER FOUR
KATHRYN: CHANGING TIMES

Kathryn sat dutifully next to her mother in the church. St. Dunstan's was one of the most beautiful churches in Sussex. Small and not particularly unusual from the outside, it was the interior that made the little church so outstanding. Dating far back to the sixteenth century, one could see the ancient baptismal font by the altar. As a child, Kathryn loved to come and look at the tombs, read the long and old-fashioned names and imagine the people who were buried beneath. Now the churchyard was not such a pretty place with more and more gravestones from the poor soldiers from the new war. But inside was a blissful place to be. She imagined herself and Bertram holding hands at the altar, looking into his sparkling green eyes and plighting their troths to each other. How proud she would be that he was hers for life. As the vicar carried out his sermon, Kathryn felt too tired to listen and take note. She was far more interested in the spring sunshine streaming through the magnificent stained glass window to the left of the altar. As she stared blankly up to the window, her eyes felt tired and she closed them for a moment. A feeling of complete and utter solace took hold of her and for a few moments her heavy eyes were relieved of any ache and her mind was quiet.

It was her mother that woke her. Mrs Beaumont gently took hold of Kathryn's hand to nudge her awake as they stood to sing *Breathe on me Breath of God*.

'Sorry mother,' said Kathryn embarrassed. 'I forgot where I was for a moment.'

Kathryn's mother just smiled knowing how hard she worked. Kathryn was brought down to earth with a heavy heart again as she knew she would have to share her worries with her mother over a lunch. She was not particularly thrilled about it, but she had to ask her mother's advice about where else she could seek work if she had to leave Dallington Place. If the rumours were to be believed and the war would still drag on indefinitely, the Fitchs were thinking about closing down Dallington Place until the war was over. It was clear from what Mrs Potts had been stating, and not very mindfully either, that the

Fitchs might well take themselves off to their hunting lodge in Norfolk. A smaller house that only needed a half of the staff that Dallington Place's great sprawling rooms required. All week the staff had been wondering, who would be asked to go if this was true and who would be asked to take severance pay. Kathryn was well aware she was in a difficult position. If she was asked to go to Endelwise Manor in Norfolk, she could not take up on the offer. She could not leave her mother especially as her health was so bad. So she would have to take severance pay, which would only last her a month or two if she was lucky. Now she was paying rent on her mother's cottage with her wages. She knew if the worst came, then she must look for alternative work.

Mrs Beaumont took Kathryn's arm as they walked past the tombs down the ancient cobbled stones, down towards the light of the wide open wooden doors and out into the welcoming spring sunshine. 'You seem distracted darling,' said Mrs Beaumont looking up into Kathryn's eyes and squinting from the rays of the sun. Mrs Beaumont oozed charm and even now she managed to hold a conversation with Kathryn and nod at the vicar at the same time without actually talking to him but holding his interest with a friendly smile. Kathryn nodded at the vicar, too tired to make pleasantries.

Kathryn smiled sadly at her mother realising how small and frail she seemed to have become. Kathryn not tall herself, towered over her stooped frame. She patted her mother's arm with great fondness. 'I am well, Mother, but I fear I need to talk to you over a cup of tea and hear some of your much needed wisdom. Shall we have lunch in the village at Mrs Jerobaum's teahouse? She needs our money if anybody does,' said Kathryn.

'Just a light sandwich for me, nothing too expensive,' said Mrs Beaumont aware not to spend too much of Kathryn's money.

As the pair walked away from the church, Mrs Beaumont turned to look at the little dwelling for the last time that day. 'You know it is a lucky church that one. Every married couple I know that has been wed there are always blessed with lots of children. I hope you and Bertram will be as fortunate,' her mother continued.

'I hope so mother,' said Kathryn suddenly feeling a little unsteady on her feet and needing something to eat as quickly as possible, as they entered the teahouse. After helping her mother with her coat, Kathryn sunk into the corner booth. She felt slightly chilled even though it was probably the warmest day of the year so far.

Judith Jerobaum was busy serving a couple of customers at the till, but Kathryn and her mother were the only people sitting down to lunch. Mrs Jerobaum waved and smiled when she saw it was Mrs Beaumont. As soon as she was finished serving the other customers she rushed over to the two women with menus. 'How are you, Judith?' asked Mrs Beaumont noticing how thin she had become.

'Well, business is terrible as you can imagine, and what with my John gone now, it is just the young lad and me. Money is tight to be frank with you, I may have to find some other income soon,' continued Judith.

'I am sorry to hear that,' replied Mrs Beaumont, generally concerned and upset to see such a nice lady in obvious distress.

'And how are you, young lady? I hear you are engaged, is that right?' Mrs Jerobaum turned her attention to Kathryn.

'Yes I am,' replied Kathryn feeling a flush to her cheeks.

'Well, I do not know where the time goes, do you Abigail?' smiled Mrs Jerobaum at Mrs Beaumont. Kathryn always smiled when someone called her mother Abigail rather than Mrs Beaumont.

Mrs Beaumont shook her head. 'It's a tough time too, what with everybody losing their positions and wages. Kathryn here is in the same position,' she continued.

'Are you not working at the big house anymore then?' asked Mrs Jerobaum surprised. Kathryn shot her mother a look of annoyance.

'Mother, please do not tittle tattle,' she whispered.

Mrs Jerobaum looked amused at the exchange between mother and daughter. Kathryn felt she should explain and begrudgingly told Judith of her own worries.

'So you will be looking for work then?' asked Mrs Jerobaum, admiring this young woman's independent spirit.

'I think I may have to if things continue as bad as they are,' replied Kathryn, hoping that Mrs Jerobaum would not get into it any further.

'Well, let me take your order and I will be back to sit with you. I do not think anybody else is coming in today, and look, it is starting to rain. Well that is it then.'

The women watched Mrs Jerobaum go behind the counter and fetch a sandwich for Mrs Beaumont and a lemon crumble for Kathryn. After making their cups of tea, she settled down to join them for a cup. 'You know, there is a munitions factory needing female workers in a place called Cliffe at Hoo on the Hoo peninsula,' said Mrs Jerobaum helpfully, looking at both.

'Good gracious Judith, she is not that desperate yet!' exclaimed Mrs Beaumont rather taken aback by the idea.

'Well Abigail, you may be shocked but we are all in this boat together and if things do not pick up here, I may have to ask for work there myself,' said Mrs Jerobaum, a little surprised at Mrs Beaumont's reaction. 'Times are tough and any work should be welcomed work.'

'Judith, you are not serious,' Mrs Beaumont continued looking aghast. A munitions factory was no place for a woman.

'Mother please, let Mrs Jerobaum explain,' said Kathryn looking sharply again at her mother. Placing the teacup down with some force and splashing the contents messily in its saucer.

Mrs Jerobaum stood up and waved her hand. 'Wait a minute, I need to find something.' She disappeared behind the counter again.

'Kathryn, do you know how dangerous those factories are? Just look at what happened to those poor men working at the Faversham factory three weeks ago. There were no women killed as it was a Sunday, but at least a hundred men were killed. Terrible, just terrible that explosion,' whispered Mrs Beaumont now concerned that Kathryn might consider working in a factory. Kathryn just listened as her mother continued. 'And you know what they blame for that explosion? The weather. I ask you, blame the weather when there is no one else to blame. Apparently all of France could hear the noise of the explosion!'

Kathryn took a bite of crumble, chewing slowly, her heart beating fast. Just as they had finished their last bite, Judith came rushing back to their table. 'Got it!' she exclaimed, holding a piece of paper out in front of them.

'What is it?' asked Mrs Beaumont.

'The address I got from Betty Millen. She told me of the factory only yesterday. She said she was going to try her luck for employment there. All the factory workers are going there as soon as possible, you know, the women from the Faversham factory,' explained Mrs Jerobaum.

'Luck, is that what you call it Judith? I do not know what has become of us,' said Mrs Beaumont with clear disgust on her face. 'Lloyd George and his emancipation of women! If that is emancipation working in an atmosphere of sulphur and poisons and the promise of being blown up. Lloyd George says it is a time to be singing. Singing I ask you?' she continued.

'Mother, calm down and drink your tea, Mrs Jerobaum is trying to be helpful and besides, I want to hear about it. Look at what Bertram has to go through every day. It is hardly as harsh as that,' said Kathryn, trying to calm her mother down.

'Well, your Bertram has not sent you a penny I see,' continued Mrs Beaumont, displeased that her daughter's new fiancé was not offering his support.

'Mother, you really are talking out of turn, you know I do not like to ask him,' said Kathryn, now feeling embarrassed to have this discussion in front of Mrs Jerobaum.

'Pride will not help you my girl,' her mother rambled on.

'Come, come, you two, I didn't mean to stir up trouble for you, it's just that the wages are excellent apparently and you would have more freedom than you have already,' said Mrs Jerobaum trying to placate them.

Mrs Beaumont, aware she should have kept quiet, did just that, but by her pursed expression it was clear she was outraged.

'How much do they earn?' asked Kathryn with a feeling of excitement welling inside her. Better wages and more freedom sounded good to her.

'Well, I am not sure exactly, but it is the same as the men's wages and you are also paid danger money,' said Mrs Jerobaum.

A huge sigh of indignation came from the muffled Mrs Beaumont. 'They say the new light railway you would take to get there is most comfortable and quick. Although you would have to rise early at five o'clock, but I dare say you are used to that. And they clock off at two or three in the afternoon. You could be home with your mother by five and have the whole evening off, and maybe Saturdays and Sundays too,' Mrs Jerobaum continued.

Kathryn could not contain her excitement. She would travel all alone to Kent every day and be home in time for tea. It was incredible to think she could have every evening to do as she wished.

'What is this clocking off business?' asked Mrs Beaumont, now interested.

'I would get home to spend the evening with you mother, would not that be nice?' said Kathryn looking at her mother hoping that she would see this as an opportunity for a better life.

'Of course it would darling, but it is the danger I do not like,' replied Mrs Beaumont her voice filled with worry.

'Well, I would like to do something more for the war effort,' said Kathryn looking at her mother, having already decided that she would find out more about the Hoo factory.

'That is very noble of you, but can we not think of something else?' asked Mrs Beaumont, aware she may have already lost this battle.

Kathryn was now dreaming of a large salary, a different life with more freedom. 'Who can I ask about this work at the Hoo factory, Mrs Jerobaum?' asked Kathryn.

'Look here, take this paper, it has the name of the General Manager, Mr Devlin McAlister. Apparently he owned and ran the Faversham factory and has now moved on to the Hoo factory. They are interviewing next Saturday at the town hall, be early, mind!' said Mrs Jerobaum delighted that Kathryn was interested despite her mother's resistance.

Kathryn placed the piece of paper safely into her bag. Her mind was now in a whirl with all sort of thoughts. She wanted to go back to Dallington Place and write to Bertram about the news as soon as possible.

It still had not stopped raining, in fact it was now bucketing down. As Kathryn checked her reflection in the large mirror by the door of Jerobaum's, she hoped her hair would not become too frizzy in the rain. Not that she had anyone to impress at Dallington Place. Mrs Beaumont was upset they had gone out to lunch at all. Kathryn on the other hand was thrilled. It felt like an adventure of her own and she kissed Mrs Jerobaum on the cheek as they left and said their goodbyes. Besides, what harm could it do if she worked there for a couple of months, just until she found something else? Even the rain could not dampen her spirits. It had been a long time since she had had any happy thoughts.

'Look at you, you are a drowned rat,' said Mrs Potts, opening the door to the staff entrance and dragging the sopping wet girl in. Kathryn wanted to share her news with the other staff, but before she could say anything, Clara, who had clearly been crying, told Kathryn she was needed upstairs as soon as possible to have a talk with Lady Fitch. As Kathryn dried her hair, and despairing of its frizziness, gave into the tension of the day as she sat on her bed and wept. She knew what the meeting with Lady Fitch would be about and the tension in the air was just too much. She knew she must hurry now and not keep her employer waiting, but in her heart of hearts, Lady Fitch was more than an employer, she was more like family. It dawned on her just how fond she had become of Dallington Place and all its comings and goings, if not for the hard work. Steadily she took the steep back stairs and made her way down to the drawing room.

An hour later, she felt very alone in her bedroom. Clara was still being comforted downstairs by Mrs Potts so Kathryn decided to take advantage of the quiet to write to Bertram and tell him her news. As she took a piece of the headed notepaper and as her pen hovered over the crisp cream parchment, she hesitated over how she would begin her letter. She could not decide if she should tell him yet that she would be leaving Dallington Place. Lady Fitch had made it quite clear that once the war was over, there could possibly be a place left for her to pick up again and maybe become a lady's maid like she had once hoped at Dallington Place. But this idea had lost Kathryn's interest now that new and more independent opportunities were possibly in the offering. Kathryn was comforted to know that any correspondence could be delivered and collected to and from Dallington Place. Some of the staff would be still be in residence to keep a watchful eye over the property. The family would be moving to Norfolk over the next couple of months. Kathryn thought it was perhaps wise not to worry Bertram, but tentatively tell him that she may look for other work. As his correspondence would be safely arriving at Dallington Place, it was best that they kept to this arrangement. Letters being sent to and from a well-known and well to do address were more than likely to reach their destination. Nervously smoothing out the paper she began to write.

21ˢᵗ May 1916

My dearest Bertram,

I have much to tell you, but as always rushed to put pen to paper, it is always the case to find some spare time to write. I always like to think upon what I say as not to worry you and to keep things light to lift your spirits. From my own selfish point of view, I am relieved to hear from your last letter that you will be receiving some much needed time off. How lovely for you and I hope you enjoy your rest. I am sure I will hear all about where you are staying and what the French family is like. I would love to know if they live so differently from us. As I write this, I know you are away from any dangers and that gives me such comfort. I know I will sleep well until I hear you are back on the front line again.

I spend my Sundays with my mother as you know and this Sunday was the same, except for the talk in church and a tea at Mrs Jerobaum's. I have heard that many girls and men, for that matter, in service are leaving their jobs and finding work independently. Of course I am worried about my future, but do not worry, as I have many people looking out for my welfare and the good Fitch family have my interests at heart.

Lady Alison is marrying in June and although I am looking forward to the wedding, I wish it was you that would be accompanying me to St. Dunstan's. My mother though is greatly looking forward to it and I must not let on that I would prefer it was your arm in mine and not hers. Mrs Jerobaum may have to close her teashop too. Life is changing too fast Bertram and I am changing too, although for the better I feel.

I cannot wait for your next letter and I will finish now, as I want to put this letter in the early morning post.

Bless you my darling, keep safe,
Your Kathryn always

As Kathryn signed her name, she felt ashamed she had not let Bertram know that she would be interviewing for the factory job on Saturday. She knew he would not approve, but although he would understand why she would be taking the job if it was offered, Kathryn knew it would make him uncomfortable and it would worry him. Licking the envelope and sealing it, her lips felt dry. She sipped some water from her drinking glass before she got into bed, but the dryness in her mouth and the nervousness in her stomach did not subside and she did not sleep well that night.

CHAPTER FIVE
BERTRAM: BILLETED TO FRANCE

Kathryn's letter arrived at the battalion headquarters a few days before Bertram finished his leave. The last couple of days had been an opportunity for Bertram to sit out in the warm sunshine and write to Kathryn. Berenice's son had taken to following the British soldier around and was sitting at his feet whilst Bertram wrote his letter to Kathryn.

18th May 1916

Dearest Kathryn,

I have been brought back from the front line and I am staying in a small village called Mesves-sur-Loire near St. Eloi. I am being housed by a French family and they have a young son called Sebastien who has taken a shine to me. When I write my poetry to you, I recite it to him and it makes him laugh. I hope it is the accent he is laughing at. So I enclose the poem I wrote about waiting. I am done waiting here now and I am rested and ready to go back.

The last ten days have been enjoyable although I came here alone without my friend Robert Alton Weaves, who was to be billeted with me. I believe he has been sent back to a hospital in Gravesend (I leave the address at the bottom of the page). If you could possibly spare some time to visit him and see how he is, I would be so grateful. He had a badly broken leg and I hope he will be returning here in a couple of months. I also enclose some money. Not much I know, but it will help you, especially for travel expenses if you or your mother needs it. I have picked up quite a bit of French, understanding more than speaking it.

The boy, Sebastien, has the most jet black hair you have seen, dark eyes and a beguiling smile. He makes me believe in the future again and of what you and I could have in time. He has cheered me up no end, after seeing so much horror on the battlefield. There have been so many tear gas grenade injuries in our battalion, Kathryn, and that is why we have been taken off duty for so long. I am enjoying my newfound freedom. Everything seems so light and warm here. Only a few miles away it is different. This is paradise compared to the acrid greyness of the front line.

Something else I want to share with you is that I visited an American hospital in St. Eloi. A friend did me a favour so I promised I would visit the men there. I found it more interesting than I would ever have thought, Kathryn. I met a man there called Alexander Pillard. I believe he was brought up in the Americas, but is of French extraction. His mother is American. We got along famously as my interest grew when I realised he was a journalist. He has been reporting on the war since 1914 and written about the Triple Entente Alliance. It would definitely be a job that would interest me, and I am going to see him again on Wednesday before I leave so he can give me some names and addresses of people with connections. I have been writing reports on what I have seen already and maybe they would be of interest to somebody.

Here is my poem
Waiting, I hope you like it.
Goodbye for now and God bless.
Your Bertram

Waiting by Bertram Wright, waiting to go back to war.
Even the sun appeared this afternoon,
but I am done waiting.
Smoke in hand to relieve the boredom,
at precisely two o'clock I sit across from the Valley.
I sit on a grassy bank, feeling the comfort of my new boots,
a light upon the darkness,
A poppy amongst the fields,
inhaling the aroma of the tobacco, I sit,
Sebastien at my feet.
He plays leisurely with the laces,
I wonder who wore these boots before.
A hand cupped underneath his chin.
A frown upon his brow.
You do not leave here, he says.
"Partir pas, mon ami!"
I pat him on the head.
I am done waiting.
A slight touch on the shoulder, too sad to see.

Too intimate, as a son and a father would be.
How many boys have lost their fathers, Kathryn?
I am done waiting.

Bertram put the letter in its envelope and placed it in his left coat pocket. He had forgotten to write the address of the Gravesend Hospital, where Robert was. He quickly retrieved the letter, scribbled the address from his notebook and resealed the envelope. Taking Sebastien's hand, he jumped to his feet. His limbs did not ache anymore. The few days' rest had done him good. His sore throat was not as bad as it was. Was his voice ever this deep, he wondered. Maybe not he thought, as he pulled the little boy by the hand down the side of the hill and towards home.

He would say his goodbye to Sebastien's mother. Hopefully he would be back.

Berenice was waiting for them by the side of the house. 'Maman, maman,' the little boy cried with tears streaming down his cheeks. By the worried look on her face, she must have been fretting where they had been all this time. To Bertram's surprise, she threw her arms around him. Enjoying the feeling of a hug from such an attractive woman, he did not pull away. The two of them stood there by the side of the house in a tight embrace. She then pulled away, conscious that perhaps Sebastien was watching. Bertram took this friendly embrace as one of relief that they were back safely and her eyes were full of tears. He went to kiss her on the cheek for being so kind to him over the last ten days. Berenice caught his lips with hers as he bent to kiss her. She was so tiny he almost stooped. Again Bertram did not pull away and felt her soft rosy mouth on his. A mouth that could cure all ills that befell them. A longing took hold of him and as she led him back into the house, he felt part of his life fall away. The worry, the loneliness and the longing for female company were gone in that moment and deed. He knew he would be back and shutting the gate behind him, the Bertram that he thought he knew so well, was a mystery even to himself.

As an army truck turned into the dusty track of the hospital and Bertram climbed out, he was a different man to the man that had visited here a few days ago. He was back with a fervent mission. He knew it to be selfish, but that made him even more excited and determined. Alexander Pillard was going to help him change his life. The hospital had a cooler feel to it today. A new round of injured soldiers had arrived, and no one asked any questions as to who Bertram was and who he was here to see. Nurses and doctors were running back and forth and hearing the cries of some of the soldiers turned his stomach for a moment and made him stop and wonder what he was doing here. A young nurse came running up to him that second, with bedpan in hand, she handed it to him and then vomited in a corner. Bertram just stood, he did not move, he did not comfort her. When she had regained her composure, she turned to him, took the bedpan from him, embarrassed at her own weakness. Bertram leaned against the cool blue paint of the walls and closed his eyes. He wanted to be back in England, not here in a stenching hospital wracked with death and ruin. Then the thought of going up in an aeroplane, of achieving his desires to be a reporter, and that urged him on and down towards the bed of Alexander.

Bertram reached the end of the bed to see Alexander fast asleep with a book open flat across his chest. He was lying under a blue hospital blanket, it was gently moving up and down as Alexander breathed. Bertram did not have to wake him, the young journalist was soon rubbing his eyes and conscious of someone watching him, woke up quickly. 'Bertram old boy, good to see you,' said Alexander sitting bolt upright and holding his hand out to shake Bertram's.

'On the way back to the war zone I am afraid, thought I would take time to say hello once more,' said Bertram as he shook the man's hand.

'Well, I am afraid it is going to be a goodbye as I am out of here tomorrow and back to New York,' announced Alexander loudly as if to be proud to be American.

'Well it is a good thing you are better, glad I caught you before I left for the trenches,' said Bertram offering a friendly smile.

'Sure, sure,' said the American knowing full well Bertram had come back to show him his notebook. 'So let us have a look at this work of yours then,' he continued.

Bertram put his bag down and fumbled about in the clean washing that Berenice had kindly done for him. He thought of her for a second, her hanging out the washing yesterday in the sunshine. Her silhouette and her pretty long black hair, half tied up in a bun, the rest flowing loosely and seductively down her back.

'Here,' said Bertram opening the pages of some of his poems from the front line, including a few love poems to Kathryn. 'There are also some diaries on what we have been doing whilst on and off duty.'

Bertram watched the man study his work. Alexander then placed the book down and took off his reading spectacles that had still been perching on the end of his nose whilst he was asleep. 'What do you think?' asked Bertram apprehensively as if his life was depending on Alexander's opinion.

'I think they are fabulous! I think you could go to your commander at the battalion and see if you could start your own battalion newspaper.' Bertram listened with excitement. Alexander asked Bertram to pass him his own writing folder in the side cabinet. Bertram was surprised to see so much paper stuffed into such a tiny cabinet.

'Well, I have had to do something whilst I have been in here,' said Alexander laughing at the expression on Bertram's face. 'There is only so much flirting one can do with the nurses and besides I am married.'

Bertram smiled but it was an uncomfortable one. He felt a surge of guilt creep over him. Poor, trusting Kathryn, he thought, if only she knew. As he handed over the folder, a photograph fell out. Bertram retrieved it from the floor and handed it over to Alexander. 'Oh yes, here I am flying with a French ace pilot and aerial photographer Pierre Le Sierre. A colourful chap he is!' Alexander smiled to himself. 'Listen here,' said Alexander passing Bertram a piece of paper with a name and some personal details on it. 'Lieutenant Jacob Jacobson, that is who you need to find, he will take you up in his triplane. Now there is an experience you will never forget!' Alexander's voice was full of excitement as he was talking about aeroplanes.

Bertram's eyes lit up with hope. Could he possibly be able to do this? To write about such an experience would be incredible. 'Make sure there are three of you, you need a spotter to keep an eye out for enemy fire. You fly quite low, you know,' said Alexander. Bertram was not afraid, there was nothing about this conversation that made him afraid. Being free up in the air and seeing things most people could only imagine, how could one be afraid?

After an hour together and being ushered on by one of the matrons, the men shook hands and made a pledge to see each other one day in the Americas. As Bertram opened the door of the ward, Alexander called out to him: 'Come and see me in New York anytime!'

Bertram just smiled and wished Alexander the best, but he had a gloomy feeling he would not be seeing the American again. As he walked out of the hospital and onto his lift back to the trenches, he realised how naive it was to make pledges in the middle of a war. No one knew if they would survive one more day, let alone making promises to each other.

Bertram tried not to think of Kathryn. As he arrived back to the cold damp shelter where he was to be stationed for a couple of days, half a mile from enemy lines, he was handed a letter by his commanding officer. It was late and not the time to bring up friendly banter about the battalion having a newspaper. He recognised the blue insignia of Dallington Place and began to read Kathryn's letter. As he lay in the near darkness, tears welled up in his eyes. For he could tell Kathryn was struggling with her words and he realised she was keeping things from him. It was an optimistic letter trying to cover up heartache, he knew her so well. As for his own heart, he was not sure if it ached or it was just beating to keep alive. Did anything else matter at the moment, he thought. Then the shelter went into darkness and he fell asleep.

Orange Lilies of Dallington Place

SOPHIE CLOUD

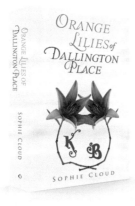

Size:	(234 x 156)
ISBN:	9781848979598
PRICE:	£8.99 / €10.99
CAT:	HISTORICAL FICTION / WAR / ROMANCE
FORMAT:	PAPERBACK
RIGHTS:	OLYMPIA PUBLISHERS
TERRITORY:	WORLDWIDE
IMPRINT:	OLYMPIA PUBLISHERS

ABOUT THE BOOK

'I forge ahead, further west I tread,
from England's green and native birds,
a bird of prey, flies high above the Madrone Tree,
from the scorched mountain top.
An absurd looking raptor,
somewhat akin to me.'
In 1916, as a call to arms to the Western Front, Kathryn Beaumont, a maid and Bertram Wright, a soldier, fall in love by the magnificent manor house 'Dallington Place', in rural Sussex, England. When Bertram goes to war and sets his sights on becoming a journalist and aviator, can Kathryn, his fiancé, wait patiently for him to return?
With the twists and turns of life, Kathryn and Bertram are inextricably linked throughout the war, with Kathryn becoming a strong and resourceful woman. Can Bertram return to her and put his demons and traumas of war aside?
With an array of intriguing characters, *Orange Lilies of Dallington Place* is a story with great insight into the opulence of the age as it unfolds to 1940.
This novel will warm your heart, touch your soul and make you smile.

ABOUT THE AUTHOR

Sophie Cloud's particular interest lies in the idiosyncrasies of a person's character after studying Psychology at university, which she has channelled into *Orange Lilies of Dallington Place*. With the light and shade of her characters, it brings a new and never-ending fast-paced story. Sophie loves the meaning of people's names and places and is always fascinated by the coincidences that have appeared whilst working on the story.
Sophie's other interests are military charitable causes, and the history of Britain, France and America has fuelled her desire to write the book.
Coupled with her poetic skill set, her knowledge of the era has brought exciting experiences and opportunities which are woven into her novel.
Sophie Cloud resides in London with her family.

Olympia Publishers
Tel: 0203 755 3166 **Fax:** 0207 002 1100

E-mail: pressrelease@olympiapublishers.com
www.**olympiapublishers**.com

CHAPTER SIX
KATHRYN AND GERALDINE

Kathryn woke unusually late. Clara had known she had the day off to attend her interview at the town hall, so she had not woken her. The sun was streaming through the gap in the curtains and she knew she must have overslept. Hearing footsteps on the gravel driveway, she jumped out of bed, pulled on her dressing gown although she soon realised she did not need it to keep out the chill. It was a warm day and as she opened the window, she could see an automobile approaching. Kathryn could tell it was Henry the chauffeur, who was talking to Lady Alison outside moments later. Lady Alison's high pitched voice was so distinctive and excitable. It was Ned Stedford that was approaching in his green open top automobile, but it was stalling, and then it finally broke down before the final stretch of the driveway. Kathryn could see Lady Alison and Henry running towards the smoking engine. She had hoped perhaps Henry would drive her to the village, but it looked as if it would be out of the question, if Henry was needed to fix the engine. She would have to walk now, and she had better hurry up, she thought, not to miss the interview. She would have to leave breakfast and just put some clothes on and go. How she had wanted to fix her hair properly before she left. There was no time. She had laid out her clothes last night, thank goodness, so she quickly dressed, put some rouge on her rather pale cheeks, not too much, plaited her hair and fixed it securely with a pin on top of her head. There, she thought, it would have to do, not approving of her outfit. Her blouse was too floral and her shoes rather worn. She only owned two hats. One smart for a wedding, that her mother had bought her, a dove grey with small pink flowers nestled in the brim. The other was plain, more fitting for a maid. She pulled it on, tucking in a few stray curls. At least it would keep the sun out of her eyes. Shutting the door, she collected her thoughts. Making sure she had enough money with her just in case, she shut her purse and ran down the servants' stairs.

'Oh, you do look smart,' called out Mrs Potts to the now perspiring Kathryn as she fled the kitchen, with a buttered scone that Mrs Potts had shoved into her hand. She was too nervous to eat and as

53

she ran down the drive, she did something that she would not normally do – she placed the soggy scone in the bushes, hoping at least some lucky animal may enjoy the cook's delicious pastry.

She hoped the party now peering into the green automobile's engine had not noticed her. They had not. A steaming, smoking engine was far too exciting for Lady Alison to be distracted. Kathryn could see Mr Stedford making wild gesticulating movements with his arms and Henry was already opening a toolbox and rolling up his sleeves. Kathryn hoped the weather would not turn as she had not brought her coat. It was too heavy for the spring. Then an enticing thought entered her head. If she was making good money in a new job, perhaps she could afford a spring coat. Just like the one she had seen advertised in a French magazine. Lady Rosalyn and Lady Alison had brought back many magazines and fashionable clothes on their visit to Paris a couple of years ago. Lady Alison had swooned over a particular coat by designer called Erté. Only last week Lady Alison had distributed the magazines around the maids' quarters just to lift the spirits and show them some glamour in this austere time.

As Kathryn approached the village, a tall man, not young, maybe of about forty years of age tipped his hat at her. Lost in thought, it took her a moment to acknowledge him. She gently smiled and was rather embarrassed to realise he was walking across the road towards the town hall as well and, the fast walker she was, she was almost in step with him. As she went to reach for the door handle, she could see him reaching in his pocket for a large number of heavy silver keys. 'I am locking up, miss,' he said. He must have realised why Kathryn had such a forlorn look. 'If you are here to interview for the munitions factory, then I am afraid you are too late. My secretary has left for the day. If you want to come down to the Hoo factory on Monday, you can,' he continued.

'I am on duty on Monday, I cannot,' said Kathryn with tears beginning to prick her eyes. She could not believe she had missed the interview opportunity.

'Nurse are you?' he asked giving the door handle another pull to make sure it was secure.

'No, I work at the big house, you know Dallington Place,' she said warming to the man with a kind face.

'Sorry, I just presumed, you just look, well, the sensible type,' he continued.

Kathryn not sure whether to take this as a compliment, decided to leave the conversation there and then, when a young girl with shiny red hair and freckles bounded up the stairs and almost bumped into Kathryn. 'Not too late am I for the interviews?' she asked with an eager puppy dog look in her large brown eyes.

The man looked skyward, took a sharp intake of breath and then, because he liked the look of Kathryn, placed the keys in his velvet coat and held out his hand to introduce himself, 'Devlin McAlister, general manager of the Hoo factory. You two I suppose are looking for employment?' He looked at both girls.

'Geraldine,' said the red haired girl taking the man's hand, which was meant for Kathryn.

Kathryn followed suit and shook Mr McAlister's hand. 'Kathryn Beaumont, pleased to meet you sir,' she said shyly.

'You two know each other I presume?' he asked expecting a prompt reply. The two girls looked at each other and Geraldine gave Kathryn a look as if to, say yes.

Kathryn cleared her throat nervously. 'Yes we do, sir,' she continued.

'You can vouch for this Geraldine?' he asked again, unsure of the nervous looks the girls were giving each other.

'I have references, sir,' Geraldine hurried to say.

'Well, if you are keen to work, be sure you are down at the factory on Monday. It is not easy work mind, but there are bonuses for the hard workers,' said Mr McAlister looking at both girls.

'I will not be able to start for a couple of weeks, I will have to serve out my notice until the end of the month,' explained Kathryn, now feeling the blush riding up her cheeks.

'That will be fine, just bring references from Lord and Lady Fitch, that will suffice,' said Mr McAlister, now looking weary and making his way down the stairs.

Kathryn noticed he had a limp as he made his way down. She had not noticed it before. Kathryn started down the stairs after him. 'You know Lord and Lady Fitch, Mr McAlister?' she asked surprised.

'Yes, I do, I know them well,' Mr McAlister slowed down to look at Kathryn. Tipping his hat at both girls, he walked off lifting his hand behind him as if to dismiss them.

Mr McAlister was not at all what Kathryn had expected. She had heard stories about the general manager being a rather off-hand boss at the Faversham factory. This man had a kindly face and manner. It served her right, making a judgement on pure gossip about a person's character. Kathryn turned towards Geraldine, who was busy writing down the address of the Hoo factory from a notice that was still attached to the door of the town hall. She took out a pen from her purse and ran up the stairs. She had forgotten she too needed the address. 'Do not worry Kathryn, I have got the address. Let us have a cup of something to celebrate, thank you so much for vouching for me,' said Geraldine with a big relieved smile on her face.

Kathryn noticed that she was even prettier when she smiled. 'You are very welcome,' said Kathryn sensing the girl needed the job as much as she did. 'There is a teashop just around the corner, let us go there,' said Kathryn wondering if Mrs Jerobaum was working that day. She hoped that she was not. She did not want her mother worrying if Mrs Jerobaum told her she had seen her. Kathryn was surprised to find the teashop closed. She rang the bell just in case but to no avail.

'Listen, maybe it is for the best, I should really be getting home,' said Geraldine.

'Which way are you going?' asked Kathryn, hoping to have some company on her walk back to Dallington Place.

'I need the station; which way is it again? I have a terrible sense of direction,' asked Geraldine. Spotting a bench on the side of road, Geraldine suggested they swap addresses. She gave Kathryn the factory address and her own address.

Before Kathryn placed the piece of paper in her purse, she took a glance at the address. 'You live in Bexhill?' Kathryn asked surprised.

'Yes. I think I had better go, I do not want to miss the afternoon train,' said Geraldine now eager to go.

'How long did it take you to travel up today?' asked Kathryn intrigued. Having barely been out of the village herself, now she had met a girl of her own age, freely travelling back and forth on her own through Sussex. Kathryn was impressed.

'Two hours,' replied Geraldine.

'So why did you come all this way for an interview when you could have gone to the Kent site instead?' asked Kathryn.

'I've been nursing a lady up here of late. Sadly she has gone into a home now. That is why I need to find a position very quickly. I came up here today to say goodbye to her. Jane Portersfield, do you know her?' asked Geraldine.

'That is why you look familiar, I have seen you at church,' realised Kathryn.

'Yes, St Dunstan's. I used to accompany Miss Portersfield every other Sunday,' said Geraldine now pleased that she had met such a lovely girl like Kathryn.

'I used to go to church with my fiancé,' said Kathryn with a wry smile. 'Now I accompany my mother,' she continued.

Geraldine acknowledged how Kathryn must feel and smiled back at the pretty maid. She picked up her large brown satchel and backed away from Kathryn towards the entrance of the station. 'I will take a look at the ring next time I see you,' Geraldine exclaimed as she waved and rushed off. Kathryn watched the girl run, her red hair streaming unfashionably down her back. Kathryn really liked her and it had been good to chat to someone of her own age who was not employed at Dallington Place.

It had been a successful day and Kathryn could not wait to tell Mrs Potts all about it. When she rushed through the back door, she could see a brown envelope sitting on the kitchen table. It always made Kathryn's heart leap out of her chest when she did not recognise the envelope. Mrs Potts was bringing some clothes in from outside, caught sight of Kathryn's worried expression. 'It is all right love, I can see it is Bertram's handwriting. He has just changed the style of envelope, that is all,' said Mrs Potts.

Kathryn had to sit down. It did not get any easier, receiving mail. As each day went by and letters arrived at Dallington Place, there was always the worry they could be from the War Office. Then her life would be over… She put her head in her hands and wept with relief.

'There, there, you daft girl, everything is alright! Did your interview not go well?' asked Mrs Potts as she gave Kathryn a reassuring squeeze on the shoulder.

'Actually Mrs Potts, it went really well and I made a new friend, who is going to work with me at the factory. It is just everything is changing and I do not like change. I am not brave, like the Geraldines of this world,' said Kathryn between huge sobs, hunching her shoulders even more.

'Now you have got me confused, who is Geraldine?' Mrs Potts quizzed, with a funny expression on her face that made Kathryn laugh. 'One minute you are crying, the next you are laughing!' smiled Mrs Potts. 'We are going to miss you here you know,' she continued. Mrs Potts put her plump arm around Kathryn and kissed her on the cheek. 'I will make us a nice cup of tea and then you can open your letter from that lovely man of yours. Do not forget, we have Lady Alison's wedding in a couple of weeks, so there is lots to look forward to,' said Mrs Potts with a kind smile.

Kathryn dried her eyes and sipped her tea. She felt better and happily opened Bertram's letter. She loved the poem he had written to her and showed it to Mrs Potts.

'My, he calls you his Lily, it must be love,' she smiled and gave Kathryn a wink.

Kathryn read of Bertram's fondness for the little boy, Sebastien and she tried to picture them sitting in the French sunshine, in a little French village not far from the Somme. It was hard for her to picture the reality, but in her imagination it was a pretty village, where she imagined everything to be exotic and so different. As she read on, she hoped by the time he came back to her, she would still be interesting to him. He seemed to be full of new ideas and she was interested in his visits to Alexander Pillard in the hospital and his ambitions to fly. She loved his letter and as soon as she had read it, tucked it into the pocket of her skirt to keep it close to her. She then settled down with Mrs Potts to discuss Lady Alison's wedding. Clara joined in too, she had just come back from evensong at St. Dunstan's. Kathryn lay in bed that evening, she made a mental note to herself that she would visit Bertram's friend in Gravesend. She would be brave and travel there alone in a couple of weeks just before she was due to start at the factory. Besides, she had to get used to travelling on a train on her own. Bertram would be proud of her. Maybe she was braver than she first thought.

CHAPTER SEVEN
BERTRAM: THE BATTLE OF THE SOMME

Adjusting back into trench life had not been easy this week. Bertram had hoped he would have had the time to contact Lieutenant Jacob Jacobson, but as soon as he was back in the trenches, the work had been constant. As he settled down for five minutes peace in the damp and noisy shelter, there were ten men sleeping there that night, he wanted to write Kathryn a long letter. The men were instructed to write several letters over the next few days. As soon they would be marching to Ypres, they would not have the opportunity to send any letters for a while. Drinking a mug of tasty cocoa, just right and not too hot, Bertram tried to imagine Kathryn at Dallington Place. His memory was fading, or was it his eyes, he thought. He could not picture his Kathryn tonight and it made him sad. He sat with his head in his hands. He knew she had delicate hands and a perfect posture, but he could not picture her face. It was a blurred memory, mixed in with the features of Berenice's face and her feminine charms. Rubbing his eyes, he held the pen over the paper and paused. He decided not to see Berenice for a while. Next leave he would not go back to Mesves-sur-Loire. He needed time to speak to Lieutenant Jacobson and besides, Berenice was becoming demanding of his spare time. He did not have the strength to argue with her and it would be a good excuse to maybe finish things with her. Feeling better about things, Bertram set to write. He managed to write no more than three letters until the lights went down in the shelter.

May 30th 1916

My dearest Kathryn,
I am looking forward to tomorrow. Another day to start afresh, and be grateful for many things. Extra rations are arriving, and we hope to stock up on bacon, bread, biscuits and condensed milk, my favourite. There may be some rum if we are lucky. We are in our dugout shelter, which has taken quite a few days to dig. It is damp and my feet are cold, and today we were issued with gas masks to protect

us from phosgene gas. Not a pretty picture. I was instructed to shave off my beard, and now I look younger but my eyes look older, Kathryn. I have seen too much with them. My eyes are tired. I wake every night with the sound of mortar bombs going off. I dream of cheese, I wake in disarray. Cheddar cheese is what I dream of. I hope I do not depress you with too much talk of war.

Dearest Kathryn,

Try not to worry about me, although I wish I was with you to comfort you and you to comfort me. I am safe and that is very important that you know this and hold on to this. We have not moved from here for two weeks. This letter has turned into three, as we have been told we will march to Ypres soon and I will not be able to correspond for some time. I wrote this poem tonight, I hope you like it. The boys have put my scribblings and poems up on the shelter wall. It keeps my mind off the hunger and my belt buckle moves up a notch every two days or so. I think I am thin now, but I do not have the time to tell.

Yours always,
Bertram

Astride The Valley of The River Somme by Bertram Wright
If I was a giant, I could hop between camps,
a shadow of a go- between good and evil.
I would have one foot on solid ground,
the other in no man's land.
Foreign and grim this no man's land,
an enemy we are sure to fight,
I fear a war we cannot win.
If I was a giant, I could see for miles,
quarries and safety nets, where our men could hide.
We are too open and too exposed,
just these trenches to wallow and take some pride.
But what good is pride, when only extinction is the outcome.
If I was a giant I could hear the enemy approach.
I could cover John Miller when his time came upon him.
I would cover his body to shield him from the dust.
To protect his body from pain and anguish.
Yet here I am a mere mortal with small eyes to watch,
no signal I can help with, no voice I can alert.

If I was a giant, I wouldn't tarry long.
I would stride my way back from the river Somme.
One step, two, I would be there with you.
So my dear, I fear I am not a hero.
A man of little stature, a man of little worth.
Except you think of me not, so I do have the lot.

As Bertram squinted in the midnight darkness, although his eyes were tired and strained, he wrote with his left hand and in his right he held a gift for Kathryn. Leaning over his letter, he had to keep it short. Paper was scarce and he had used up more than his usual quota for his scribblings and musings on the daily habits of his fellow comrades.

My dearest Kathryn,

My last letter to you for a while. I do not know when I will be able to write again, but know that I am thinking of you and most importantly, I am sending this gift of a sweetheart brooch, which is my engagement token to you. When I am back in your arms, I will present you with a ring that is fit for a princess. This will do for now so you know my commitment to you is sincere and when you wear it you will think of me. Think of me, whilst a pin lies amongst the fold of your blouse. A piece of my love you wear, in reverie that marks our hold and treasured pledge. I see you dancing in your Sunday best, a brooch marking my stamp above your breast. Circling and laughing around the room you dance. This pin, this easy wearing badge, will not I hope lance the love we share. Keep it close, whatever closeness is these days…

Yours forever,
Bertram

Folding the letter three times and smudging the writing, Bertram pinned the brooch to the bottom of the letter. It tore slightly, but he was too tired to care. He sealed it in a large brown envelope and placed it next to his gas mask ready to hand it in in the morning. As he wondered how long it would take to arrive at Dallington Place, his eyes started to close and his thoughts wandered unyielding to Kathryn.

Dearest Kathryn,

Of course we are eating! Everything is rationed and I am sure with our diet of bacon, eggs and some occasional ham, our nutrition is still fairly good. I cannot equate the wages though, so meagre. To think of such a small salary, to lay down your life for the country. It

*would be an honour, says our colonel. I am not sure I agree with him.
I plan to stay alive, write my journals and keep on writing to you. I try
to keep positive but Kathryn, there is so much debauchery here.
Nothing seems real anymore. I hope you are real to me. I hope you
enjoy the present I am sending you. Wear it every day if you have
permission.*

*Please tell me how life is at the beautiful Dallington Place. I want
to hear of the weddings, day to day life, I want to hear about happiness.
A different world to where I am, Kathryn. I feel I am in the dark and
cannot see the light. My eyes grow dim. Please remind me of that
pretty place. The place where we fell in love. Keep reminding me.*

 Yours,

 Bertram

He did not send this last letter, he held it close as he fell asleep. He
wanted to send it, but it was too honest. Too honest for Bertram. He
held on to it and kept it in his breast pocket.

At first light, maybe half past four in the morning, the men were
ready to march. Their route would take them past the canal and along
the railway lines. There would be hours of marching for their unit, and
they all had extra food last night. Relieved by his letters to Kathryn,
Bertram could relax his mind about her. As he, along with his
comrades, did not think of much. He was not thinking of Berenice
either. He thought of his friend Robert Alton Weaves. He should have
been with us now, Bertram thought. And a smile spread across his lips
at the thought of him in the hospital bed in Gravesend with pretty
nurses at his beck and call. He wondered how long before Robert was
able to return to duty. In one month, maybe two. He missed his young
friend.

As the dim light grew into daylight, as they trudged their way
towards Armentières, Bertram was aware of his brown boots kicking
up stones and soil and the scurrying of rats in and around the train
tracks. By midday, gunfire could be heard steadily, although this was
nothing to be alarmed by. A constant noise to remind them that, yes
this is war and yes we are defending. Not a battle of dread at this
moment, that this would be your last day on this earth. The unit were
backing up the dominating observation position in front of Ypres.
There were other British units already there to pin down the area.
Canadian troops had been there for a while. To Bertram's surprise, he
heard the roar of engines and flying low above them, two aeroplanes

dipped their wings and then disappeared out of view behind layers of woodland. He watched the aeroplanes disappear with envy. Canadian aircrew, he wondered. Could he possibly be able to go up there one day with them? Was Lieutenant Jacob Jacobson up there now?

They arrived where the British and Canadians were entrenched at Armentières and it was not as basic as he had imagined. An army camp almost like a house had been built by a canal and men sat idly on a wooden jetty, smoking and talking. The unit passed them and the commander signalled to the forty-two men to stop and take note of where they could rest and what work was to be carried out. Bertram put down his back pack and sat by the canal edge, wanting to pull off his boots and plunge his feet into the icy cold water.

A Canadian commander, Horace Bearsley was speaking to Bertram's commander, Colonel George McGovern, shaking his hand and as they disappeared in to the man-made stone house, the unit were at ease. Water was handed out and Bertram lay in the muddy grassland his eyes averted to the copse, where he had last seen the aeroplanes disappear. He wondered if he was nearer to tracking down Flight Lieutenant Jacob Jacobson, the friend of Alexander Pillard.

As the days turned to weeks, the units were there to dig out new posts and shelter ready for assaulting troops and airborne activity. The physical labour, although the toughest and most exhausting on his body he had ever experienced, he felt free emotionally. Having no one to look after, no women to worry about, not even Robert to watch over. He could have been happy actually. The only threat were the phosphine gas attacks, that could be imminent, but word at the moment was that it was fairly quiet from enemy attack and the men could at least rest at night.

It was early one morning as Bertram lay in his bunk dozing, he heard raised voices. Canadian voices. A man named Jacob was mentioned and Bertram unmistakably knew this would be Flight Lieutenant Jacob Jacobson. Could Alexander Pillard have told him about some upstart called Bertram Wright? As he pulled on his boots, he could hear his name being called by Colonel McGovern. He shot to his feet.

CHAPTER EIGHT
KATHRYN AND THE WEDDING

Kathryn finally had some time to herself to get ready for the wedding. No one had managed to have more than a few hours' sleep the night before and come to think of it, there had not been much time to sleep most of the week, she mused. Admiring her reflection in the small oval mirror hanging by the door, she smiled at herself. Normally she was not vain at all, but today she did notice how radiant she was looking. Surprised by this as she was feeling so tired, she realised it was because she was happy. She was going to have the whole day to relax and enjoy the wedding and also she was excited about the prospect of working at the munitions factory. How her life was changing, she thought, as she patted some delicate pink rouge onto her cheeks and sparingly applying a little to her lips. Clara had managed to get some from a friend in the village and both girls were keen to try it today. Wiping away the excess colour from her mouth, she smiled at the thought of her mother's disapproving glance as they sat in church together. She felt pretty for once.

Henry, the chauffeur, had been sent to collect Kathryn's mother and Lady Fitch's dressmaker from the village, a much-loved friend of the family, and to take them to St. Dunstan's. Placing her cream straw hat on her head, she was pleased with the result of her look for the day. Even her unruly hair was behaving itself. She knew Clara was coming to get her once Lady Alison was ready. Kathryn had helped her bathe and wash her hair last night and it was Clara's duty today to set her hair. As Kathryn peered out of the bedroom door to listen to any comings and goings, she heard familiar footsteps running full steam up the passage way. 'Oh Kathryn, you should see Lady Alison, she looks so beautiful! Let's set off as quick as we can to get a good seat in the church,-I forgot to say you have a package downstairs, looks interesting!' said Clara with a knowing smile.

'Really?' asked Kathryn, her eyes wide and her heart beating fast.

'Must be from Bertram, I expect,' said Clara opening her closet and putting on her spare pair of shoes. 'Comfortable shoes, Kathryn, unfortunately we will have to walk and set off now. Henry told me the other two automobiles are needed elsewhere,' she continued.

'Henry told you that this morning?' asked Kathryn realising that Henry and Clara seemed to be talking a lot lately. Clara nodded pretending not to notice Kathryn's keen interest in her budding romance. Kathryn changed her shoes too, disappointed she could not wear her best pair. 'Listen, I will take a bag and we can hide it in the church. Here, put your good shoes in it and we can change once we are in the church,' Clara handed her bag to Kathryn. Her attention was elsewhere, she was dying to get to the kitchen and pick up her parcel.

Out of the door as quick as a flash, the girls ran down the back stairs down to the kitchen, where Mrs Potts was putting her large bonnet on her head, looking flustered. Normally Mrs Potts was a calming influence, but today she had not had much to do as the wedding breakfast was to be held at Rutland Hall, a smaller house that belonged to Ned Stedford's mother. Spending time on herself appeared to have made her nervous. Rutland Hall was nearer to the church and everyone thought it was practical as it did not have Dallington Place's impressive but long driveway. It would have taken all the guests nearly an hour to organise themselves into automobiles after the ceremony. The walk to the church would take Kathryn and Clara nearly half an hour.

'You girls better go now, there's nothing else for you to do,' hurried Mrs Potts, giving Kathryn her package and ushering them out the back door. With all the thoughts on Kathryn's mind, she had not thought to bring a shawl. She had presumed it would be a warm day like yesterday, but in fact there was a distinct chill in the air. It was too late to go up and fetch it, especially now as she did not want to disturb any of the wedding party.

As they set off down the long driveway with Kathryn clutching her package, they saw Henry returning to pick up Lady Fitch and Amabel, her youngest daughter.

Henry waved, looking rather flustered. Clara could not help but laugh at the hapless flustered fellow doing his utmost to make the transport to the wedding go without a hitch. 'I think I can see storm clouds ahead,' Kathryn pointed out to Clara just as she tore open the sealed envelope.

They walked quickly, holding on to their purses, umbrella and various pieces of paraphernalia. 'I wish for once we could have got a ride to church!' exclaimed Clara, as she watched Kathryn tucking the letters from Bertram into her purse but also clutching something else.

'Oh my goodness, that's beautiful!' said Kathryn excitedly, admiring the pretty brooch that Bertram had sent her. 'I love it, just love it, pin it on me please, just by my collar.' The girls stopped for a minute so Clara could attach the sweetheart brooch.

'I have heard about these, you must be one of the first girls to receive one, how utterly modern of you, Kathryn!' said Clara almost jealously.

'Well I am not the only one who has a beau by the looks of things!' said Kathryn, making Clara flush with embarrassment.

'He is handsome, is he not?' said Clara, adjusting the pin on Kathryn's collar and standing back to admire it. The pretty brooch was made up of two entwined hearts with the words "The Lord watch between me and Thee when we are absent one from another".

'He is the most romantic man, your Bertram, is he not Kathryn?' said Clara. Kathryn smiled a smug smile, knowing her Bertram was about the most perfect man she could wish for. How she wished he was with her today.

As the girls reached the entrance of St. Dunstan's, the rain began to fall. Giggling with relief they had missed getting wet, they ran into the church. Kathryn looked for her mother and noticed she was sitting with a middle aged man. She could see her mother nodding animatedly. His grey hair a little too long on his collar and his thick set shoulders moving unnaturally swiftly as he talked to her mother. Kathryn recognised it was Mr McAlister. Placing her hand on her mother's shoulder, Kathryn indicated to her she would sit behind as there was not enough room on the end of the pew. Kathryn sat behind her mother and Mr McAlister and when he turned around to greet Kathryn, she felt herself flush with embarrassment. 'Good to see you here Miss Beaumont,' said Devlin McAlister in his deep and husky voice. She noticed him looking her up and down with an almost whimsical look on his face. His eyes stopped for a moment as he noticed the brooch, and then he turned around as Mrs Beaumont continued chatting to him.

'Who was that?' asked Clara, elbowing Kathryn playfully in the ribs.

'It is Devlin McAlister, he owns the munitions factory, where I am going to work on Monday,' answered Kathryn feeling rather unnerved.

'The Devlin McAlister?' replied Clara looking surprised. Kathryn nodded willing Clara not to say anymore in case he overheard. Clara leaned over to Kathryn and whispered: 'He is not what I would have expected!'

Luckily before Kathryn could reply, a young couple with three small children asked Clara if the rest of the pew was free and they squeezed past the girls, talking loudly. The smallest child, a little boy of about three years of age was now crying and muttering about wanting to go home, and only pacified when Kathryn asked his mother if he wanted a sweet from her purse. The little boy unwrapped the sweet with great concentration, and as he sat quietly now, he gazed up at Kathryn with a look of great admiration. Kathryn patted his head and the little boy put his hand in hers. Kathryn could barely move now, squeezed into the crowded pew. The rest of the church was filling quickly and she observed with interest Ned Stedford's family, as they hustled and bustled into their seats. There were some very glamorous women finding their seats and Kathryn looked at their clothes with interest. She hoped no one would notice her plain and old shoes and wished she had put on her best ones. She had no room to move, let alone change them under the seat. She felt hot under her collar as she looked at Devlin McAlister's neck directly in front of her. His shirt was a pale blue and rather rich of texture. He was wearing a light green jacket, rather casual for the occasion, as if he had nonchalantly slung it on moments before, without a care for form or fashion.

His neck was rather broad, she thought, and she could see as he talked a slightly protruding vein moved quickly as if he was nervous. Kathryn tried to distract herself from her direct view and looked to the ceiling. She noticed the criss-crossing of the wooden beams above, which opened up to reveal the beautiful stained glass of saints surrounding the Virgin Mary. She loved this view and had often sat in almost this exact spot to gaze up at the ceiling. A loud voice distracted her and a formidable woman with an American accent was tapping her cane on the granite floor as she made her way to the front of the church. A handsome young man was escorting her and as her hands trembled, she clung on to him. Kathryn got the impression she was not frail in spirit. The young man looked like Ned and Kathryn thought perhaps this was Ned's younger brother. He led the old lady to the front pew and Kathryn watched with interest how her glimmering diamond drop earrings swung about her neck catching the light and encasing the old lady in superficial glamour. Apart from the earrings, her attire was purely functional; a velvet jacket to keep out the chill and a rather dowdy black heavy skirt, which barely moved as she shuffled to her seat. Perhaps she had dowdy shoes on like her own. Maybe dowdy was the new fashion Kathryn thought with a smile, perhaps in the Americas anyway. Not at Erté, where satin and lace were all the rage if you had the money. Ned Stedford's family still had a lot of money, not like some of the gentry in England, who were suffering like the rest of everyone. Not quite in the same way but having to cut back on expenses, which they had not ever had to do before. Kathryn was in the opinion that perhaps this was better and in some ways made people more equal and kinder to each other. If it was not for the war, she doubted whether she would have been invited to the wedding.

Stopping herself in her tracks as she did not want to think of the positives of the war. Not when her Bertram was so far away. Tears sprung in her eyes unexpectedly as the music started and everyone stood up for the first hymn. Do not cry, do not cry, she told herself. Trying to distract herself, she watched Lady Fitch standing alone without Lord Nicholas. Kathryn watched as she opened her handbag discreetly to take out her handkerchief to dab the corners of her eyes. Kathryn was relieved she was not the only one that was feeling emotional. She watched Ned shuffling awkwardly waiting for his bride. His best man, his brother, stood beside him giving him a gentle pat on the back to soothe his nerves as his hands nervously held onto the hymn book. Lady Alison was at least ten minutes late and everyone was beginning to turn around and look to the doors for signs of her and her bridesmaids. 'I hope Henry has not had a problem with the automobile!' whispered Clara to Kathryn. As Kathryn turned around again she caught a glimmer of gold. It was indeed Lady Alison. On her head was the beautiful family coronet and her dress the colour of pale gold satin lapping around her ankles in folds of the heavy shiny expensive material. Around her neck was a single string of pearls and a veil hung lightly over her face and moved eerily in the wind as she picked up her train and walked over to her father to walk up the aisle. Sir Nicholas looking proud, handsome and distinguished welcomed her delicate white hand as she looped it through his arm. Taking her bridal posy of red roses and blue forget-me-nots with her other hand, she stood for a moment to catch her breath and to wait for the young bridesmaids to join in line behind her. The music of Mendelsohn's Wedding March began, everyone turned around to watch the beautiful Lady Alison walking down the aisle to join her groom. Ned nervously smiled at his brother when he saw her. His dark eyes lighting up and his gesturing to his brother was uncharacteristically animated. His relief was palpable that she had arrived and maybe the usually confident Mr Stedford was shaken for a moment wondering if his bride would arrive at all, Kathryn thought.

Kathryn almost forgot where she was for a moment as the ceremony continued. She thought of herself and Bertram at the altar instead. As people rose to their feet to leave the church, Kathryn's feet were almost rooted to the spot, as if her body did not want to leave the church. It was only the little boy tugging on her skirt that made her sit up and take notice that everyone in her pew were trying to leave to get the best advantage point to throw petals at the wedded couple.

Standing by the church gates, Kathryn and Clara waited for Mrs Beaumont, who was being accompanied by Mr McAlister. Kathryn waved at her mother to let her know they were going to walk on ahead to Rutland Hall. Many people were already in their automobiles and the girls set off quickly, eager to get some refreshment at the reception. As they walked, Clara turned to Kathryn. 'Are you alright, you are looking awfully pale?' she asked.

'I am fine, I just need something to drink, I was rather squashed in there,' replied Kathryn avoiding eye contact with Clara. The ceremony made her realise how much she would like to get married to Bertram.

As the girls walked towards a large white marquee in the majestic garden of Rutland Hall, the sun began to shine on them, casting an admiring eye on the perfectly cut lawn and sweeping gardens. But the sun also uncovered flaws of the old hall and revealed large clumps of moss on the imposing stone stairs to the house. Time had taken its toll on the stunning house. Mrs Stedford lived in London most of the time and only resided at Rutland Hall at monthly intervals. Repairs were often overlooked, but maybe now with Ned and his new wife moving in until their planned departure to the Americas, Rutland Hall would have its much deserved upgrade as the new couple have made it their temporary home. Money was never a problem for Ned Stedford, although in these austere times it would have to been renovated discreetly.

As she sipped her wine, Kathryn watched how carefully the waiters walked down the stone steps. Carrying silver trays, they were terrified they were to slip on the wet moss and drop the glasses. Lady Alison mingled with the guests and her golden dress twinkled in the sunlight. She heard her mother's voice behind her and saw that her arm was still entwined with Mr McAlister's. She could hear her chatting merrily away about the weather and how lucky they were now the sky had cleared in time for the reception. 'Is that not right Kathryn?' she said still looking for Mr McAlister for approval.

'Yes mother, we are all grateful for that, especially me as I did not bring my shawl,' said Kathryn.

'How lovely your brooch is Kathryn,' Mr McAlister said, making her feel so self-conscious as she felt his eyes once again look her up and down. 'May I call you Kathryn, Miss Beaumont? I am sorry, it seems so informal, but your mother has been telling me all about you and I feel I know you already,' enquired Mr McAlister, hoping that he was not imposing on her inappropriately. 'You may call me Devlin,' he said extending his hand to shake hers.

'Pleased to see you again Mr McAlister, Devlin, what has my mother been saying?' asked Kathryn, feeling Clara's eyes upon her, almost judging her. There was a long silence as wine was passed between them and Kathryn took a large sip to comfort herself. This man was making her uncomfortable and she knew she had to keep her nerve as she was working for him on Monday.

Clara broke the silence to say she was going in search of someone, and Kathryn knew who. 'So Kathryn, I hear congratulations are in order on your engagement,' Mr McAlister continued.

How Kathryn wished that sometimes her mother would keep things to herself and not tell everybody every miniscule detail of their lives. 'Thank you Mr McAlister,' she said touching her sweetheart brooch. 'My fiancé, he is away in France.' She did not want to talk about Bertram to him and thank goodness he realised this and changed the subject.

'Well, I look forward to you working for us at the factory,' continued Mr McAlister with a softer smile.

'I am looking forward to it too and tomorrow will be my last morning at Dallington Place. That will be sad,' said Kathryn her mind now filling with sadness to say goodbye to a part of her life.

'Indeed, indeed,' he replied.

'It is a surprise to see you here, Devlin,' Kathryn's mother interrupted.

'Well yes, I have been a friend of the Fitch family for many years,' replied Mr McAlister turning to Mrs Beaumont. Looking Kathryn squarely in the eyes he began telling his story of how his father used to fish on Sir Nicholas's land, and he was caught poaching there as a lad. His father was then asked to work there as a junior ground man, a sort of punishment until he was eventually a paid up member of staff. He eventually met Devlin's mother back in Ireland, a distant cousin, on a fishing and hunting trip organised by the Fitch family. His parents married and had Devlin in Ireland and then returned to England and settled in Dallington village. His father went out to Australia to make his fortune in the Australian gold mines, met another woman and never returned. However, his father left Devlin his fortune and in turn, Devlin ploughed the money right back into buying local businesses and then the munitions factories. As Kathryn listened to the story, now more relaxed after a couple of glasses of wine, she wondered why Devlin McAlister was being so frank with her.

Walking with her mother to Mr McAlister's automobile later that evening, her mother pulled her aside when Mr McAlister was saying his goodbyes to the Fitch family. 'He is quite taken with you Kathryn, I can tell that,' she nodded to Kathryn knowingly.

'And how do you know that mother dear?' said Kathryn giggling and rather tipsy.

'He had shown you his hand, that is why!' she retorted curtly.

'Well, he knows that I am engaged so he cannot be serious and besides, I will be working at his factory. I really think he is just being friendly,' replied Kathryn now looking at her mother more seriously. She could not even imagine Mr McAlister other than as a future employer.

'Friendly or not, he likes you, and I find him endearing and very likeable,' her mother chattered on. 'And not short of a few bob either!' she continued smiling at Kathryn.

As the automobile pulled up outside Mrs Beaumont's house, Kathryn helped her tired mother out into the dark and chilly night. Helping her into the cottage and saying goodnight, Kathryn was surprised Mr McAlister was still waiting for her outside. Calmly smoking a cigar and leaning against the driver's door, he was staring into the night sky thinking thoughts perhaps he should not have been having. 'I know you do not have a shawl so perhaps I can drive you to Dallington Place?' he asked as Kathryn reached the automobile. She thought to herself that Mr McAlister was rather a thoughtful gentleman, having remembered that she indeed did not have her shawl and the night was getting rather chilly.

Later that night, the little maid sat ruefully at her desk. This was the last letter she would write from Dallington Place. She was no longer a maid, but a factory girl, starting on Monday. A secret she would have to keep from Bertram for the time being. She began writing her letter slowly and carefully.

24th June 1916

Dearest Bertram,
Well my dearest, I have so much to tell you about the wedding of Lady Alison Fitch and Ned Stedford. It was so exciting and even exotic with different foods, some from the Americas, and unusual accents and clothes to feast your eyes on. To have a day to relax and enjoy with friends was truly wonderful. I am sure you can appreciate that, especially when you are billeted out and you too can enjoy time with friends. I am still wide awake and there are still people arriving and leaving Dallington Place as I write. I cannot sleep with the excitement of it all. It is way past midnight now and I will be up again in a few hours to tidy up with Mrs Potts.
Lady Alison looked so beautiful in a golden dress fit for a princess! There were so many diamonds twinkling in St. Dunstan's, it was bright enough in there without any candles. The church just sparkled and was packed to the brim. I wish you had been there. Clara and I sat together behind my mother. We were squashed into the pew and I sat next to a little boy too and his family. Ned Stedford was so handsome yet so nervous. Not what I would have expected as he seems of such a collected character. The wedding breakfast was held at Rutland Hall. Although smaller than Dallington Place, it was more convenient from the church. Oh Bertram, it had the most magnificent lawn and a large white marquee stood in the middle. That is where we were served drinks! Me served drinks, I could not believe it either. I have never tasted such a beautiful wine. Of course I was modest in my behaviour, but I certainly giggled with my mother, who loved every minute of it as did I. I wore my gorgeous brooch, which I adore, thank you so much! I have received so many admiring glances for it.
Lady Alison and Mr Stedford, Mr and Mrs Stedford now, I must practice the new title for Lady Alison, are going to live at Rutland Hall until they move to the Americas next year. Everyone was gossiping about how Lady Alison will adapt to life over there. Apparently summers there are so very warm. I do not know much about Texas, but they will live on a ranch that Mr Stedford wants to expand with horses and cattle. At least Lady Alison can horse ride. The Fitchs are still adamant that Lady Alison, I mean Mrs Stedford, should not go but Ned feels it will be a good move in the long run, as the war could just carry on for so long. I suppose I can understand that, can you? But Bertram, I know you talked of travel so much, and about your hopes and dreams to travel the world, but for me, England is my home. Lady Alison is so

brave. Like you. I have to try to sleep now. I am going to read and read again your letters tomorrow. I am sleepy but happy you are busy and safe.

    Keep writing to me,
    Your Kathryn

CHAPTER NINE
BERTRAM: IN THE SKIES

29TH JUNE 1916
Take Flight in the Black Sheriff by Bertram Wright
There were sixty-eight of us, now forty-two.
The last left behind us, so we can forge ahead.
Some injured, some dead,
my friends, my comrades,
with tales left unsaid.
I will write for them,
the tales I know and have witnessed.
A ghastly mix of loss and sadness, of scenes obscene,
lives snuffed out.
Men with such a vigour, youth, a wasted oblivion.
I gulp down life and rise above the clouds.
Listing men and actions,
some proud and some mundane.
No one else will tell their story as I climb and soar
a hundred feet,
to win and sometime fold to defeat.
A hard landing for us all.
The plane judders safely back to land.
My lungs expand to the fear and cries,
where we go and where we arrive,
could always be our demise.
But I will rise and not fail.
I will not finish my life,
here in France's clay soiled land.
A handful, a mighty handful of England's grace,
will return, at last to their loves,
and vows to their country.
God speed.

Bertram sat on the grass, nervously waiting for Jacob to give the all clear to take off as he did his last checks on the triplane. He wrote quickly, scribbling his poem, desperate to finish before they had their orders to take flight, once again.

Dawn was approaching and Jacob Jacobson shook his head at the imposing but incredibly fragile looking triplane. The engine was not going to start. Bertram stood by to offer assistance to Flight Lieutenant Jacobson. Bertram was more nervous about not being able to fly today. He knew it was not a fighter mission and he was there to take photographs, but right now his heart was beating fast with annoyance. He did not want this opportunity to pass.

'There is always tomorrow,' said Jacobson, realising that "The Black Sheriff", his triplane, was probably going nowhere.

Bertram stood beside the triplane feeling defeated. He would have been seated in the gunner's position but today he would be taking aerial photographs instead of firing. Bertram traced his hand over the single synchronised Vickers machine gun, wondering how much training he would need to be able to use it. Jacobson could see what was going through Bertram's mind. 'That you use as of necessity. You do not hesitate when someone's firing at you,' he said also admiring this powerful machine. He patted Bertram on the back to console him as he shrugged his shoulders. 'Perhaps it is best so that I can give you some training today,' he continued in his Canadian accent, 'Besides, I would like you to meet Monsieur Pierre Le Sierre, who is an ace pilot with The Lafayette Escadrille, the French Air Service and he is one of the best aerial photographers. He and his squadron are bringing more aeroplanes in today from Dunkirk. If you do not go up with me today, I am sure Pierre will take you with one of the newer aeroplanes tomorrow,' said Jacobson.

'Sir, with no disrespect to Monsieur Le Sierre, I would rather go with you. I trust you are a good pilot,' said Bertram feeling rather disgruntled.

'Do not worry, rookie, if that is what you want, so be it, but meet Pierre anyway. He is great fun and loves to boast about all his successes, you will see. Maybe you will change your mind,' continued Jacobson, as he picked up his leather jacket and walked to the back of the aeroplane. 'Time for breakfast, rookie,' he said turning to look at his aeroplane, kicking the ground and then walking back to the headquarters.

Bertram writes of his experience of flying over No Man's land and seeing German troops on the ground from a small triplane.

Can You Take Me Up? By Bertram Wright

Soldier, soldier, here I am.
Flying low, yet high and mighty am I,
over the land of the Somme.
Can you see me soldier, soldier, and
dare you shoot me down?
I am a writer, who will write your name down.
If you fall, soldier, you will become nothing but a
name under my wings.
Fire at me, as we swoop across the muddy plain.
I see you there, soldier, soldier.

The heady mixture of the French and British units and the French and Canadian naval squadrons proved to be challenging. Fifteen aeroplanes had arrived from Dunkirk that afternoon and twenty aeroplanes were to follow. The plan was for Pierre La Sierre to show Bertram the ropes. To teach him all he knew about photography above the clouds, in the space of an afternoon. Monsieur Le Sierre was not what Bertram had expected. A tall and quiet man with an angular face had greeted Bertram with a kiss on each cheek. Bertram was aghast at this, his wiry moustache tickling his face. Le Sierre's French accent and the lack of the English language certainly did not help matters, but as they sat in their quarters with maps spread out on the makeshift trestle tables, there was a lot of finger pointing. Bertram had been let off duty to build some makeshift buildings for more ground crew that were arriving.

Sitting here with commanders and flight lieutenants, he was almost being pampered with mugs of rum and free cigarettes. This had not gone unnoticed with his own unit and there was definitely an air of jealousy and resentment from them. A few had taken to ignoring him, but Bertram did not seem to notice. As far as he was concerned, he was doing what was right for him. His obsession with flying and writing about the war from an aerial perspective had engrossed him.

Lying in his bunk that night, knowing he would be flying tomorrow in the early hours, brought him great satisfaction. He was thrilled at having a purpose in this war and being able to write about it. It was a cold evening and a fog was expected in the morning. Only if the weather had cleared by four hundred hours, would they fly.

The British squadron had arrived too with fifteen aeroplanes. More French had arrived two hours after, but with only eight aeroplanes. Two from their squadron had been shot down. One pilot was killed yesterday and another seriously injured from friendly fire. Pierre explained that the pilot had been shot down from friendly fire but he had managed to save the aeroplane and himself although he had had bullet wounds to his legs. One of the squadron had fired from straight above and a bullet had hit both of his legs. Incredibly for the time being he was still alive, saving himself and his wingman. Landing safely away from enemy lines. Lucky for them but an occupational hazard, Pierre stated, looking at Bertram to test his mettle. Bertram looked away almost disinterested. Nothing was going to put him off.

It was not until the next morning, when he woke just after six o'clock, that he realised they were not flying that morning. Annoyed and knowing he would be in for a day of digging and forging a barricade for the river, as high tides were predicted and storms lay ahead. He wanted to roll over, fall back to sleep and forget everything. This was impossible, for four of the soldiers from his unit were already ready and John, a young soldier from Sussex, was kicking the side of his bunk urging him to get up. He knew Robert Alton Weaves and apparently they had attended the same village school. 'Hey Bertram, you heard from Robert? When is he getting back here, the lazy lout!' shouted John out loudly.

Bertram rubbed his eyes and feeling the cold, wrapped a grey blanket around his shoulders. He did not like John and found him immature and needy. He was always following the older men and looking for guidance. He had a penchant for stealing too. A couple of things of Bertram's had gone missing since sharing a dug out with him. Twice he had to buy a new lighter. Bertram had known it was John after going through his pockets, when he had wandered off looking for a free cigarette. He had not let on that he knew and had taken the lighter back only to find it was missing again the next day. 'Do not know when Robert will be back, but I would imagine in a week or so,' replied Bertram. 'Why?' he then asked, getting annoyed.

John shrugged and then proceeded to spit out of the window. 'Dirty rain, dirty country,' he retorted, looking out at the water and seeing the mud flow. Kicking the door open, he disappeared leaving Bertram to get ready. Nothing on the ground was going to make him hurry. Wearing the thick pair of trousers he hated and tying up his heavy boots, he thought he may just find Jacobson before he was set to work.

Bertram could not find Jacobson but chanced upon Le Sierre drinking a mug of coffee outside the commanders' hut, one leg balanced against the flimsy tin door frame, the other foot tapping in the sticky mud. 'No, go today Wright. Tomorrow we go on an aerial reconnaissance mission over Salient, South of Ypres,' said Le Sierre taking a sip of his coffee. A smile spread across Bertram's face. That was all that he needed to know and he was now getting excited about tomorrow. An observation mission, harmless but interesting, thought Bertram. How wrong he was.

Bertram sat at his typewriter recalling the last few days on 5th July 1916:

Saturday 1st July 1916

0400 hours. Aeroplane engines start. Our mission as aerial observers to report to the ground before fighter planes go in over the enemy lines.

0500 hours. Over the Somme, cloudy skies.

0530 hours. Skies beginning to clear. Three aeroplanes flying together aloft for an hour and a half. Reporting to the ground of any sight of effective bombardment from 1,000 feet.

Twenty fighter planes to follow. Rate of climb at 200 feet per minute. Fighter planes from French, Canadian and Royal Flying Corps (RFC) squadrons.

0600 hours. Flying low below 1,000 feet over the enemy lines.

0630 hours. Spot German defenders protected in their dug outs. Sightings reported back to base. Aerial photographs taken by Watson Air Camera.

0635 hours. Spot our soldiers closing in fast, close to enemy lines and dug outs.

0645 hours. Sufficient photographs taken, return to base. No retaliation from German air squadron.

Bertram rubbed his sore eyes, it had been a tough few days. He thought of home and Kathryn and longed to be held by her. He tore the piece of paper out of the typewriter and replaced it with another to write a letter to Kathryn. For him it was his way of expressing his anger and devastation at what he had witnessed.

5th July 1916

My darling Kathryn,

I so look forward to your next letter but in the meantime I have so much to report to you. Firstly, I had my first flight in an aircraft. It was a triplane, the wonderfully named Black Sheriff. Flight Lieutenant Jacobson took me up and it was a mind numbing experience. It takes your breath away as you climb up fast amongst the clouds. Cold air hits your lungs and I wondered if I would survive. It would have been almost worth it if I had not. I did not know it, but the battle over the Somme started that morning, and I had no idea of the danger we could

Orange Lilies of Dallington Place

SOPHIE CLOUD

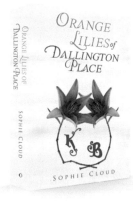

Size:	(234 x 156)
ISBN:	9781848979598
PRICE:	£8.99 / €10.99
CAT:	HISTORICAL FICTION / WAR / ROMANCE
FORMAT:	PAPERBACK
RIGHTS:	OLYMPIA PUBLISHERS
TERRITORY:	WORLDWIDE
IMPRINT:	OLYMPIA PUBLISHERS

ABOUT THE BOOK

'I forge ahead, further west I tread,
from England's green and native birds,
a bird of prey, flies high above the Madrone Tree,
from the scorched mountain top.
An absurd looking raptor,
somewhat akin to me.'
In 1916, as a call to arms to the Western Front, Kathryn Beaumont, a maid and Bertram Wright, a soldier, fall in love by the magnificent manor house 'Dallington Place', in rural Sussex, England. When Bertram goes to war and sets his sights on becoming a journalist and aviator, can Kathryn, his fiancé, wait patiently for him to return?
With the twists and turns of life, Kathryn and Bertram are inextricably linked throughout the war, with Kathryn becoming a strong and resourceful woman. Can Bertram return to her and put his demons and traumas of war aside?
With an array of intriguing characters, *Orange Lilies of Dallington Place* is a story with great insight into the opulence of the age as it unfolds to 1940.
This novel will warm your heart, touch your soul and make you smile.

ABOUT THE AUTHOR

Sophie Cloud's particular interest lies in the idiosyncrasies of a person's character after studying Psychology at university, which she has channelled into *Orange Lilies of Dallington Place*. With the light and shade of her characters, it brings a new and never-ending fast-paced story. Sophie loves the meaning of people's names and places and is always fascinated by the coincidences that have appeared whilst working on the story.
Sophie's other interests are military charitable causes, and the history of Britain, France and America has fuelled her desire to write the book.
Coupled with her poetic skill set, her knowledge of the era has brought exciting experiences and opportunities which are woven into her novel.
Sophie Cloud resides in London with her family.

Olympia Publishers
Tel: 0203 755 3166 **Fax:** 0207 002 1100

E-mail: pressrelease@olympiapublishers.com
www.olympiapublishers.com

have been in. As we turned a sharp left, taking my stomach with it, we lowered by a few hundred feet, and all of a sudden we saw German soldiers waiting to entrap our men. I later learnt that our soldiers, that we had spotted reaching the enemy lines were sadly all killed. A whole battalion, the Irish fusiliers, all of them wiped out. I had not come across any of the poor souls before, I did not know any of them, but still I have an ache in my heart for their poor mothers. I ache everywhere. My throat is still on fire, which only the cold rush of fresh air in the skies seemed to reduce its fervent annoyance. I cannot remember the last time I had a bath.

The last few days have been equally hard to bare. Many men from our battalion have lost their lives, some critically injured and sent back to England. The stretcher bearers were brought in from another battalion, as we had lost too many of our own. No one from the other battalion recognised a soldier from our unit and I uncovered the wax sheeting that covered his broken body. It was John Miller, who shared my quarters here. Such a shock, I can tell you. I thought of him as such a wiry fellow, one that could dodge bullets, you know. It could be anybody's time, and that's the fear, the fear of the unknown.

The first taste of gas is upon us here, and it is something you cannot get out of your skin. I am on stretcher duty tonight, pray for me Kathryn. Layers of skin have been penetrated and there is nothing I can do about it.

Yours always,
Bertram

Depressed, Bertram sat contemplating what he had written. Perhaps he should not send the letter, it was too grim. Getting up to stretch his legs, he was startled, when the door swung open and a familiar face greeted him with a wide toothy grin. Robert Alton Weaves was back and Bertram's depression lifted for a while.

CHAPTER TEN
KATHRYN: PASTURES NEW

Leaving Dallington Place was never going to be easy. As she sat on a plush, scarlet velvet chair waiting for Lady Fitch to return from her morning walk, Kathryn apprehensively looked to the carriage clock reminding her she was late for her afternoon train. How many times she had dusted that clock, as it had rung out to remind her dinner would soon be served. The long sweeping green and gold curtains hung luxuriously framing the most beautiful and familiar view of the grand lawns of Dallington Place. Kathryn's favourite view in the whole world. How happy she had been working here for the Fitchs, and a lump in her throat rose quickly. She reminded herself, she would be back here to collect her letters from Bertram. There was no need for tears.

Two black spaniels bounded into the drawing room and immediately jumped up at Kathryn and busily sniffed her hands and her small brown luggage set. Almost suspiciously curious as to why the young maid was leaving. 'Kathryn my dear,' called a lovely voice from the hallway. She could see Lady Fitch fussing with her umbrella. She had been unfortunate to get caught in a quick shower. Brushing her heavy, black brocade jacket, wiping away imaginary water droplets, she danced into the room and held out her arms to Kathryn. Lady Fitch hugged her and then moved briskly over to the mantelpiece to smell the large vase full of orange lilies. There was an abundance of flowers in the house ever since the wedding and Kathryn was allowed to take a small bunch with her today. Mrs Potts had arranged them perfectly.

Lady Fitch sat down opposite to Kathryn, placing her hands into her lap and sighing. 'I do miss Lady Alison and all the young people are now moving out of Dallington Place,' said Lady Fitch with a heartfelt sigh. 'Kathryn, what are we to do?' she asked with a small smirk on her face.

'I do not know Ma'am, but they will return to Dallington Place, I know that for sure.'

'You are so right, I must cheer up, that rain has dampened my spirits! Did you enjoy the wedding, Kathryn?' asked Lady Fitch knowing the answer.

'Yes I did, thank you. It was the most wonderful day, my favourite day, with the exception of course of Bertram proposing to me,' replied Kathryn shyly, remembering her place and hoping she hadn't been too familiar.

'Ah yes Bertram, I hope he is well,' said Lady Fitch now looking at Kathryn more closely. She had always thought the young girl was very attractive and sensible and would marry well.

'Yes very well, and he sent me this brooch in his last letter,' said Kathryn, proudly showing her sweetheart brooch.

'Young love, nothing quite like it! I hope Lady Alison is enjoying her honeymoon,' Lady Fitch looked into the distance for a minute, as if she was sad and a little uncertain of the future. Her brows narrowed as she turned her attention back to Kathryn.

'So is it tomorrow you start at the factory?' enquired Lady Fitch changing the subject.

'Yes Ma'am, I am very nervous and sad to leave here,' said Kathryn, now filled with sadness.

'Well I am sure you will be well looked after by Mr McAlister. We have known his family for a long time,' said Lady Fitch looking wistfully out to the garden again. 'Now Kathryn, two things. I hear from Mrs Potts that you would like your letters to be kept here from Mr Wright, is that correct?' continued Lady Fitch.

'Yes Ma'am, if that is all right with you. You see, I have not told him of all my plans yet. In case I may move address or something, at least I know they will arrive here safely,' said Kathryn, looking at Lady Fitch. She had been so lucky to have worked for such kind people.

'Yes of course, very sensible. My goodness, do any of us know where we will be living a year from now?' said Lady Fitch, searching for a handkerchief in her handbag. 'Sir Nicholas and I will be leaving for Norfolk at the end of the week, but you can always collect your letters here on a Saturday. Evans will be looking after the general upkeep of Dallington Place as Mrs Potts will be retiring. He has our Norfolk address so anything you need, please do not be afraid to ask,' said Lady Fitch.

'Thank you so much, you have all be so kind to me.' Kathryn could barely hold back the tears.

'You have been a good worker and a cheerful presence in the house,' continued Lady Fitch digging again in her handbag for something else. She handed a white envelope containing Kathryn's references and then she leaned over and placed a small black box into Kathryn's lap. 'Here, open it and you better hurry as I think that is Henry tooting outside.'

Kathryn could not believe it. A present, this was too kind. The flowers would have been enough. Her little hands shook as she opened the box to find a little sparkling hairpin. 'It is so lovely Lady Fitch!' replied Kathryn almost lost for words.

'Well, put it in your hair, it will keep it in place whilst working at the factory.' Kathryn and Lady Fitch smiled at each other with the full knowledge that both of them had difficulty in taming their curls on the best of days.

Kathryn looked behind her as the automobile swept her down the long driveway, left into the village and then to the train station. She would not be back to Dallington Place for weeks, but it would not be long. Lost in her thoughts, she had not noticed they had arrived at the station. Henry helped her onto the Gravesend train, tipping his cap. 'See you soon,' he said. Tears were running down his cheeks as he walked backwards through the archway and out of sight but still whistling and waving back to Kathryn. Though sad to see Kathryn leave, Henry was excited about meeting up with Clara in the village that afternoon.

The journey took longer than Kathryn had expected and she was especially weary from the wedding and the goodbyes at Dallington Place. Trying to keep her eyes open for most of the journey had proved difficult, the heat in the train was unbearable. It had become a very warm afternoon and she was already running late. She had to be back at the station in a couple of hours so she could get back to her mother's. Kathryn had no idea where she was and hoped the hospital was within walking distance from the station. She clutched the now wilting lilies in one hand and the address that Bertram had given her in the other. 'Could you tell me where St. James Military Hospital is please?' asked Kathryn to a surly looking guard who stamped her train ticket.

'You can see it from here,' he said pointing to a row of buildings to the left of the station. 'If you walk through that alleyway you can get to it quicker. It is the building with the tall chimneys.'

Relieved it was not far, she set off following a crowd of people through the gates and out to a welcoming cool breeze. It was good to have some time to herself, she thought. Her life would become more like this now she was no longer a maid at Dallington Place. As tired as she was, she treasured the moments to be by herself, and hold her destiny in her own hands. This frightened her and she wished she was brave, but she felt proud of herself for finding her way here.

The hospital was smaller than she had expected but she had learnt from a lady in her train carriage that there were many of these small military hospitals dotted around the country. It was pot luck which one the soldiers ended up in. Luckily it had not been too far for Kathryn to travel. She walked up to the tiny reception area where two nurses were sitting behind a long desk. 'Can I help you?' asked one of them, making Kathryn feel as if she should not have been there. Suddenly one of the nurses got up quickly and ran towards the double doors. Maybe there was an emergency going on Kathryn thought. As the doors swung open, she could hear some cries coming from the ward and for a split second Kathryn wanted to run away.

'I would like to see Private Robert Alton Weaves, if you would be so kind,' said Kathryn to the other nurse sitting behind the desk.

'Ah,' said the nurse looking through her notes. 'You are Miss Geraldine Weaves, his sister? I recognise you from the other week.'

'Me, no my fiancé Mr Wright is a good friend of Mr Weaves. He asked me if I would come and visit him.

'Just a minute, I think maybe Mr Weaves had been discharged.'

'Discharged?' asked Kathryn, now feeling foolish. She was too late. She should have telephoned first.

'Let me just check my notes.' The nurse's spectacles perched on the end of her nose moved up and down as she scanned a list of names. 'Yes just as I thought, he was discharged ten days ago.' Kathryn now feeling disheartened, sat down opposite the desk. Just as she was about to leave, she watched a redheaded lady go up to the desk.

It did not occur to Kathryn for a minute who it was. The conversation was heated and as Kathryn listened in she was amazed. It was Geraldine, her nurse friend, who she would be seeing tomorrow at the factory. 'Why did you discharge my brother?' she was asking, almost shouting. She was sniffing and dabbing at her eyes with her handkerchief.

'I am sorry Miss Weaves, but really it was not our decision. The doctors felt his health had improved and his leg had healed as much as it was going to. He was insistent to go back to war. There was no reason to detain him and we need the bed. Surely you can understand that,' the nurse spoke calmly, clearly having dealt with emotional relatives on a regular basis.

'But when I left two weeks ago, they said he would be here indefinitely. Doctor Platt said he was worried about his mental state of mind and wanted to keep him here indefinitely,' said Geraldine now barely able to speak through tears.

'Well, I am sorry, Miss, but Doctor Platt is working in London at the moment,' said the nurse shrugging.

Geraldine shrunk back on to the seat next to Kathryn. She put her head in her hands and wept. 'Geraldine?' said Kathryn slightly embarrassed to disturb her.

Geraldine turned to look at Kathryn, her face all scrunched up and exhausted. For a second she did not recognise her and then all of a sudden her face relaxed. 'Kathryn is that you? What on earth are you doing here?' she said with relief in her voice.

'It seems I was visiting your brother,' said Kathryn sympathetically looking at despaired Geraldine.

'Sorry what, I do not understand!' sniffed Geraldine, looking all confused.

'My fiancé Bertram is a good friend of your brother. They are in the same battalion, can you believe it? He asked me to look in on him, I had no idea he was your brother!' said Kathryn.

Taking the information in, Geraldine dabbed her eyes and let out a slow whistle. 'Well I be, what a coincidence! Am I happy to see you,' said Geraldine, now managing a smile through her tears.

'I am sorry about your brother going back to war, but listen, if he is with Bertram he will be fine,' said Kathryn hoping this would re-assure her.

Geraldine smiled, showing her large, white, slightly protruding teeth. 'Yes of course, that is good, but he is my baby brother and I worry about him so, sometimes he is so naive.'

Kathryn nodded, after all he is only eighteen years old. 'Let me cheer you up and have something to eat somewhere and talk. I do not have to be back for another hour,' suggested Kathryn to cheer up Geraldine.

'Are you going back to Dallington Place tonight?' asked Geraldine.

'No, I have left there, I live with my mother now as of today,' said Kathryn pointing to her bags on the floor.

'Are you still going to work at the factory tomorrow?' asked Geraldine looking surprised.

'Yes, and I am so looking forward to it but I am exhausted. How about you?' replied Kathryn with an excited smile.

'Absolutely! I feel one hundred and ten years old, do you think life will get any easier?' asked Geraldine now laughing.

'I hope so,' replied Kathryn, relieved that Geraldine's mood was shifting. 'If we get something to eat! Here, take these flowers, they were for your brother,' said Kathryn, putting the orange lilies on her lap. 'They are from the Fitch's wedding, I thought perhaps I would see you there.'

Geraldine instinctively hugged Kathryn. 'It is so good to see you! I know just the place where we can talk and you can tell me your news and all about the wedding. Why do you not stay with me tonight and then we can travel to the factory together in the morning? You look about as 'done in' as I feel and it will be so much easier for you,' suggested Geraldine.

'I would love that,' replied Kathryn smiling at Geraldine's lovely thought. 'But my mother will wonder what has happened to me if I do not go back tonight,' she continued.

'Well, we could telephone the lady I used to work for from here and she could send out her man to your mother's house and pass on a message to her,' said Geraldine, willing Kathryn to stay. Kathryn could not resist not staying at Geraldine's.

The girls walked to the nearest tearoom to recover from the afternoon's shock of Robert not being at the hospital and the incredible coincidence of bumping into each other. Kathryn's feet were beginning to ache. She could not wait to sit down and have something to eat and drink. Whittles of Gravesend was the most popular tearoom in all of Kent. Kathryn knew the large white envelope containing her references from Lady Fitch also contained her wages. She had not had any time to open it and now was about as good a time as any to see how much money she had in the world until next month.

The girls settled to a small table in the middle of the room as it was very crowded. Most of the tables by the windows were occupied. Some by lovers and some men in army uniform sat with their loves discreetly by the corners of the room. Kathryn tried not to stare and take too much notice of them, as this would upset her too much. She stared down at the pretty white tablecloth for a moment before rummaging into her bag to check her wages.

'Shall we just order a pot of tea for the moment until we know what we want to eat?' asked Geraldine turning to Kathryn as a young waitress stood impatiently by their table. Kathryn nodded as she took out a letter that Lady Fitch had given her. She opened it and read it to Geraldine.

25th June 1916

Dallington Place

Dear Miss Beaumont,

I have written two references for you, contained within this envelope. I hope this will suffice.

Lady Fitch and I wish you all the best in your future endeavours and wish to stress upon you how much we appreciated your services to Dallington Place, how conscientious a maid servant you have become. I understand from my dear wife Lady Fitch that you will be working at the Hoo factory in due course. We have been assured by Mr McAlister that you will be well looked after there.

If you need anything, please do not hesitate to come to Dallington Place and contact Mr Evan, our housekeeper. I understand you will be visiting occasionally to collect your letters from Mr Wright. Mr Evan has been made aware of this.

I have also included another month's wages to tide you over, which I hope will be very useful. I am sorry you will not be coming with us to Endelwise Manor. The offer still stands as a ladies maid there, although I know you cannot leave your mother so this is not feasible for you.

Thank you for your services and we wish you the very best.

Kind regards,

Sir Nicholas Fitch Esquire

'Another month's wages Kathryn, you are so lucky!' said Geraldine trying to be discreet in the noisy room.

'I know,' smiled Kathryn now looking through the menu. 'But you know it is not just for me, it is for my mother as well. Bertram sent me some notes too. I am going to save those for our future together,' said Kathryn carefully placing the envelope back in her pocket.

'I cannot save anything.' giggled Geraldine. 'As soon as I have it, I spend it on silly things. I know I should be more sensible like you, but you know I want to live for the moment, none of us know what is around the corner!' she said looking upset again. 'I would send some to my brother if I knew where he was Kathryn.' Tears were running down Geraldine's face as she snatched the menu from Kathryn to hide her eyes. The stain from the orange lilies on Geraldine's hands transferred onto the white tablecloth. She scratched at the tablecloth nervously, trying to remove the stain.

'Do not worry Geraldine, he will be with Bertram, as I said, I have a feeling they are together. Can you believe it, of all the coincidences Robert is your brother! I will write to Bertram tomorrow and ask if Robert is back with the battalion. I suppose there is no reason for him not to be there,' said Kathryn reassuringly. 'Would he not write to you and tell you?' she continued.

'Our Robert, no he is not one for writing,' replied Geraldine with a wide toothy smile again. 'Let us choose what we want or we will be here all night,' hurried Geraldine feeling tiredness descend on her again.

Kathryn woke listless and worried in the night. She was not very good at sleeping in a strange bed. Sharing a bed with Geraldine, who wriggled and snatched the eiderdown was not ideal. In some ways she longed to be back in her little bed at Dallington Place, at least she knew what to expect from the next day. Tomorrow would be so unnerving although exciting. She looked at the clock. It was four o'clock in the morning. It felt cold although it was summer. She shivered and felt out of place in this little holding in the town. She was used to village life and as she tiptoed to the window and carefully peeped out of the curtain, she was surprised to see people in the street already out and about. Had they gone to sleep at all, she wondered. As the dusky air whistled through the open window, she felt her spine tingle and a feeling of unease took hold of her. It was not for herself but for Bertram. She must have sat there for an hour until she woke Geraldine up at five. Kathryn was already dressed in what she thought would be appropriate for work.

Geraldine sat up in the bed, her red hair falling about her shoulders, making her look younger and paler than usual. 'How long have you been up?' she asked sleepily.

'Not long,' replied Kathryn guiltily. 'Do I look presentable?' she took a swirl in front of Geraldine.

'You always look presentable, not a hair out of place!' said Geraldine observing a shiny pin in Kathryn's hair.

As they walked quickly to catch the train, Kathryn carrying all her worldly belongings, and trying to take a bite of some not so fresh bread that Geraldine had stored in her cupboard. They talked and laughed along the way. Geraldine teased Kathryn about Mr McAlister. 'Oh dear, Mr McAlister could not keep his eyes off you!' Geraldine nudged Kathryn with giggle. 'Did you see those bushy eyebrows? They almost had a life of their own!' said Geraldine nearly falling over with laughter. Kathryn just looked up the to the sky and sighed at her friend's silly observation.

Arriving half an hour later at the factory gates, which were opening at six o'clock, they joined the queue outside with at least forty women. Kathryn noticed most were fairly young women, not much older than herself, some were older. Some pretty, some looking weary and worn. Some with wedding rings and others without. An argument started between two women and the girls craned their necks to see. It was about someone's husband who had run off with another woman in town. From what Kathryn could hear, the two women were both rivals for this man's affections. She looked away. How sad she thought, what the war does to people. Everybody fighting, even on the home soil. Just in the nick of time, they were ushered in, with some jostling from the women in front. Their names were ticked off the list and they were issued with hats and overalls. As Kathryn and Geraldine helped each other into their new surroundings, they were blithely unaware, this was to become an almost home to them for the time being. There was a community feel to the place and once you entered in, it was hard to escape.

CHAPTER ELEVEN
BERTRAM: RETURN TO MESVES-SUR-LOIRE

'You have timed that with expert precision, Robert!' declared Bertram patting his friend's back with genuine warmth. 'Good to have you back, how is the ol' leg holding up?' he continued looking at Robert, who was struggling to stand still on his bad leg.

'Not brilliant to be honest, but I could not take that hospital they sent me to in Gravesend. My sister Geraldine will kill me, but I had to get back here. I am a soldier after all,' said Robert looking Bertram square in the eye. Surely he knew the feeling.

'That you are my dear fellow, that you are,' said Bertram as he watched Robert limp over to his bunk. 'Well, one more night and then we will be billeted out to Mesves-sur-Loire again,' declared Bertram biting his bottom lip and stifling what he wanted to tell Robert. It can wait, he told himself. 'So how did they pass you fit if you are still limping?' he asked instead.

'Well, it only plays up when I am tired, it was a bad break though. I did not think they would send me home, I was hoping to stay in Calais. But there were few surgeons and as I had a sister living near Kent they thought I would be better taken care of at St. James's hospital in Gravesend,' said Robert as he stopped and turned to Bertram. 'Maybe they wanted me to discharge myself from the army, but that was never going to happen Bertram! Being a soldier is my life. Anyway, I can live with the guilt that I did not tell my sister that I had left. She would have kicked up such a fuss, being a trained nurse,' he continued, easing himself up on the bed to rest against a hard and uncomfortable pillow. Hitting the firm bolster and then pushing it off, he laid back to listen to what Bertram had to tell him.

'Listen, you have nothing to feel guilty about, I am sure your sister will understand. I know all about guilt and what you have done my friend is nothing, believe me, it is me that should feel guilty,' said Bertram resting his hands on his lap nervously playing with a lighter.

'You? What have you got to feel guilty about?' asked Robert, taking Bertram's statement lightly. Bertram pressed the lighter to his lips, tapping it slowly against his dry mouth.

'I am no saint Robert, and perhaps I should not tell you, but you know I stay with Madame Comte, we are lovers…'

Robert closed his eyes and did not say anything, until he had digested what Bertram had told him. 'I am going outside,' said Robert with a look of disdain for his friend. He was shocked to hear this especially since Bertram had been so fondly talking about his fiancé Kathryn. Watching his friend limp to the door, Bertram now regretted telling him. It was unnecessary to burden his friend, how selfish he could be sometimes, he thought.

Robert did not return for an hour. Bertram had fallen into a fitful sleep. Rubbing his eyes and clearing his sore throat, he wanted to catch his friend's attention. But Robert did not want to talk about it. 'I have just heard about John Miller, you should have told me,' he snapped at Bertram, still not looking at him.

'Sorry, what can I say, I have things on my mind,' snapped Bertram back. His friend was beginning to annoy him; how sanctimonious he was becoming.

'I am going to call it off with Berenice, so please drop it!' Bertram barked at him. 'Come with me tomorrow and stay with me at Berenice's and I will prove it to you,' he continued now having calmed down.

'It is not that I do not believe you, I am sure you will, but I have a sister and if someone did that to her, well I would want to chop their block off!' declared Robert, casting a telling look at Bertram.

Bertram cleared his throat nervously. 'It was a mistake, it will not happen again. Let us not talk about it anymore. We have tomorrow to prepare for, you'd better get some rest,' said Bertram hoping to change the subject.

Next morning, primitive gas masks were passed around the camp. Bertram could see Robert was nervous. 'It will be fine, just a few hours out there, get a few men out and then we can be well away early tomorrow morning on the train to St. Eloi,' said Bertram trying to comfort his friend. Bertram knew the only reason they were being ordered to do stretcher duty that night was that too many bearers had fallen in the last few days. Bertram had a plan. He was not going to hang around. He would do his duty and get the hell out of there.

As darkness fell, shells and gunfire could be heard surrounding them. As they stoically ascended the hilly ground having covered at least two miles, with Bertram and twenty-five men from their battalion and Robert lagging behind, they knew they were near the enemy lines.

Just one body and then I am out of here, thought Bertram to himself, the words going over and over in his head. Robert was none the wiser and each weak step he walked, his body shook with every nerve in his being. He kept looking behind him as if death was following him. He could not settle and keep his mind on his job in hand. His heart was beating and sickness was enveloping him. Bodies were beginning to be strewn around them. They smelled gas, the word went up from command and the men were suddenly running to the left of Robert and then to the right. His head was spinning, he could not move. 'Move!' shouted Bertram, as a shell hit to the right of them. Bertram and Private Hammond pulled a young officer onto their stretcher, and out of the corner of his eye, he could see Robert pulling on his gas mask, scratching at his head and waving his arms around. Bertram had to keep going. Lifting the officer out of the black confusion with Hammond in the front, they ran. They ran for their lives and Robert was nowhere to be seen. Where did he go, thought Bertram as he and Hammond ran through the small woods towards the lights of their camp. The officer, who had been screaming in pain to the noise of the shelling had grown silent, like the silence now engulfing them. Their gas masks still eerily pulled down, covering their stricken faces, as they reached the trucks that would take the injured officer to the nearest hospital. There was not time to patch up his wounded leg and bloody arm. The men would never know if he survived.

Bertram arrived back to his dug out, only to find Robert sitting on his bunk, shaking and being violently sick. And when he was not being sick, he rocked to and fro, whining and crying. 'You need hospital treatment. I will take you outside and see if someone can take you,' said Bertram looking worryingly at his friend who appeared to have lost his mind.

The train journey to his billet was a lonely one. Bertram took out a piece of paper to begin to write to Kathryn, but all he could think was how he was going to break things off with Berenice. Screwing the paper back into his pocket, he was aware of how black his fingernails were. How he longed for a hot bath and a woman's touch. Could he resist Berenice, he wondered. How he had hoped Robert would be with him. He would have kept his promise to him if he had been with him.

Berenice's outstretched arms were a heaven from the hell he had succumbed to. She looked different, prettier if that was possible. Her black hair shiny and her face more youthful than he had remembered.

He had not seen her for a few months and she had missed him more than he expected her to. She was thirty-two but her maturity and age only increased his desire for her, and she behaved like a twenty-year-old girl around him. This he did not see or realise that she was in love with him.

The week he spent with her and Sebastien was blissful. His guilt resided in the back portals of his mind. Away from the stress of living in a time of war, only once when he left the house to take a walk, he was aware of the reality of his wartime existence. Seeing soldiers at the local café brought him down to earth and back to now, the summer of 1916 in war-torn France. The weather was hot and sitting in the shade in the little back garden with Sebastien at his feet, he could have been as far away from the Somme as anywhere in the world. Lavender bloomed by the corners of the walled garden, ready to be harvested and filled into pillows that Berenice sold at the local shop. She was a good seamstress and in the evening she would light three or four candles behind her wicker chair and embroider cushions and silks for her friends. She would look up every now and then and smile at him, and twice during an evening she would get up and fetch him some cognac for his sore throat, until his eyes were heavy and then she would lead him upstairs, her warmth radiating from her whole being and taking him to her bedroom. A room filled with cosy tapestries on the pale grey walls and an iron bedstead in the middle and on it a mattress with a will of its own. Not once did he think of Kathryn or Berenice's husband, it was make believe and that is the way Bertram wanted it. He could cope with no more just now, until the last afternoon they spent together.

A knock on the door at two in the afternoon confirmed one thing and that was the end of their time together. Berenice's husband was back, having stopped off for a drink at the local watering hole. Berenice's older sister, Solange, had warned them of his impending visit. A small and plain woman much older than Berenice, she could not look Bertram in the eye. She would brush past him and out to the garden to help Berenice hang out the washing. Not once did Berenice flinch or come into the house to order Bertram to go in a hurry. Perhaps she wanted to be caught, he thought, as he watched their heated discussion. Solange would nervously eye him with a sideways glance and squint almost at the height of his navel. Her aged fingers would wag at Berenice who would shake her head and tut and shrug her shoulders until finally she would leave to find Bertram upstairs

93

packing his few belongings. She had tears in her eye as she hugged his waist tightly from behind.

Bertram waited patiently across the street. Sitting on a neighbour's stone and crumbling wall, his hat tipped privately over one eye as he watched for this man that was so reviled. Sebastien knew Bertram was still there. Up and down the front path he bounced his ball, only glancing at Bertram to check he was still there. A tall man in scruffy clothes opened the gate and once Sebastien recognised his stepfather, he went over to him dutifully. Alphonse Comte brushed his stepson's hair with his heavy hand and Sebastien followed him to the house. The door of the cottage opened and Sebastien looked over to Bertram discreetly before disappearing inside.

Was that the face of a deserter, or was this man just of weak will and an alcoholic, thought Bertram, finally getting up to leave. He threw his backpack over his shoulder and he walked to the station, relieved that the heat was subsiding. But in his heart a burning sensation of loss took hold of him. Would he see Sebastien again, he wondered. That sweet boy, I wish he was mine, he muttered to himself. Knowing he had a photograph of the little one moved him on, back to the dust and darkness of the battalion.

Bertram stopped to talk to three men that were relaxing by a worn down truck. Propped up against it all three men were laughing and joking. Bertram wanted to join them and enjoy their cheerful chat. Bertram knew Officer Alfred T. Simkins from way back when they were enlisting. Alfred had been made an officer because of his good education and he had applied to a university just before the war. The lads teased him for his upper class vowels however, he got on with everyone and although an officer now, he still managed to have time for the lower ranked soldiers. As soon as he saw Bertram approach, he offered him a cigarette. 'Looking well there, Private Wright!' he said acknowledging how rested Bertram must have looked. Bertram liked this man as he knew full well there was a lot of jealously regarding his flying and 'time off.' He still had time for Bertram.

'Thanks, I have just returned from Meves-sur-Loire,' said Bertram, happy to inhale the cigarette slowly and pleasurably.

'Got yourself a lady friend here then?' asked the older soldier with a sleazy grin on his face.

Bertram could not tell if he knew something. Maybe Robert had blagged. Damn him, thought Bertram. 'What? No, just had a good rest,' he replied unconvincingly.

Alfred smirked and stubbed out his cigarette under his heavy boot. 'No loyalty here,' he said turning round to the men as if dismissing Bertram. 'Tell him the story of Whisper, now there's loyalty for you,' said the older soldier sarcastically.

'What is his problem?' mumbled Bertram annoyed, feeling the pulse on his neck beat faster and his hands sweat. He was fed up with the men's attitude here. 'Who is Whisper?' asked Bertram turning to Alfred trying to keep calm.

Alfred had now stopped and turned back to Bertram. 'Well, as rumours go apparently last night, a messenger dog called Whisper owned by the Essex Regiment, a right little runt terrier, caused a ceasefire. The Germans ceased firing for a good two hours so he could run behind the enemy lines and pass on his message. It gave our squaddies time to retreat and that little dog saved hundreds of lives. The Essex Regiment were a lucky bunch of bastards last night!'

Bertram always squirmed when Alfred swore. As educated as he was, it just did not go well with his accent. Bertram wanted to laugh. 'Phew, a man's best friend!' he winked at Alfred.

'Talking of best friends, have you seen Private Weaves anywhere?' asked Bertram, hoping that Robert was around.

'Ah there is a problem there, I am afraid. I think he has only gone and got himself court-martialled,' said Alfred biting the end of another cigarette and spitting it out. 'Damn bloody fool,' he continued.

'What? Our Robert Alton Weaves, tell me that is not true,' Bertram looked at Alfred in disbelief.

'It is I am afraid; they've got him down with the Commander to make a statement. He will be fine ol' chap, good chap that, just a misunderstanding,' said Alfred reassuringly.

'I have got to go, see what I can do,' said Bertram suddenly feeling drained.

'See you then, by the way keep up the good work, hear you have been doing some great stuff with your battalion newsletters, officer material Bertram!' said Alfred waving him off.

There was nothing more Bertram could do that evening. Finding Robert had not returned by late evening, he went to speak to Commander McGovern, who was sitting in the officers' mess drinking rum and playing cards with Monsieur Le Sierre and some other officers he did not recognise. Monsieur Le Sierre had one eye on some plans that were lying on the floor by his feet, as well as playing poker with the three other men. Commander McGovern, usually an approachable man, seemed agitated that Bertram wanted to talk at this hour. 'It is about Private Weaves, Sir, could I have a few moments please? Sorry to disturb you.' Bertram could see the commander rolling his eyes at the other men in annoyance at ruining his card game.

'Yes Private Wright, make it quick,' he said swigging down what was left in his glass.

'Sir, I am here in defence of Private Weaves, who I believe has been court-martialled today,' said Bertram nervously looking at the commander.

'Yes, sorry business that,' said the commander arrogantly pushing his hair off his face.

'Will someone hear his defence? I do believe the man is ill. He had only just returned from hospital in Kent and they believed he was not ready to return to duty, Sir,' explained Bertram.

'That is very noble of you Wright, but Weaves returned to duty of his own accord. You can petition to be a "prisoner's friend" but you will have to be pretty sharpish about it. I will write you a letter of pardon and you will have to get to Labourse in the next couple of days. That is where he has been sent,' said the commander now warming to Bertram's dedication to help his friend.

'Already?' said Bertram his face going quite ashen, having realised the severity of the situation.

Commander McGovern shrugged. 'Pick up the letter from me tomorrow and you can make your way there, that is all I can suggest.'

Bertram looked at him in gratitude and sighed in relief. 'Thank you, Sir, I will see you tomorrow,' said Bertram thankful that the commander was so accommodating.

'Right you are, I will have it here by noon, now goodnight,' said the commander without any emotion on his face.

As Bertram walked to the door, Pierre Le Sierre followed him out. 'Private Wright, do you have a cigarette on you?' he asked Bertram who was firmly shutting the door behind them. Bertram fumbled in his pocket for one for himself and one for Le Sierre. Lighting their cigarettes and not saying anything for a moment, they inhaled the fumes and the cool night air. The air was relatively clear tonight, an unusual silence near the woods made Bertram nervous. No lights could be seen, alighting the sky with red and orange flames. 'Had any more flying time?' Le Sierre suddenly asked.

'No, I have not seen Jacobson for a while. And you, have you been up?' asked Bertram, now looking at Le Sierre and trying to figure out what he was after. 'Non, but in the next few days, we may be onto something,' replied Pierre looking uneasy. 'There is a mission commencing soon, Jacobson is returning tomorrow. Maybe you would like to go with us, or maybe not. It could be very dangerous,' Le Sierre continued looking at Bertram, unsure if it in fact was a good idea at all.

'I will be there, count me in,' said Bertram immediately cheered up.

'Good, good, well bon nuit,' The Frenchman said, turning his back on Bertram and going back to his card game. Bertram sat there for a moment, smoking and trying to relax and not think of Robert. He will be fine, he muttered under his breath. He will make a statement and he will be fine.

Bertram tried to sleep but he was too hot and his nerves were jangled. He could not get away from his worrying thoughts so he got up at four in the morning, took his pen and wrote to Kathryn.

14th July 1916

Dearest Kathryn,

I loved to read your news about the wedding and what fun you have been having. I shall admit my jealousy, as in my mind's eye, you look so pretty dancing at the wedding and having so many admiring glances from good looking fellows, I cannot rest. I miss you my dear Kathryn.

I have some sad news, my comrade Private Weaves has been court-martialled and sent to Labourse near Calais. I have a permission to follow him there, to see if I can help in any way. I am sorry I have not written for a while. I was billeted once again near St. Eloi and desperately needing the rest, I did nothing but sleep and eat. I arrived back today to hear the news of Weaves so things are bad here.

Will write soon when I have more news. Write to me quickly, it makes me so happy.

Yours truly,

Bertram

Bertram sealed the envelope and jumped in his seat in a shock when Le Sierre suddenly burst into his dug out. 'Bertram, we are going up this morning, now in fact, so grab your things and we will get a lift to the airfield,' hurried Le Sierre.

'Now?' said Bertram pulling on his flying jacket and trousers.

'Oui, no time to lose, now or never, we have to be up in the skies by 0500 hours,' continued Le Sierre.

'Will we be up there long?' asked Bertram, worrying that if he went, he would miss the chance to go to Labourse for Robert.

'You afraid, Private Wright?' asked Le Sierre, now getting visibly annoyed that Bertram was so hesitant.

'No, no, it is just I have to be here by noon to meet with Commander McGovern,' said Bertram, following Pierre out into the warmth of the morning.

'I should think we will be back by 0700 hours, no later,' replied Le Sierre now getting curious about this meeting with Commander McGovern.

Still carrying Kathryn's letter he stuffed it into the pocket of his flying jacket. Flight Lieutenant Jacobson was waiting for them in the truck. Shaking Bertram's hand firmly, he then tapped on the shoulder of the driver. 'We are going now!' he commanded.

CHAPTER TWELVE
KATHRYN: THE CANARY GIRL

25TH JULY 1916

The last few weeks had gone by so quickly, Kathryn had not had much spare time to visit Dallington Place to collect any letters. She had promised herself she would stay home, spend the next days off with her mother and visit her friends in the village. Her work at the factory, although arduous, was peppered with time off at lunchtime, where the girls could relax, gossip, make new friends and widen their social lives. They had been invited to a few dances, one in Gravesend and another one the previous Saturday evening in a small village hall at Sharnell Street. Some of the men from the naval base at Port Victoria had been invited and Kathryn and Geraldine had had the most fun in their lives. Kathryn wanted to pinch herself. Her independent spirit was growing and she loved that she had enough money not to worry about her mother and even have some money left over to buy herself a few pretty dresses. To save money and to relieve her fatigue, she had stayed with Geraldine Saturdays and Sundays and only travelling back to Sussex during the workdays. There at the dance, Geraldine had met a handsome naval engineer called William Lovet. He had seen the girls arrive as he stood by the grand piano in the village hall. He had been instantly attracted to Geraldine's red hair and as he danced with her all evening, felt he was falling in love with her and her vivacious personality already. Kathryn had danced with his friend Joe but wearing her sweetheart brooch so he was aware she was someone else's girl. At the end of the evening William and Joe walked the girl's back to the station at Sharnell Street and they arranged to meet them on Sunday at eleven o'clock at Port Victoria's marine base.

Seeing Port Victoria from the train, Geraldine combed her hair and took out her red lipstick. Admiring herself in her small mirror, she touched her skin softly. 'Do you know Kathryn, as soon as I have a whiff of my skin turning yellow I am out of that factory! That TNT[1]

---

[1] Trinitrotoluene (TNT) was first prepared in 1863 by German chemist Julius Wilbrand and originally used as a yellow dye and later as an explosive. British female shell workers during

is dangerous stuff and have you seen the state of Mary's mother? I know, she has been demoted to another, safer area of the factory, but she may have to leave if her condition does not improve,' Geraldine chattered on not even expecting a reply from Kathryn. 'We are all canaries[i], Kathryn, just for how long that is all,' she continued smacking her lips together and pouting.

Kathryn looked idly out of the train window at the lush marshlands. The sun beginning to twinkle on the blue water, the marshy grasses bending in the breeze. Birds in flocks landing on the water and taking off one at a time. Their wings outstretched and free floating, they were flying in the same direction as the girls towards Port Victoria. Out perhaps to the Isle of Grain and then across the Channel. Kathryn's thoughts wandered to Bertram and what he may have thought of her gallivanting with naval men on a Sunday.

Geraldine was up and walking to the door before Kathryn had time to dissemble the quagmire of her thoughts. 'Come on sleepy, let us have some fun!' announced Geraldine excitedly as she jumped down onto the platform. The Southern train at 1308 hours departed once again along the fens, leaving the girls stranded to the mercy of the admiralty. The girls headed towards the pier, which they could see in the distance. 'Shame it is closed to the public at the moment,' said Geraldine reading the warning signs at the station. 'You know Queen Victoria came to the pier quite frequently,' she continued.

'Where are we going?' asked Kathryn, feeling the heat in her blue dress. Geraldine had been more sensible wearing a light yellow cotton dress. She looked very pretty and free today although Kathryn questioned the length of her dress.

'To the marine depot,' Geraldine called out, running along the pebbled and potholed road, her yellow dress billowing out behind her in the breeze. She looked like a canary bird against the backdrop of the fens, thought Kathryn hot and bothered. 'William said he would wait for us by the gate. Look he drew me a map, he said it was only a ten minute walk,' said Geraldine now out of breath, turning the map up one way and then the other. Kathryn caught up with her, mopping her brow and hoping her hair was not turning into one large bird's nest.

There was a marshal at the gate of the marine base. 'May I help you, ladies?' he asked politely tipping his hat.

World War I, who handled TNT, were called the canary girls because of repeated exposure turned their skin an orange-yellow colour, reminiscent of the plumage of a canary bird.

'Yes, thank you, we are here to see Mr William Lovat, he is supposed to be meeting us here at the gate,' said Geraldine still out of breath. Kathryn was sure the marshal was staring at her wild hair amused.

'Your names please?' he asked still staring at her.

'Kathryn Beaumont and Geraldine Weaves,' stated Kathryn, trying not to catch his eye. 'Ah yes, Captain Lovat is waiting for you just inside that door there, to the right,' the marshal pointed to the door of the barracks.

'Captain Lovat!' whispered Geraldine, poking Kathryn in the ribs as the marshal opened the iron gates with just enough room for them to fit through.

Surprised to see William not in uniform, Geraldine smiled at the young man in his white shirt and soft brown trousers. He returned her smile, showing white but crooked teeth and a warmth spread across his face, his brown heavy lashed puppy eyes glinting at the girls. 'Would you like a cup of tea and then I can show you out to the hanger, where we are working on my aeroplane?' he offered.

'Yes please!' said Geraldine, although confused about what he meant by his aeroplane. Picking up a flask of tea as they walked through the naval base, and eventually finding some cups, they walked out through to a large open space, where in front of them stood a large aircraft hangar. Both girls gasped impressed by this magnificent view of aircrafts. Kathryn was amazed by all this life going on behind the iron gates. 'Is Joe here?' asked Geraldine nodding to Kathryn.

Annoyed by her friend's directness, Kathryn raised her eyebrows at Geraldine, and a relief took hold of her when William explained he was on duty today. Thank goodness, she thought to herself. Sipping their tea as they walked, they heard a large rumble of engines coming from the hangar.

'I will show you my baby I am working on,' said William excitedly, pointing to a small biplane in one corner of the hangar. There were many men working in the hanger that day, some off duty because this was their hobby, their life, it was down time to them. 'I am checking this one for its maiden flight today, it is called the floatplane,' explained William.

'You are?' asked Geraldine, now impressed that William sounded to be a skilled pilot.

'Yes indeed I am, that is why I asked you girls along, interested?' he asked with a wide grin.

'Love to watch but from a safe distance, thank you!' replied Geraldine smiling. She was rather afraid of heights, let alone flying.

'It was designed to intercept German Zeppelins,' explained William, keen to impress the girls with his knowledge. 'You can watch from the pier if you like, it is being carefully supervised. The Royal Navy has taken it over but if you are with me they will let you on,' he continued, realising that there was no chance getting Geraldine up in the air with him.

'Really? I feel like Royalty!' smiled Kathryn. 'I saw a few of those Zeppelins going over Tilbury docks not so long ago.' Geraldine joined in.

'They are hard to detect at first as they fly so high,' explained William. Kathryn shuddered. She was fully aware airships were arriving more often in the skies. Like silver cigars, hanging almost motionless once finding their target, except for the bombs that they dropped causing havoc over all our cities and in London a few days ago. She began to admire this man, whose legs were now sticking out under the undercarriage. If these aeroplanes could bring the airships down before they reached the shores of England, all well and good she thought.

'Zeppelins light up the skies momentarily in the fog before they strike at night, when the moon is not visible. Now there is the challenge, to spot the buggers before they get you!' William shouted out from the undercarriage.

The "White Fairy" in all its novice glory was wheeled out on to the tarmac. The girls had long been dispatched to the pier at Port Victoria. A crowd had formed, some wives of the aviators, apprehensively sitting on benches with white handkerchiefs ready to wave. Thirty or forty men gathered in front of the girls to get a better view as the biplanes and seaplanes took to the skies and demonstrated what they could do for the expectant crowds. Everyone on the pier that day had to be accounted for and the other town folk were kept behind barriers for safety and not let on to the pier at all. The Mayor, Julien Wiggans, declared the flight's arrival as a band played from the local naval military band.

Kathryn squinted in the bright sunlight as five or six aeroplanes zigzagged the sky above.

'Can you see William's floatplane?' she asked Geraldine who was now jumping up and down with excitement as a roar of the little aeroplane could be heard. It came in fast towards the pier, circled around it and then disappeared behind some clouds out of view.

'Did you see him?' squealed Geraldine proudly at her friend.

'Just about,' said Kathryn still waving her white handkerchief at any aeroplane she could wave to. 'Did he say where you will meet him afterwards?' asked Kathryn bemused that it was all over so quickly.

'I think he has to go back to duty but he knows where to contact me,' replied Geraldine with a smile. 'He is very dashing is he not? I love the fact he is so knowledgeable about his aircraft and you can see that he loves his job with a passion,' she continued now looking little downcast for a moment.

'Do you not like working at the factory, Geraldine? I was beginning to really enjoy it, the freedom and everything,' said Kathryn feeling unsettled by Geraldine's apathy towards the factory.

As the girls made their way to the platform and waited for the Gravesend train, Geraldine turned to Kathryn taking hold of her arm. 'I am missing nursing, Kathryn, I want to do more for the war effort.'

A notice firmly stuck on the side of the wall to the entrance of the station had not gone unnoticed by the girls. It read:

IT IS FAR BETTER TO FACE THE BULLETS
THAN TO BE KILLED AT HOME BY A BOMB.
JOIN THE ARMY AT HOME AND HELP TO STOP
AN AIR RAID.

Kathryn knew Geraldine was tired so she did not ask any more questions that evening. She did not want to spoil the wonderful day they had had. Both tired but with healthy, flushed cheeks, they walked arm in arm to Whittles for tea. An early night was called for as Monday was always an early start.

Kathryn noticed that Mr McAlister had been keeping more of a watchful eye on her factory floor this week. Twice he had approached her station and asked if she was enjoying her work and was she taking full safety measures. His undue attention was beginning to unsettle her and when the bell went for lunch, she gleefully rushed away to find Geraldine.

By Wednesday lunchtime, a notice had been put in place warning the women that there was going to be some change around at the factory. Some job losses, and some posts would be moved around. The reasons being some people were on sick leave, others had left their jobs and the factory staffing numbers were being cut due to shortage of money. 'The factory is in money difficulties?' Kathryn asked

Geraldine, who was now amongst a group of women gossiping about who would be next to lose their job.

'I hear some of the older ladies are being let go, and it is terrible as their husbands are either too old to work or are away at the war. They will be destitute if they have to go,' said Sarah, who was working on the post next to Geraldine.

'Is there not some kind of union we could go to, if the worst comes to the worst?' piped up Laura, whose father and brother had just been killed in the battle of Jutland. 'I cannot take this anymore, the loss and the uncertainty of it all! My mother is ill because of this, I cannot take any more bad news,' she said tearfully.

'Bloody Mr McAlister, he has no feelings for the rest of us,' said Margaret, who worked on the floor above Geraldine and Kathryn. Making the bags for the dangerous materials was considered an easier job and most sought after. She was aware that her job was envied and the girls on the floor below her had the most dangerous job of all as the shell fillers. Kathryn was surprised to hear the other ladies talk about Mr McAlister in such a way. She had known the rumours that he had been unpopular at the last factory he managed before it was bombed, but she thought his popularity had risen again. Maybe it was just around the aristocracy that he was popular, she thought, not with the lower classes.

Kathryn sat away from the ladies to eat her lunch. Too much gossiping was giving her a headache. As she reached for some brown bread and cheese wrapped tightly and carefully by Geraldine last night, she heard cries from outside in the courtyard. Startled, she ran to the window.

'Zeppelin, Zeppelin!' shouted Devlin McAlister now running towards the factory door to warn the women.

'Everyone out!' screamed Kathryn. Girls dropped their lunches as the siren started to go off. Covering their ears and running for the courtyard, Mr McAlister ran past Kathryn, as fast as he could with his limp. Shouting at all the women to get into the shelter on the other side of the courtyard, was quite impressive to watch.

Kathryn stood at the entrance and waited until all the ladies had got out. Geraldine ran past her grabbing her hand. 'No wait, I am going to wait for Mr McAlister!' she shouted back to Geraldine, whose face was as red as a beetroot.

'Come on Kathryn, do not be stupid,' she shouted back, shocked that Kathryn could be so foolish to let go of her hand.

'I will be along in a minute,' shouted Kathryn back, willing for Devlin to hurry back down the stairs as quickly as possible. A quiet rumble could be heard from above and doors began to shake. Kathryn looked up in horror to see an enormous silver cigar shaped airship hovering over the building.

'Kathryn, what the devil!' shouted Mr McAlister, as he almost did not see her there by the doors as he ran down the bottom stairs missing the last two. By now he was limping badly and taking Kathryn's hand he shouted they had no time and dived for cover in the flower beds behind a tin toilet to be used for emergencies if there was a water shortage. Two explosions encased them, one after another. Devlin had thrown his body over Kathryn's as two bombs hit the site, narrowly missing the main munitions building and the shelter. Ear splitting explosions, kept them immobile and Kathryn could swear that she could hear Devlin's heart beating as he squashed her to the ground. She was aware of her cheek against the gravelled ground, his heavy arm over her head pushed it further into the sharp earth. But she would not have moved even if she could. There was something unworldly keeping her still and lying there. She did not know how long she had been there until she heard a shout from a soldier from the Home Guard saying the airship had moved on and it was safe to surface. It was a miracle no one had been killed.

The following week, as Kathryn walked up the imposing driveway to her beloved Dallington Place, tears sprung to her eyes for the first time in weeks. She was safe back in the folds of the manor house she knew so well. Mr Evan was pleased to see her and excitedly told her of two letters that had arrived for her. 'How are Lord and Lady Fitch, in good health I hope?' enquired Kathryn, longing to hear some good news.

'In good health Ma'am, but Norfolk took quite a hit from those Zeppelins. Missed Endelwise Manor, mind!' responded Mr Evan.

'Oh thank goodness,' said Kathryn touching her bruised and cut cheek. 'Here, I will make you a cup of tea as you have come far. You can sit here and read your letters,' said Mr Evan with a kind smile.

'Thank you Mr Evan, I am tired I must admit,' said Kathryn gladly taking up his offer.

Sipping her tea, Kathryn read Bertram's account of his flying and she proudly imagined him in the triplane, like William flying over the Peninsula and Port Victoria in his floatplane. She ripped open the next letter and her heart stopped for a moment. Tears flowed in shock as she read the news of Robert being sent to prison. How was she going to tell Geraldine? Was there any respite to this war, she wondered. In a trance, she left Dallington Place walking towards the village. She did not remember crossing the little white bridge and she did not stop to watch the flowing stream as she always did. She just put one foot in front of the other until she reached her mother's cottage and fell into her arms, tearful and exhausted.

CHAPTER THIRTEEN
BERTRAM: THE GERMAN AIRSTRIKE

Fifteen aeroplanes were waiting patiently. Bertram knew this was a highly charged mission. The plan was to forge an attack on a German aerodrome, but the men were aware there were German Fokker fighter planes already in the skies. Without an attack from the German squadrons, they could get near the aerodrome. Bertram's mission was to take as many pictures as he could and log all the aircraft that he could see. Any losses from their squadron, as well as on the German side, were to be meticulously recorded. Eight aeroplanes were from the RFC squadron at Gosport, three from the Canadian squadron. Flight Lieutenant Jacobson's aeroplane and Pierre's aeroplane accompanied by Bertram were joining the convoy. Two aeroplanes were left without pilots. Bertram did not ask why, but he already knew. Men that had not made it back from yesterday's attack. Their two-seater Vickers F.B.5 also known as the "Gunbus" planes were waiting in vain for their fallen pilots, who like vulnerable feathered birds in the sky, had taken the full force of bullets. Skilfully landing their unmarked aeroplanes and then bowing out on friendly soil.

Bertram pulled on his goggles and sat behind Pierre. Giving Bertram the thumbs up sign, they made their way down the grassy runway and slowly taking off, turning sharply out across the valley. The continuous buzzing of their comrades' aeroplanes behind, above and beside them built an assuring cocoon around them. Bertram breathed calmly, reassured that the Frenchman was a skilled pilot and he knew there was no other place he would rather be at that moment.

Suddenly, out of nowhere, a brightly coloured Fokker plane dived in front of them shooting at any of the squadron that were in his path. Bertram had never seen anything like it before. The German pilot's skill as an airman could not be matched by any of them. He was shooting continuously and shot down two RFC aeroplanes almost simultaneously. Bertram strained his neck around if he could see which ones they were. Who were these fallen pilots, he thought. This lone, daredevil fighter that had the gall to just appear out of nowhere, alone and full of fight. Bertram knew that German pilot Max

Immelmann, nicknamed as "Eagle of Lille," had been shot down a month ago, so who was this pilot he wondered. There was a rumour that his brother was flying to revenge his death. But that is just what it was, just a rumour. This was someone new and how many more of these German aces were out there this morning, he thought. The colourful ghost disappeared as fast as he had dawned. But another slow humming fighter appeared above them. Flight Lieutenant Jacob Jacobson was quick with his guns. Three German observation aircraft appeared through the clouds. Stealthily they followed the RFC squadron and Jacobson fired from his Black Sheriff, receiving rapid return fire from the Germans. A battle ensued and two of the enemy aeroplanes were struck. Nose diving elegantly, then a trailing fire fled behind the stricken aeroplanes, plotting their demise. Bertram watched mesmerised, poetical words springing to his mind as the aircrafts reeled out of control and out of sight.

Reeling, Squealing Colourful Ghosts.
Out of the blue, I watch for you.
Eliminate the elite, enmesh our crew,
down to wasted land.
Ennobled Pilot, you win.
Chapfallen we have become.
By Bertram Wright

Bertram wanted to reach for his notes and write his thoughts and words down, but he was aware that Pierre was now following orders to abort the mission. They were outnumbered and the only way out was down. Pierre's sudden jolt to the left and a steep descent, Bertram knew they were going down to the unknown. Following the safety of Jacobson's aeroplane, the "Black Sheriff", they followed him down. Luckily visibility was clear and a few minutes later Pierre and Bertram landed at Abeele Aerodrome. Bertram jumped down from the aeroplane, his legs uncoordinated as if through nervous energy, whipped off his goggles and Jaeger fleece-lined aviator jacket and walked as fast as he could over to Jacobson. Checking his watch, he was surprised to see it was mid-morning already. Close call, my friend,' said Jacobson looking over to Pierre who was waving him on as he checked his flight controls. 'Loved every minute of it, except when we lost some aircraft. Do you think they stood any chance of survival?' asked Bertram already checking his flight records.

'Doubt it,' replied Jacobson looking stern and saddened. 'Do not think about it, we have to move quickly. We will have to stay here the night, move the aeroplanes into the hangars and then tomorrow we can set off at dawn again back to base. We need the aeroplanes checked. I thought mine might have taken a hit on the left wing. Not sure,' he said removing his gloves.

'Tomorrow? I was supposed to meet up with Commander McGovern at noon,' said Bertram feeling nervous.

'No other way I am afraid; things could be worse. Sorry cannot help you old chap, unless you get a lift or take the train,' said Jacobson now wondering what this meeting with McGovern was about.

Pierre ran up to the men and put his arm around Bertram. 'You got your taste for aerial battle then?' said Pierre patting Bertram on the back. 'Good you did not lose your nerve!'

Bertram put a smile on his face to hide how he was feeling. 'Let me take a photograph of you and Jacob,' said Pierre excitedly as the adrenaline still pumped through his body. Bertram posed with Jacobson, both pulling their goggles back on top of their heads. Smiling for the camera, Bertram's mouth twitched with unease. He reciprocated and took a photo of Pierre and Jacob. Giving the camera back to Pierre, the men walked over to the base to search for some early lunch. Bertram made his excuses for a few minutes to see if he could find someone to take him back along the Ypres road.

Outside an ambulance had pulled up, preparing to transport some men to the hospital. 'Can I hitch a lift with you, going back along the Ypres road?' asked Bertram.

'Sure,' said one of the ambulance crew in an American accent, 'any airman doing their duty is welcome! But the only transport is horse and wagon. These two men are going to the hospital at St. Omer, you can go we them. We could use the help,' he continued. 'Hurry though, we are on a tight schedule, these guys are going now,' said another one of the ambulance crew, an Englishman.

There was not time for Bertram to say goodbye to Pierre and Jacobson. He helped the crew load an injured soldier, his head bandaged and his leg in a splint. Bertram sat beside him, offering him a cigarette. The soldier took it gratefully. The wagon swung around and as they passed the base, he saw Pierre in the distance. Bertram waved frantically and just in time Pierre spotted him. He run the distance of the field and tossed a wrapped bread roll onto Bertram's lap. 'Bon voyage!' he shouted out waving the wagon on until it reached the end of the field.

Passing over some cobbles, Bertram noticing the soldier wince in pain as the wagon bumped its way across. Out along the road, lined with tall oak trees, Bertram nervously puffed on his cigarette. The sun was beating down, his eyes were heavy and on the last puff of the cigarette, as it fell out of the corner of his mouth, he fell into a deep sleep.

Woken up some hours later, he was aware of a commotion around him. There were trees being felled by the side of the road and strong South African accents were booming right over the wagon. Bertram looked to his left, where there were large oak trees, falling by the side of the wagon. One had fallen right across the road. Four South African soldiers were trying to move it out of the way. Their horse had reared, but luckily stopped in time otherwise they would all have been goners. Bertram checked his watch and promptly swore. It was three in the afternoon, where had the time gone? He had missed his appointment with Commander McGovern. 'Where are we?' he asked of his fellow soldier.

'Delville Wood, I think,' replied the poor soldier. That is not too far, Bertram thought to himself. 'Think I will get out and walk from here!' replied Bertram jumping down from the wagon. Watching the muscled bound men as they vied in groups to chop down the trees, he walked on his way, his panic suppressed by few hours of sleep.

'What do you mean he is on leave?' asked Bertram his mouth parched. After walking a mile back to the base he went straight to the officers' lodgings.

'As I said, Private Wright, Commander McGovern left on leave for two weeks. You have missed him by a couple of hours, I understand you had an appointment with him?' asked a stern looking officer.

'Yes Sir, but I got caught up in an airstrike and had to land at Abeele. Has he left me a letter for permission to have leave to defend my friend Private Weaves?' asked Bertram his tone becoming more impatient.

'Let me see, there does not seem to be anything here for you,' replied Officer Lowden, busily adjusting a typewriter on his desk.

'But Sir, I appeal to you, please ask someone else, it is imperative I go to Calais immediately to help Private Weaves,' Bertram shouted back at the officer.

'I can assure you Private Wright, if you take that tone with me, you will regret it!' the officer shouted back at him with a thundering face.

'I am sorry, Sir, but I am late back and worried I am too late to save him, please can you understand the predicament I am in!' pleaded Bertram, trying to keep himself calm.

Officer Lowden took a deep breath. 'Wait here, Wright, I will see what I can do.' A few minutes later, Officer Lowden came back full of apologies and carrying a bundle of letters. Passing them over to Bertram, who took them quickly and ripped open the official looking one. His eyes skimmed over the words. He had permission to leave for three weeks but no official statement declaring him "prisoner's friend".

'All right Wright you can leave now,' said the impatient officer.

'Sir, just one thing, Commander McGovern has not signed me on as an official prisoner's friend, is there anything else I can do?' said Bertram defeated.

'I can sign the letter on the bottom for proof with time and date, but that is all. I suggest you hot foot it to Calais and see what you can do there!' said Lowden nonchalantly.

'Thank you, Sir,' replied Bertram knowing this officer's signature would not make any difference.

'And Private Wright, I suggest you enjoy your leave and go back to England to see your family!' Officer Lowden continued with half a smile on his lips.

'Yes Sir,' replied Bertram, realising he was being ungrateful. It was not Officer Lowden's fault that he had missed his appointment.

Bertram packed a few belonging, including the two other letters. One was clearly from Kathryn and the other he had no idea who it was from. He walked towards the truck depot and waited for his ride to Labourse. He would not get there much before midnight. He knew that he would be too late to see Robert tonight.

'May I see Prisoner Robert Alton Weaves please?' Bertram asked the formidable looking guard. He was guided through to a section where Robert was being held. Bertram had not slept all night, having had to spend the night in the truck. Both men looked as bedraggled as each other, each noting each other's dishevelled appearance. Trying to put each other at ease was impossible. Bertram explained what had happened during his flying mission and he was sorry he was too late to retrieve the prisoner's friend statement from Commander McGovern.

'Do not worry Bertram, I know I will be all right. They have told me to make a statement, and I will plead my case. They know I was only just out of hospital. Still I should have listened to my sister. Will you let her know by the way, I have her address written here,' said Robert handing over a piece of paper and looking downcast.

'Of course I will but you must stand up for yourself. Take this letter and make sure you explain everything,' said Bertram giving Robert a reassuring smile as he handed over the letter. 'Have they got you for desertion?' he asked sympathetically.

Robert nodded yet avoiding Bertram's gaze. He was so ashamed. 'They call it "fleeing in the face of the enemy" but Bertram I did not flee, I just could not move and I do not remember the rest or how I got back to camp,' said Robert quietly.

'As long as you make a statement, you will be fine, do you hear me Robert?' said Bertram firmly. Robert nodded feebly. 'Have you eaten much?' Bertram noticed how pale Robert was.

'No, I am not hungry!' he cried in desperation.

'You have to stay strong, do you understand? I cannot come into court with you without McGovern's permission, but I will stay here until you are let out,' said Bertram comfortingly, noticing the desperate state his friend was in.

Robert's eyes were downcast. 'Thank you my friend.' Bertram tucked Geraldine's address into his top pocket. 'I will come back in the morning to see you. Eat something, I will make sure they give you some food,' said Bertram patting his friend's limp arm. 'See you tomorrow,' Bertram called out as he was led out of the corridor, to freedom. Freedom, he thought. Once I get Robert out of here, I will go back to England. The thought gave him some hope.

The next morning after finding some lodgings with some other soldiers in town, Bertram made his way back to the prison. The guard looked at him with a quizzical look. 'I was here yesterday to visit Private Weaves, my name is Bertram Wright,' said Bertram.

'Yes I recognise you,' said the guard almost haughtily. 'I am sorry for the loss of Private Weaves.'

Bertram's heart jumped a beat. 'What, no I am here to visit him and find out when he will be in court,' he said with his heart pounding.

'You are mistaken, they tried him yesterday afternoon and he was shot at dawn,' continued the guard, getting uncomfortable with the line of questions.

'That cannot be, I only saw him yesterday, you have the wrong person!' said Bertram feeling tears prick up into his eyes and a tight hand around his throat.

Two men in uniform came into the room and asked him to sit down. 'I am Officer Dowling, you were a friend of Private Weaves?' asked one of the officers.

'Yes, I am a friend of Private Weaves and I had a letter, which I gave him from Commander McGovern. Did he not give you the letter?' said Bertram, struggling to keep his voice coherent as panic was taking over him.

'No, I am sorry, we received no such letter and I am afraid your friend refused to make a statement. We asked him to write his case clearly, but we could see his guilt was written all over his face,' continued Officer Dowling without any emotion or mercy.

'Guilt? What guilt?' said Bertram, as anger was taking hold of him. 'He was only eighteen years old for goodness sake and a good man and soldier. He was suffering with his nerves, that is all. He was clearly ill,' said Bertram trying to make sense of this mess.

'He deserted his post, his officer and commander had clearly stated this and without a statement pardoning his behaviour. We had no option but to execute him,' continued Officer Dowling.

Bertram could barely stand as his trembling legs carried him out through the prison gates and onwards towards the port. His friend was gone and what would he say to his sister? Reaching the winding road that lead into the town, Bertram grabbed hold of a small oak tree that stood alone, as he felt his legs buckle underneath him. He let out a primeval scream so high pitched he wasn't even sure he had heard it himself. His ears were ringing and his head was splitting. He slumped down to the ground, collapsed in a heap, his body heaving with sobs. How he wanted to go back to the arms of Kathryn. Kathryn, he thought, she was the answer. He must get back to Kathryn.

He must have lain there for hours until he heard voices and two men on bicycles stopped to see if he was alive. Bertram nodded not understanding them and sat up holding his hand up as if to tell them he was all right. Sitting up and noticing a stream a little further from him, he walked down to it and bathed his swollen eyes. The freezing water brought him to his senses, but he knew he was not the Bertram of old. He was older, wiser and a hardness had enveloped him in the last few hours. Taking the letters from his pocket, he read Kathryn's letter. He felt a shell had formed around him, a jacket of steel, no emotions could penetrate. For the words from Kathryn were shocking but Bertram was not shocked. He read that Geraldine was in fact Kathryn's friend and how she had asked Bertram to look after Robert. He took out his notepad and wrote as steadily as he could about what had happened to Robert. He owed this to Robert. This was the last conversation he had had with him. He must let Geraldine know. But he did not let Kathryn know he had leave and was coming back to England. He could not face her. He took out the other letter. Expecting it was from Berenice, he found it was not. It was from her husband. Someone must have translated for him, it read:

Dear Soldier,

I am aware that you have been keeping my wife and her sister company whilst I am away on business. I thank you kindly, but from what my wife tells me you have become somewhat a pest, so I write to say, and warn you, to leave my family alone. We are very happy and are very excited at the news of Berenice's pregnancy.

So please, Monsieur Wright I do not want to see you anywhere near Mesves-sur-Loire.

I wish you well.

Monsieur Comte

Bertram sat still for a moment, and then screwed the letter up and threw it in the stream. His face motionless, he walked up the bank, onto the road, and continued his journey towards London.

CHAPTER FOURTEEN
KATHRYN: THE HUNDRED OF HOO

SUNDAY 1ST AUGUST 1916

Later that evening on the Gravesend train, Kathryn consoled herself with the knowledge that perhaps Robert was safer in prison than he was serving on the front line. It was clear from what Geraldine had told her of Robert's illness, he was not ready to go back and fight. Arriving back at Geraldine's place, Kathryn had taken her hand and made her sit down. At first she had not taken the news well and raved and ranted what a fool he had been to discharge himself. She blamed him for his silly behaviour as she paced up and down the small room wringing her hands and crying. 'Tell me Kathryn, he will be all right, he is all I have got. I do not have a good feeling. The silly boy, look at the mess he has got himself in!' said Geraldine. Kathryn hugged her and told her Robert would be fine. Perhaps, she suggested, they could talk to Devlin tomorrow to see what he could suggest to help him. If that did not work, she would ask the Fitch family for help.

The next couple of days went by in a whirlwind. There was much clearing up to do in the factory and the busy chores and hard labour took their minds off Robert. Devlin had advised the girls to sit tight and wait for a few days for any news. He then promised to call the war office by Friday if they had not heard anything. On the Thursday evening, William dropped by the factory just as it was closing. He was relieved to see that both girls were fine and well. He had not been told of the attack on the factory until he had returned from a mission in France that morning. He came as soon as he could. Taking the girls for dinner at Whittles, he managed to cheer Geraldine up and promised he would put a call through to Calais tomorrow to check on Robert.

Kathryn smiled happily for Geraldine who obviously was sweet on William. As she watched them talk, and hold hands under the table, her thoughts wandered to Bertram. How she had noticed his letters growing more distant and less frequent. Then her thoughts ran to Devlin, who had saved her life last week, how calm and caring he had become. But he also made her slightly uncomfortable in front of the other women. She knew she was being singled out. He had even offered to put her on light duty away from the ammunition and install her upstairs in the sewing department instead. She had refused at first but now she was beginning to relent as his persistence carried on. His watchful eyes on her all day made her blush and she knew she liked his attentions.

By Thursday she found herself being taught the ropes to sew cartridge bags. Her conscience was numb with the worries that surrounded her. She had allowed herself be led down a path of least resistance. And by the evening Devlin had escorted her home and insisted on taking her out to dine that evening. She could not refuse, she owed him her life. Promising Geraldine she would not be too long, she took Devlin's arm and sauntered down the steep white steps of Geraldine's lodgings and turning right towards the promenade. It was a warm night, but for some reason dusk had come early.

In the shadows, a man watched the two of them from across the street. Slowly dragging on his cigarette and then stamping on it, leaving the remains in the gutter, he walked up the white steps and knocked on the door of Geraldine's home. Geraldine ran to the door, thinking it was Kathryn having forgotten her shawl. The man watched the young woman prudently through the stained glass window of the door. Geraldine was taken aback when she saw a man standing there. He gazed at the redhead, recognising the same toothy smile of Robert's. Pausing before he spoke, he took in the girl's beauty and skittish spirit.

'Can I help you?' she asked this green-eyed stranger.

The man shook his head, and in a low and gravelly voice said: 'No thank you, I have the wrong address.' Shiftily walking away, his hands in his pockets, his head bowed. He looked back once, to notice Geraldine's manner, worried, her head cocked to the side, wondering if she had met him before.

Geraldine sat by the window, waiting upon Kathryn. Normally she would have busied herself, maybe sewing or making herself something nutritious to eat, but tonight she could not pry her eyes from the road. The silvery lights from the promenade reflected back on to the black surface, mesmerising her. She willed Kathryn to come back early, but Kathryn took her time.

Geraldine had fallen asleep when eventually laughing and high octane voices could be heard from the street. Geraldine woke with a start, when she heard the key turning in the door. Her face paling, she jumped to her feet and ran to hug Kathryn with tears in her eyes. 'What on earth is it?' asked Kathryn already feeling guilty for leaving her friend.

'I had a dream, Kathryn, about Robert, and this man, not in my dream, knocked on the door and there was something about him, frightening, and I just got the feeling that something had happened to Robert,' said Geraldine looking pale.

'Which man?' asked Kathryn, worry starting to take over.

'Just a man that was lost and knocked on the door just a few minutes after you had left. There was something familiar about him. I know I am being silly but Kathryn we must find out how Robert is tomorrow!' Geraldine gave her friend a pleading look.

'Yes of course, but I think you have got yourself overwrought, let me make some tea and we will think what we want to do,' said Kathryn calmly.

When Kathryn woke she realised Geraldine had not slept all night. Pulling on her dressing gown, she rushed into the sitting room to find Geraldine white as a ghost with grey shadows under her eyes, sitting at the table leaning over a newspaper. Her hair in need of washing hung in lanky streaks. 'Have you not slept at all?'

Geraldine shook her head. 'I have been making plans.' She looked up at Kathryn with an ashen face.

'What sort of plans?' asked Kathryn, now very worried about her friend.

'I have to keep busy, otherwise I will lose my mind with worry!' Geraldine cried out as she buried her face in her hands. Kathryn understood this, but what was she up to? She did not look at all well. 'I have made up my mind, I am going back to nursing, I do not want to turn into one of those tired and sick women in the factory. Well, it is all right for you, having a safe post upstairs with Mr McAlister keeping a loving eye on you! Or are you calling him Devlin now?' said Geraldine sarcastically.

Kathryn was surprised by Geraldine's tone. She had not heard her friend so resentful before. 'Geraldine, I am not in love with Devlin, he is just being kind to me!'

Geraldine shot up in her seat and looked right up to Kathryn. 'Well, that maybe but where is your fiancé when you need him!' Geraldine's words stung her and her eyes smarted with tears. Kathryn turned away from her friend so she would not see her cry.

As she dressed as fast as she could, she knew Geraldine was right. How few and far between his letters were now and how short and blunt they were too. Maybe he was forgetting her and fixing her eyes on her reflection in the mirror, maybe he was right to do so, she thought. Her hair was a mess and she did not know how to make herself glamorous like those models in the French magazines. Maybe she was easily forgotten, she decided. Running to the train station, her thoughts swirled on in her mind. But did not Devlin find her attractive, she thought, feeling a little more confident.

After reporting to her post and letting one of the deputy managers know that Geraldine was unwell, Kathryn decided not to think on it too much, except she had promised that she would ask Devlin to contact the war office. At lunchtime, waiting for a quiet moment when the other women could not see her knocking at his door, she stood outside Devlin's office willing him to hurry up and answer it. 'Come in!' he answered briskly with a touch of annoyance. 'Oh Kathryn it is you, I thought it was Mr Jeevers, with the reports,' his tone instantly softening. 'How are you getting on?' he said ushering her in and pointing to a large leather chair.

Sitting down with her hands neatly and stiffly on her lap, she tried not to catch his eye.

'It is about Geraldine,' she began as she noticed a framed photograph of a curly haired woman in her thirties placed proudly to the side of his desk. 'Please, if you would be so kind, to try to find out what has happened to her brother Robert Alton Weaves. She is making herself ill over it and she fears the worst,' pleaded Kathryn now looking up at Devlin.

He must have been looking directly at her all this time as their eyes met briefly. 'Yes, yes of course I will, I said I would, did I not?' he said with an almost mischievous twinkle in his eye. Kathryn felt self-conscious and her cheeks blushing. She wanted to thank him for dinner, but she could not take her eyes from the lady in the frame. Devlin noticed her glance, got up and opened a file behind him. With his back to her, he quietly told her that that was his first wife. 'She died in a tragic accident, I am afraid,' he said with his voice deepening. Turning around to see and hear Kathryn's response, she hesitated. 'Yes first and only wife, if that is what you are thinking,' he replied bluntly.

'No, no I was not... I just did not realise you had been married before,' said Kathryn now feeling embarrassed.

'No?' he said again with the same impish look he had shown earlier. 'You think no one would be brave enough to marry Devlin

McAlister, do you Miss Beaumont?' he said yet again with that mischievous twinkle in his eyes that Kathryn was becoming accustomed to. 'With my ruthless infamy and a gammy leg! Eh, Miss Beaumont?' he continued.

'I know nothing of the kind, Mr McAlister!' said Kathryn feeling a little intimidated.

Devlin walked over to her chair, slightly limping as his leg was still causing him pain. Slowly he sunk down on one knee and grabbed Kathryn's hand. Pulling away her hand from his, Devlin's face smarted as if she had just hit him. 'Mr McAlister, I have a fiancé whom I am very happy with, please do not ask anything of me!' said Kathryn bewildered and shocked.

Devlin did not say a word for a while, just stood up and walked back to his desk. 'There is the door Miss Beaumont, you had better get back to work, I will let you know of my progress with Robert Alton Weaves,' he replied, busy looking through his file.

'Thank you,' said Kathryn relieved she still had a job, yet she felt a dagger in her heart. She truly hoped she had not hurt Devlin's feelings. Closing the door behind her, she shivered and walked quickly past some of the ladies returning to work. She noticed them whispering and pointing. She did not want to work here anymore, just like Geraldine.

Working a little later than usual and picking up a food parcel from Whittles she passed a neighbour in the street. 'Kathryn, I am so pleased I bumped into you, I have just come from visiting Geraldine. We have had the doctor in. Terrible, terrible news about her brother.' Before she had finished her sentence, Kathryn started to run. Catching her heel in the pavement she winced as she ran up the white steps. She found Geraldine calmly sitting in the kitchen, having washed her hair, but her tearstained face revealed her true manner. Putting down her bag, Kathryn grabbed the brown envelope that was in front of Geraldine on the table and folded open the telegram inside.

It read:

The Military Secretary regrets to inform Miss Geraldine Weaves that Private Robert Alton Weaves has died in Calais.

Placing the telegram down on the table, Kathryn sat beside Geraldine, holding her hand and they sat there in silence. A single tear fell down Geraldine's cheek and she moved her hand to touch her face, her nails slightly digging into the flesh of her cheek. 'Kathryn,' she spoke at last, 'I do not know how he died! They did not say...I have to know.' Kathryn pulled Geraldine's hand away from her face, before the sharpness of her nails could penetrate her pretty face.

'We will find out, do not worry,' she said hugging her friend.

'I am sorry about this morning,' said Geraldine another tear escaping.

'It's fine, and you are right, I do not know what has become of Bertram either,' said Kathryn holding on to her friend tighter.

Chink chink, a chink in my armour,
and let the chimera of death let go of my hand.
I will wash away the ghostly apparition,
that has taken hold of our men.
By Bertram Wright

Sipping on some tea, Geraldine showed an announcement in the local newspaper to Kathryn over the table.

WOMEN WANTED TO JOIN FIRST AID NURSING YEOMANRY. INTERVIEWS HELD IN LONDON.

'Come with me Kathryn and we can see what has become of our men, I cannot stay here now and do nothing. I have to go to Calais to find out about Robert and to see if I can get a nursing job out there in the frontline. I will feel Robert's life would not have been in vain,' said Geraldine with a persistent look.

'Me nurse, but how?' asked Kathryn interested and worried at the same time. 'I must admit, it would be good to get away from the factory. You were right, Devlin declared his feelings for me and it is too much to take in,' she continued, thinking back to that fateful moment in his office.

'He asked you to marry him?' asked Geraldine her eyes widening. Kathryn just nodded. 'What did you say?' Geraldine was desperate to know.

'I suppose I was rather sharp with him and explained I could not even think of it as I was engaged to someone else,' said Kathryn slowly as she watched Geraldine's face for a reaction. She herself was still trying to process Devlin's sudden declaration of love.

'Life is short Kathryn, and he has a lot to offer!' Geraldine could not believe her friend would turn down such an offer, a chance to become a real lady and a wife of someone like Mr McAlister.

'You sound just like my mother; I have to say she took quite a shine to Devlin at the wedding!' laughed Kathryn at her friend's excitement. Wanting to change the subject of Devlin, Kathryn asked how she would train to be a nurse.

'They will train you in first aid, and apparently they need drivers too,' said Geraldine referring to the newspaper announcement.

'Me driving an automobile or truck? I like the sound of that! If Lord and Lady Fitch knew, they would be surprised that one of their little maids of Dallington Place could be a driver on the battlefields,' smiled Kathryn of the thought of seeing the surprised faces of the Fitchs.

'I am going to go to London on Saturday and sign up,' said Geraldine, the light returning to her eyes for a few moments.

'It is too soon Geraldine, why do you not spend the weekend with me at my mother's? I have to go to Dallington Place to see if I have any more letters from Bertram. I will show you around the place, it is so beautiful and restful at this time of year. Why don't you go to London on Monday? I will cover for you,' pleaded Kathryn.

'Maybe you are right, I am still shaky on my feet,' said Geraldine, as she got up to go to bed. Blowing the candle out on the table, she wished Kathryn a goodnight's rest.

'You too,' said Kathryn, feeling for her friend who looked so worn and sad.

Not yet sleepy, Kathryn began to write a letter to Bertram, asking why he had not written a loving letter in a while. She found her mood had altered towards him. Tears of frustration pricked her eyes. She was angry with him and why had he not protected Robert, she wondered.

10th August 1916

Dear Bertram,

I have just received the desperately sad news of Robert. Neither Geraldine or I can understand what has happened to cause his death, both of us sad and terribly confused. I only hope you were near him and gave him some comfort. You had mentioned in one of your last letters that he had returned to the battalion, did you see him in prison?

Bertram I am also sad that I have not heard from you in a while, but I hope to receive a letter from you soon and for you to say that you still hold me dear.

Please reply and put me at my ease.

Your forever loving

Kathryn

Kathryn could not bring herself to write the envelope. She placed the letter inside her diary to post it later.

CHAPTER FIFTEEN
BERTRAM: FLEET STREET, LONDON

11TH AUGUST 1916

Alexander patted Bertram on the back as they left the Evening Standard's formidable building. 'Well done, looks like you have got yourself a column! Bertram Wright, the war correspondent, from a private to high flyer,' said Alexander passing his friend a cigar to celebrate.

'Thank you for meeting me here, I do not know if I could have gone in there without you,' said Bertram sincerely relieved that he had met up with Alexander again.

'Easy, once you have got the hang of how they do things in there, they were pretty impressed with your writings and accounts of the flying,' continued Alexander genuinely pleased for his friend.

'They want me to do more of the flying, apparently it goes down well with the readers,' said Bertram at last letting himself feel a little smug.

'They pay pretty well as well, always a bonus. And talking about being well paid, let us go to my club in Mayfair and spend some of your earnings already,' said Alexander with a wink.

'Steady on my friend, I have not been paid yet!' said Bertram laughing, 'although there's a cheque in the post.'

Alexander rolled his eyes. 'It is on me idiot! I will just charge it to my publisher, he is used to it by now anyway.' The men walked towards Mayfair happy to enjoy the clement weather and each other's company. Reaching the Gelding Club, Bertram paused for a moment on the marble steps. Alexander jumped into the revolving doors with his usual glib manner. Bertram looked over his shoulder, aware he was leaving his past behind him, and a new life was opening up to him. The young man at the reception desk ushered the dark and charismatic Alexander into the club, tipping his hat at Bertram. 'Afternoon Sir.'

Bertram nodded back, unfamiliar to being treated in this worthy manner. 'I could get used to this,' said Bertram with a broad smile.

Bertram felt the full extent of his hunger as they perused the menu while sipping their whisky. He caught his reflection in the frosted glass above the leather chairs. How hollow his face had become. His frame barely filled his old, brown, almost mud-coloured suit. He hoped to replace it as soon as his money came in. 'Two guinea fowl and a vegetable platter please,' Alexander ordered their food as Bertram watched the young maître d' scurry around nervously for a pen. Alexander was obviously a very good customer, Bertram acknowledged.

Both men inhaled their cigars and then simultaneously sipped their drinks while they discussed their own experiences of the war so far. 'How is the injury?' asked Bertram admiring the form of his journalist friend.

'No problems now, I am as good as new! Good food and rest has done me wonders. You my friend need to do the same by the looks of you,' Alexander casted a worrying look at his diminished friend.

'I have had some rough times lately but I will get over it,' said Bertram not believing in his own words.

'May I dare ask if there is a lady involved? I remember you had someone when we first met,' enquired Alexander.

'Yes that is right, but well I… do not know… the war I think it has put a wedge between us. I do not know what I want anymore. I did want marriage, but now it seems I am moving further away from it, I mean her,' said Bertram with sadness in his eyes.

'Is it over?' asked Alexander.

Bertram took a glug of whisky. 'Looks that way I am afraid, but I try not to think about her. You are married right?' said Bertram trying to deflect talking about himself.

'On paper, but I have not been back to New York for months now. My wife, she is done with me I think!' exclaimed Alexander.

Bertram observed a glimpse of sadness in his eyes. 'Really?' asked Bertram surprised.

'Ah no, Sarah, and me we go back a long way! Childhood sweethearts, she is Brooklyn born and bred. And she is a looker too. I will win her back,' said Alexander confidently as he leaned back in his armchair, blowing a ring of smoke over the table.

'Good for you,' said Bertram little insincerely, as jealousy crept into the forefront of his mind. Men like Alexander always get what they want, he thought, as a picture of Kathryn with that man on the steps of Geraldine's home flashed across his mind. 'Another whisky I think, Alexander!' he announced rather loudly.

'So what are your plans now? Going to stay in London for a while?' asked Alexander.

'Think so, maybe two or three weeks and then I am going to sort out my paperwork so I can enlist with the RFC. Going to learn to fly solo!' replied Bertram excitingly.

'Can you do that?' asked Alexander surprised.

'Yes that is the plan. I can be seconded to the Royal Flying Corps. They cannot refuse me especially with all the journalistic work I have been doing. Did I show you some of the photographs from my first mission as an observer?' asked Bertram.

'Let me see,' said Alexander, watching impatiently as Bertram rummaged through his bag for the aerial photographs.

'These ten pictures I have given to the Evening Standard. That is the first one, with Flight Lieutenant Jacobson, it is rather overexposed. It was first light and we were waiting to try to repair the aeroplane. Jacobson leaned over the motor, his face away from the camera.' Alexander had a closer look at the picture.

'Is that my old friend Jacobson? Difficult to say if it is him with his goggles on and his thick sheepskin lined Fug aviator's boots that go well over his knee. Love the picture, can I take it back to New York and get it published there?' he asked.

'Yes sure, you take it, I owe you,' said Bertram delighted.

'I will get quite a pretty penny for that,' Alexander smiled. 'Like that one,' he said leafing through the portraits of the airmen when they had just arrived at Abeele Aerodrome. There was a great one of Pierre grinning like a Cheshire cat with his arm around Jacobson. 'I recognise him! French, right?' asked Alexander.

'That is Pierre Le Sierre. An ace pilot and photographer. He taught me so much about aerial reconnaissance, great chap,' said Bertram full of gratitude to the Frenchman.

'Yup, I met him in New York a couple of years ago. Quite the ladies' man,' said Alexander, waving at the waiter to pour them another whisky.

'Really? I would never had known, quite the dark horse!' said Bertram surprised.

'Oh I've got quite a few stories on him!' said Alexander with a sly grin. 'Talking of ladies, now you are in town for a while, I have my cousin Winnie over from Texas staying with me at the Ritz and her sister Marjorie. I bought them tickets to see the new musical in town called Chu Chin Chow by Oscar Asches. We could go too, do you fancy it on Wednesday night?' asked Alexander.

'Sure! Sounds good, it would be nice to have some female company,' replied Bertram delighted about the kind invitation.

'Hands off the ladies though, they are my cousins!' barked Alexander with a wink.

'Would not think of it, I have too much women trouble as it is!' answered Bertram back rolling his eyes.

'Really?' asked Alexander looking intrigued. He really was the journalist. 'Ok, let us get out of here,' said Alexander, passing back the photographs, keeping the one back and putting it into his briefcase. Pulling out a pen and paper, he jotted the address of the theatre and time for Bertram. 'It is at her Majesty's Theatre. Be there for seven o'clock. Oh, by the way, where were you flying to in this picture?' asked Alexander pointing at another picture.

'That was for a reconnaissance mission over the Salient, but we had to abort it, took off again the next day though. Listen, take that one of Pierre as well, that was a good day. Jacobson managed to shoot down two German Fokker planes on that mission,' said Bertram.

'Thanks I will, that is a great picture. See you Wednesday,' said Alexander as he got up to leave.

'See you Wednesday! By the way Alexander, you do not happen to know a good doctor in town do you, whom I could get a quick appointment with? Have this awful sore throat that's been going on for months, only the whisky seems to help,' said Bertram as he stood up ready to leave as well.

'Sure, I will write the number down here.' Alexander tore a page out of his notebook, scribbled on it and handed it to Bertram. The men left the club, but not before Bertram had used their telephone to make an appointment with the doctor. He then walked towards Piccadilly, noting he had just passed the Ritz hotel and walked towards Victoria to his lodgings.

The lights had already gone down in the theatre and Bertram had already missed the drinks beforehand. 'Sorry, sorry…' he said, aware he was treading on people's toes in the darkness. Alexander was waving furiously amongst some disgruntled older ladies. Bertram found his seat few seats from Alexander, next to an attractive lady. 'Jorie,' she whispered in her American accent. 'Bertram,' he whispered back settling into his seat, nodding a hello to Alexander. A shush came from behind him and Jorie let out a large humph. Her sister next to her on the other side started to giggle and they were shushed again. As the curtain went up, Bertram turned to Jorie, to look at her properly in the light. Her profile was pretty and what he noticed more than anything was how blonde her hair was. It was tied in a bun and how she wore it reminded him of Berenice. His thoughts ran to her and he could not concentrate on the performance. Wondering if she was truly pregnant or was it something her husband had said to warn him off her? Berenice had told him that she did not sleep with her husband anymore. Was it all lies? He wanted to find out. His thoughts were interrupted by the vigorous clapping of the young lady beside him. As she reached down to the floor for her purse, he noticed the back of her neck. How long and slender it was. When she stood up she was almost the same height as he was. She was like an elegant swan as they walked to the exit and into the bar.

'Winifred Doubletree,' said Alexander's cousin grabbing hold of his arm and leading him towards the bar. Bertram was startled by how forward these American ladies were. Winifred ordered two lime sodas for herself and her sister and two brandies for the men. Bertram knocked back his brandy and began to relax.

'Kind of forward, are they not? said Alexander. 'But I like it, they are spirited and fun!'

Bertram watched the ladies jostle for position at the bar. 'Sorry I was late, I had to get to North London for an interview with the Royal Flying Corps and then I hotfooted it back to Belgravia for the doctor's appointment,' said Bertram apologetically.

'How did it go?' asked Alexander, gesturing to his cousins to join them. 'Well, I have to have a medical with the RFC next week, so as long as I pass that I am in. Just wanted the doctor to give me the go ahead, do not want the boys in uniform sniffing about thinking I have trench fever or something,' continued Bertram.

'And do you?' asked Alexander looking rather horrified.

'Nope, do not think so, he told me to get some rest and relaxation, and plenty of sleep. That should do the trick and clear it. No sign of infection. Just had the damn thing since I was in the trenches. Sure it is nothing,' said Bertram.

'You are lucky that is all you have got, heard some nasty things about syphilis being caught amongst the soldiers,' said Alexander mindfully, stopping short his topic of conversation before the ladies could hear them.

'Just going to the restroom,' shouted Winifred over in her loud voice. Jorie joined them, sucking rather loudly on the straw of her lime and soda.

'So what brings you to London, Jorie?' asked Bertram genuinely interested in this pretty and loud American.

'Apart from visiting my favourite cousin over here, I have never been to London and I am looking into joining the Suffragette movement,' replied Jorie grabbing Alexander's shoulder.

'Quite the emancipated woman, my cousin!' said Alexander playfully nudging her on the cheek.

'I just love England, it is so quaint,' continued Jorie, still looking directly at Bertram. 'So Bertram what do you do, the same as Alexander?' she asked her huge blue eyes widening with interest of his reply.

'Sort of except next week I am learning to fly. I have just returned from the trenches, where I have been writing my journal and I have had some experience flying and photographing the Somme from fifteen thousand feet,' said Bertram clearly enjoying Jorie's attention.

'Wow, how exciting! Well when you learn to fly maybe you could teach me too!' she said clapping her hands in excitement. 'We have just got back from staying in Sussex. My sister is a writer; Gwendolyn Doubletree is her nom de plume, do not tell her I told you. She was just very interested in the writing set there. Do you know Sussex, Bertram?' asked Jorie, her bright blue eyes twinkling with interest.

'I do, very well Jorie, it is where I am from and so is my battalion,' replied Bertram.

'What a coincidence, Alexander did you hear that? Bertram is from Sussex!' Jorie called out to her cousin. Alexander just rolled his eyes at his cousin and all her excitement. 'Winnie hear this, Bertram is from Sussex!' she turned around to Winifred as she bustled back to their little party.

'Sister dear, I think the whole of the theatre knows by now that Bertram is from Sussex,' laughed Winifred at her sister's loudness. The girls burst into fits of giggles, before being interrupted by the theatre bell sounding off to make their way back to their seats.

Bertram did not remember an evening where he had had so much fun. The girls were a hoot and he hoped he would see them again. 'It has been very nice to meet you, Bertram, Winnie and I are hoping for an invitation to your flying club,' said Jorie, shaking Bertram's hand.

'Jorie, I do not think Bertram can just invite anybody there, it is not his club!' laughed Alexander at his cousin's eagerness.

'Oh nonsense little cousin, of course we will visit. May we Bertram?' asked Jorie.

'I will do my best to get you gals an invitation when I am settled,' said Bertram smiling at the girls.

'See Alexander, you can be a bore sometimes!' said Jorie literally jumping up and down with enthusiasm.

Alexander opened the door to their taxi. 'The Ritz, please', he said to the driver. 'Can we drop you off anywhere, Bertram?' he offered.

'No thank you, I think I will walk,' said Bertram politely turning down the offer. The taxi sped away with the girls waving to him from the back. His head clearing from the brandy, he walked passed Buckingham Palace and onwards to his digs. He was in good spirits, knowing that this time next week he would be installed at Hendon doing what he loved. He even managed a little whistle. How refreshing his companions had been tonight he thought.

His happiness was short lived though, as after packing his bags the next day and getting ready to leave, he thought he would go out for an early dinner before coming back to collect his bags. Grabbing his raincoat, he walked down Victoria Street picking up a paper on the way. As he walked he turned the pages nonchalantly until something caught his eye. It was his photograph of Pierre Le Sierre standing proudly next to Jacob Jacobson with a broad grin on his face. His first thought was that they had printed his article already, until he noticed the headline.

TOP FRENCH FLYING ACE KILLED BY ENEMY FIRE AT ST. SAVEUR

His face went pale, he could not believe it. He had only talked about Pierre to Alexander a few days ago, and suddenly he was gone. Ducking into a small hotel he asked to use their telephone, hoping to catch Alexander at his club before he returned to New York. 'You seen the paper?' he asked Alexander, with anger dwelling.

'Yup. They have not even had time to print it in New York yet. What an absolute shame, and quite what his two wives will think now?' replied Alexander, ignoring Bertram's annoyed voice.

'Two wives?' asked Bertram.

'I will explain when I see you. Got to catch my train. See you in a month, sorry about your friend. Bertram, got to dash.' Bertram placed the receiver down. Is this war going to get everyone, he thought. Not feeling hungry anymore, he slowly walked back to pick up his bags. He wanted to get out of there and leave immediately.

CHAPTER SIXTEEN
KATHRYN, THE NURSE

30th OCTOBER 1916
Kindly Nurse
Sacrificing Soldier
I hear the thunder of war
calling me back to the trenches.

Kathryn had come straight from London to Dallington Place. Wearing her new khaki uniform of the First Aid Nursing Yeomanry, she felt a different person standing outside the familiar imposing doors. Even Mr Evan did not recognise her straight away, looking the young woman up and down, taking in the official looking uniform. 'Oh my goodness, it is you Miss Beaumont, I did not see it was you for a moment!' exclaimed Mr Evan at the door.

'I am not sure I recognise myself!' said Kathryn smiling warmly. She was rather proud of the uniform and she loved her cumbersome riding skirt. When she walked into the building, she walked a little taller than the young maid that had first walked down the servants' steps of Dallington Place for the first time.

'So when do you travel to France?' he asked, taking her one piece of luggage and placing it under the mirror in the hallway.

'I am starting out early tomorrow, back up to Charing Cross and then Folkestone to Calais,' she replied.

'How exciting!' said Mr Evan now slicing some lemon cake and offering Kathryn a piece.

'It is exciting but I am nervous too. Hopefully when I meet up with my friend Geraldine, I will feel more at ease. Look, here is my nursing certificate,' continued Kathryn proudly taking it out of a large envelope and passing it to Mr Evan.

'I am very impressed and you have passed your driving test too!' Mr Evan nodded approvingly.

'Yes that is what I will be doing when I am out there. Once I have gained some experience, I will be driving the ambulance,' she replied while enjoying her tea and savouring the taste of the lemon sponge. 'This is delicious Mr Evan,' said Kathryn with a mouthful of the cake.

Mr Evan was clearly pleased that Kathryn had not lost her appetite. 'Would you like to take some food with you? I have plenty of cake left,' he offered.

'Thank you, that is very kind,' Kathryn said as she watched him place a large portion into a tin box. 'Do not let me forget your letter, it arrived this morning,' said Mr Evan.

Kathryn was sure the letter was from Geraldine but she hoped it was from Bertram. 'Here, it is, I do not recognise the handwriting but it is from France,' said Mr Evan.

'That is Geraldine's handwriting,' said Kathryn forcing a smile. 'I will leave you to it, I have some correspondence to take care of. Ring for me when you are ready to leave,' Mr Evan took that awkward smile as a cue to leave her to read the letter in private.

'Thank you Mr Evan,' Kathryn gave him a grateful smile. She settled down to read Geraldine's letter. It was surprisingly long, and as she quickly scanned the news she could not believe how busy her friend had been.

5th October 1916

My sweetest friend,

I cannot believe I have been here nearly two months already. I presume you will be passing your Nursing Certificate shortly and you will be on your way out here soon. I have so much to tell you, and the hardest thing of all was to find out about darling Robert. As soon as I arrived in Calais I wanted to go to the prison at Labrouse but I was not able to and it took me a further two weeks of hard work before I was allowed a day's compassionate leave to travel there. I had a terrible feeling Kathryn about what had happened to him on my way there and it was the most frightening place. I was led into an interrogation room, where two officers explained what had taken place. The greatest shock of all was he was shot for 'deserting his post.' Kathryn, I could not believe it and I broke down and wanted to scream at everyone there and then I remembered I was in my uniform and I had to be civilised. But I did make a statement and explained that I was his sister and that I was a nurse and I was a witness to the fact that Robert was suffering from 'shell shock' as they call it now. When I was nursing when the war first broke out, we had some fellows coming to the hospital with such an ailment, and the Swiss doctor who was in charge of our ward, was studying such a medical phenomenon.

Anyway, I explained this to the officers and they did not seem to take me seriously at all. But I said I wanted answers and they would look into this matter. I know Kathryn that he could have died on the battlefields from his wounds like any other soldier, but I knew my brother and the last thing he was was a coward. He was a brave soldier and that's all he wanted to do from the age of six. Our father had a best friend that had served in the Boer War and Robert would sit on this man's knee when he came over to our house to drink whisky of an evening. I think his name was Sergeant Jonty, a funny man with an enormous moustache and he would fill little Robert's head with exciting war stories. That was it for Robert, that is all he wanted to do, and when his schooling was cut short, being a soldier was a dream for him.

They have promised to keep me informed of any information regarding a 'mistake' that may have been made, which gives me some comfort. They also mentioned that a friend had visited and that must have been Bertram, which also comforts me knowing that he probably did as much as could have to save our Robert. The only way I have coped my dear is to throw myself into nursing and hopefully save lives... I will not go into details of some of the grim tasks that we have had to do, but I am hardened now to life's shocks out here, and bitter moments as you could imagine.

But there is also much camaraderie here, and some days can be almost fun. Note there are things planned for Christmas and some revelries from the troops will be really looked forward to. So not all doom and gloom, so do not hesitate to come!

My day usually starts early and for example two weeks ago I had to drive with a fellow nurse one hundred and twenty miles to Cajeux, we hadn't been to bed at all. We picked up some wounded, bandaged them as best we could, put them in the back of the ambulance and drove back to Calais again. We had to stop every twenty miles or so to tend to any cries for help or comfort them as much as we could. My map reading skills have really improved and you would have been proud of me as I drove through the night with my eyes almost shutting. But I did not mind, as I have not been able to sleep properly since I arrived here and finding out about Robert. To keep going until I fall over is the best medicine. You know me, I have so much energy!

The fellow nurse that I mentioned is a girl from Belgium and her name is Aurelie. Can you believe it she is a Countess? Me, mixing with a Countess! The thing is Kathryn, here we are all charwomen and equal. And even the higher ranked soldiers seem to respect us now, as it has become more apparent, the good work that we do. There is also a journal that is written about us so we are very well-known now and our khaki uniform is quite infamous!

There was also an amusing story written in the journal this week about a soldier who had been missing and then turned up with no memory of who he was. Hundreds of women replied to the announcement to say that he was their very own husband!

This week we have been blessed with a mobile bath unit and we can wash 250 soldiers per day in it and sterilise their clothes. Myself and Aurelie have been doing this together, and I am becoming the fastest bed bather in all of France!

I must go, cannot wait to see you in Calais as soon as possible. Please can you bring out some custard powder and maybe some bully beef if at all possible.

> *Love and kisses,*
> *Yours truly,*
> *Geraldine*

Kathryn, surprised and saddened by the truth of Robert's death, sat still slowly sipping her now cold tea and was only jolted back to reality by the grandfather clock in the hallway loudly striking five. She rang the butler's bell and she let herself be amused by the fact that this was the first time she had ever rung the bell at Dallington Place. It had always been her that had scurried to her master or mistress at the calling of the bell. 'Are you ready to leave?' asked Mr Evan, appearing in the room. Kathryn making sure she had her papers with her and the cake box, slowly walked through the house, taking in the comforting furnishings and familiar smells. There was a little dust here and there but Kathryn, who would have balked at this previously, found it endearing that the house was somehow suffering a little like the rest of them. Even the edges of a few elaborate rugs were fraying, as staff had left and belongings and furniture moved out quickly, snagging the ancient décor. A sad exodus, the family leaving as soon as they could. A new silver framed photograph of Lord and Lady Fitch with their two daughters did not pass by Kathryn's prying eyes.

Remembering Geraldine's request for custard powder, Kathryn asked Mr Evan if he had any. Mrs Potts would have had some in stock she was sure. As Mr Evan telephoned for a driver to pick up Kathryn, she stopped to take a closer look of the photograph when Mr Evan's back was turned.

'The station is it?' he asked, catching her peering into the picture, as he stepped back into the hallway.

Embarrassed, she answered she was going back to the village to visit her mother. Her nosiness had not gone unnoticed by him. 'It is old Johnson's boy that is going to drive you,' said Mr Evan wiping away some dust from the bureau under the mirror and moving the corner of the silver frame back an inch to align it in place.

'Henry is not working here anymore?' asked Kathryn, having forgotten all about Clara's budding romance with the young chauffeur.

'No, he went to war about three months ago, no one has heard of him since, but I think Clara has married a boy in the village, your mother will know,' Mr Evan informed her not wanting to gossip too much.

'Married already? Poor Henry...' said Kathryn feeling sorry for him.

'Yes, well life is changing far too rapidly Miss Beaumont!' said Mr Evan, now also feeling compassion for Henry.

'And the Fitchs, are they all well?' enquired Kathryn, changing the subject.

'Yes, very well and there is some exciting news on the horizon, I believe. Lord Fitch is visiting tomorrow but I can guess what it is.' continued Mr Evan. Kathryn followed Mr Evan's eyes back to the photograph and she inspected Lady Alison's form. Was it her imagination or had she gained a little weight? The family were sitting under a large oak tree in the grounds of Endelwise Manor and were all beaming with pride as if they held on to a wonderful secret. Breaking the silence, an automobile pulled up outside and Kathryn reluctantly left her beloved house once again.

Kathryn could still feel her mother's arms wrapped tightly around her. Her small bony fingers had almost left an imprint on her upper arms. They knew they would not be seeing each other for six months and she was under no illusion that Kathryn could be in grave danger out in France. Smoothing down her warm skirt over and over again as if to brush away some imaginary dirt, she nervously sat alone in the carriage to London. The train paused at a station, a girl in the same uniform as Kathryn opened the partition doors of the carriage and briskly walked in. She sat opposite Kathryn, extending her arm and shaking Kathryn's hand firmly. 'Daisy Meers,' she said in a clipped accent wearing bright red lipstick. Daisy stopped talking after a while when she realised that Kathryn was rather lost in her thoughts and did not seem to want to engage in a conversation. She shrugged her shoulders and took out her book.

Kathryn closed her eyes and tried to sleep. She knew she would probably be sleep deprived from now on, and thought it best to rest now. But her thoughts flickered from Bertram and then to Robert. Checking to see if the letter from Bertram was still firmly in her coat pocket, her unease left her, full in the knowledge that her love had written and just in time. Mr Evan had sent a car to Kathryn's mother's house that very morning before she left, knowing what a letter from Bertram would have meant to her. She had not noticed that the postmark was from London. Discarding the envelope, she had placed the letter safely in her breast pocket. She had placed her sweetheart brooch, which she had not worn for a few weeks, under her jacket and out of sight. It was pinned tightly to her blouse. Taking out the letter and opening it, she was aghast at how few his words were. He explained about Robert in a matter of fact way and there were no loving words to make her feel special. What had happened to him out there? Maybe he had met someone else. Then she went cold. That was it, nothing else could explain his coldness. Feeling ill, she stood up and reached over to the window, pulling it down she breathed in some fresh air. The countryside flew by as she rested her head against the glass. She stayed there motionless until they arrived in London.

Eventually arriving at Folkstone, she and Daisy disembarked and waited on the platform. These were her instructions from Lieutenant Elsie Danners in London. There were eight of them huddled together as the wind and rain whipped around the station. Strangers yet comrades at the same time. 'One more train to wait for I am afraid,' said Lieutenant Crawford who looked very efficient and capable, her short hair tipping up around her cap. She pulled out a folded piece of paper from her front pocket. 'I will call your names one by one and tick you off the list. Miss Beaumont?' Kathryn shot up her hand. 'Good, Good, I have a parcel for you sent from London.' Kathryn took the brown parcel recognising the handwriting. It was from Devlin. Her mother had told her he had dropped by her house when Kathryn was away in London, to ask her advice on a present. Her mother, ever so practical, had suggested a blanket and by the feel of the package, that is what it was. How on earth he had managed to send it to the

Yeomanry and have someone bring it to her was incredible. How did this man do these things, she thought. She was impressed.

Eventually three trucks picked them up and took them to the docking station. She hoped Geraldine was there to meet her at Calais.

CHAPTER SEVENTEEN
BERTRAM: ALEXANDER'S BETRAYAL

Running towards the airfield, his heart was pounding. He was late for his first solo flight and his instructor was waiting for him. The telephone conversation with his editor Jeff "Budd" Buttersfield at the *Evening Standard* had not gone well at all. 'Wright, what do you think you are playing at, giving away our photographs, and worst of all, to Alexander Pillard? Christ Wright, he has printed some tittle-tattle tale about the women in Pierre Le Sierre's life alongside your photograph. For God sake, it makes our story look like peanuts!'

Bertram was dumbfounded on the other end of the line. He could not believe what he was hearing. 'Bertram Wright,' shouted the editor down the phone, 'if you make another mistake like this you are out, do you understand me?'

Bertram could imagine Buttersfield's face, sweating profusely, his fat cheeks puffing out and his broad neck straining in his too tight discoloured shirt, constricting his breathing. 'Sorry Budd, it will not happen again,' said Bertram stuttering away, worried he may lose his chance to report again.

'You make damn sure it does not Wright, stay away from that Alexander Pillard, he is trouble. He's only interested in number one,' huffed Buttersfield.

Bertram was shocked that Alexander could do this to him. Out of friendship, Bertram had allowed him to print his photograph but not with such a calumny of Pierre. Pierre did not deserve that. Bertram realised that he would have to be wary of Alexander from now on, and maybe not be so upfront with him. After all he was a journalist.

As he boarded the aeroplane, Bertram was relieved to have something to take his mind off the confrontation with Buttersfield. All the mental notes he had taken to avoid trees bordering on the aerodrome, racing through his mind. Obvious of course but vital, as a few students had overshot the runway before. 'Take the machine into the air with precision,' his instructor had told him. 'You are now on your own,' he said getting out from the passenger seat.

Putting his goggles back on and having been given the all clear, Bertram set his aeroplane off down the runway. Respecting the wooden aeroplane, he lifted it gently up into the air, turning slightly to the right because the propeller of the aeroplane revolves to the left. This was the first test that Bertram had to pass today. He looked down and could see his instructor watching his manoeuvres. He moved the rudder bar now to straighten the aeroplane and climbed a little higher. Not too high, as he was instructed. Relaxing his arms but keeping a firm grip on the bar to prevent the biplane from tilting sideways, he passed over a copse flying straight over a road with a tram trundling along. He wondered whether the people inside could see him. Now coming into land without any awkwardness, Bertram was relieved to have finished his first test. The little biplane came to a standstill just a few metres from his instructor.

'Thought you were not coming back, Wright! Could have made that a little easier, you did not have to go over the road,' said the instructor clutching his clipboard. Bertram was not sure if he was annoyed with him or not.

'Sorry sir, I was just enjoying it,' said Bertram disgruntled that he may have yet again broken some rules.

'Right, there we have it,' he said signing Bertram's sheet to hand over the plane and get back to base as he wrote on his notes. 'I will let you know by this evening if you have passed,' muttered the instructor as he walked away.

'Thank you Sir,' replied Bertram, hoping that he had not ruined up his chances to pass with that last manoeuvre.

'It will be on the mess noticeboard.'

Bertram strolled back to base, feeling confident in his ability, but not sure of the final decision the instructor may have taken. He could tell, the instructor thought of him as too sure of himself, so could make him take the test again. He truly hoped not, as this weekend his friends were coming to see him. It was just the girls as Alexander was still in New York, but Bertram was looking forward to seeing Jorie and her sister, Winnie. 'That is much improved, Wright, now next time listen to my instructions,' said the instructor clearly pleased that Bertram had taken his advice and done what he had been asked.

'Yes Sir and thank you,' replied Bertram, relieved that he was finally doing something right. Having been made to take the flying test again for not obeying the rules, Bertram nervously made his way back to base to find Jorie waiting for him in the refectory. She had arrived earlier and was having a cup of tea and eating cake with some of the men. Bertram glanced over at them. How engaging she was. Sitting there in her all white frock and grey overcoat looking pretty as a picture, as she amused the men with her trials of becoming a suffragette.

'Bertram, I hear you have been in trouble,' she said with a naughty twinkle in her eye.

'I was going to take you out to lunch,' he said giving her a brotherly peck on the cheek.

'Oh how lovely, well let us go. I do not like to waste time!' she said with a giggle and excused herself from the fawning uniformed men as she took Bertram's arm.

'So how is life as a suffragette?' asked Bertram turning to Jorie as they walked out of the base.

'I have only been one for a week but I am enjoying it enormously,' she said with a wry smile. 'Firstly, being an American, I do not really qualify as a full member, but I have been handing out leaflets over the last few days and then last night I attended a meeting in Westminster. One of Winnie's friends has been battling to get the vote for women for years. Even her family now disown her with all the antics she has been up to. Anyway, things are moving forward and last night the meeting was about setting a formal meeting with Asquith,' explained Jorie excitingly of her new role in the women's organisation.

'Impressive,' said Bertram listening intently.

'You see, with the war it has demanded a vote for every soldier but many soldiers have lost the right to vote as they do not qualify as householders. It is almost as if tables are being turned. The only ones who are left here to vote are the women. So it kind of makes sense to give women the right to vote. The Government is facing up to it slowly but I think it will happen eventually,' explained Jorie with such conviction.

'So you have been busy, that is good,' said Bertram steering Jorie into his local restaurant. She chatted so animatedly it was hard for him to get a word in. As they found themselves a table, Bertram realised that he was really enjoying her company. She was bright and interested in everything. 'So where is Winnie?' asked Bertram, surprised not to see her sister.

'Oh, she met some chap in Sussex, a writer, so she is staying with his sister. Ever the romantic,' she continued rolling her eyes.

'And you?' asked Bertram, 'do you want to marry?' as he looked at Jorie.

'Me? Good heavens no, I like my freedom, and I do not want children,' replied Jorie, shrugging her shoulders.

Bertram raised his eyebrows, what an unusual response for a young woman. 'You may change your mind one day,' he said inspecting Jorie's face for a sign of hesitation.

'Never,' she said defiantly.

'So tell me about Texas,' asked Bertram, eager to change the subject. 'I hear Lady Alison has married into a Texan family?' He had heard from Kathryn the latest news of Dallington Place.

'Well, I come from a close family, with lots of cousins and aunts always at our house. My father runs a stud farm so I grew up with horses,' said Jorie.

'So you can ride well? I have never been on a horse,' asked Bertram, intrigued to hear more about this American way of living.

'Yes, sure thing, I will teach you to ride one day if you take me flying,' said Jorie, hoping that Bertram would agree.

'It is a deal!' responded Bertram delighted with this idea.

'We live in a fairly small town called Santa Anna. It is real pretty but not an awful lot to do except horse riding for us gals! Maybe I will take over the farm one day, as my sister is not interested. She is far too intellectual! And you should feel the heat of the Texan summer. It is nothing how you would imagine,' Jorie chattered on. Bertram wanted to close his eyes and imagine he was in a different place and time with Jorie. 'Hey you, are you listening?' asked Jorie, nudging Bertram with her elbow.

'Sorry I am sleepy, I could not sleep last night,' said Bertram, embarrassed.

'Thinking about me, were you Bertram?' she said nudging him again playfully.

'No, my exam actually. You are off limits to me, Alexander made me promise,' said Bertram looking at Jorie.

'Do you always do what Alexander tells you?' said Jorie teasing him with a twinkle in her eyes.

'Maybe not now, in fact I am quite angry with him. He took the photograph I gave him and printed it, which I had agreed to, but then he made up some not very pleasant story about Pierre La Sierre and printed that with my photograph,' responded Bertram, regretting again to have trusted Alexander.

'Pierre?' asked Jorie confused.

'A friend of mine, who apparently was leading a duplicitous life and instead of an obituary, Alexander wrote some tale about his private life,' said Bertram looking away so Jorie would not see his displeasure with her dear cousin.

'Oh that is Alexander for you, do not take it personally. He is just the journalist through and through. Just do not tell him your secrets!' laughed Jorie, without realising that Bertram was rather upset.

'Noted, thanks!' Bertram managed to say. He did not want this to ruin his relationship with Jorie.

'I will not tell if you do not,' said Jorie mischievously her eyes yet again twinkling at him.

'That is enough Jorie, I have enough woman trouble and besides, you are too young for me,' said Bertram not seeing the funny side of the situation.

Jorie stuck out her chin defiantly as she continued to eat her lunch. Eyeing him throughout and after finishing her last mouthful, she continued. 'What woman trouble?' she looked at him with curiosity.

'Jorie, enough I told you, I will tell you another time when I know more myself.' Bertram was not in the mood to talk about the women in his life, not the least to Jorie. Smiling and shrugging her shoulders, she took her napkin, wiped her mouth and flounced off to the ladies room.

A few hours later after they had said goodbye at the station and promised to meet again with Alexander and Winnie in a month's time, Bertram found himself feeling uncharacteristically lonely. Was he homesick for Sussex, he wondered. One month to go and then he could go back home.

NOVEMBER 1916

'Pilot Wright?' said Alexander shaking Bertram's hand vigorously. Jorie ran up to him and gave him a hug. 'Winnie is on her way, she stopped off at a corner shop. So where is the aeroplane?' asked Jorie looking across the airfield.

'It is in the hangar. I cannot take you flying today I am afraid, but you can sit in the aeroplane if you like,' said Bertram smiling at Jorie's enthusiasm.

'Show me how you fly, Bertram!' said Jorie eagerly jumping into the seat behind Bertram. He pulled the rudder as if to manoeuver the plane to the left. Jorie squealed with delight and excitement.

'If we really cannot fly today, well, let's go and have our picnic!' said Jorie, jumping down and catching the hem of her skirt on a screw on the door. 'Well, that has torn it,' she said laughing, when she caught Winnie's expression.

'Will you be careful, if you had fallen you could have really hurt yourself,' shouted Winnie at her sister's carelessness.

'Me? Never. Look at the times I've fallen from horses,' remarked Jorie cheerfully. 'So can we go flying tomorrow, Bertram?' she asked, willing that he would offer to take her up in the air soon.

'First of all, I would not be allowed yet and secondly, the weather conditions are not right. But one day I will, I promise Jorie,' said Bertram looking at Jorie with a sly smile.

'Spoil sport,' Jorie looked disappointed with a deep sigh.

'Jorie, poor Bertram has only just got his wings, you do not want them taken away from him already?' said Alexander sympathising with Bertram over his sulking cousin. 'And where do you suppose we should eat this picnic, outside in the freezing wind, Jorie? Is there somewhere we could go, Bertram?'

Winnie turned to Bertram, while delving into her shopping bag to show Jorie what she had bought. 'There is a folly behind the copse, I flew over it yesterday. However, it is at least a mile to walk,' warned Bertram as he pointed to the woods on the left of the base.

'I love the idea of having a picnic outside in the cold. It's always hot in Texas and too hot to eat. We have some wine, that will warm us up,' said Jorie examining the cups Winnie had bought. 'These are not suitable for wine, Winnie,' she called at her sister. 'Sorry but that is all they had in that corner shop.'

Alexander wrapped his scarf around his neck, as he followed the girls and Bertram out onto the path alongside the woods. As the girls walked on ahead, Bertram took the opportunity to ask Alexander why he had betrayed Pierre's memory like he did.

'Oh come on Bertram, do not tell me you have a conscience!' barked Alexander at Bertram with a patronising look.

'I try when I can!' answered Bertram back rather haughtily, casting a disapproving look at his friend.

'Do you now, Bertram, you sure about that?' asked Alexander rather shiftily. He was making Bertram feel uncomfortable and so he changed the subject.

Calling to the girls to slow down, instead they ran on ahead as if egging the men to catch them. Jorie could run, there was no doubt about that. Bertram thought she must be the fastest female he had ever seen. He watched her run, her hair unravelling out of its bun. Her cheeks flushed with happiness and youth, her tiny hands moving swiftly. He remembered how tiny Kathryn's hands were, her small waist and delicate mouth. Was Jorie as pretty as Kathryn, he thought. His Kathryn, he almost said to himself, but she was not his anymore. It was clear there was another man in her life now. Thinking about the man he had seen leading Kathryn away that day. Thoughts of Kathryn disappeared as they ran up the steps of the little white folly. Although its doors were not open, it sheltered them from the rain. Winnie lay down a small checked blanket, just big enough for two. Jorie poured everyone a small measure of wine into small cups. As Bertram sipped his wine and began to relax, he watched Jorie dance in the rain, the raindrops sliding down her face, her giggling resonating around their stone shelter. Perhaps he was in love, he thought. A crush perhaps, but tomorrow she was leaving for the Americas. One can admire someone and not do anything about it, he decided.

Mr Evan could see the young man in an airman's uniform sitting on the bench under the lime tree. Just staring at the large house, and not moving for the last half an hour. If he did not knock on the door in the next five minutes he would go out and see who this man was for himself. Not that he wanted to go out into the cold again, sensing that he had a nasty cold coming on from working in the garden yesterday. Pulling on his warm hat and overcoat, he shuddered, then walked out to the far side of the garden. 'Can I help you?' he said to the man and then promptly sneezed.

'Bless you,' said the airman. 'My name is Bertram Wright and my fiancé works here. Kathryn Beaumont? I thought perhaps the place was deserted, there did not seem to be anyone about,' he said looking at this kind faced man.

'Ah you're her Bertram, Miss Beaumont collects her letters from here every so often, but she will not be back here until March I should say,' replied Mr Evan and he took a closer look at Bertram. Rather dashing looking young man, he thought.

'March?' said Bertram looking astonished. 'No, you must have the wrong person, Kathryn works here.' Mr Evan took a deep sigh.

'Not anymore, the Fitch family have moved to Norfolk for the time being. They will not be back here to live for the foreseeable future, although Lord Fitch is making a trip up from London today. He should be here any minute if you would like to speak with him. I am the caretaker, Mr Evan,' he offered to shake Bertram's hand.

'Well, I do not want to trouble anyone,' said Bertram dumbfounded.

'No, no trouble, would you like to wait in the cottage with me until Lord Fitch arrives? We do not want to be seen waiting in his house. I need to get warm again, think I caught a cold yesterday,' offered Mr Evan pointing to his cottage.

'Thank you Sir, much appreciated,' replied Bertram gratefully, wondering why Kathryn had not told him she was working in Norfolk.

Just as they were crossing the grass, an automobile pulled up in front of the manor house and Mr Evan rushed across the lawn as quick as his legs could carry him. 'Sir Nicholas, so good to see you,' he said opening the automobile's door for him and helping Lord Fitch with his luggage.

Bertram had caught up with him and he loitered by the majestic columns of Dallington Place. 'Ah Mr Evan thank goodness, I so could do with a cup of tea,' said Lord Fitch with gratitude after a long drive.

'Right you are my Lord, just let me open the front door, I have been in my cottage most of the day, I caught a cold yesterday,' hurried Mr Evan as he balanced the luggage and opened the front door.

It took a few minutes whilst Lord Fitch paid the driver and swung around for him to notice Bertram standing by the door. 'By heavens, it is Bertram Wright, Miss Beaumont's fiancé, I did not recognise you in your airman's uniform!' said Lord Fitch delighted to meet the young man again.

'Good day to you, Lord Fitch, I hope you do not mind the intrusion but I came to Dallington Place to find Miss Beaumont and I find she is not here,' he removed his hat and offered his hand to shake Lord Fitch's hand. 'No of course not, no trouble at all. She has been working at the munitions factory at Hoo in Kent since we left for Norfolk. It was very unfortunate that we had to let go all our staff,' he replied, having a closer look at Bertram.

Mr Evan interrupted. 'I do beg your pardon Sir, but can I remind you that Miss Beaumont has now moved to France and she is working for the First Aid Nursing Yeomanry there.' Mr Evan noticed that Bertram's face had gone ashen.

'Oh yes, yes, I forgot,' said Lord Fitch.

Bertram stood there, all agog. His mind racing, without being able to make sense of what he had just heard. 'Come, come Bertram, hurry through the door, let us talk in the sitting room. Mr Evan would you make us a pot of tea please.'

Lord Fitch motioned Bertram toward the sitting room to the left of the entrance. 'Right you are, Sir,' replied Mr Evan as he disappeared to the kitchen. Bertram followed Lord Fitch into the sitting room, he noticed some furnishings had dustcovers on. How could the Fitchs leave such a beautiful house behind, he wondered.

'Please sit down Bertram, so good to see you again. I must say, I have been following your column in the *Evening Standard*. I see you have been making quite a name for yourself. Take your coat off and sit down.' Lord Fitch motioned him to sit down on the chesterfield opposite to him.

Bertram carefully placed his raincoat over the back of a chair, something he would not have done a year ago. There was always a servant on hand to take one's coat. He settled down on the plush velvet couch. Bertram's head began to pound. Kathryn out in France, what was this nonsense, he thought. 'I am afraid Sir, Kathryn and I have lost contact over the last few months. I presumed she was still working here.' Bertram looked at Lord Fitch rather embarrassed not to be aware of his fiancé's whereabouts.

'No, she has not worked here since just after the wedding. I gave her a good reference and off she went to work at the munitions factory owned by Mr Devlin McAlister. Do you know him, Bertram? He's an old family friend of ours,' enquired Lord Fitch, not aware of Bertram's changed expression.

'I think maybe I have seen him, yes,' he answered, his jaw twitching with anger. Trying to lighten the conversation, he asked Lord Fitch about his daughter's wedding.

'Yes it was a marvellous beautiful day. I am going to be a grandfather soon, very pleased about that,' Lord Fitch beamed with pride.

'Congratulations, Sir,' said Bertram offering a genuine smile.

'Thank you, except against my dear wife's wishes, they have moved to Texas in the Americas. None of us are pleased, but that is life. So how is the war keeping you, Bertram? You look very well,' observed Lord Fitch, not wanting to get into more detail of his daughter's rather sad departure.

'Thank you Sir, yes I have been training with the Royal Flying Corps. In fact, I am going to my new air base at All Hallows in Kent tonight,' replied Bertram.

'So you will be going back to France?' asked Lord Fitch, moving the tea tray that Mr Evan has just brought in and placing it between them.

'Maybe in a few weeks, I haven't been informed yet,' responded Bertram as he gratefully helped himself to some steaming hot tea.

'No, of course not, all hush hush, I suppose,' said Lord Fitch giving a knowing wink.

Mr Evan knocked on the door to say Lady Fitch was on the telephone. 'Listen Bertram, I am going to have to take this call, please take your time and drink your tea. Is there anything else I can do for you?' asked Lord Fitch as he stood up.

'Not really Sir, but if you hear from Kathryn, would you please tell her I called,' replied Bertram, grateful that Lord Fitch had so kindly spared his time.

'Yes, yes, quite,' Lord Fitch trailed off as he opened the door. Suddenly he turned around and smiled at Bertram. 'Keep going with the column, it is very interesting,' he continued.

'Thank you, Sir. And thank you very much for the tea and your time,' said Bertram politely.

'All the best,' said Lord Fitch as he walked to the next room to take the call.

Alone in the sitting room, Bertram couldn't stomach the tea. Why on earth had Kathryn been lying to him all this time, his mind raced. In France, his Kathryn? He could not believe it. This did not sound like the Kathryn that he had known.

He could not even remember his journey to Kent. He felt numb. He signed himself into his new base and promptly went to his quarters to get some rest. Perhaps this day had been an awful dream. Tomorrow things would be different.

CHAPTER EIGHTEEN
KATHRYN: LAMARCK HOSPITAL, CALAIS

Kathryn was relieved at last to have received a letter from Geraldine. Exhausted and tearful, she opened the letter hoping for good news. Working at the Lamarck hospital had certainly been an experience for Kathryn. It was not the hard graft of scrubbing and cleaning, she was used to that, but it was the constant flow of the soldiers arriving and not being able to always make them better. It was the injuries and how many young soldiers there were, that Kathryn found the most difficult. One more day to go and then the hospital was closing down. She was waiting for her instructions of where she would be sent next. She knew that she would have a few days of leave around Christmas time and she wanted to spend that time with Geraldine.

Instead of driving trucks and ambulances, she had been put on basic nursing at the hospital. It had been a daily grind of not even one day off and she felt suffocated. She wanted to explore some of France. Geraldine had tried to see her a couple of times, but each time she had been redirected on emergencies as her bathing wagon had been called to duty. She missed the structure of working at the factory, and even she admitted that she missed the puppy dog eyes of Devlin McAlister. She had to admit, she enjoyed his attention and devotion. She thought of Bertram every day, but it was pure anger on her part. She knew she had to find him, even if it was to put her mind at rest and find out the reason his love had cooled towards her.

Kathryn was not disappointed by Geraldine's letter. It read:

1ᵗʰ December 1916

My dearest friend,
I hope this letter finds you in good health. I am writing with my new address and as soon as you have a few days leave, please come to see me here, as soon as possible. So many times we have got so near to Lamarck Hospital and then we have had to turn around. I always cry on the return journey not to have seen you. I hope you have had

word of this, I think so as Daisy Meers told me, you had been looking forward to seeing me and then disappointed. She is working here alongside me at Méricourt-l'Abbé. I am here indefinitely so come as soon as you can.

Love always, your friend,
Geraldine

Kathryn wanted to cry with joy. She had four days leave, and she had been working so hard that she had little time to spend her meagre salary so her purse was full and so was her heart.

10ᵗʰ December 1916

Lamarck Hospital, Calais
Dear Geraldine,
So pleased to hear from you my dear friend. I hope this letter arrives before I do. I am hoping to come to visit you on the 20ᵗʰ December, I am planning to arrive at Heilly station at midday. I was due to have just a few days of leave, but now the hospital is closing down earlier, I can stay longer over Christmas. Since I have no more work here, perhaps I can come and work at Heilly hospital with you?

I so look forward to seeing you and spending time together over Christmas.

Lovingly your friend,
Kathryn

As the train pulled in at Heilly station, Kathryn was relieved to see her friend waving and running along the platform, looking at each carriage as it edged nearer to its stop. The journey had been long and with many stops. Some injured soldiers being dropped off at hospitals and others carried on board. Some soldiers who were not injured, had asked Kathryn about her uniform and what she did. Kathryn was about to alight the train, when she saw Geraldine rushing past, her skirt billowing out behind her and a scarf covering up half her face. Her red hair always visible and making her conspicuous. A soldier standing nearby kindly lifted Kathryn's heavy bag from the train to the platform, and Kathryn not recognising him at first, thanked him without looking up.

'Kathryn, it is me, Henry, did you not recognise me?' said Henry beaming at Kathryn in his uniform.

'Oh my goodness Henry, I am sorry I did not, you look so mature in your uniform!' said Kathryn astonished she had bumped into him. 'Can you wait here for a moment, Henry? I have to catch up with my friend,' Kathryn said keeping one eye on Geraldine, who was flying down the platform.

'I am going on to Mesves-sur-Loire, look me up, here,' he said tearing off a piece of paper, writing his address on it. Kathryn hugged him quickly and promised she would.

'Take care,' she called as he scrabbled back on the train and back to his seat before someone else took it.

Kathryn called out to Geraldine, not daring to leave her bag. Luckily she heard, turned around and ran back. 'I thought perhaps you were not on the train, Oh Kathryn, it is so good to see you!' said Geraldine hugging her friend. 'I have some days off and I was hoping I could work here at Heilly Station Hospital with you after,' said Kathryn.

'Yes, you should be able to, Aurelie is going home for a month. You could at least take her place for a while,' said Geraldine picking up Kathryn's bag. 'Goodness what have you in here?' she said as she struggled to lift it up.

'My worldly belongings! A bit pathetic really, it is all I own!' said Kathryn rather heavy-heartedly.

'Hey, you sound down,' said Geraldine putting one arm around her friend's shoulders. Kathryn turned to wave goodbye to Henry as he was calling out from the open window. 'Who is that?' asked Geraldine intrigued.

'Henry, he was the chauffeur at Dallington Place. He used to court Clara, the other maid I worked with. Shame really, he is really nice and apparently she recently married someone else. I wonder if he knows…' said Kathryn, looking back to take one last look at Henry as the train moved along.

'Where is he going now?' wondered Geraldine out loud.

'Mesves-sur-Loire, do you know it? It is where Bertram was billeted out to a few times. He would describe how pretty and peaceful it was and so, I know he was happy there. I know it is not far, perhaps we could visit Henry, he gave me his address,' suggested Kathryn, realising that her friend seemed to have taken interest in the young soldier.

'That would be lovely, a quiet day's visit away from here,' said Geraldine, liking the idea of visiting Mesves-sur-Loire. 'There is a concert tomorrow night, some of the troops are putting on a show and a few girls from the Nursing Yeomanry are too. There is a group of them that travel and perform plays and songs. Perhaps we could go out to Mesves-sur-Loire the next day, but I have to be on duty on the 26th,' said Geraldine suddenly feeling weary. 'This war is getting to me too Kathryn, do not worry it is not just you. And do not forget I was a nurse long before you ever did anything like this. I still find it hard. You never get used to the awful sights of suffering and not being able to save everyone. It plays on my mind all the time.'

The girls walked through the market square and sat for a rest on the stone edge of the village fountain. 'Make a wish,' said Geraldine as she dropped a silver coin into the water.

'Do you know a soldier's wage is a shilling per day, not much is it? Are their lives not worth more?' asked Kathryn feeling melancholy.

'I think you need some sleep. Why not have a rest this afternoon and then we can come down here tonight for a drink,' suggested Geraldine, realising how tired her friend was.

'Sounds wonderful!' said Kathryn cheering up.

'If you decide to stay longer and work here, there may be a place in the village you can stay with the other girls. Aurelie has been staying there, just above the barber's shop,' said Geraldine, pointing at a building just across from them.

Kathryn peered up to the purple shuttered windows, wondering what it would be like to live in Heilly. 'Come back to the hospital now and then we can enquire later. I am still on duty until tonight,' said Geraldine, as she stood up to go.

Shivering, Kathryn got into Geraldine's bed in the nurse's quarters. She was exhausted, and it took Geraldine a while to wake her. 'Sorry I am late, I had to drive over to Boucy and we had to wait an hour for some soldiers coming in from the train,' chattered Geraldine happily, perched on the edge of the bed.

'What time is it?' asked Kathryn feeling numb, her nose was freezing.

'It is nine o'clock, but if we hurry, we can still get a drink in the village. Wrap up warm though because it is snowing!' continued Geraldine.

'It is?' said Kathryn surprised, as she got out of the bed to look out of the window. 'How pretty!' she said in astonishment as large snowflakes fell from the sky.

Taking care not to slip on the settling snow, their arms linked and bodies huddled together, they made their way to a small tavern a few streets away from the hospital. A frequent meeting place for soldiers and nurses, both French and British, the tavern was dimly lit with a roaring fire. A local old man propped up at the bar, looking somewhat a sea captain of old, tipped his cap when he saw the girls entering. Geraldine smiled at him and then quickly ushered Kathryn to a little table for two, before someone else took it. People were piling in because of the biting wind and falling snow.

As Kathryn took off her gloves, she paused for a moment to look out of the window beside her. She wondered how the soldiers were faring in the trenches on such a cold night. Five days to Christmas and not a lot to look forward to in the middle of the battlefield. Selfishly she was relieved that she was not working out there and could not believe her luck to be with her best friend at long last. They ordered meat stew, which Geraldine bragged was the best she had ever tasted. 'You look so much better after your sleep,' said Geraldine, taking off her hat and coat. At last Kathryn's face had some colour and the warmth of the fire lit her alabaster skin, making Kathryn's face look almost doll-like with her fine features. Kathryn smiled at her friend's compliment and then noticed a soldier by the bar watching Geraldine with interest. He was wearing a Canadian Expeditionary Force uniform, she recognised the badge on his cap that he was holding on to. A party of young soldiers and their nurse girlfriends came through the door. Their chatter and laughter making the proprietor, Monsieur Lappett, wave his hand for them to hurry in and close the door to keep in the warmth.

One of the nurses knew Geraldine and she came over to greet the girls. 'Lesley,' introduced the pretty girl herself. She had a rather drunken soldier in a firm grip as he swayed slightly. His arm bandaged and a newly acquired pink scar under his eye, he looked worse for wear. Kathryn shook Lesley's hand. 'Do not mind him, it is just Greg!' said Lesley, pushing his face away as he tried to kiss her. 'He is a handful! I better go and find us a table, but just wanted to ask you to come to the play tomorrow. Geraldine, are you coming? I have to count the numbers!' said Lesley cheerfully.

'Of course I am and Kathryn's coming too,' replied Geraldine, trying to get a word in edgeways, but giving up, she shrugged and took a mouthful of the stew.

'See you tomorrow then!' Lesley waved as she and Greg stumbled towards the bar. She tried to prop Greg on a rather precarious stool next to the sea captain. The old man and Greg eyed each other warily, only to go back to their own worlds a moment later.

Kathryn pondered for a moment whether to bring up the subject of Robert. Seeing her friend's smiling face surrounded by friends, she decided against it for now. 'This stew is delicious, you can really taste the onions,' said Kathryn keeping the conversation light.

'Well, we will not be kissing anyone tonight, that is for sure,' jested Geraldine, wanting to tell Kathryn all about William and how he had been keeping in touch. She did not want to brag and upset Kathryn so she kept quiet.

'Have you been kissing anyone?' asked Kathryn almost reading her thoughts.

'Not quite, but William keeps in touch,' she shrugged, trying to make light of his fervent ardour for her.

'That does not surprise me Geraldine, come on, tell me, I do not mind if you do. Life goes on and it goes on without Bertram.' It was the first time Kathryn had said his name without wanting to cry. Were her feelings waning, she thought. 'He writes to me and says that he is thinking of me a lot. I did not want to say anything to upset you,' said Geraldine with an embarrassed look on her face.

'I know, but right now I do not know my own feelings about anything or any man anymore, so do not worry, I am swinging with the punches! It is this war, nothing shocks me anymore,' said Kathryn. 'I know that is how I feel and I am just grateful to be alive,' she continued, wishing she just had not said that. Realising she had put her foot in her mouth and not wanting to depress Geraldine, she changed the subject to Devlin. She did not want to talk about him either, but it was a good excuse to chatter about something else. 'You know Devlin wants to marry me, what do you make of that?' asked Kathryn, looking at her friend's reaction.

'Well, I think you could do worse!' said Geraldine, ordering another pitcher of wine.

'I have not kissed him you know, but when the bomb hit the factory site that day, and he covered me with his body to protect me, we must have lain there for almost an hour, it felt like it anyway. I could feel his heartbeat and his hot breath on my neck. I am ashamed to say I liked it, and I do not care, I have said it now!' said Kathryn downing her glass of wine in one go so Geraldine could fill it with the new wine from the pitcher.

'There is so much we have not talked about. I have to say, I think there is something very attractive about Devlin… for an older man!' said Geraldine kicking her friend under the table.

'Lance Corporal Weaves?' the soldier, who Kathryn had noticed before, interrupted them. He towered above their table and Geraldine did not recognise him for a moment. Kathryn took in the Lance Corporal title with interest.

'Sammy, is that you? You look so well!' squealed Geraldine with delight and stood up to hug the soldier. 'When did you return to duty?' she asked him.

'Last week but I wanted to thank you and the other girls at the hospital for getting me out of there, when you did,' Sammy said.

'That is all right Sammy, it is just our job, and I'm surprised you remembered me!' Geraldine laughed, now blushing.

'How could I forget your flaming red hair? I was in such pain but I kept looking at your red hair and well, it just took me somewhere else, if you know what I mean.'

Geraldine blushed at the young Canadian's words. 'Thank you, I am thrilled I could help you,' she smiled.

'The driving was less impressive!' winked the Canadian playfully.

'Hey, that's cheeky!' laughed Geraldine, offering the tall and lanky soldier a glass of wine and asking him to sit down with them.

'Well, I think I will, thank you,' he said tapping his knee as if demanding it to bend on will, as he slowly sat down with some discomfort. He placed his cap on the windowsill, his eyes were drawn to Kathryn. He turned to her, fixing his gaze to the sincere blue eyes, and told his story of how Geraldine and Aurelie had rescued him and few other soldiers from the front line. How they rode a hundred miles with them in the back of the little ambulance as the soldiers cried for help and comfort throughout the night. Geraldine had been made Lance Corporal Weaves for her efforts that night. And as the candles burned in the tavern, Kathryn listened to the story and she knew she could not have been more proud of her dear friend.

A large makeshift tent was put up for the Camblewell Players. A band was playing in the corner to the right of a bar. It had stopped snowing, only to be replaced by torrential rain. A soldier serenaded a young nurse with an accordion, who eventually agreed to dance with him. The play tonight was a comedy and the travelling troupe of actors were keeping everyone's spirits up. They travelled to different barracks and hospitals from Calais to Verdun. Some of the men were dressed as women. One of the actors dressed as a nurse was handing around a tin to raise money for their transport to the next posting. Sammy the Canadian, had accompanied them tonight. They sat at the bar trying to hold a conversation as the band grew louder competing with the sound of the pelting rain. There must have been at least a hundred people there tonight and it was far from cold with all the body heat in the tent. Kathryn looked around her, feeling calm and almost happy to be surrounded by good company. Men mingled with the few women that were there. Kathryn observed the injured men making the most of their time away from the war, almost relaxing, but with a haunted look on their faces. Rum seemed to be the drink of choice and most were getting quite drunk and some quite rowdy.

There were raised voices on one side of the tent towards the entrance. A young soldier, who had drunk too much, was desperate to get back into the tent to watch his actor brother perform with the Camblewell Players. His commanding officer had ordered him out but he was not having that. He was shouting that he had not seen his brother in many months and demanded to be let back in. There were whistles for the play to start but the play was postponed for another few minutes whilst someone went to fetch the brother of the drunken soldier. Eventually the lights went down and the play started to rapturous applause. The thunder of clapping eventually drowning even the loudest speaking actor and the play finished without a finale. The band started up again, only to have to stop as part of the tent was giving way to the mud and three inches of rainwater.

'Have you seen Lesley?' Geraldine asked Sammy, surprised that she had not turned up after being one of the major organisers of the event.

'She had some bad news of her husband, injured at Fort Douaumont in October. His health was deteriorating quickly. She left to see him this morning, Greg told me,' said Sammy.

'I did not know she was married!' said Geraldine with her eyes wide with surprise.

'No one did, least of all Greg, he is pretty upset. He thought she was the girl for him, but she belongs to someone else,' said Sammy poignantly.

Kathryn was now milling in the mud with everyone else as they queued to get out of the tent, she raised her riding skirt as she walked so it would not get dirty. Looking up, she felt someone's eyes on her.

Catching a man's eye across the far side, near where the band were packing up their instruments, her heart quickened. It surely cannot be, she thought, thinking she had seen Bertram for a moment. Sammy caught hold of her arm. 'Hurry up Beaumont, there are people behind you,' he said laughing at the way she was wading desperate not to get her riding skirt dirty.

'Geraldine, I thought... I must be dreaming, I thought I saw Bertram,' said Kathryn to her friend almost out of breath.

'Where?' Geraldine suddenly stopped and swung around to look.

'The far side near the band,' said Kathryn now grabbing Geraldine's arm. She was suddenly feeling lightheaded. As both girls turned to look again, they caught sight of the back of a man with fair hair and tall like Bertram.

'Is that him?' asked Geraldine, not knowing what Bertram looked like.

'I cannot see, there are too many people,' said Kathryn, feeling panic rise in her as she had to keep walking. There were too many people behind her for her to stop. Outside the tent, Kathryn did not want to leave. She wanted to wait a little in case Bertram would pass by. But the rain was making it impossible to see. 'Geraldine I am seeing things I think, my imagination is going wild. It could not have been him, let us go. He was not a soldier, he was not wearing a uniform. It could not possibly be him,' said Kathryn, trying to convince herself more than anything.

Geraldine did not tell Kathryn that she had seen the man earlier on in the evening, loitering by the back of the tent. She had thought he was one of the actors, but now she recognised him as the man who had knocked on her door. He had disappeared as soon as he had seen Geraldine, but this time she had locked eyes with him. Such beautiful green eyes could not be forgotten, with such pain etched in them. Walking back to the hospital arm in arm with Kathryn, she wanted to forget what she had seen. That man, that stranger who appears like an apparition. He unnerved her and she did not know why.

CHAPTER NINETEEN
BERTRAM, THE JOURNALIST

DECEMBER 1916

Bertram opened his journal. He would write the last entry for his column before the New Year. The offensive now stopped for winter, Bertram was staying at a base just south of Cambrai. It had been the busiest month yet for him. After flying from Farnborough in Kent, where he had finished his training, he had been immersed in reconnaissance missions and getting to grips with his favourite aircraft yet, the Sopwith 1½ Strutter. Unfamiliar at first and somewhat nervous, the little aeroplane had captured his heart for its new agility and improved viewpoint. A fantastic aeroplane for his observer and gunner, Flight Lieutenant James Morley Junior, or affectionately known as M. J. The young observer and he had made a formidable partnership over the last four to five weeks. Full of energy, M.J., who was only nineteen years old and from Yorkshire, chatted away continuously, which put Bertram at ease early in the morning. They were preparing their aircraft for the various missions from early November. He would nag Bertram to check everything to the last minute detail, and then declare 'Let us get this Tripehound off the ground!' Or just Hound, as the aeroplane was affectionately called. It was officially called the Dark Star written in black behind the wing. Bertram looked through his notes, his listed missions, his comments and the photographs. One he especially favoured that was taken by M.J. above Beaumont Hamel. He named it The Desolate Land. Bertram began to write his column:

Battle of Ancre, Beaumont Hamel through adversity to the stars: 13th -24th November 1916

by Flight Lieutenant Bertram Wright.

13th November: Our Flight in the "Dark Star".

He jotted down descriptions of the view they had had on the 13th November as they flew over the fields. Unable to fly on the 12th due to dense fog during the day, in the morning of the 14th, the mist had cleared and an early mission of two squadrons flew contact patrols. Revealing the conquest of Beaucourt on the ground to the north west, their flights gave the position of 157 German batteries.

German infantry were harassed from the air. German troops spotted in a ravine north of Beaucourt were heavily bombarded by the British, Bertram wrote.

Flying over Beaufort Hamel, a fortress village, which was located, captured and subjected to gas bombardment as Bertram and M.J. observed the desolate land.

15th November: Pockmarked country, we observed from 5,000 feet.

The Poppy enriched land that was, now winter was creeping in. Floods, mud and biting temperatures, a bleak and desolate land. On return, M.J. and I had to prepare ourselves for another flight, having no time to rest or eat. I was due to be an observer in a Vickers fighter plane piloted by Captain Snell. I did not know him well but respected him as one of the best fighter pilots. Ten Vickers' fighter planes left together, making low attacks by machine gun on railway stations, trains and road transport in Marcelcave area. Later I found out it was one of the best aerial strikes of the whole autumn winter offensive. Our men were praised. Two observers were injured, including M.J., who was observing for Captain Mitchell, but he was not badly hurt. As we flew behind Captain Mitchell, I saw a German bomber on his trail. My quick observations enabled Captain Snell to fire at the German bomber to distract it from Captain Mitchell's aeroplane, and it seems my observation might have saved Captain Mitchell and M.J. The German bomber instead redirected and stealthily bombed the airfield of La Vieille.

As I had an air-to-ground transmitter on board, I was able to quickly warn the base at La Vieille and a dummy landing ground was illuminated as a ruse, which was machine gunned by the German bomber. Craters were left undamaged and no more damage done to the airfield. No more lives lost, just wasted German ammunition.

Behind the scenes, Bertram's work was being noticed and praised. His name was being bandied about by some of the high rankers of the Royal Flying Corps. Captain Snell and Captain Mitchell both praised his quick observations. Bertram continued his column about the 16th and 17th November:

16th November: Good flying weather, but the devastating fire on trenches full of Germans. Two more of our aircraft squadrons lost.

Bertram placed a photograph of M.J. underneath. The young man, with his thumbs up sign standing next to the Lewis guns on board the

Dark Star. He had his moment of glory and England would see this young man in their newspaper. Bertram wrote on:

This column is dedicated to James Morley Junior, injured in the line of duty over Beaumont Hamel. A Hero recovering well.

Gathering up his notes for the column, ready to be posted, Bertram packed his bag for the final time before Christmas. Leaving the base with a spring in his step, his good work behind him. He would take a train to Heilly station and meet some fellow RFC's for an evening near the village of Méricourt-l'Abbé for dinner and light entertainment before he would visit Berenice in Mesves-sur-Loire tomorrow. He would forget about Berenice tonight, get drunk and relax and not think what he would discuss with her tomorrow. Seeing the snow fall, he pulled on his winter flying coat, but wore his civilian clothes. No uniform for a few days, that suited him well. He did not want to draw attention to himself. He wanted to lose himself, intoxicated, sink into the shadows and watch the merriment. Nothing to think about, just to observe.

Slipping on an icy patch on the road, he was unnerved to meet Solange on the way, she had given him the all clear to meet with Berenice. Alphonse was away for two days, she had told him. Knocking on the weathered, grey door, Berenice had already seen him through the frosted glass window, the shutters half open, as they banged in the wind. She opened the door pleased to see him. 'Café?' she asked drawing him close to her. Her belly full, he could feel the swell. Her face rounder but sweet, she tasted of coffee. Pouring some cognac into the black swirling mixture of coffee she handed it to him in a chipped blue cup. They sat together in the kitchen, she rubbed his frozen fingers, blowing on them and kissing them trying to warm them up. As she then stood up to light the fire, he held his head in his hands. 'The baby is mine?' he asked looking up at her in desperation.

'Yes it is yours,' replied Berenice, her eyes alighting with passion.

'And so what do you want from me?' he asked.

Berenice could not answer. Looking up and turning his chair towards the fire as she stoked the flames as if to raise the flames to calm her lover. She could tell he was desperate. He was not a man that could let this go.

Grabbing her around her waist and pulling her onto his lap, he stroked her cheek and took the iron from her hand, putting it back down carefully he clasped her warm hand. 'Do you want to leave your husband?' he finally asked. He was expecting a simple answer, but she slipped from his lap and walked to the kitchen sink to pour her own coffee away.

'No, I cannot leave my husband,' she said quietly. 'That would be impossible, I have Sebastien, I have my house, my sister and my life here in this village,' she said still looking over the kitchen sink and not wanting to face Bertram.

He looked surprised and wounded. 'You want me to leave?' he asked with sadness in his words.

'Never, no, I want you, that is not what I said,' she replied in broken English, trying to find the right words.

'You cannot have both lives, Berenice. Is there a future here in France?' asked Bertram, now getting little agitated at Berenice's indecisiveness.

'It will be what it will be, I cannot leave my home, as hundreds would do the same,' said Berenice finally turning around to face Bertram, still leaning back on the kitchen sink, her arms folded defensively over belly.

'I cannot stay in France Berenice, this is not my home,' he replied with tears in his eyes. She threw the mug into the sink, it clattered loudly with the other mugs and plates that lay there.

'Then nothing…,' she turned to him, her black eyes ablaze with anger.

'What do you mean?' asked Bertram confused by her erratic mood as she ran up the stairs bursting into tears. He followed her to her bedroom, tripping over a large pair of men's shoes. They sat holding hands on the edge of the bed and then he slowly unbuttoned her collar, first her neck, then her chest. Each button pinching his fingers as it unhooked the material that held her swelling bosom. He put his head against her chest as she cradled it. There was no solution and he accepted this. His heart was frozen, frozen in time since he had first trodden on French soil. He wanted to go home. He closed his eyes and fell asleep.

The next morning he was woken by Sebastien who was pulling on his shirt sleeves. Bertram turned over in the bed, the curtains were already open and he could see snow falling again.

Berenice was making breakfast and as he sat by the fireside, he could see she was in no mood to talk. Quietly she went about her business, taking a fresh loaf of bread out of the stove, placing it in front of him. She did not talk, she had nothing to say. He could see she had not slept well, and she was worried. Looking at the kitchen clock, he knew Alphonse was returning soon. Sebastien had told him. The young boy had made it quite clear that he did not like Alphonse. Bertram was beginning to understand how things were between Alphonse and Sebastien. The boy kept out of his stepfather's way. To Alphonse, Sebastien was to be tolerated, nothing more. Another man's child that he was bringing up and providing for. He would pay for his clothes and food but that was it. There was no love lost between them.

Bertram did not want to leave Sebastien, he had a quiet connection with him. He could not explain it but when the boy would sit at his feet or quietly sit reading across the kitchen table from him, there was a peace between them, a sense of belonging. This was something Bertram had never experienced even with his own family in Sussex. His parents had long since died and his much older brother had left home when he was only five years old. He had only once seen his brother again at his mother's funeral. Bertram last heard he had joined the navy and married a woman in Naples in Italy.

'You have to go,' said Berenice eventually, sitting next to him with her chin in her hands. Drinking his black coffee and eating the bread, he took her hand once again.

'Come with me to England, Sebastien can come too. We can be a family all of us,' he said.

'And my sister, her husband, my aunt in the next village?' she said almost mocking him. He knew what she was saying. She was French, she could not possibly perceive living in a country she did not know. Her ties here were too strong, and perhaps she loved Alphonse after all. He could only think this to be true. They had been together for eight years, he provided for her and Sebastien, that was all she expected.

'You could be happy with me?' stated Bertram questioning her dark eyes, seeing if there was a flicker of emotion, or even love for him perhaps that would bring her around. Tears flowed quickly and knowing Sebastien was watching them, she rose from the table. She slapped her thighs sharply and turning to him, she repeated the word 'Happy.' She was fine here, she was not expecting more out of life. 'You have to go,' she said again, turning to the kitchen sink, her back turned. Bertram fetched his bag from the bottom of the bed upstairs and slowly walked down the stairs to the front door. Sebastien behind him, he turned to look at Berenice.

She took off her apron and stood beside him for a moment. Smoothing down his coat, she unlatched the door. 'Wait,' she said, turning to the coat stand. She picked up her shawl and clumsily put it around her shoulders. Bertram affectionately pulled it across her chest and then placed a hand on her belly. 'The baby, will you be all right with the baby?' he asked, looking at Berenice with a dwelling sorrow, having to leave her and their child behind.

'Alphonse…' she started her sentence. Bertram nodded as he turned to walked away. But as he walked out into the cold morning air, she caught his hand and held it firmly. She stood on her tiptoes and kissed his lips. She heard the gate open and for an awful second she thought it was Alphonse. Instead a young woman was walking fast towards them, in a green uniform and shouting in English. Berenice let go of his hand.

CHAPTER TWENTY
KATHRYN: RETURN TO DALLINGTON PLACE

February 1917
Dear Kathryn,
I am sorry that you have had this wait, but I am full of admiration for you, and was put at ease by your last letter, that you were being discharged at the beginning of March, you were well and looking forward to coming home.

Everything here has been arranged and your mother is overjoyed that you will be returning home in a matter of weeks. I have the marriage license in my possession. Business as usual at the factory, keeping me busy, which stops me worrying about you.

I look forward to seeing you on the 18th, and I will be there to pick you up as arranged. My new automobile will have a passenger at last!
Until then,
Devlin

Kathryn placed the letter back into the pocket of her green jacket. She would be home soon and butterflies filled her stomach. Today was the 18th March and looking at her wrist watch it was nearly two o'clock. The train was pulling into the station. She peered out of the window but could not see Devlin.

Waiting, sitting on the platform bench she nervously looked at her watch again. She hoped he had not had a change of heart. Only at that moment she knew she had made the right decision. The thought of him not turning up made her stomach turn. Even more than the day she had seen that woman with Bertram. Her thoughts flickered back to that day. The riddle now being played out before her eyes began to unfold. Passing a stone cottage on that day in Mesves-sur-Loire she remembered smiling at the young lad with the black hair and black eyes as he bounced his ball on the cobbled front path. Out of the corner of her eye Kathryn watched the couple kiss on the doorstep. Geraldine noticed too, and pulled Kathryn to come away, towards the road and anywhere from where they were at that moment. Kathryn could picture the way the women looked at Bertram, she had that image playing over and over in her mind for weeks after. A pregnant woman, older and more beautiful than herself, reached up to kiss her Bertram goodbye. It was a kiss between lovers. Long, shiny, black hair fell exotically down her back, her back arching slightly as she tipped her mouth up to kiss him. He was wearing a uniform she did not recognise but his fair hair was unmistakable. Shocked and not knowing what she was doing, her body moved past the boy, as if she was floating down the cobbled path, palm outstretched as if to strike. Geraldine caught her arm as it swung in the direction of Bertram. The woman with the black hair screamed with such emotion demanding to know who this mad woman was. Kathryn remembered screaming back herself. 'Who is she?' 'Who is she?' she found herself screaming at the woman. Geraldine was there to pull her away.

Sighing, she remembered Bertram reach out his hand to her, but the woman pulled him back, pulling at his coat tails, crying and stumbling behind Bertram as he tried to follow them up the slippery, icy path. 'Leave him, he is not worth it!' Geraldine was saying holding Kathryn up and pulling her along.

'Get me out of here!' Kathryn remembered saying to Geraldine as she buried her head in her shoulder. 'Get me out of here. I want to go home,' she cried.

'Kathryn I am so sorry, there was a truck full of sheep on the Darton Road crossing, I could not get here any quicker,' said Devlin pulling Kathryn into his arms and softly planting a kiss on her cheek. Kathryn wiped away a tear, he didn't see it, as he picked up her bag and in his take charge sort of way hurried her out of the station. 'The vicar is waiting at St. Dunstan's for us and your mother!' said Devlin out of breath.

'Of course,' she said smiling the broadest smile of contentment at Devlin. He looked well in his suit, which was probably new from the Savile Row and smelling of his favourite Astor cologne by Geo. F. Trumper from Curzon Street. His hair was shorter, it suited him, she observed in the passenger seat of his glamorous automobile. The leather seats smelt expensive. Wearing his cream leather driving gloves, he drove the automobile efficiently, the car wipers moving rapidly as the rain fell. Kathryn felt oddly comforted by the rain. The heater was turned on full and Kathryn stopped shivering. She was home and it was her wedding day.

'Stop here please Devlin, just for a moment, I need some air,' she suddenly said to Devlin, touching his arm.

'Are you unwell?' he asked nervously. 'No, there is just something I need to do, on the bridge, give me a moment please,' she said.

Devlin pulled over just before the little white bridge. 'Here take the umbrella,' he called, as she opened the door, sensing that she needed a moment alone. He did not want her to get soaked in the rain.

'No thank you my dear, I do not need it, not after what I have been through,' she said smiling at him lovingly.

He stopped the car engine and watched Kathryn through the glass. He thought how small her feet were and how neat her waist was. How he loved everything about her. The way she walked briskly over the bridge and then stopped pensively. He could not quite see what she was doing, he wound the window down and heard something hit the flowing stream. She had thrown something in the cold waters beneath. She ran back to the car slamming the door shut, looking triumphant. Wiping away the rain from her pink cheeks, he did not say anything, he would ask her later.

'Ready?' he smiled at her.

'Ready!' she replied touching his hand fondly.

Driving past the driveway to Dallington Place and down the hill to St. Dunstan's, Kathryn's mind raced. If someone had told her she would be marrying someone other than Bertram, she would have laughed at them. Now she was proud to be marrying this kind man, who had proved his love with his devotion. Passing the hedgerow and the lime trees, she did have a moment of sadness, her eyes misted a little. Turning her head away from Devlin to look at some cottages that bordered the churchyard, she noticed some building work had taken place. Her mind then wandered to her dress and whether it was appropriate to be married in her nursing Yeomanry uniform. Devlin had assured her that it was fitting and that she should be proud of all she had accomplished.

Vicar Sanderson stretched out his hand as he welcomed them into the little church, asking how they were, and what uniform Kathryn was wearing. Kathryn looked for her mother, who was sitting in the front pew. Tears filled her eyes, how she had missed her, and how frail she seemed as she slowly got to her feet when Kathryn approached. They hugged and did not need to say anything, the love in her eyes said it all. Her mother passed her a pretty posy and Kathryn had never felt happier. It was her moment now and she would be a married woman from this day onward. As she watched her mother move along the pew, Kathryn had one regret, that Geraldine was not there. She knew Geraldine was making her way back to England just as they were taking their vows and they would see each other soon. The vicar turned to Kathryn with warmth in his eyes as Devlin slipped the simple gold band on her finger.

'Where shall we go for our wedding breakfast?' Devlin asked Kathryn, lovingly looking at his new bride.

Raising her eyebrows at why he was suddenly stopping outside the row of cottages they had passed earlier. 'Why are we stopping here?' asked Kathryn, puzzled as to why he smiled to himself smugly as he walked around to the side of the car to open her door.

'This is your new home Mrs McAlister,' he announced taking her hand and placing his coat around her shoulders. March winds had really picked up today and the lime tree branches blew in the furious wind. Her hair flowing freely around her face, Devlin liked her hair loose and around her shoulders. She perused the two cottages that had been knocked through to build a large house. A large willow tree stood behind the house and Kathryn held on to the catkins, as Devlin put his arms around her waist. 'Look there,' he said pointing to a clearing in some farmland in the distance. 'You can just see the rooftops of Dallington Place from here.'

Kathryn stood still for a moment, taking in the cool air but feeling the warmth and manly arms of Devlin around her. He held her like he would never let go. Oh how safe and loved she felt in his arms. Planting a kiss on her cheek, he pulled her quickly around. 'Come, I will show you around the inside of the house. It is ready to move into, I hope you like the decoration,' he said faltering for a moment to find the keys in his suit pocket.

'Did my mother know about this?' she asked, knowing by the cool blue walls and the pretty cream and blue armchairs that were newly bought, that she may have helped Devlin with the colour scheme.

'It has four bedrooms!' he said opening another door to a small kitchen.

'A separate kitchen, how lovely,' she said excitedly, thinking of all the happy times she will have there, baking for Devlin. A large black Aga took most of the room up, filling the house with warmth.

Upstairs, she looked inside all the bedrooms, the larger one already had Devlin's overcoat on the back of the door. Her small bag with all her worldly belongings had now been placed by the windowsill. She spied the large bed and she felt nervous. Tonight she would spend her first night here as a married woman. She looked over to him and he read her thoughts, taking her hand and leading her downstairs so as not to make her uncomfortable. Maybe he was as nervous as her, she thought. 'So what are we going to do with all this space?' she asked smiling at her husband, who had obviously been working hard to make it special for her.

'Maybe you could have a lady's maid,' he said cheekily.

'Me? Devlin, seriously no, I am quite capable of looking after myself and my home,' she said, taken aback by Devlin's suggestion. She did not want anyone waiting on her.

'No Kathryn I was not suggesting you could not, but you are a lady now... of sorts,' he said looking at his wife lovingly.

'I see, what because I am married to a gentleman?' she said and gave Devlin a little nudge with her elbow and reached to give him a kiss on his cheek.

'Of course. We could fill it full of children and when we have so many, we will build on another cottage,' said Devlin laughing as he opened the curtains in the drawing room. Kathryn looked at the view. She could not quite believe that she had her own house with the view of her beloved Dallington Place a mile or so away. Standing by the window looking out on her small garden. A garden of her own, she thought. Then she imagined the children she would have with Devlin running around filling the place with noise and laughter. She had not thought about children at all really. She was still young but she wondered if Devlin would want them straight away. Of course he would, she thought, he was not getting any younger. A man of forty would want his own children quickly at that age.

'I thought we could go into town, and have dinner, would you like that?' asked Devlin tentatively, wondering if she was too tired. 'Or we could stay here, and sit by the fire. Mr Evan has kindly sent over some food, a wedding present from Dallington Place,' he said.

'Really, how kind, I must thank the Fitch family,' said Kathryn, thinking of them fondly. 'Do you know how they all are? I must write to Lady Fitch immediately and give her my new address,' she continued.

'Lady Alison had a little girl, I do believe her name is Dawn,' said Devlin, now looking closely at Kathryn to see her reaction about the baby.

169

'How beautiful! I wonder what life is like for them in Texas,' she said with a big warm smile. Her mind wandered to the exotic land of Texas as she looked out of the window.

'Well, you can write to them tonight and tell Lady Fitch all about your new home. I have some writing paper in the bureau, I have not filled the house with too much furniture as I knew you would want to choose that yourself,' Devlin said, sitting down next to her on the large cream divan in front of the fire.

'Can I make us a pot of tea? I want to try out my new kitchen,' she said jumping up excitedly. 'I think it would be lovely just to stay here,' she said squeezing his hand lovingly.

'Let me just re-park the automobile around the side of the house, I will not be long,' he said pulling on his overcoat, as he noticed the rain starting to lash the windows of the cottage.

As she stood in her kitchen, and poured some hot water into the teapot, for a moment she thought of Bertram. A feeling of guilt swept over her. A feeling she knew as irrational. What if she had stayed in France and let him explain what had happened with the French woman. Would she ever know, she wondered as she heard the front door shut. Picking up the tray of tea, and seeing the back of Devlin's head as he sat relaxing by the fire, she knew she was not in love with Bertram anymore. This man before her, this kind, gentle and generous man was the one she loved. She would have a family with this man, here in this house and nothing or no one could change that.

21st March 1917, Willow Tree Cottage
Dear Lady Fitch,
I hope this letter finds you and your family in good health and congratulations on the arrival of your granddaughter. I expect you have had many celebrations and will soon be able to see the baby once this war is over.

I have recently returned from the war in France and I do not know if Sir Nicholas has informed you, that I have become Mrs McAlister! I am a very proud and a happy wife to my lovely husband Devlin. I have enclosed my new address where you can write to me.

I look forward to seeing you soon at Dallington Place.

I want to thank you so much for my happy times at Dallington Place. I have never forgotten how kind you and Sir Nicholas were to me and for introducing me to my new life. I would never have met

Devlin had Sir Nicholas not supplied me with a good recommendation
to work at the factory.
  Yours Truly,
  Kathryn McAlister

Kathryn put down her pen and sealed the letter in an envelope, realising it was getting late. It was still raining, but she would risk the cold, for she wanted to post the letter today. Putting on her new cape that Devlin had bought her yesterday, she started out on the road, hoping the rain would die away as quickly as it had arrived. A half an hour walk over some fields behind Dallington Place, and then another ten minutes' walk to the village. She had noticed the automobile that had sped out of the Dallington Place driveway as she approached the crossing. She was not close enough to see who was it. But he had noticed her, and with a cold chill inside him he did not stop to greet her. Bertram instantly knew it was Kathryn. Someone that he used to know and love. The long winding drive from Dallington Place took him all the way back to France. He did not glance back.

Lime Tree by Bertram Wright
Doth what they bring, the March wind and rain,
as love escapes the hollow of the lime tree,
where hidden blossoms are budding come spring,
I came to claim you, but you were not mine.

CHAPTER TWENTY-ONE
BERTRAM RETURNS TO ENGLAND

24TH DECEMBER 1918

Walking over to his own cottage with Bertram carrying his son, Ernest, in his arms, Mr Evan assured them that Mrs McAlister would be arriving soon at Dallington Place. She was due to open the doors to the staff preparing for the village Christmas party. 'I will make you and your boy something to eat.' Mr Evan kindly said unlocking the front door, taking his time with his fingers still feeling the icy nip in the air. 'Looks like snow, you made it on time, you and your boy!' Bertram nodded, feeling the cold too and relieved he had made it to Dallington Place before dark for his son's sake at least. 'Did you say you had flown in this morning?' asked a rather surprised Mr Evan. 'Yes and then we took the train, the baby boy could do with a sleep,' said Bertram, looking for a suitable place for Ernest to sleep. 'Does Mrs McAlister know you are coming to the Christmas party?' asked Mr Evan busying himself in the small kitchen.

'No, I am afraid she does not, it is merely a social call,' said Bertram beginning to feel uncomfortable.

'Perhaps then I should telephone her first?' suggested Mr Evan.

Bertram nodded, covering the boy with his coat. 'Are Lady Fitch and Sir Nicholas in residence?' asked Bertram.

'No, I am afraid they are not. The last year or so Lady Fitch has been quite unwell, first with a bad chest infection and then a fever. She is recovering well, but has been told to stay put for the foreseeable future. Endelwise Manor is a smaller house to manage, easier for her. Mrs McAlister has been running the social side of Dallington Place for Lady Fitch while she is convalescing,' Mr Evan continued.

'I see,' said Bertram looking away.

Mr Evan nodded and then looked to the little boy. 'How old is he?' he asked.

'Nearly eighteen months,' replied Bertram, gently looking at his sleeping son. Mr Evan gave him a quizzical look unsure of why Bertram Wright wanted to see Kathryn. He was surprised to see Bertram again, knowing how angry he had been when he had told

Bertram last year of her marriage to Mr McAlister. Bertram had been so furious, Mr Evan was afraid now for Kathryn. Maybe he should suggest she talk to her husband first before seeing Bertram. 'If you excuse me, I just have to make a few calls. Please sit here by the fire and I will be back presently,' said Mr Evan as he walked to the next room. He then dialled Mr McAlister at his factory. When he returned, Bertram was gone, having left Ernest asleep. He was making his way through the snow up to the entrance of Dallington Place. There was nothing Mr Evan could do to stop him, he could not leave the boy by himself. He stood at the window, waiting for the drama to unfold.

Kathryn had let Bertram into the drawing room, just when Devlin's automobile was racing up the driveway at full pelt. 'Berenice's husband will not accept him and I have nowhere to take him for now,' explained Bertram to Kathryn, sitting on the large chesterfield, whilst Kathryn sat nervously opposite him. She was relieved when she saw her husband's automobile arriving.

'Where is Ernest now?' asked Kathryn as Devlin marched into the room.

'Back in the cottage with Mr Evan,' he replied embarrassed.

Devlin marched over to where Kathryn was sitting by the window and placed a protective hand on her shoulder. 'Can I help you Mr Wright?' asked Devlin in his most authoritative manner.

'I was just telling Kathryn about my situation, and that of my son, Sir,' replied Bertram as he looked at Devlin to perceive his reaction.

'What is his name?' asked Devlin, still his manner giving nothing away about his feelings for this man that stood before him and Kathryn. Bertram looked tired and dishevelled. Older than his years, in fact looking not a lot younger than Devlin himself. Kathryn eyed him too and was shocked at the way his hair had grown grey at the temples, his eyes had a haunted look about them, with dark shadows underneath, almost masking the beauty of those green eyes.

'His name is Ernest,' Bertram replied, clearing his throat.

'And his mother? Can she not care for him?' asked Devlin almost pained to interfere and know of the situation.

'She has been unwell and her situation is far from easy. It is her husband, you see. Ernest is my son,' said Bertram.

'I see,' said Devlin impatiently judging Bertram. 'And how long do you propose for him to stay with us?' he continued.

'Until I get myself settled. I am thinking of accepting a job in New York,' explained Bertram nervously.

'You have no other relatives that could take him in England?' asked Devlin.

Bertram bowed his head. 'No, I am afraid not.'

Kathryn looked up to Devlin. He could tell what she was thinking. 'Kathryn, do you think Lettie could fix us a drink, a tea perhaps,' Devlin asked his wife, so he could have a moment with Bertram. Kathryn walked over to the bell, and Lettie, a girl from the village, who was there to help with the Christmas decorations, appeared on the door. Kathryn asked her to prepare a tea tray.

Devlin rubbed his chin and looked at Bertram. 'How old is he?' he asked Bertram. He was about to answer but suddenly paused and walked towards the door.

'I can see you are busy, I am sorry to have troubled you,' he said looking at Kathryn with a pitiful look.

Devlin looked at Kathryn and he said quietly but firmly, 'We will take him.' Devlin walked over to Kathryn and put his hand on her shoulder. She took his hand and patted it reassuringly. Bertram was surprised by this man's answer. He walked back across the room to shake Devlin's hand. 'Now now, there is no need for formalities, you say a month or two?' enquired Devlin, fetching a piece of paper. 'Here, write your details where we can contact you,' he said as he handed Bertram a pen and paper.

'I am afraid I have no address at the moment, but I will be back to collect him,' said Bertram, looking for Devlin's approval.

Kathryn searched Bertram's face, but there was no emotion. Devlin looked outside where the snow was now settling. 'Bring the boy over, before it gets too cold. He is with Mr Evan did you say?'

Bertram nodded again and then reached into his bag that was slung across his body. 'I will not stay to say goodbye, he will not stop crying if he sees me leaving. It is best that I go now,' said Bertram, unable to look Kathryn in the eye.

'As you like,' said Devlin, his patience wearing thin with this strange man that once had been his rival for Kathryn's affections.

'Kathryn, please be so kind and give this to Geraldine Weaves,' said Bertram handing Kathryn a brown box. 'There were some belongings of Robert's I managed to recover,' he continued.

'Oh, thank you Bertram, this will be of comfort to her.' She took the box and placed it on her desk.

As Bertram reached for the door, he turned around with a worried look on his face and said, 'You will not forget will you, it is important.'

Kathryn nodded at Bertram compassionately. 'Of course Bertram, I will not forget, she will be arriving here in an hour, you could give her the box yourself,' she continued.

'I doubt she will want to see me!' he said.

Kathryn gazed at him. He was such a mystery, she did not understand him at all. Bertram looked into Kathryn's eyes for the last time, almost to see if he could trust her on following his request. She locked eyes with him for a moment and she knew she would never see him again. He slammed the door shut, on purpose or accidently, Devlin drew a sigh of relief that Bertram was gone. 'What a strange man, he seemed to care more about that bloody box than of his own flesh and blood,' said Devlin as he stood by the window and watched Bertram walk down the drive in a hurry. 'Where he is going this time of evening, I do not know.'

Kathryn walked over to Devlin and wrapped her arms around Devlin's waist as they watched Bertram's sorry figure disappear between the trees. 'He is a troubled soul, there is no doubt about that. Must have been the war, it is done that to more than most,' said Kathryn, pulling her shawl tighter around her shoulders.

'So let us get this little boy then,' he said following Kathryn out of the door.

Geraldine and William were the first to arrive, and Kathryn hugged a very pregnant Geraldine. 'Thank goodness Mrs Lovat, you are the first to arrive. I need tell you something!' said Kathryn excitedly, her face flushed with emotion. She pulled Geraldine into the study as the men went into the dining room where Mr Evan was serving the drinks. 'You are not pregnant Kathryn, really tell me quickly?' Geraldine asked wide-eyed.

'No, no nothing like that, but we just had a visitor!' she looked at Geraldine, keen to tell her the full story.

'A visitor, who Kathryn, do tell, you are worrying me!' said Geraldine fervently.

'Bertram,' said Kathryn coldly.

'Bertram! What did he want?' asked Geraldine shocked.

'He left something for me and something for you. He is gone now, no need to worry. Here, let me show you upstairs. We better be quick, the other guests will be arriving soon,'

Kathryn hurried Geraldine to follow her. 'Wait here a moment,' said Kathryn as she left Geraldine at the foot of the stairs to go back into her study to fetch the box. As the women reached the bedroom door, Kathryn put her finger to her lips to shush Geraldine. In the darkness, with just a little side lamp lit, Geraldine could distinguish the features of a small adorable child. His thick fair hair hung in short ringlets against his olive skin. Geraldine's eyes were agog. Kathryn took her hand and pulled her out of the bedroom.

'Whose child is he?' she asked but had already guessed by the time Kathryn had shut the door.

'Bertram's and Berenice's,' replied Kathryn candidly. 'He just left him here with you and Devlin, just like that?' asked Geraldine surprised. Kathryn nodded.

'He said he would be back!' said Kathryn not meeting Geraldine's eye.

'What, the reliable Bertram Wright just left his child and he is coming to collect him, when?' continued Geraldine as she could not believe that anyone could just walk away from their child.

'A month or two,' replied Kathryn still avoiding Geraldine's gaze.

'Kathryn, you know what this means?' Kathryn nodded. She did not believe he would be back either. 'And Devlin, he is fine with this?' asked Geraldine her eyes welling with tears.

Again Kathryn nodded. 'For the time being, I think that he is.' Geraldine looked at her friend and grabbed her hand.

'Well, you married a remarkable man, Kathryn Beaumont.' They embraced each other to offer mutual support. Kathryn could sense that Geraldine was in an emotional state.

'I did indeed and so did you!' as she held her friend tighter.

'I know, I know and now look at me,' laughed Geraldine through her tears pointing at her belly.

'Listen before we go downstairs, I have to tell you that Bertram left you some things of Robert's.

'He did?' said Geraldine, needing to sit down all of a sudden.

The loud doorbell of Dallington Place rang out, and Kathryn passed the box to her friend.

'I'd better go and introduce the guests. Wait here for a moment, sit on the seat there and I will be back,' she said as she helped Geraldine to sit down.

Kathryn raced down the stairs to greet her guests and lead them into the dining room. She touched her husband's arm as he was talking to the vicar. 'Devlin my dear, I will be back, I have to see to Geraldine upstairs, do you mind?' He nodded and smiled at her as she rushed back up the staircase.

'I have heard that Dallington Place might be for sale, have you considered putting an offer?' asked Vicar Sanderson.

Devlin turned to the vicar with raised interest. 'Is that so,' he said.

Geraldine had already opened the box and was sitting staring at the contents. 'What is in it?' asked Kathryn worried by her friend's expression.

'A medal!' cried Geraldine, tears now flowing down her cheeks. 'Bertram wrote me a letter, I will read it to you.' Kathryn sat next to Geraldine.

Dear Geraldine,

I have left you this medal as I feel it belongs to you and Robert. I heard the good news that he had been pardoned and I was so pleased for him, and for you. But for me, I am not pardoned. I am a changed man from this war and the only way I can express this is by leaving my Victoria Cross to you. It is the only way I can pardon myself. I do not feel a war hero or someone that deserves this reward. Someone as brave as Robert was, who did not defend himself because he felt not worthy. He was ashamed of not being able to read or write.

His so called friend, who could write for a living, could not save him. I am guilty of this.

The only way I can unburden some of my guilt is to leave my most precious symbol of this war and return it back to the man that should have been honoured for it instead.

I hope this leaves you with some comfort.

I am so sorry. Robert loved you with all his heart.

Keep Kathryn safe.

Bertram Wright

Tears ran down Geraldine's cheeks and she held her belly. 'Kathryn, I do not blame Bertram, Robert would not have wanted that.'

Kathryn squeezed her hand. 'I know.' Kathryn realised that Bertram must have been in such an emotional turmoil. Kathryn took the medal from Geraldine's hand and placed it back in the box. "For Valour, in the face of the Enemy" was inscribed on the back. Geraldine shut the box and held it close to her chest. They were all brave, she thought. It was hard to distinguish one person from another who had fought in their own way for their country.

Later that night, as their automobile drove over the white bridge on the way back to Willow Tree Cottage, Kathryn thought of her sweetheart brooch that she had thrown into the fast flowing stream. She thought of the wasted lives and feelings of all that had been in France with her. Then looking to the back of the automobile, where Ernest slept peacefully, she realised that although unexpected, not all of it was wasted. Lives had sprung from it, new beginnings and a love that was not temporary.

Willow Tree by Bertram Wright
Encase me in the willow,
for I will not weep.
Judge me by the billow,
so not to keep.

Open your arms,
and let me walk amongst the spaces.
Do not fold your branches,
so thin are the traces.
I can disperse, in a fair swoop,
as the wind blows; I will return.
A spore is let loose,
I am more than before.
Each particle travels,
not sure where to land.
Unravel sweet catkin,
forty seeds venture forth.
Lost in a myriad,
of openness and kind.
Where do you go,
What do you find?
To seek your growth,
you cannot be pinned.
Each North, South, East and West,
lovely resting place; forlorn but free.
A soft landing, a mating mound,
A quiet spot, a lofty croft.
A meadow, a stream,
A bird, a scene,
it doesn't make the difference,
Of places, time, or sight.
Rights are abound,
Everything goes to ground,
a branch and tree,
weeping willow encase me.
Test me, and I will revolt,
a horse, a wild gripping colt.
A spirit of life that cannot be withheld,
felled me,
And you will know every length of your leaves,
will shed a tear.
It is right when the storm takes,
you will bend, but will not break.
Be open, and then closed,
the only way to be, is flexible with me.

CHAPTER TWENTY-TWO
CHRISTMAS, 22nd DECEMBER 1933

Kathryn tapped her fingers nervously on the ornate marble panelling of the hearth as she waited for Dawson to enter the sitting room with some tea. The cool surface of the hearth had a soothing effect on her. A place she stood by often, thinking and looking out to the lime trees on to the great lawn of Dallington Place. A spot which held much solace for her. She had become a popular figure in the community although of late she had been rather reclusive. 'Sebastien, are you hungry? Dawson will not be long,' she said, aware of the silence between them. The young man with the dark eyes glanced at her sideways. His olive skin and good looks should have looked unfamiliar, but they were not. She remembered him from that day at Mesves-sur-Loire, running down the path from Berenice's house. He had looked at her now just as he had all those years ago as a young boy. She did not need to ask any questions, it was him without a doubt, but the American accent was a surprise.

Dawson interrupted the moment and Kathryn instructed him where to place the tea and cake tray. Sebastien watched Kathryn like a hawk, his eyes lingered on her body and then he studied her face. He liked her eyebrows, the way they danced happily above her small blue eyes as she firmly told Dawson they were not to be interrupted. He noticed she was not very tall, her newly fashioned heels hardly making her much above five foot. It was her posture that made her statuesque. She held her back straight and her neck was long and slender. She was not a traditionally pretty woman, her features were not even, but she was undeniably attractive. There was a luminosity about her skin. Age had not diminished that and her smile was engaging. As she sat back down, she pushed some curls away from her forehead and he noticed how small and exotic her hands were. She poured the tea with an air of authority. There was a nobleness and intelligence about her, a knowing look as if she could make any problem surmountable. She was safe and Sebastien liked safe. No wonder his father had fallen in love with her.

Kathryn, aware he was staring, started up the conversation again. 'So why have you come to England, Sebastien? Are you visiting family, friends?' she enquired.

'No Ma'am,' he answered avoiding her gaze. 'I am sorry to tell you that my father Bertram, passed away. He left these letters addressed to you,' he said. Reaching down into his bag by his feet, he pulled out a thick bundle of envelopes and passed them to Kathryn.

Sebastien did not see Kathryn blanch. She sat further back on her chair, her back pushing into the velvet cushions. Her lips were dry and she took a sip of tea before reaching out for the letters. Her hands shook slightly as she placed them on her lap. 'Thank you, I am sorry for your loss,' she said now looking down onto the neat bundle of letters addressed to her at Dallington Place.

'Perhaps he never meant to send them,' said Sebastien interrupting her thoughts.

Kathryn raised her eyebrows. 'He was always writing, now we know he was writing to you. I think he missed writing for the newspaper once we moved to Santa Anna,' he continued.

'Santa Anna?' asked Kathryn distracted.

'Yes Texas, that is where we lived,' replied Sebastien, noticing the skin on Kathryn's neck had blushed and she nervously clasped the double row of pearls around her neck. She reached for her handkerchief. 'I thought perhaps Bertram went to New York, that is where he said he was heading after he left Ernest with us,' said Kathryn dabbing the corners of her eyes before composing herself.

'I was ten, I cannot remember much. We stayed in New York with Alexander Pillard's family for a while, I do not know for how long,' he explained.

'I remember Bertram mentioning Alexander Pillard,' Kathryn said interrupting him.

'Then we moved on to Texas to visit Jorie and we just stayed. I started school and father and I helped Jorie with the horses at the ranch,' continued Sebastien.

'Jorie?' asked Kathryn, her voice dry again.

'Yes Jorie, my stepmother. She and father had met in London during the war one summer. They had this thing where she would she teach him to ride horses if he taught her to fly an aeroplane.'

Kathryn's eyes grew larger. What was this life of secrets Bertram had kept from her? Grasping the bundle of letters her hands began to perspire. 'So you never went back to France, Sebastien?' she managed to ask.

'I had nothing in France, my mother Berenice had left with another man, and so Bertram took me with him. Maybe I asked to go with him, I cannot remember. It was so long ago and I was happy to be with someone who gave me some attention. Bertram was always kind to me,' Sebastien trailed off lost in his thoughts.

As she watched Sebastien bite into a piece of cake, her thoughts turned to Ernest. Had he come back to meet his brother, did he know about Ernest, she wondered. How could Bertram have left Ernest and taken someone else's son with him? Seems like she really had not known Bertram at all. He was a mystery to her now as he was during the war. Getting up to open a window, she was reminding herself how lucky she was that Devlin had come along when he did. Opening the window slightly, she breathed in the fresh air, her cheeks now cool and her throat less dry. It looked like snow, just like the evening when Bertram had arrived and left Ernest with them all those years ago. When Devlin had raced up the drive knowing Bertram was keeping his wife company. She smiled to herself, he was not here to rescue her now. She missed him dearly but suddenly she felt full of confidence. 'Are you staying Sebastien? Snow is beginning to fall,' she asked as she swung around and caught his gaze fixed on her.

'I would like that very much, that is very kind, Ma'am,' said Sebastien politely getting to his feet aware that Kathryn seemed tired.

Gathering the letters and placing them on the bureau, she turned to Sebastien. 'Were they happy, Bertram and Jorie? she asked.

'I remember the good times, the laughter. We flew in the aeroplane quite a bit. Father taught Jorie how to fly and me too. They were fun times, but then father began to retreat into himself and he was drinking too much.' Shrugging he continued, 'Jorie and I were left to run the stud ranch, it was hard work. I think she became quite resentful of him,' he said.

Kathryn could see a glimmer of sadness in his eyes. He studied Kathryn's face and saw that she looked hurt. 'I sound hard on him, but we were all angry in our own way. He could have made it easier on himself and us,' Sebastien explained. Kathryn nodded. She understood that. 'I think he was in a lot of pain, you know, turmoil in his mind,' continued Sebastien.

'Yes,' agreed Kathryn, 'that I did know, … the war,' she did not finish her sentence. Reflectively, Kathryn rang the bell for Dawson to show Sebastien to his room.

Sebastien looked Kathryn sharply in the eye, 'Do not think he did not love you – he did,' he said with wisdom beyond his years whilst reaching out to touch her arm gently.

Kathryn blushed but she was not sure if it was because of the electricity between them as he had brushed her silk blouse with his hand or that he was too forward with his words. 'Just one thing Sebastien, do not think I am alone here. I have Dawson and other staff here and Ernest will be returning tomorrow… my son,' said Kathryn firmly noting the young man's flirtatious manner.

Sebastien strode to the door and as Dawson opened it, he turned to Kathryn with a half-smile and flicked his dark hair out of his eyes. 'I would never imagine a woman like you Kathryn would ever be alone,' he said. And with that he disappeared through the door. The comment had not gone unnoticed by Dawson, as he led the young man the long way to his bedroom, through the old kitchen and up the backstairs to the attic.

Kathryn sat pensively in her bed. There were so many other questions she wanted to ask Sebastien. She would ask him tomorrow over breakfast, she decided. She had placed Bertram's letters on her dressing table and was curious what they would contain. She looked away and snuggled under the heavy eiderdown. She wanted to telephone Geraldine but it was too late. She could hear the clock strike eleven o'clock and she closed her eyes. Instead of tiredness she felt a new rush of energy surge through her. It was good to have someone new staying at Dallington Place. She had to make preparations, it was Christmas after all.

Kathryn slept late the next morning. It was unusual for her as she was normally an early riser. She could have sworn she had heard footsteps on the gravel underneath her bedroom window during the night, but she had soon fallen back to sleep, thinking it was a fox. The snow had not settled, she was pleased to notice. Even the sun was shining this morning. She rushed to get dressed, wondering if Sebastien had already had his breakfast.

Downstairs, Libby the young cook was rushing about looking flustered. 'Where is Dawson, Libby? I rang but no reply,' asked Kathryn anxiously. It was unlike Dawson not to be up by this hour.

Even though he was quite old, he was always up and about by nine most mornings.

'He is at Willow Tree Cottage with the young American man, Ma'am,' replied Libby looking nervously tying her apron around her waist.

'What?' said Kathryn surprised. 'I am afraid something has happened to the automobile and Jonas had been knocking at the front door for an hour to get your attention. I think the automobile got stuck in a ditch,' continued Libby.

'Good Lord Libby, what on earth was Mr Comte-Wright doing with the automobile?' exclaimed Kathryn.

'I do not know Ma'am, you will have to ask Mr Dawson.' responded Libby looking uncomfortable. She disappeared back to the kitchen to continue with breakfast preparations.

'It was Mr Dawson's automobile he went out with?' Kathryn called back to Libby as she grabbed her automobile keys from a kitchen draw.

'Yes Ma'am,' replied Libby as she was kneading the bread dough.

Thank goodness it was not her Morris saloon. Disgruntled and confused, she pulled on her overcoat. Although it was a bright day, it was certainly chilly. Walking over to the stable block behind the house where the automobiles were kept, her mind was whirling. What was she thinking, letting a stranger in her home, she thought to herself. How naive she could be sometimes. Nothing changes, Geraldine always told her off for being too trusting.

As she drove out from the long driveway of Dallington Place, she could see a figure in the distance. She squinted in the bright glare of the sun. For a minute the figure reminded her of Bertram, with a straight posture wearing a long black coat. My goodness, she realised, it was Ernest. What on earth was he doing on foot, she thought. As she drove closer she honked the horn and a familiar wide toothed smile appeared as Ernest waved enthusiastically. Kathryn pulled over. 'Get in darling, you must be frozen. Why did you not wait for a lift?' she asked as Ernest sat next to her in the passenger seat.

'I telephoned the house this morning, but no reply so I just thought I would walk. I thought maybe someone would come along eventually!' he said smiling at his mother.

'Oh Ernest, I have missed you, always the optimist! I am so sorry, I did not think you would be arriving until this afternoon, I overslept,' said Kathryn kissing him on his cheek.

'That is not like you!' said Ernest with raising his eyebrows.

'I know, well we had a visitor yesterday and now I am about to rescue him. He seems to have got himself into trouble with Dawson. Do not ask! Honestly, that poor old man, he must be fed up with us all,' said Kathryn rolling her eyes.

'You look well, Mamma!' said Ernest pleased his mother was in good form. Perhaps a little drama is what she needed, he thought.

'Thank you dear,' said Kathryn turning to Ernest, recognising his expression that was just like Bertram's. The way his hazel eyes twinkled and the skin creased in the corners.

'Mamma, I promised Carlyon I would go over to Bishops Cross this afternoon for a party. You do not mind, do you?' he asked feeling little guilty to suddenly arrive and then leave so soon. He knew how she had been looking forward to spending time with him.

'No, of course I do not, but you know what, instead of Christmas at Geraldine's, how about Christmas at Dallington Place? Roberta is home from London and I thought I would ask the Richards as well.' said Kathryn.

'Sounds good,' replied Ernest, looking at the automobile in the ditch outside Willow Tree Cottage as Kathryn pulled up in front of it. Kathryn sighed. She could see three men in the ditch, peering into the engine. Slamming her car door shut and pulling her coat apprehensively around her, she walked over. Her beautiful navy blue Wolseley Ten looking very sorry itself, one wheel buckled in the snow.

Seeing Kathryn approach, Dawson tentatively got himself out of the ditch. 'So sorry Ma'am, I think the Wolseley will need to be pulled,' he said to Kathryn. 'Ernest, good to see you,' said Dawson wiping his greasy, oily hand to shake the young man's hand.

'Anything I can do to help?' asked Ernest patting the old man on the back. Kathryn looked intently at Sebastien, who was looking guilty and rather shifty.

'Dawson, we will give you a lift back, Jonas can you get the car towed?' asked Kathryn looking at the farmer's son who lived in one of the cottages on the estate. He helped his father, Richard Mullins, to run the farmland at Dallington Place.

'Yes Ma'am, the trucks on its way,' said Jonas wiping his oily hands on the sides of his work overalls.

'Sebastien, are you coming?' asked Kathryn shooting an angry look at the young man. She felt like asking Sebastien to walk back to the house after causing all this trouble. Sebastien scuttled out of the ditch and followed rather sheepishly to Kathryn's Morris and jumped in the back seat next to Dawson.

Back in the car as they drove up the drive, Kathryn watched Sebastien's face in the rear mirror. He looked tired and drawn, his dark eyes looked sunken with worry. He had a streak of oil down the side of his face. 'I hope no one got hurt,' said Kathryn swerving slightly as a pheasant landed in front of them and rushed across the road.

'So sorry Ma'am, I took Sebastien out early for a ride this morning. He wanted to look around the land,' said Dawson, realising his mistake. He should have asked Kathryn's permission first.

Kathryn could feel herself frown deeply, giving herself a sharp headache. 'I am so sorry Kathryn, please do not blame Dawson, it was all my idea. I just wanted to get a feel for the place,' said Sebastien bowing his head in shame.

Kathryn shot Ernest a look. He was looking bewildered at this stranger with an American accent as much as Kathryn was stunned at the audacity of this young man. 'Well Sebastien, we will talk inside. Dawson, you look as if you need a stiff drink,' said Kathryn casting a look at poor Dawson.

'I will park the Morris for you, Mamma,' offered Ernest, knowing his mother was about to lose her temper, which rarely happened. Kathryn took off her coat and practically threw it at the coat stand. 'Libby!' called Kathryn marching towards the kitchen. Libby ran out taking off her apron on seeing the men.

'Ma'am, breakfast is served in the morning room,' she said timidly.

'Good, thank you Libby, please get the men some brandy with their coffee,' said Kathryn as she walked into the morning room.

Libby was staring at the handsome Sebastien, who flicked back his hair and gave her a wink. Turning bright red in the face, she hurried back into the kitchen. Kathryn was convinced that Sebastien was laughing at the girl. Ernest rushed up the impressive staircase with his luggage to his bedroom. 'Do not forget to ask the Richards if they would like to join us for Christmas, my dearest,' Kathryn called after him.

Ernest changed into his favourite lounge suit to make an impression on Carlyon's family. Bishops Cross was a large manor house in the neighbouring village once owned by the Bishop of Sussex. He was looking forward to mingling with prestigious political figures and delegates from London.

Kathryn ushered Sebastien into the morning room. 'Before you say anything else, I want you to know this is my house. I do not know what you are up to but you could have killed poor old Dawson. He is nearly seventy-five you know,' she said anger rising up.

'Like I said, I am sorry, I was just curious. My father had talked so much about Dallington Place for all those years and I wanted to see the grandness of it all for myself,' said Sebastien realising he had overstepped the mark and Kathryn was not a woman to be messed with.

Libby entered with a tray of brandy coffees, Dawson behind her. 'I will not trouble you Ma'am,' he said feeling uncomfortable.

'Dawson, please have a drink and sit down will you. I think you should not work today. You have had quite a shock,' said Kathryn motioning Dawson to sit down.

'Actually Ma'am, we rather slipped into the ditch. It was quite icy this morning, the wheel went and that was it. It happened in slow motion. Neither of us were hurt,' he said eyeing Sebastien.

'Well, I think you two seem to be in cahoots. Thank goodness no one was hurt.' She was relieved. 'Dawson, I could do with some help for shopping in the village tomorrow morning. Libby said that we are short on basic supplies. So rest today and we will start again tomorrow,' said Kathryn. 'Then both automobiles will be taken so Sebastien cannot get his hands on them,' she said imperiously lowering her eyes at Sebastien.

'Yes Ma'am,' said Dawson slugging back his coffee and getting up to leave. Dawson passed Ernest in the hallway, who was on his way to the morning room. 'Good to have you back Sir,' said Dawson smiling at the young man as he patted him on the back.

'Ernest, this is Sebastien. If you have not worked it out already, he is your half-brother from your mother Berenice,' said Kathryn, her nerves now soothed with the brandy.

The two young men eyed each other eagerly. There was nothing physically alike about them, one dark and the other fair. Sebastien being a fair bit older, although not taller, obviously appeared more mature. It was not until they smiled at each other, that Kathryn could see the resemblance and the same perfectly straight gleaming white teeth. Kathryn had thought perhaps they would have seemed uncomfortable knowing of each other's existence but she could see there was a bond there, even in the first few seconds of meeting each other.

Sitting down for breakfast, the two sat opposite each other. Their conversation was light and friendly. Kathryn watched both of them intently. It was surreal really, she thought, sitting here without Devlin at the head of the table. She wondered what he would have made of Sebastien. Kathryn busily buttered her toast, her ears pricking up when Ernest asked Sebastien what he planned to do in the future.

'I have not quite figured that out yet,' he said turning his gaze to Kathryn. I thought perhaps I would stay in Sussex or maybe go to Paris for a while.'

Kathryn raised her eyebrows, putting down her knife with a sigh. 'And you Ernest, what are you studying?' asked Sebastien.

'I am going to study English and literature at Oxford next autumn, I would like to become a journalist,' Ernest answered.

Sebastien eyed him suspiciously. His dark brows pinching above his narrowing eyes. 'Just like Bertram then,' Sebastien answered back, looking to Kathryn for her reaction. She knew he was being provocative and avoided his gaze.

'Mother, I have to pick up Carlyon at lunchtime and take her to this party. Is it alright that I take your Morris?' asked Ernest feeling the need to leave the house. The news of a brother was so sudden and he needed time to digest.

'Well, you may as well, I am not going anywhere today darling,' replied Kathryn. 'What are your plans, Sebastien?' asked Kathryn turning to Sebastien. 'Well, I was going to go to London. There is a jazz band I wanted to see and I was hoping to meet up with Alexander Pillard, who is staying in Soho for a few days. I wondered... would you like to accompany me Kathryn?' he asked bluntly.

'Sorry Sebastien, what did you say?' Kathryn was not sure she had heard Sebastien correctly.

'How about you and me take a trip to London? You said you have not been out much lately,' continued Sebastien with a mischievous smile.

Kathryn looked to Ernest, who was now pretending he had not heard the last of the conversation. 'That is very kind of you, but no thank you Sebastien,' replied Kathryn with a half a smile. Sebastien shrugged his shoulders.

Ernest looked at his mother. He thought for a moment. 'Mamma, why do you not go to London? You could meet Mr Pillard and talk about Bertram. You have not had a fun day out for so long, maybe it is time,' said Ernest wanting his mother to enjoy yourself a little.

'Ernest!' exclaimed Kathryn.

'Besides it is Christmas, and you could do some shopping. What harm would it do? I could drop you two off at the station and pick you up from the last train tonight. It would be fun, besides you could pick up that waistcoat I wanted from Jerome's that I liked?' continued Ernest, hoping this would encourage her to go.

Kathryn looked to Sebastien, who looked as if he did not care whether she decided to go or not. 'Fine, thank you Sebastien, I will take you up on your offer. But can we not be back too late tonight?' said Kathryn finally realising that it would do her good but little unnerved to be alone with Sebastien.

'That is fine by me as long as you do not mind me staying another night here at Dallington Place?' said Sebastien.

'No, of course not. Ernest would like that, would you not?' replied Kathryn.

Ernest did not answer, he just munched on his toast. 'I am going to telephone Carlyon and tell her I will pick her up at twelve,' he just mumbled.

'Right, I will instruct Libby to have the day off since we are all out for the day, ' said Kathryn rising from the table. She hoped she could persuade Geraldine to spend Christmas at Dallington Place instead.

'So Carlyon is your girl, Ernest?' asked Sebastien as they stopped outside the station.

'No, just a friend from school,' answered Ernest although he was not sure that was quite true. He did like Carlyon but felt she did not return his feelings.

Sebastien flicked his cigarette ash out of the window and got out of the Morris. He stepped back to open the back door for Kathryn, who had sat in silence the whole journey. She had second guessed herself on agreeing to go to London with Sebastien. What if someone should see them, who would she say Sebastien was, she thought to herself. She was feeling the cold, her black velvet coat was too thin and she had not brought her scarf. At least her cloche hat was warm and she pulled it further down over her hair, it covered some of her face. She did not want to be recognised. She may have changed her mind, but for the intriguing thought of meeting the infamous Alexander Pillard, it was too good an opportunity to miss.

The Brighton Belle had been sitting on the platform for almost fifteen minutes. Sebastien opened the door of the carriage to help

Kathryn to get on. He noticed her neat ankles as she climbed the stairs up to the plush seats. After extinguishing his cigarette and throwing it out onto the platform, he took his place opposite Kathryn and watched her unbutton the top buttons of her coat.

CHAPTER TWENTY-THREE
KATHRYN: LONDON LIFE

The restaurant was crowded. Well it would be as it was Christmas. Nicotine filled the air. Sebastien looked about him anxiously for Kathryn. He knew Alexander was going to be late but Kathryn should have been finished at the hair salon by now. The show at the Trocadero was about to start, he had not wanted Kathryn to miss the beginning.

Kathryn meanwhile was anxiously looking at her watch. The coiffeur working late at Christmas time had been especially recommended to her by Nora Parker, who she had accidently bumped into at Harrods. Kathryn was starting to regret letting Nora, the wife of the Mayor of Dallington village, into persuading her to get her long hair cut into a marcel wave. 'Only Victor can do it for you, in Chez Victor's a hair salon next to Harrods,' insisted Nora, a wealthy lady, who had sent one of her assistants along to book Kathryn in at five o'clock for a 'Marcel' and the ladies had then promptly settled into the café bar at Harrods for a long chat with coffee and cakes. Nora, who liked to gossip about who she had had lunch or dinner with that particular week was now telling Kathryn all about Charles Digby Junior, the son of the Harrods founder, who had given Nora a special tour of Harrods one Christmas as a child and how very charming he had been. Her parents had been family friends of the founder Charles Henry Harrod.

'Look,' Nora squealed at Kathryn, 'how cute is the Harrods' business card?' and passed the card promptly over to Kathryn. 'They have asked me to do the grand opening of Harrods sale in January. Apparently Harrods[2] is the store to be seen in now, Kathryn, will you accompany me?' Nora pleaded.

Kathryn smiled at Nora's enthusiasm. She was like a breath of fresh air. Kathryn was very well aware that Nora was not everyone's cup of tea. A real social climber, and she never stopped talking but Kathryn liked her very much. 'Of course I will. It sounds tremendous

---

[2] In 1917 Harrods' managing director and Gordon Selfridge made a bet as to which store would make the most profit. Upon losing, Mr Selfridge offered a gift, a silver replica of Harrods store which has a pride of place on the lower ground floor in Harrods.

fun,' said Kathryn, knowing that it was about time she came out of hiding at Dallington Place.

'I am so sorry about your loss of Devlin, Kathryn,' Nora gets momentarily serious.

'Thank you Nora,' said Kathryn patting Nora's hand in her soft grey gloves.

'But it was a long illness Kathryn, it must have taken its toll on you,' Nora continued.

'I suppose so, but I did not think of it like that, he was my husband,' replied Kathryn inconspicuously brushing away a tear with her grey gloved hand.

'I know, I know, but after the General Strike it was hard on all of us, especially your Devlin,' Nora continued.

'I do not think he ever got over it, Nora, to be honest,' Kathryn said not wanting to discuss Devlin anymore.

Nora nodded and then applying her bright red lipstick and changing the subject in a flighty manner, noticed the time. 'Oh Kathryn, you are going to be late for Victor, let us hurry and the next time I see you, it will be here again!' quipped Nora as she dashed off, with a spritz of perfume she had just purchased, and she was gone with her assistant hard on her heels. 'Merry Christmas, Kathryn,' she called back as she marched around the corner.

Kathryn entered the lift, her heart beating fast. Should she really cut all her hair off, she thought to herself. How Devlin had loved her long hair. Kathryn knew though she could not turn up at the famous Trocadero restaurant to meet the infamous Mr Pillard looking like a country scarecrow. The sophistication of London was rubbing off on her already and she wanted to impress. It was dark outside now and as Kathryn hurried around the corner, she turned back to look at the imposing Harrods store with its fancy illuminations. England was back on its feet again, she thought. After the War and the General Strike maybe it was a time for people to enjoy themselves again. Spend a little money, have fun. It was the time to be young and pretty.

Kathryn had overheard pretty shop girls at Harrods gossiping about a colleague, who was being courted by a wealthy gentleman and was due to go to French Riviera for a little jaunt. How liberating, she thought to herself. Lost in her thoughts, she stepped into the road and had to suddenly jump back to avoid getting run over as a horse and cart raced past.

Kathryn could have taken her hat off inside the Trocadero, but she chose not to. The kind lady in the cloakroom had taken her coat and another had shown her to her table. Kathryn noticed glamorous women sitting around tables in shiny gowns with fancy, long silver cigarette holders. Equally attractive men were pouring champagne and everyone seemed to be laughing through the haze of smoke and gaiety. Sebastien waved when he saw Kathryn, admiring her blue dress, which was very fitted and sashayed as Kathryn, moved towards him.

'Alexander will not be here until nine o'clock, he sends his apologies. Something to do with work, but here, take this glass,' said Sebastien passing Kathryn a rather full glass of champagne. Sipping it, she took a glance at the evening's programme. *Revels in Rhythm* in black letters stood out. 'Have I missed them? I so wanted to see the dancers,' asked Kathryn looking at the programme.

'No they are not on yet, there has just been a band playing and a troupe of dancers, I do not know who they were. Here, choose something to eat," said Sebastien taking a menu from the waiter and passing it to Kathryn.

'Just something small for me, I am feeling rather nervous at meeting Mr Pillard,' she said gulping down the champagne. 'It had been a long day, Sebastien. I bumped into an old friend who persuaded me to buy a new dress and have my haircut,' said Kathryn between mouthfuls of champagne.

'I picked up Ernest's waistcoat for you, and I chose a new suit, what do you think?' said Sebastien proudly touching the lapel of his new grey suit.

'Very dapper, Sebastien,' said Kathryn. She could tell by the cut of the cloth that the suit must have been expensive.

Kathryn was beginning to relax and enjoy herself. She could not take her eyes off the other customers, let alone the dancers and singers. She was mesmerised by a younger couple, who seemed to be having a tremendous row in the corner bench, and the young lady was now crying as the man stormed out. Kathryn's heart went out to her, she had seen that same hurt expression on herself many years ago. The waiter interrupted her thoughts and Kathryn ordered her food. As Sebastien pondered the choices changing his mind several times, Kathryn wondered what his life must have been like growing up with Bertram. Although at times Sebastien seemed self-assured, there were times like now when he could not make up his mind what to choose. She could see someone who was perhaps a little lost. She also reminded herself that he had had the experience of living with Bertram. Something she had once wanted so much but it was not to be. Here was a young man that had lived a life in a sense that she would have had. She was not sure if she envied him or felt sorry for him. Perhaps it was more the latter, she decided.

Making conversation, Kathryn asked Sebastien whether he had known the Fitch family.

To her amazement he said that he did. 'Yup! Their daughter Dawn-Marie is a good friend of mine. She learnt to ride at our stud farm. She is quite the looker too!' said Sebastien with a twinkle in his eye.

'Lady Alison, do you know her too?' asked Kathryn rather surprised that the Fitches had never mentioned it.

'Yes, her ladyship, she is quite the old dragon!' said Sebastien giving Kathryn a cheery wink.

'Sebastien! I am sure she is no such thing.' Kathryn glared back at him.

'Well, she is rather high and mighty, not too friendly. Maybe she just does not like me," said Sebastien.

Kathryn nodded, but did not say anything. She wanted to be loyal to Lady Alison, and discreet. We have kept in contact all these years, she writes to me, every few months,' said Kathryn.

Sebastien agreed but looked uneasy. Changing the subject, he grabbed Kathryn's hand and placed it on the lapel of his suit. 'So what do you think of the cloth then? I hope you do not mind but I put it on your bill,' he said sheepishly.

'What Sebastien, you did what?' Kathryn exclaimed claiming back her hand and clenching her fist under the table.

'Well, I thought I could work at Dallington Place and pay you the money back,' he said shrugging his shoulders.

Kathryn could feel the heat in her cheeks rise and her throat was getting so dry. Thinking of an answer, she was about to speak, when a booming voice was audible and a large man came into view hovering in front of Kathryn and Sebastien puffing on a huge cigar.

'Alexander Pillard, please to have your acquaintance Mrs McAlister at last.' The man reached out his hand to Kathryn. Flustered Kathryn looked up to see a larger than life man, with a thick grey moustache matching his salt and pepper hair. Surprised Kathryn shook his hand as he exhaled a large ring of smoke, which rose steadily above their table. 'My, Mrs McAlister you are quite the beauty Bertram used to talk of,' Alexander said flopping into the large black leathered armchair next to her.

'Thank you, Mr Pillard, you are most kind! It is lovely to meet you at last,' said Kathryn blushing shyly.

The large man then shook Sebastien's hand and ordered himself a martini from a passing waiter. 'This is the best seat in this joint, I reserved it yesterday, are you enjoying the show?' he asked looking Kathryn squarely in the eye.

Kathryn not wanting to catch Sebastien's eye, looked directly at Alexander. Although she was nervous, she answered him assuredly. She chose her words carefully not wanting to reveal too much about herself as yet. There was a likeability to this man, with his overweight stature and laughing eyes. 'I am loving all the glamour of tonight, Mr Pillard, I have been too long in the country I fear. It has been good to visit London again,' said Kathryn.

'Please, Kathryn... if I may... Please call me Alexander,' said Alexander again looking straight at Kathryn. She could see Sebastien was trying to get a word in edgeways, but she was having none of it. She was so cross with him.

'I am sorry to hear about your husband, I hope you are coping well?' asked Alexander in a deep and caring tone.

'It has been two years now, so yes I am recovering well. I have good friends that see that I am kept busy and of course we have Dallington Place to run,' replied Kathryn now looking at her hands, to avoid Alexander's gaze.

'Of course, the infamous Dallington Place. I would love to see it one day,' Alexander said still looking at Kathryn.

'You would be most welcome, Mr Pillard,' responded Kathryn looking back at Alexander with a smile, ignoring Sebastien's obvious irritation.

'Well, it is good to be busy, I do not think I could ever retire. I love my job as a reporter, and could never give up the travelling bug. London, Paris, New York, that is the life for me Kathryn,' said Alexander with large whooping laugh as he slugged his Martini in one go.

As Alexander ordered his meal, it gave Kathryn a chance to go to the ladies room. She wanted to check herself in the mirror. Aware how attracted she was to this man, she wanted to remove her hat and show off her new bob. She felt the men's eyes on her as she made her excuses and walked across the room. After putting the finishing touches to her make-up, she returned to the table and both men gave her an admiring glance. Sebastien trying desperately to make amends and commenting on her hair. Self-consciously she slid back into her chair.

'So Kathryn, Sebastien was telling me how beautiful Dallington Place is. I must say, I do not know the Sussex countryside,' said Alexander yet again looking Kathryn square in the eye.

'Well, Alexander, how long are you in London?' asked Kathryn genuinely interested.

'I plan to be here over Christmas, I have booked myself into the Dorchester Hotel.'

'How about Christmas with my family in Sussex then? I have quite a house full now and it would be an honour to show you my home,' suggested Kathryn now excited about Christmas with all her family and friends around her.

'Well, thank you Kathryn, I would love that very much,' answered Alexander raising his glass to her. Out of the corner of her eye she could see Sebastien squirming in his seat, rather uncomfortable about this friendly exchange.

'Sebastien will be there of course, will you not Sebastien?' said Kathryn rather too bluntly now looking at Sebastien. She did not mind that he was going to be there but it was his presumptuous manner that she could not stand.

Before Sebastien could answer, Alexander carried on talking. He talked about his life in New York, how too he was recently widowed and how much he enjoyed living in Paris for six months of the year now.

'So would you like to come down tomorrow? There are few trains running and I have Dawson who can pick you up from the station,' offered Kathryn hoping that Alexander would say yes.

'Dawson? Is that your fancy man, Kathryn?' Alexander asked, his blue eyes twinkling with interest. 'I too have ladies that take my fancy, but I am fancy free now, I am not with Pearl anymore,' he continued with a smile.

'Good grief, no Alexander! He is my butler, and my driver I suppose. He is seventy-five years old,' said Kathryn barely unable to stop laughing. She could tell that Alexander Pillard was quite the lady's man, but she liked his straightforwardness all the same.

'Now Kathryn, Sebastien was suggesting you should have some horses at Dallington Place, maybe a stud or a riding school,' said Alexander now suddenly appearing serious.

'Oh, did he?' replied Kathryn trying not to sound riled. She did not like the idea that Sebastien was discussing her Dallington Place without her knowledge. 'Well, we could think about it, there is always room to find ways to make money, I admit it is an expensive house to run,' replied Kathryn thinking she could not believe that Sebastien had spoken behind her back.

'Well, young Sebastien here seems to think it would be an idea to import the horses from America and bring them to Dallington Place,' continued Alexander.

'Goodness, all these ideas being bandied about without my prior knowledge, said Kathryn now looking at Sebastien.

'Oh, Kathryn, I am begging your pardon, I thought perhaps Sebastien had already mentioned it to you,' hurried Alexander to reply.

'No, Mr Pillard, Alexander, Sebastien had not,' said Kathryn sternly looking at Sebastien. Taking a sip of wine and thinking for a moment, she did think it sounded interesting. 'I will think over that idea, Sebastien, but I think it is for another day to discuss.' It was too much for Kathryn to think about that evening. Here she was with these two men that she hardly knew, discussing the future of Dallington Place. It did not feel right to discuss these things without Devlin. There were these moments, when people were intruding, when she missed his reassuring voice and sound advice.

'Excuse me Mr Pillard, there is a trunk call from Paris for you, it is urgent, please come to the reception,' announced the waiter, who had now appeared at the table.

'Interesting,' said Alexander now composing himself and politely nodding at Kathryn as he followed the waiter to the reception.

'Sebastien, I think we should leave soon, we must not miss the last train,' said Kathryn feeling tired. She wanted to get out of the smoky atmosphere. She knew Ernest would be waiting for them at half past ten. As they got up to leave, they could see Alexander ushering them to hurry to the reception. The show was still continuing. Three girls in sparkly short trousers, now singing and tap dancing on the stage. Kathryn dipped her head as if to make herself smaller as she passed tables full of people mesmerised by these attractive girls with their long legs and swirling batons.

'I am so sorry Kathryn, I am going to have to pass on the invitation for Christmas. There has been a train crash just outside Paris, between Lagny-sur-Marne and Pomponne. I am going to have to work back in Paris on this one. Maybe in the New Year, if the invitation still stands?' said Alexander kissing the back of Kathryn's hand.

'Of course, I understand, what a shame, and I hope the crash is not too serious,' said Kathryn disappointed that Alexander would not be coming over for Christmas after all.

'It looks bad I am afraid, I have to make my way back now,' said Alexander with urgency in his voice now. 'Sebastien old chap, look after Kathryn and au revoir until we meet again,' said Alexander as he firmly shook Sebastien's hand. Now tipping his large grey hat, Alexander rushed out of the Trocadero and out into the rainy London street.

Kathryn quietly contemplated the day's events as they sat in the train out of London. Sebastien had fallen asleep and she watched the rise and fall of his chest, his face even more handsome asleep than awake. His face always animated made him appear strained and worried, now asleep he seemed peaceful, like a young boy. She had been inclined to reprimand him once more, but as she let her thoughts run, she thought perhaps he needed work and a place to call home. Perhaps he was seeking a base for a while. He was as vulnerable as the next person and maybe his charm was all for show. If it was Ernest in his situation, she would want people to reach out and help him. She had to admit the idea of the horses was exciting. She was not a horsewomen herself, but the romantic notion of horses at Dallington Place appealed to her. Perhaps she needed a new project and financially it could not do any harm. As the train drew into the Lingfield railway station, she could see Ernest waiting patiently in his automobile. She would ask his advice on the idea she decided.

CHAPTER TWENTY-FOUR
ERNEST: COMING OF AGE

CHRISTMAS EVE 1933
'RAIL CRASH HITS PARISIANS, FOG TO BLAME. 230 DEAD,'
Ernest announced, reading out the headline over breakfast.

'That is why Alexander had to return to Paris, Ernest,' said Kathryn raising an eyebrow at Ernest's interest.

'If I had been with you, I would have gone to Paris with him!' Ernest said wistfully.

'Well then, I am glad you were not. And how is Carlyon, looking beautiful as ever?' asked Kathryn changing the subject.

'Of course Mamma, but she has no interest in boys, men my age. She was telling me of an admirer that had already proposed, a widower with five children,' said Ernest with disappointment in his voice.

'My goodness, is she going to accept?' questioned Kathryn, wondering why Carlyon was so hesitant.

'No I do not think so; I think she loves the drama of it all. His wife was killed in the war, driving an ambulance, like you did Mamma. She feels sorry for him, that is all,' said Ernest.

'Poor Mrs Richards must be at sixes and sevens with all her pretty daughters and their shenanigans. Is Carlyon coming tomorrow with Mr and Mrs Richards?' asked Kathryn wanting to change the subject.

'Yes, she is looking forward to it and meeting Sebastien. She kept asking me about him, and how exotic he must be being French-American. Where is Sebastien anyway? If he makes a move on Carlyon, I will punch him on the nose!' exclaimed Ernest with such a conviction.

'Ernest, you will no such thing! Do not worry, I will tell him to behave in my house,' said Kathryn sternly.

'Mamma, you sound cross,' said Ernest, looking at Kathryn's preoccupied face.

'Well, I am a little. You see, Sebastien suggested to me over dinner that we should introduce horses to Dallington Place. It is not that I am against the idea, it is just that I find him rather presumptuous.

But he does need a job, and I do need the help. What do you think?' asked Kathryn looking at Ernest for clarity.

'Mamma, I agree with you, I do not want a stranger muscling in on our home, but I suppose he is not a stranger, is he? And I like the idea of having a brother,' said Ernest liking the idea of Sebastien coming to live at Dallington Place.

'I like him too Ernest, but it has just been the two of us here for the last two years, and well, I know we need to breed some life into Dallington Place, he is right there,' said Kathryn as she tried to picture Sebastien on the grounds of Dallington Place.

'Horses would be expensive, Mamma, you have to be careful, with the money father left you,' Ernest implored.

'I know, and your schooling too and your future career. I wish you would come home after school and run the estate, but I know where your heart lies," said Kathryn watching Ernest shrug.

'I would leave school now and go to Paris if I could, and work for the *Populaire* newspaper,' said Ernest as he got up, taking his newspaper with him.

'Ernest, do not grow up too quickly, everybody leaves here, it breaks my heart!' said Kathryn hoping that Ernest would stay just a while longer to keep her company.

'I am never leaving Dallington Place Mamma, do not worry. If I go, it will be just for a while! I have to spread my wings,' said Ernest as he kissed her on her cheek.

'You sound just like Bertram," said Kathryn smiling. 'It is good that we have had some time to talk alone,' Kathryn said admiring Ernest's young zest for life.

'Not alone anymore,' said Sebastien at the door of the breakfast room. Brushing his hair out of his eyes with a sleepy yawn, he wished Kathryn and Ernest a good morning as he wasted no time in helping himself to the side dishes of bacon, eggs, toast and jam. Kathryn watched as Sebastien tucked into his breakfast wondering how long he had been standing by the door. 'Come Sebastien, sit yourself down, we need to talk,' said Kathryn authoritatively, motioning him to sit next to her. 'Sebastien, I wanted to say, if you have something to discuss with me regarding Dallington Place, please do so in private. Talking to Mr Pillard without my knowledge was very wrong,' she continued, avoiding eye contact with Sebastien.

'I am sorry, Kathryn, I just got carried away with ideas, and Mr Pillard was the one that brought up the business ideas,' replied Sebastien keeping eyes on his breakfast feast.

'Is that so?' asked Kathryn intrigued.

'Yes, he suggested if you needed a financial backer, he would be very interested in the horse idea,' replied Sebastien, now looking up at Kathryn.

'Well, that is for me and Alexander to discuss next time Sebastien, I see how the conversation could have materialised. But Sebastien, if you are to stay on here at Dallington, you must earn your keep in the meantime,' said Kathryn thinking about the soaring cost of running the household.

'I would like that very much,' Sebastien smiled at Kathryn, who was still avoiding his gaze. Sometimes Kathryn felt he lingered too long on her features or her figure. It made her slightly uncomfortable. Placing her coffee cup down, she suggested that they first start with over-seeing the stable block but not until after Christmas.

'Let us enjoy Christmas and I need some help organising everything here today,' said Kathryn starting to feel overwhelmed about the Christmas festivities.

'What time are the guests arriving?' asked Sebastien, looking at his pocket watch, which had once belonged to Bertram.

'Well, the tree is arriving at one o'clock and then the guests are arriving after five," said Kathryn anxiously ringing for Dawson. 'I have some shopping in the village to do and I could do with help with the menu if you like,' said Kathryn as she got up from the breakfast table.

'That is just fine by me, and if you do not mind, I would like to suggest a Texan dish. Maybe I can cook it for your guests myself,' offered Sebastien wanting to impress Kathryn with his cooking skills.

'Really Sebastien, you can cook?' asked Kathryn, now seeing this young man in a new light.

'Love it!' answered Sebastien, taking a piece of toast and getting up from the table too. 'I will go into the village with you and Ernest and pick up the ingredients. My mamma, she was a great cook and she encouraged me to cook from an early age in France. When we had our enormous kitchen on the ranch in Santa Anna, Jorie and I would try and learn new recipes together,' Sebastien fondly reminisced. 'I could do a casserole for dinner. I am used to cooking for many as we had fifteen cowboys working on the land most days, plus the occasional hired help,' he continued.

'I am very impressed Sebastien, I would like that very much. We could perhaps have something to eat after midnight mass at St. Dunstan's tonight,' suggested Kathryn. 'I would love to hear more about Texas, Sebastien, it sounds so interesting and different to anything I could possible imagine,' said Kathryn genuinely interested in the culture and the life Sebastien had led.

'I have got many stories that would entertain your guests,' replied Sebastien with a smile.

'All in good time I think, Sebastien,' said Kathryn rather wary now of Sebastien's gossip. 'I am going to find Ernest, let me know when you want to go out,' said Sebastien almost running out of the breakfast room. Kathryn watched him go and thought how much young energy he had. There was so much life in that young man. His intelligent face and bright sparkly brown eyes darting about his face expressively. Maybe she thought he would have the initiative to run some sort of horse farm here. Make a successful business at Dallington Place. There was a lot to think about but first Kathryn wanted five minutes peace. She had something else on her mind and that was Bertram's letters.

Admiring her new hairstyle in the mirror, Kathryn paused for a moment as her hand rested on the pile of letters. Drawing a deep breath she picked up the first letter. Her hands shook as she opened it.

August 1920, Texas

Dear Kathryn,
We arrived in Santa Anna yesterday with Sebastien. How different America is. The accents, the manners. Our journey has been a long and arduous one. Sebastien and myself are feeling weak. Sebastien had been suffering from stomach problems for most of the sail. Luckily on board there was a doctor. It appeared the water and food did not agree with him. Nothing serious. He is only ten years old and he seems to hide his anxiety well. Leaving his home country of France is quite the adventure. I felt disorientated as we stepped off the ship. Eventually arriving at our destination where Jorie was waiting for us. The heat of the midday sun was intense, our clothes stained with sweat and anguish. I am surprised she recognised us! There was this girl I hardly recognised too. Her face flushed with excitement and from

riding horses in the Texan sun. Bright red cheeks and a pearly white smile, her hair almost white from the atmosphere. Wearing jodhpurs, standing astride, waving on top of her horse and a trap cart. All I could think of was sleep, when I should have been as animated and joyful to see her as she was of us. She scooped up Sebastien into the back of the wagon and I sat next to her as we made our eight mile journey to the ranch.

Jorie was talking constantly and showing me views and subjects along the way. But I found it hard to focus except on one thing and that was the Madrone tree. Its bark twisted and grey, reminded me of how I was feeling. I spied a bird circling above us and then it settled on the branch of the tree. Wiping sweat from my brow and squinting in the rays of the sun, I thought how poignant it was. Free and healthy and at home. Not like us. Jorie pointed out the neighbour's ranch. We were three miles outside Santa Anna now.

I asked about the Fitch and the Stedford families and Jorie told me they lived five miles north of us on a cattle farm. She knew them well. Then we passed the Amos and McClerron's farm. She told us how all the eleven siblings had married siblings from a neighbouring farm. Now there were twenty-three young children running around there. Almost a community in itself. A large Irish catholic family, which was thriving and growing. Noting how anything thrived in this heat, I could not form an opinion of the place just as yet but I sense I do not dislike it. Jorie tells me of the new immigrants from Europe and the influx of the Mexicans to work on the cotton farms, lured with the promise of money and power. The oil industry is booming too for those that are willing to work hard, much money is guaranteed. As we pull up to the gated entrance of her farm, two cowboys ride by and open the gates for us. They tip their Stetsons at us, with hardly a look of curiosity to who we are. Jorie tells me it is Dale and his son Roger, long-term farm hands here. She reminds me our deal that I must learn to ride and she will learn to fly a plane. Dale will teach me apparently. The house quite a way down a dusty track is quite the surprise, not what I had been expecting at all. As I had watched the few houses along our route, this one stood out as monied and beautiful. Designed by a Mexican architect friend of Jorie's grandfather, it was based on an idea Jorie's grandfather had of a French chateau. I expected to see a one-storey ranch house, but this was spectacular. Three stories on one side, white - or as white as it could be with the dust - although it had recently been painted. Long French windows had a full view of the farmland and it is almost castle like, a French chateau or an Italian villa.

Jorie explained her grandfather had been in the navy and travelled through Europe. He met Jories's Texan grandmother in Italy, her family being one of the first to claim land in Santa Anna. Apparently their family was the wealthiest of settlers then and the house reflects this. Quite breathtaking. Jorie tells me she will give us a tour of the estate once we are rested, maybe tomorrow. I am worried about Sebastien, who needs his bed immediately.

Until then,
Bertram

Kathryn put down the letter and picked up the small piece of paper that was enclosed with it.

Bertram had enclosed a poem written on an unusual paper. Stained around the edges as if tobacco stained fingers had eagerly rubbed at the edges of the parchment, slightly torn in parts along the bottom edge. As she unfolded the paper, a light corn colour mixture, dust or maybe earth, fell onto her skirt and spilled onto the desk. Kathryn shook out the paper away from her so no more dust would fall on her skirt. It was a poem, which he had called The Madrone Tree.

The Madrone Tree by Bertram Wright
Dusty, hot and red licked land
Unfamiliar view,
But in my mind's eye
A memory of you,
less I forget.
I forge ahead, further West I tread,
from England's green and native birds,
a bird of prey, flies high above the Madrone Tree,
from the scorched mountain top.
An absurd looking raptor,
somewhat akin to me.
Once it was I above the lime tree,
now this predator mocks me.
Grounded, feet of lead am I.
I will regain my wings and be free.

Kathryn held the poem to her chest for a moment and then suddenly she could hear Ernest calling her. The automobile was running outside; she could hear it now. Grabbing her purse and her stole, a renewed energy surged in her. Bertram may have gone, but his life and story lived on. It made her happy to think she could get to know him better now. There was never an ending. She was aware there was a new beginning taking place at Dallington Place this Christmas and it would never be the same again, in a good way.

'It is a suffragette necklace, Kathryn, do you like it? See the stones represent freedom and dignity, purity and hope,' explained Geraldine as she admired this sparkling piece of jewellery. Kathryn held the pretty pendant up to the light to see white, green and purple stones in their glory against the gold of the delicate filigree of the design.

'Ernest, please help me with this darling,' asked Kathryn waving at Ernest, who was in a deep conversation with Roberta. As poor Ernest was trying to open the catch to put it on, without luck.

Sebastien came to her rescue. 'Here, I will help you,' he said carefully placing the pendant around Kathryn's neck. His flirting did not go unnoticed, Geraldine and William exchanged looks. Kathryn dutifully bent her head forward so Sebastien could fasten the clasp. He seemed to enjoy touching Kathryn's neck and lingered a little too long fiddling with the clasp as he eyed her long white neck and milky skin.

'Are we opening our presents now, Mamma?' asked Ernest now pouring drinks for everyone from the silver decanter by the fire.

'Oh, it was just a thank you present really,' said Geraldine with a broad smile. 'Kathryn, I thought it appropriate, because I want you to have hope in your new project at Dallington Place. No more suffering, just fun and success!' she said smiling at her friend.

'Exactly Geraldine,' said Kathryn smiling at her dear friend and raising a glass to everyone. 'Merry Christmas and here is to our new business ventures at Dallington Place.'

Everyone raised their glasses: 'To Dallington Place, they all chorused. Sebastien was also toasted for the delicious casserole he had made, which had been a great success. It had raised Carlyon's interest in him rather, but she also noticed he could not keep his eyes off Kathryn. Kathryn looked particularly lovely tonight, her burgundy velvet dress fitted her every curve and her hairstyle suited her so well. Matching lipstick, which she did not normally wear, gave her glamour. She normally liked to dress down, and not stand out from the crowd.

Ernest had turned his attentions to Roberta, knowing now that Carlyon would never be his. Roberta had matured into a real beauty and she seemed equally enamoured with him as he was with her. As he turned off the lights of the drawing room after everyone else had retired to bed, he quickly changed the seating plan, which his mother had set out earlier on the large dining room table ready for their Christmas lunch tomorrow. He placed Roberta's place card next to his and put Sebastien next to Carlyon. He could have Carlyon, he thought to himself, he did not care anymore. Ernest could not now stop thinking about Roberta. How she giggled at his every joke and stood beside him meekly in the church, finding the correct page for them in the hymn book and smiling adoringly at him. She really was sweet, he thought to himself and looked forward to seeing her in the morning. He wished he had bought her a present today. He had chosen a red silk scarf for Carlyon, but now wished he could give it to Roberta instead. He would ask his mother's advice tomorrow. Maybe she had something he could give to her.

CHAPTER TWENTY-FIVE
ERNEST'S PROPOSAL

Kathryn could not sleep. Her mind was ticking over. Was she prepared for the Christmas gathering, had she bought in and ordered enough food for everyone? Poor Dawson had gone down sick with the flu the day before, and everyone was taking turns to visit him in his cottage with food parcels and to prepare hot drinks for him. Kathryn hoped that no one else would go down with it. Sebastien had volunteered to cook with Libby. Kathryn was doubtful that the two could cope but ever the optimist, she hoped everyone would be understanding.

Vicar Sanderson and his wife were arriving for lunch at one o'clock. Had she ordered large enough turkeys, she thought to herself. There would be eleven people for Christmas luncheon. Just as her mind wandered on to Boxing Day hunt drinks and food after the day's meet, she stopped herself worrying anymore. Putting on her bedside lamp and propping herself up on numerous pillows, she put on her reading spectacles and opened another of Bertram's letters.

Sunday 5th September 1926

Dear Kathryn,

Horses... not my thing but Jorie insisted I must learn to ride if I am to be of any use here at the ranch. As we walk amongst the stables early in the morning, there is a window of coolness in the air as she teaches me of the different breeds of horses. Her favourites are the Quarter Horses, but apparently Arabian horses bring in the most money for racing and breeding. I have to admit the Arabians are the most beautiful and almost majestic, I cannot deny that. Jorie lets Frank, the young and skilful stable hand, take an Arabian called Unicorn, that is a four-year-old stallion and bred at the ranch, into the show ring. Jorie tells me she broke him in gently and he is very much a big love of hers. I feel somewhat jealous now. This magnificent beast, its pure white beauty with a pearly, almost luminescent coat and long wavy mane making its way around the ring showing himself off as he pranced about, his nostrils wide, blowing hot air. His head

swooping up and down as if to say, 'Look at me, how beautiful I am.'
As Frank brings him over to us to the side of the fence, he stood at my
height and he looked into my eyes, maybe looking for my lost soul. As
he looks at me squarely his dark and intelligent eyes penetrate deeply
through me. His huge silvery tail rises and then he is let free by Frank
and off he goes again prancing joyfully around the ring, with strength
and speed, agility and elegance. I envy the stallion – he is wild and
has his freedom.

> *Unicorn by Bertram Wright*
> *The white Stallion in the ring,*
> *his legs clapping hard down on to the sand,*
> *like Thunder striking the mountains.*
> *Shiny coat, that gallops passed, I hear an Indian beat,*
> *a heartbeat onto the very soil that habituates here.*
> *A hymn to the rhythm of the land,*
> *that swells with pride and oozes out of the pores that fertilises it.*
> *A temper kicks up the sand,*
> *his head lowers like the wings of my plane dipping,*
> *his tail pointing skyward as if coming out of a tailspin.*
> *His heart pounding, his nostrils flaring to the air of freedom.*
> *Animal not to be tamed.*
> *I am at one with this beast.*

We can rise slightly later now as the temperature in the mornings
is getting cooler. We do not have to rush our chores in the morning.
The business of running the ranch keeps us busy all day, which does
not please me. I wish to pursue my flying in the afternoons, but Jorie
insists that we work until the late afternoon, leaving me no time to fly.
I feel my sense of freedom disappearing, I am trapped like a wild
stallion, fighting to get free from the stable.

Kathryn paused and put the letter down. She tried to imagine
Bertram in this foreign land, standing relaxed by a white fence in the
middle of dusty grounds and heat rising around him. Early morning
mist mixed with smells from the desert tracks and a sandstorm in the
background ready to engulf the inhabitants that live and work there,
making them perspire from their hard day's toil. The very opposite of
the cold, the rain, the wind and the damp here.

She imagined what Jorie would look like. She imagined a pretty young woman with fair hair and with an American look about her. She wondered if her imagination had captured the woman's likeness. She appeared so different to Kathryn. She imagined someone loud, who never ceased to talk and laugh. Gregarious and fun loving, an extravert unlike herself. Someone able to bring Bertram out of his sullen mood swings.

She jumped out of bed, pulling the eiderdown with her for warmth as she searched for her shoes under the bed. Pulling on her warmest coat, she headed out to the courtyard behind the house and walked briskly to the stables. Unlocking the old padlock she turned the key, which was stiff at first, before it clicked open. There were two old automobiles of Devlin's parked together and clearly not cleaned for years. Kathryn tried to look beyond them and then walked past them into a large partitioned stables she did not know even existed. She counted eighteen boxes, nine on each side. She had no understanding of how they would work on a day to day basis. This was new territory for her. The number of boxes was probably enough to start with and maybe if they expanded the barn that backed onto them. And perhaps they could build a ring like the one Bertram had described in his letter, and a riding arena. She would have to ask Sebastien for advice.

The air was sharp this morning, a deep frost had settled but no snow thank goodness, she thought. She sat down on a barrel that had decayed and was covered with spider webs. Unknown to Kathryn, a small spider crawled up and onto Kathryn's nightdress. She brushed something away with her hand and stood up. She felt a tingle up her spine as if someone was watching her. She called out into the back of the stables. She thought she saw a shadow. She shook her head. She was tired, she knew that. Her mind had not really switched off since Alexander and Sebastien talked about the business opportunity of having the horses at Dallington Place. Locking the door, she hurried back to the house. That almost ghostly presence had made her feel uneasy. She crept back to the house unnoticed and went to sleep for a few more hours. She fell asleep as soon as she laid her head on the pillow and was unaware at first of Ernest trying to wake her to open her Christmas present. 'What time is it?' she asked sleepily.

Ernest smiled. 'Five past eleven!' he shrieked, eager to get started with Christmas presents.

'Oh no Ernest, why did you not wake me?' said Kathryn realising that she had slept so late on Christmas Day.

'I just did! Mamma, you needed the sleep and everything is under control. The turkeys are cooking well; Sebastien took care of it. Libby was crying a while back as Sebastien was shouting at her, but I soothed things over and everyone are friends again,' said Ernest smiling at Kathryn, clearly proud of his efforts.

'What, why did you not wake me earlier?' said Kathryn worried about her guests.

'Stop fretting Mamma, you will upset yourself. I want you to open your present, here,' said Ernest passing her a rather heavy present wrapped in red tissue paper.

Kathryn sat up in her bed. 'Pass me my spectacles, there is a dear,' she said pulling her shawl around her shoulders.

Unwrapping the present, Kathryn gasped. As she unfolded the tissue she could already make out what it was. Kathryn held a lucky horseshoe made from heavy brass and held it up so she could read the inscription. "Dallington Place Riding School. Opened Christmas 1933". 'I just love it Ernest, thank you so much,' she said leaning over to hug him.

'We are nearly ready for the opening, my dearest Ernest. Thank you so much, it is all very exciting,' she continued giving him a loving look.

'Mamma, I was going to ask you, I like Roberta very much and was wondering if you had something I could give her as a Christmas present?' he asked bashfully.

'Well, let me see,' smiled Kathryn, getting out of bed and walking over to her dressing table. 'I think a piece of jewellery would be a lovely gift,' she said turning the key in the ornate chestnut box. 'A ring would be nice, what do you think?' asked Kathryn, picking up two and holding them out for Ernest to have a look at.

'I like this one, Mamma,' said Ernest delighted as he picked out the ruby ring with a single pearl, the engagement ring of Kathryn's mother.

'I agree, it would go perfectly with her red hair, and it is so lovely we can give her something that belonged to my mother, what do you think? After all Roberta is my goddaughter,' she said, smiling at Ernest.

'Would you mind Mamma, if I said it was just from me, you know as a romantic present?' asked Ernest a little embarrassed.

Kathryn took off her spectacles and raised her eyebrows. 'Ernest, you do not mean to get engaged, do you? You are only eighteen!' she laughed.

'No Mamma, but it would be nice to have a sweetheart,' he replied with his hazel eyes twinkling.

Kathryn's heart skipped a beat. It never occurred to her that there could be a romance between her son and her goddaughter, but she could not have wished a better girlfriend for Ernest. 'And what about Carlyon, have you forgotten her already?' asked Kathryn with a teasing smile.

'No Mamma, I just got bored waiting for her, and I think Sebastien has taken over from where I left off!' he said sarcastically.

'Yes, talking of Sebastien and everyone, I think I had better get dressed or they will think their hostess has left Dallington Place,' she said opening her wardrobe and taking out few of her favourite dresses to choose from. She held her blue velvet dress in front of her, looking at Ernest for approval. Ernest shrugged, kissed his mother on the cheek and left her to dress.

Carlyon had waited for Sebastien that morning. It was Boxing Day. The mist had cleared over the downs and now an eerie silence had descended over the grounds of Dallington Place. The cockerel swung quietly in its tower to the left, where winds from the east swept along the blades of grass. The branches of the limes trees creaked quietly and ghostly as Carlyon stood underneath them. She steadied herself on the old twin seat where inscriptions of a Bertram Wright, his birth and his death were written down. She slowly slipped into the warm embrace of the sweet timber as she anticipated Sebastien's arrival. He was late, but not so late to upset her too much. He walked before her arrogantly, well knowing how handsome he looked, pushing his thick hair out of his eyes he bent down to kiss his lover on her cheek. It took only a few minutes for Carlyon to hear his lament. It was not what she wanted to hear and she set off back to the house as fast as she could to hide the tears. There were already people arriving and she ran the short distance up the stairs to her room so no one would see the tears running down her cheeks.

Sebastien stayed on the bench, smoking nonchalantly, his feet up on the wooden frame, relaxed and happy. He had made it, in his view. Here he was, living the life of an English gentleman in the lap of luxury. Pretty women flocking to his every whim. Every girl turned her head at him, to his voice, his charisma. Yawning from not much sleep he watched the people arrive. Then the sounds of the hounds brought everyone out of the house. He stood up and stamped on the cigarette.

Carlyon sat high and proud on her horse, and not a friendly word was ever uttered between them again. But she would race him today, if her life depended on it. Sebastien coolly watched Ernest help Roberta into her saddle. Kathryn declined to ride, preferring to stay at the house to greet the visitors. Shame Sebastien thought, it would have been nice to ride with her. The Richards abstained too, as did Mr and Mrs Lovat. William had put on weight this Christmas, promising his wife he would exercise more. Having left the RFC, he had worked from home, and living a sedentary life that perhaps did not suit his physique. His wife Geraldine, still a beauty with red hair and fiery temper, and her daughter Roberta, now that could be a challenge, thought Sebastien. A sly smile on his face as he patted the flanks of Roberta's horse. Ernest glanced sideways at Sebastien, shooting him a territorial look. Sebastien tipped his riding hat at him with a confident demeanour.

Kathryn had watched Sebastien from the window as he sat talking to Carlyon. Her arms folded protectively over her chest, she knew what he was saying to Carlyon. There was something predictable about him, but she knew he enjoyed being a bit of an enigma to others. It was his youth that gave him away to Kathryn. She could read Sebastien, when Bertram she could not. Bertram had always been a challenge and a mystery. Even the brass inscription that Sebastien had brought and placed on the love seat under the limes, had not come as a surprise. She and Ernest had liked this choice of Christmas present but others had thought it a little insensitive to Devlin's memory. Kathryn was well aware that part of him had done it to shock the other guests, but Kathryn also knew it was his way of putting his stamp on Dallington Place. She knew he was here to stay. But it did not bother her or even Ernest. In fact, Ernest seemed to like the idea even if Sebastien was a threat with Roberta. His assertive and flirtatious demeanour could put any other man at disadvantage. Not that Kathryn would not keep an eye on him. She could see the young boy in him, the one that had run past her outside Berenice's house that day. That pivotal day in her life. Sebastien had become one with her as Bertram had. Maybe she thought by keeping Sebastien here, it would keep Bertram's memory alive. Pulling the red curtain across so she could not watch anymore. She heard the fox hounds arrive and rushed down

211

the grand stairs to meet the rest of the hunting party. Dawson was passing the sherry around on a silver tray to the riders. His hands were shaking, he was clearly nervous around horses. Not a good start, Kathryn thought, to the new business venture at Dallington Place. Everyone on the hunt had now passed through the gates and were making their way down the long drive. Carlyon sat proud on her grey horse, ignoring Sebastien behind her. Roberta and Ernest followed on behind them. Kathryn was pleased that he had learnt to ride well at his school. How handsome he looked. His blond hair curled over the edges of his riding hat, his kind face shone with pride. How happy Roberta and he seemed together and she proudly wore the ring that he had presented to her the day before.

Geraldine had taken Kathryn aside later that morning, worried it was an engagement ring. Kathryn assured her it was no such thing, but in her heart she knew it probably was. There were some things that were written and perhaps it was always meant to be between Ernest and Roberta. Life could be fleeting, she knew that, and perhaps it was best to grab happiness and not to let love drift as she and Bertram had. Other people get in the way you see, she thought.

CHAPTER TWENTY-SIX
KATHRYN: NEW YEAR'S EVE 1933

'What does the telegram say?' asked Geraldine dressed up to the nines in her red silk evening dress.

'He is coming all right but not alone I am afraid,' said Kathryn her heart sinking suddenly.

'You have gone to all this effort, had the carpets cleaned and the place gleaming for a man that is bringing a date!' uttered Geraldine looking even more put out than Kathryn.

'Oh well, what can I expect? There has been nothing between us as yet,' sighed Kathryn, looking at her dear friend.

'I know, I know, but you know he could have asked,' said Geraldine, standing by the window and watching her husband walk up to the front of the house, the gravel crunching under his boots. 'Gosh, my husband needs to diet!' joked Geraldine as she watched her husband adoringly.

'At least you have a date to my party,' said Kathryn now laughing.

'Who is he bringing?' asked Geraldine waving through the window at William.

'It does not really matter now does it? A woman is a woman!' said Kathryn shrugging her shoulders.

Kathryn had not noticed Dawson introduce Alexander Pillard around the room at first. She was distracted by a friend of William's, who knew quite a lot about horse racing and had spent the summer in Deauville. 'You could make Dallington Place into the Deauville of Sussex,' he declared on knowing Kathryn's ambitious plans.

'It is a very expensive project, I must say,' said the other man at her side, Mr Herbert Lange. He was a rather portly chap, a local historian and a retired accountant. 'If you need some advice on cost, you can call me any time. Here is my business card,' he offered, now clapping his eyes on Geraldine and his face lighting up.

As Kathryn smiled at Geraldine, she suddenly noticed Alexander out of the corner of her eye, casually smoking his cigar. Looking very sophisticated in his blue lounge suit talking to Vicar Sanderson and introducing the young woman by his side. Kathryn walked up to him.

'Alexander, how lovely to see you, why did you not come over to see me earlier?' she asked him, although she knew why.

He was uncomfortable with the idea of introducing his date to her. 'Annie Marguerite, Kathryn McAlister.'

The French woman politely shook Kathryn's hand but there was a frostiness between them. Kathryn tried to hide her jealousy but found it hard to swallow. This woman was stunning, very young and very beautiful. She was Alexander's lover and in her home.

'Annie is a dancer,' said Alexander looking rather shameful.

'A Tiller Girl to be precise,' interrupted Sebastien, who found the situation was very amusing. Alexander was well into his fifties and here he was looking tired and strained with a young dancer half his age with not a lot to say.

'Tiller Girl?' asked Kathryn pretending not to know what it was.

'Yes, I trained at the Folies Bergère and then I have been living in New York for two years working on Broadway, where I met Alexander,' said Annie Marguerite looking very pleased with herself.

'Please enjoy yourselves. Excuse me please, I have guests to attend to,' said Kathryn with a polite smile, not wanting to talk to this woman anymore.

Sebastien took Kathryn's arm and steered her across the room. 'You were rather, how do you say, abrupt with Annie,' he said, looking closely at Kathryn. 'I thought he was seeing Pearl, Pierre Le Sierre's widow. I thought they were a couple,' he continued. 'But then Mr Pillard always had an eye for the ladies, my father would tell me. Always two or three women on the go,' he said with a knowing smile.

'That is nothing to be proud of Sebastien, and Pierre's widow, surely not?' balked Kathryn at the thought.

'Oh yes, for quite a few years and she puts up with his womanising,' replied Sebastien, surprised that Kathryn had not heard of the affair.

'Well I had no idea. Had I known, perhaps I would not have invited him,' said Kathryn, struggling to hide her disapproval.

'Really? I doubt that, I can see that he fascinates you!' said Sebastien, looking for a flicker of emotion.

Kathryn hid her feelings well, he thought. 'Not so much as he is a link to the past, my past with Bertram, I suppose,' replied Kathryn.

'I hope you do not mind me asking but you never seem to mention Devlin,' said Sebastien.

Kathryn swung Sebastien a wounded look. 'Please do not mention him again,' she hissed through her teeth and waltzed off to get a glass of wine. Sebastien knew he had hit a nerve and he was truly sorry. He was about to apologise and chase her across the room, when he saw Roberta standing alone by the fireplace. He made his way towards her just as Ernest arrived by her side. He grabbed a drink from the tray and went to see if he could find Carlyon.

'ALEXANDER PILLARD LEAVES MRS LE SIERRE IN NEW YORK FOR JAUNT WITH TILLER GIRL AT DALLINGTON PLACE,' the headline read in the *Daily Herald.* Kathryn could not believe what she was reading. Who would have known that the great Alexander Pillard was being spied upon. She knew for all his gaiety and flamboyance, he liked to try at least to keep his private life under wraps. After all, she had not known he was practically living with Pearl Le Sierre in New York for half the year, when he was not in Paris. She was aware it has been two years since his divorce from Sarah. She was relieved that she had left her guests still sleeping and had escaped on the early morning train into London. She had made arrangements for Dawson to take Alexander to the station with his mistress later on. Alexander was insistent on accompanying her to London to open the sale at Harrods, but she did not want to be seen with Annie Marguerite. She promised him that they would meet for dinner that evening after she had done her charity work with Nora Parker.

Nora was waiting at the new back entrance of Harrods. 'I am sorry I am late, we had quite the party at Dallington Place last night and I had to leave all my guests behind,' Kathryn walked over to Nora full of apologies.

'You must be quite exhausted!' said Nora. She was wearing a mink and a rather bright red hat with a large osprey feather, which was slightly drooping over her left eye. Kathryn understood from Nora's comment that she looked rather understated and she did agree herself. She had been too panicked to get away this morning to worry what she should have been wearing. 'The press will be here, and I see from this morning's paper that your Dallington Place has become quite the place for lovebirds!' said Nora laughing.

'Oh, do not say that Nora, I only hope the publicity will be good for business and not have the opposite effect,' said Kathryn feeling nervous and tired.

'All publicity is good, especially as you tell me your ideas about a new business venture. I feel you should be making the most of this opportunity. We have a little time so why do we not go to the ladies' department and pick a glamorous coat and a hat for you? Mr Burbridge would not mind,' said Nora licking her lips at the thought of delving through the furs, feathers and stoles, the best Harrods had to offer.

Woodman Burbridge led the ladies through the private corridors of Harrods department store, through to the main shopping area on the ground floor. People were waving flags and bunting behind cordoned off areas. They were women and children mainly, a few older men that were not at work. Shop assistants lined the opposite side and watched intently as The Honourable Nora Parker cut the ribbon and declared Harrods sale open. Kathryn nervously followed Nora and after being introduced, was passed a bottle of champagne hanging from a rope in the ceiling. She dutifully smashed it against the new model of a Ford automobile that Harrods was selling.

Money was beginning to flood back into the country and British people were starting over, trying to put the war behind them. Men were lost but their spirit and memory not. As Mr Burbridge remembered the dead with a minute's silence and everyone bowed their heads. Kathryn remembered Bertram and her Devlin, whom she missed so much. Maybe she was tired and overwhelmed but tears began to flow. Before she could reach for her handkerchief, a man had sidled up to her and handed her his handkerchief, just as flash photography set off and they were temporarily blinded. Only then she realised it was Alexander.

He led Kathryn out through the doors with Nora in tow. Once outside, they all breathed a sigh of relief to be out of the way of the scrum of people leaving and the mayhem of the opening of the Harrods sale. 'Thank you Alexander, but I thought we were not meeting until this evening?' asked Kathryn, as she handed Alexander's white cotton handkerchief back to him.

'Miss you opening the Harrods sale, never!' he said laughing. 'Besides, I had nothing to do. I am not working today and Anne Marguerite had to go back to rehearsals. May I take you two ladies out to lunch?' he asked in his most charming manner.

'How lovely Mr Pillard,' said Nora politely. 'But I do need to discuss a few charity agreements with Kathryn, we need to change,' said Nora looking at Kathryn. She had noticed that there was clearly something going on between the two.

'Oh yes, I almost forgot, I am wearing the new Harrods' designer wears! And my purse, that is upstairs too,' Kathryn said almost apologetically to Nora.

'Well, how about I meet you two ladies at twelve o'clock at Riley's restaurant?' suggested Alexander.

'That would be lovely, Alexander,' replied Kathryn blushing.

'Au revoir until then,' said Alexander tipping his grey flannel hat at the pair of them.

As the ladies turned to go back in, Nora took hold of Kathryn's arm. 'Perhaps it is best I do not join you for lunch Kathryn. I feel there is some important business you need to discuss with Alexander,' she said with a half-smile.

'Really?' replied Kathryn surprised. Was it that apparent, she thought.

'I too have a lunch meeting in fact. I did not want to say in front of Alexander, as I did not want to appear rude, but I have an important meeting of my own.' Kathryn could not mistake the twinkle in Nora's eyes. Did she mean a romantic meeting, Kathryn wondered taking a sharp intake of breath.

Kissing Nora goodbye on both cheeks, Kathryn ran across Brompton Road, across to Trevor Square. The cobbled street made Kathryn's footing unsteady and she stopped every few minutes to steady herself. She knew that she was attracted to Alexander but she knew he was a ladies man. She knew that after this meeting, their relationship would change from a friendly acquaintance to something deeper. Whether it would be more of a serious business partnership or something romantic she was not sure, but it would change. As she passed through the small revolving door of Riley's, she remembered the last time she had been here. She had met Devlin for dinner three years ago almost to the day. He had been in town to discuss expanding a business idea of his own. It was just before he had fallen ill. Kathryn's heart began to pound. Now she was meeting another man here. Yes, it was a coincidence, but she still felt awash with guilt. As she looked around the darkened bistro, she hoped that maybe Alexander had been too busy and forgotten, then she could walk out, jump on a train and be enfolded into the safety of Dallington Place. He was not there and a sigh of relief took hold of her.

'Good afternoon Madam, do you have a reservation?' asked the handsome manager she recognised from her dinner with Devlin.

'I do, I am meeting Mr Pillard, but it appears he has been caught up with business. Thank you but I have to catch a train.' Kathryn found herself talking nineteen to the dozen with nerves to the manager, trying to convince herself to leave.

'Are you Mrs McAlister?' he asked. Kathryn nodded, now feeling trapped.

'Mr Pillard sends his apologies but he will be a little late. He telephoned a few minutes ago. Would you still like to stay, our waiter can suggest a glass of champagne while you wait?'

Kathryn was about to refuse, but then she thought about Ernest and what Geraldine had reminded her. She was not married anymore, still in her thirties and attractive. It was time to have some fun.

'Yes, thank you, you are very kind, my train can wait,' said Kathryn taking off her coat and trying not to look the manager in the eye. Trying not to feel embarrassed, she handed over her coat and let him lead her to a corner table. People were starting to flood into the restaurant now, it had begun to rain. Every time the door opened, Kathryn shyly looked up to see if it was Alexander. Eventually a large man in a grey raincoat entered in, shaking the manager's hand, his voice roaring across the restaurant. He was here and Kathryn, relaxed from her champagne, smiled warmly at him as he looked around for her.

He joined her at the table, pleased to see her there. He waved at the waiter for a menu and glass of champagne.

'The grounds are so extensive at Dallington Place, there would be no dispute with the neighbours,' said Alexander sipping his champagne and sitting back in his chair. He noticed how beautiful she looked, her cheeks flushed from the champagne, he took hold of Kathryn's hand. Kathryn did not pull away as he slowly extinguished his cigar with the other.

'You have done your homework on Dallington Place,' said Kathryn impressed as she looked into Alexander's beaming face.

'Well, I had to have some breathing space away from Annie Marguerite yesterday. I got your Dawson to drive me around the grounds before we arrived for the party. Sebastien was with me, did he not tell you?' said Alexander raising his eyebrows surprised.

'No, but that is Sebastien I am afraid,' said Kathryn biting the inside of her lip. That boy really had the cheek, she thought to herself. 'That explains why I did not know you had arrived,' said Kathryn, now excusing herself for the ladies room.

Observing herself in the mirror and reapplying her lipstick, her mind whirled with thoughts. She hoped she could trust Alexander and she knew this was the way forward for Dallington Place. There were decisions to be made on the name for the racecourse, Dallington Races was the clear winner. She would have to talk this over with Ernest. There was much building work to be done, it would take a couple of years at least, and there were questions over the surrounding cottages. According to Alexander's architect, these may need to be demolished to make way for the racecourse. A rough outline of where the racecourse would be in relation to the house had been crudely and quickly planned out. It made sense but Kathryn had known she would have to learn as she went along. This was all new to her and very exciting.

Closing her eyes for a moment as the train pulled away from Victoria station, she felt the weight of her sudden decision to agree to let Alexander invest in the new Dallington Place racecourse. Forty-nine per cent share and he would put up most of the money to begin with, until the business started to work for itself and hopefully money would pour in. Kathryn had already studied the papers that Devlin had left her, money for herself and Ernest, everything he had sorted out before he died. There were a few people she needed to talk to, including Mr and Mrs Turoc, who were mentioned in a disagreement with the factory at one stage in 1928. Kathryn remembered quite a bit of stress for Devlin at this time. The General Strike, business was not doing as well and they had cut back on their expenses. She always felt the General Strike was the cause of his bad health and worry was etched all over his face. Kathryn had asked him to step down, maybe retire but knowing Devlin as she did, she knew there was no changing his mind. He was a man that liked to be in charge and she knew he would keep working until his health finally gave up. His stubbornness had made her angry and there was quite a lot of friction between them for the first time in their marriage. But Kathryn knew she could not change nor convince this man. After all, he had changed her life for the better, she could not argue with his choices that he made. He kept the business to himself and Kathryn often wished he would have shared his worries with her.

The train was quiet and although it was good to think about the day, it left her rather exhausted. 'I have finished with Annie Marguerite,' Alexander had announced as they left the restaurant. A question that hung in the air between them was whether they would further their relationship and make it romantic. Alexander had made his intentions clear and although Kathryn was intrigued and very attracted to this large man full of charisma and charm, she found herself holding back and rushing for the train. Flustered, she waved her goodbye quickly, telling him they would meet next week. She knew he wanted an answer, but it was too soon for her.

CHAPTER TWENTY-SEVEN
BERTRAM: FLYING WITH LINDBERGH

Bertram could see the house in the distance. He knew Jorie would be watching him from the veranda. It was a hot day but clear and perfect for flying. 'If you helped me here on the ranch rather than disappearing into the skies for hours on end, things would be better between us,' she would always say. She always made herself clear, but Bertram did not listen, or he pretended not to. Concerned about his growing indifference to the ranch and his obsession with tracking the whereabouts of the pilot Charles Lindbergh[3], who was making quite a name for himself flying solo missions across the Americas, Jorie quietly stood back observing her relationship with Bertram disintegrate. Like Lindbergh or 'Slim' as Bertram referred to him, Bertram had bought himself a surplus Curtiss JN-4 "Jenny" biplane, and after having been flying again for a month over the local fields, decided to meet up with Lindbergh in San Antonio. All Jorie could do was wish him well and that she would see him in a couple of days. She and Sebastien waved him off as he took excitedly to the skies to meet up with his hero. They watched the yellow biplane ride bumpily over the Texan terrain and then lift slowly and quietly up into the dawn skies.

'Well that is it, let us get to work Sebastien,' said Jorie slapping the right thigh of her jodhpurs and then clapping her hands together as she always did when she had a lot on her plate at the ranch. It was not even five in the morning, but they were both ready to work. It was a Saturday and not only had they horses about to foal any minute, she also had to set up the barn and the house for Pedro's birthday tomorrow. Her half-brother would be turning twenty and it seems he had invited nearly all of Santa Anna to the celebrations, including some of the Fitch and Stedman family and neighbours in the surrounding farms and cotton fields. Pedro had worked on the ranch

---

[3] Charles Augustus Lindbergh, nicknamed Slim, Lucky Lindy, and The Lone Eagle, was an American aviator, author, inventor, military officer, explorer, and social activist. (Wikipedia)

all his life but now that Bertram and Jorie were married, he had taken a step back and had been living with a woman in the town. Jorie was rather worried about him. He was drinking too much so Jorie did not want him at the ranch to interfere. She had been feeling so much frustration trying to keep Pedro on the straight and narrow and trying to get Bertram interested in the ranch. Well, at least as much as he had been in the beginning when he arrived four years ago. Fortunately Pedro was keeping an eye on their father in town, but she really needed the help at the ranch. Every time she needed Bertram, he seemed to find an excuse to fly off, and it was not cheap either. Sighing to herself, luckily she had Sebastien. He knew his way around with the horses and there were also the stable hands working for her. But if the stud farm did not begin to expand, she was not sure how she was going to pay them by the end of the year. She had written to her sister in New York, who was now married to an eminent playwright, and she hoped she would come and stay in the next few months. Maybe Winnie could help her financially, she hoped. She needed to buy more horses, not fuel for the biplane.

The vet arrived at nine o'clock. Lupin, the grey mare, had gotten in trouble while foaling. Jorie and Sebastien and Grey, the stud farm manager, had all been trying to help deliver the foal, but it was well and truly stuck. They could not afford to lose another horse and now the vet's bill would be another finance to worry about. Gone were the days before the war, when their ranch was thriving. Her father fit and running the ranch, they had all been wealthy. The girls and their mother could afford to travel when times were quieter at the ranch and they never went without. Her father had money to spend like water then. Now it was about counting every dime and dollar. Her brother had decided to drum up business by having a birthday party, which he could ill afford. Why she had let him talk her into it she had no idea. It was already eighty degrees outside and Jorie was running back and forth to the house with pails of water. The tap by the stable had ceased working yesterday and the only way to keep the mare cool was to fetch water from the main house. 'Why, damn Bertram, had he gone off today of all days!' she screamed, kicking the last bucket of water in frustration. Sebastien had gone off to town with the wagon to buy food for tomorrow. It was just her and the two ranch workers Grey and Roger. The other men were out working in the field at the other end of the ranch.

'Morning!' said John Dykes, the vet pulling up in his new automobile. 'Oh, thank goodness, I thought you were not coming!' Jorie said wiping her wet hands and forehead with a cloth. As the vet walked towards her, she at first felt a wave of relief and then all of a sudden a wave of nausea. And then she did not remember anything else.

It was Sunday morning, and Jorie knew full well the party was about to start but she had strict doctors' orders to rest and stay in bed. Alison was the first to arrive at Jorie's bedside. 'If there is anything else you need do not forget to ask us, please.' Not understanding the circumstances of Jorie's financial or medical worries, she talked on and on and gossiped about this and that. Suddenly Jorie's ears pricked up when through a haze of talk she heard the words she needed to hear. 'May Dawn-Marie have riding lessons here? I hear Roger really is the best riding teacher and it would do her good to get out of her surroundings. I fear she is getting quite spoilt. I would pay you well and some of her friends are interested too,' chatted Alison on looking at Jorie with excitement. Jorie managed a smile through her sadness.

'Oh, thank you, Alison, of course I can help,' she said struggling to sit up. Alison gave her a sideways glance and Jorie knew perhaps she had an inkling of her troubles.

'Jorie, the brood mare has pulled through and the foal was born at eleven on the dot last night!' announced Sebastien, pleased to be able to tell Jorie some good news. The doctors had been and gone and asked Sebastien where his father was. Sebastien had just shrugged and said that he would be back in the next few days. One of the doctors informed him they would be back to check on Jorie in a couple of days. 'She is going to be all right, is she not?' asked Sebastien suddenly feeling worried.

'She will be fine lad, just keep an eye on her and call us if she falls ill again,' the doctor patted Sebastien's shoulder reassuringly. 'I will Sir, thank you,' said Sebastien relieved that Jorie would be fine.

'That is so good, Sebastien, I was wondering when our luck would change,' said Jorie, slowly registering the news of the birth. But Jorie looked sad and no jokes that Sebastien tried to come up with could make her smile. Maybe she missed Bertram he thought, but he was not convinced. There was something else she was not telling him and she still looked ill. Only a few days ago she had a golden tan and glistening eyes looking her usual radiant self. Now she was white as the sheet that was covering her. 'Can you manage to get out of bed?' he asked her.

She shook her head. Not even to look through the windows at the success of the day's events.

'We have made quite a lot of money from the pony rides,' he said proudly. He could not understand his father. Why would he disappear just when important things were happening at the ranch.

'How's Pedro?' she asked wearily.

'Having a great time and I almost forgot he sent you up some birthday cake,' Sebastien pulled out a chunk of cake wrapped in a napkin.

'Thank you, I will have it later dear, just put it on the bedside table,' said Jorie thankfully.

Sebastien leant over the bed and touched her hand. 'Hurry up and get better, it's quiet down there without you.' Jorie managed a smile, she knew what he meant. They were close and she had to admit he felt like a son to her.

'I will, just give me a day or two and I will be back to my old self,' she said.

'All right, I had better get back, Dawn-Marie wants me to take her for another pony ride,' quipped Sebastien as he headed for the door.

After Sebastien left, all Jorie could do was to burst into tears. She felt a mess, and inside she was breaking.

The band had started to play and Sebastien watched as people walked towards the large barn for the dance. A truckload of cowboys from the Stedford ranch arrived with their wives. They unloaded barrels of beer and a huge pig for the spit roast, running back and forth to the barn, kicking up red dust with cowboy boots. Roger, Dale and Grey were greeting the guests and delighted to see all the food and drink. Sebastien headed for the barn to make sure they would set the spit roast in the right place. The barn was filling with the locals and pony rides that Sebastien had organised, brought in some welcomed revenue. Men were dragging on their cigars outside the barn and a couple were kissing on a hay bale. Dusk was beginning to settle and as the evening drew in, the McClerrons and the Amos family were arriving on horseback to enjoy the festivities after a long hard day's work at their ranch.

Cowboy boots
on weathered land,
I miss the wet damp soil of England.
Brown boots,
are what I remember,
on French clay soil.
On England's cobbled streets,
my shiny brogues on theatre land.
I wish to be barefooted now,
and aloft in the skies.
My feet too well travelled,
and too well trod.
By Bertram Wright (returning back from flying with Lindbergh)

Sebastien was squinting up to the fading sun, cupping his hands to shield his eyes, as he spotted a yellow aeroplane making its descent over the farmland. Unicorn stomped his foot impatiently and snorted loudly with his nostrils flaring as it heard a familiar noise above in the skies. It took off, galloping around the pen with its tail held high. 'Father is back, father is back!' shouted Sebastien as he saw the little biplane come to land in the distance just in time for the sunset.

Sebastien watched Bertram jump down from his aeroplane and ran up to greet him. Bertram saluted him and passed his small flight bag over to Sebastien, as he always did, who then proudly slung it over his shoulder. Sebastien knew exactly what was inside the bag as he always helped Bertram to pack it the night before his flight. There were a metal water bottle, his wallet, maps and the pilot's logbook. They quietly walked up to the ranch house, Sebastien looking up to Bertram expecting him to say something, but he never did. The two doctors were there again to check on Jorie and as Bertram entered the house, they ushered him into the study. Moments later Sebastien heard him slamming the study door shut, cursing to himself and then walking into his own bedroom. He did not go to see Jorie and Sebastien did not see him again for another two days.

1st JULY 1934, DALLINGTON PLACE

Kathryn put down the letter and the pilot's logbook that was between the fourth and the fifth letter. Shocked, she put her hand up to her mouth. Poor Jorie had lost their baby. She felt for this woman, who like herself in her own innocence had put her trust into Bertram who by the looks of it had let her down as well. She wanted to read on to the fifth letter but it was all too much, she would read it tomorrow. She had her own thoughts to concentrate on, her new beginnings with Alexander. She snuggled under the eiderdown. It had been a good Christmas at Dallington Place and there were many more filled with family and hope. Closing her eyes she thought of the positive things that were about to begin. Dallington Races was a big yet very exciting project and she could not wait to begin on the hard work.

'Kathryn, I hope you will agree with me, I have asked Dawn-Marie to stay at Dallington Place for the summer. She is very knowledgeable about horses and will be a valuable asset to the business,' said Sebastien over breakfast the next morning.

'Yes I know,' said Kathryn always one step ahead of Sebastien.

'I have spoken to her mother who agrees with me. She wants to get to know England, her heritage and well, let us say Alison hopes that the genteel nature of ladies here in the village may just rub off on her. I do believe that Alison thinks Dawn-Marie to be as wild as the horses she loves so much,' she laughed.

'She is headstrong, believe me,' said Sebastien rolling his eyes, 'but I do not know a better horse woman. She could be a great asset for us choosing the right horses when the time comes.' He had witnessed Dawn-Marie blossom into quite an expert at Jorie's ranch in Santa Anna.

'Exactly Sebastien, we need all the help we can get,' said Kathryn enthusiastically. Her head was spinning with ideas. For four months now there were building works going on. The old stables had been renovated, plans drawn up where the new racecourse would be and the training and breeding stables were to be situated in the two barns nearer the main house. Also plans were to be drawn up for the site where the cottages stood, to renovate and extend them to make room for restaurants and a tearoom. Alexander had ploughed his money into the start of the business and only yesterday they had pored over the accounts. Kathryn, who had at last delved into some of Devlin's old account books, had some work cut out for herself. After they had taken

225

a brief walk in the midday sunshine to look where they would extend the cottages out to, they had sat down under the lime trees, and watched the tawny daylilies as they were officially known, nodding their heads in the light breeze in front of Dallington Place.

Kathryn loved this view. The little crop of the lilies to the left of the main door always looked welcoming. As soon as the warmer weather arrived at Dallington Place, there were always the lilies, the first sign of spring. The summer that Kathryn had worked there as a sixteen-year-old, she had marvelled at the orange hue of the lilies and loved to smell the scent first thing in the morning. Sometimes when she had washed the front steps of the main door, she would bend down and sniff their scent, as if by doing so she was fresh and clean, and beautifully perfumed herself. Then she would cut a few and place them on the mantle in the main drawing room for Lady Fitch. Those flowers were Dallington Place to her.

Alexander had taken her hand that morning, and she had not pulled away. He had kissed her as they walked back to the house. His arm around her lower back, discreet enough not to be seen by the other occupants in the house, but strong enough to hold on to Kathryn so that he could draw her to him, and kiss her gently and quickly but without startling her. It was not an ardent kiss of young lovers but a warm and comforting gesture and one that Kathryn welcomed. She needed support and she had got it.

That evening they sat opposite each other in her study, happy to spend some more time in each other's company before Alexander travelled to New York the next day, the fire lit and warm between them, both sipping their brandies. Something was troubling Kathryn as she sat there going through the account book. She was turning the pages back and forth. She had noticed a name that kept coming up: Mrs Turoc of 1A Willow Tree Cottage. Kathryn knew that Mr Turoc had worked at Devlin's factory for years, but they lived in the village not at Willow Tree Cottage. There were five or six cheques listed to a Mrs F Turoc. Each for the same sum of one hundred pounds, over a period of six months. Kathryn flipped over the pages, checking dates. She wondered whether Devlin had got confused, he had become ill around this time so perhaps he had made a mistake. But Kathryn knew he was always very precise and there were no other discrepancies. She flipped over two more pages, and there again, were payments, two more in the June, in which Devlin died. This time Kathryn took a sharp intake of breath. One sum was for one thousand pounds and the other for two thousand pounds. Payments made to Francesca Turoc. She was sure she had let out a small scream and looked over to Alexander, who had now dozed off in front of the fire. She slammed the book shut. It did not make sense. She had met the Turocs once at a Christmas party. He was a small man and she was rather tall with a ruddy complexion and well she could not remember much else about them. They were nice enough, but why had he been giving them, or rather her money. And why Willow Tree Cottage? Three thousand pounds had gone out in the space of nine months, that was more than she and Devlin and spent on running Dallington Place that year. It did not make sense. Thoughts were running through her head, and then she faltered. Did they not have a daughter? She remembered that perhaps they did. Was she not poorly at one stage? It was a vague memory but there was something. Yes now she remembered. That evening of the Christmas party, Dawson had told her that one of the guests had to leave early due to an emergency. She was not entirely sure it had been Mrs Turoc, but she had heard of some gossip the next day that one of the guests had left their daughter home on their own and that she had fallen ill and was now in the hospital. It was flooding back. Yes, even Devlin had mentioned it. He had sent flowers to the hospital, as one of his workers was ill. Kathryn had thought what a kind gesture. But looking at this in the accounts, it all seemed too personal. And why the change of address? Sipping her drink, Kathryn tried not to fret.

Alexander stirred his drink and looked at her with raised eyebrows. He knew her well now and could tell something was troubling her. 'You look worried my dear, what is the matter?' he asked seeing her poring over the books, her spectacles perched on the end of her nose as if she had not the time or inclination to push them back.

'It is nothing, just there is a name in these books that keeps occurring, and the person has the address of Willow Tree Cottage. It does not make sense,' said Kathryn now holding her spectacles in her hand and rubbing her forehead.

'I am sure there is a simple explanation, do not fret dear,' said Alexander getting up and wrapping his arms around her. 'Besides I am leaving tomorrow and I do not want to see you so worried before I go. Ask Dawson, I am sure he understands the mix up,' he said comfortingly.

'Mix up?' said Kathryn stiffening.

'Well you know, you said yourself that Devlin was confused at the end,' he continued, mindful not to upset her further.

Although Kathryn did not mind saying these things herself she did not like it when someone else spoke about Devlin in this way. 'Never mind,' she said stingingly, 'I will find out on my own.'

Alexander gave her shoulders a loving squeeze. 'I did not mean to talk out of turn,' he said feeling her annoyance. 'I am sorry, I am just so tired, and what with the building works in Willow Tree Cottage coming to a close. I am worn out,' said Kathryn managing a little smile. She knew Alexander only meant well.

'I know, I know, but perhaps you will rest a little now, maybe take a break?'

Kathryn looked up surprised. 'A break? No, we have to convert the barn in the next two months, and the plans are not even finalised yet,' she said.

'So where is Sebastien? I have not seen him all week,' said Alexander concerned that Sebastien was not pulling his weight.

'Well, when he moves into Willow Tree Cottage tomorrow he knows he will have to pay me rent. The only way he can afford that is if he works here with me, so I am sure he will be,' she said in a softer tone. This is what she so admired about Alexander, he was always looking out for her, making sure no one took advantage of her kindness. 'Do not forget when you are gone, Dawn-Marie is moving in. She arrives on Friday,' Kathryn reminded him. 'But I promise to take the Saturday off, show her around Dallington Place and take her out to somewhere nice for lunch,' she rested her hand on his that was resting on her shoulder.

'Good,' said Alexander.

'How long will you be gone for?' Kathryn asked nonchalantly.

'Two maybe three months,' said Alexander, suddenly feeling a surge of guilt. Realising that his life was more complicated, he felt he needed more time to tie loose ends and to adjust to a permanent move to England. However, he did not want to leave Kathryn on her own in Dallington Place for long periods of time.

'Nearly three months? Oh Alexander, I had no idea, I thought it would be two months!' she looked up visibly disappointed.

'I know, but I may have to go back to France after New York, just to tie some loose ends there. They still have my desk and if I am to retire, I need to say goodbye to my colleagues,' he said, now regretting to be travelling for so long.

'Yes, of course I understand,' Kathryn said looking weary. Three months without Alexander would seem like a year.

'I almost forgot, there is something I would like to give you!' he said, his face brightening up.

'There is?' asked Kathryn, pushing her hair back off her face as Alexander let her go and walk over to his tweed jacket. He pulled out a small black box and walked back to where Kathryn was sitting. He handed the box to her without a word. Kathryn opened it and gasped. A large solitaire diamond ring shone back at her.

'You do not have to say anything. I know it is early days and I know you still wear Devlin's ring, but perhaps you could wear it on your other hand? And when the time is right and it feels right, perhaps you will think of it as an engagement ring,' said Alexander nervously, hoping he had said the right words.

'It is beautiful and totally unexpected! And yes I will wear it, but I need a little time,' said Kathryn holding his hand and gently squeezing it.

He bent down and kissed Kathryn firmly on the cheek. 'On that note I must go upstairs and pack.' He marched out of the room, feeling taller and happier.

Kathryn sat by the fire for a few moments longer. It was her third proposal. Her first one was by Bertram under the white bridge in the grounds of Dallington Place. The second one was by Devlin at his factory, and now in the drawing room by Alexander. She could never have imagined that when she was sixteen. And now she was asked to be someone's wife again, a French-American and an exciting man at that. She sat looking at the ring, holding it up against the firelight, not realising Sebastien had entered the room. Alexander had not closed the doors and she did not hear him knock. 'Oh Sebastien, you startled me!' exclaimed Kathryn hoping he had not seen the ring.

'Oh that is very pretty,' he said admiring the ring and not realising the significance of it at first.

'We were just talking about you, wondering where you had got to. Have you organised your things to be taken over to Willow Tree Cottage tomorrow?' she asked, eager to talk about something else.

'It's not a problem, I can drive myself over there tomorrow,' he replied with a broad smile, clearly excited that he was getting a place of his own.

'Actually if you do not mind, I will come with you. I would like to oversee things there, just to make sure everything is how it should be. I have had some new keys cut too, remind me to bring those with us tomorrow,' she replied. This young man was dear to her and she was thankful for him being around to help.

'Would eleven be alright with you Kathryn? I was wondering if I could take a few books from the library with me?' he asked little sheepishly. He did not own any books himself and he found the library of Dallington Place a true fount of knowledge. He had spotted several culinary books to inspire his passion for food. And his interest of late in political topics. Sir Nicholas had left behind numerous political books including a few about the Boer War. 'Of course you can Sebastien, and we must talk about your wages. We can talk about that tomorrow, but as you know the cottage will be twenty shillings per week, which I can deduct out of your wages if you like. Of course you can eat with us at the house whenever you like and use the farm produce free of charge,' said Kathryn, hoping Sebastien would be happy with the arrangement.

'Kathryn, you have been more than kind and I hope I have not overstayed my welcome here at Dallington Place,' he said.

'Of course you have not Sebastien and I look forward to working with you on the Dallington Races. Of course you will be a manager and your wages will reflect that. We will talk more tomorrow, but I have to go and to see that Alexander is ready for his departure tomorrow,' she said as she stood up.

'What time is he leaving?' asked Sebastien, keen to run some ideas over with him.

'Early I am afraid,' said Kathryn.

'That is a shame, I wanted to discuss some things with him,' he replied, looking disappointed.

'Well, it will have to wait I am afraid. You can discuss anything with me regarding the Dallington Races, please do not forget that Sebastien,' she continued giving him a stern look. Sebastien realised that he might have stepped out of line.

'Yes of course, it was just I wanted a man's perspective on something,' he hurried to say.

'Can it wait?' asked Kathryn genuinely keen to help.

'Of course, absolutely,' he said now leaving for the door.

CHAPTER TWENTY-EIGHT
DAWN: TEXAN GIRL IN SUSSEX

18TH JULY 1934

Kathryn did not know what to expect. Alison Stedford had forwarded on some luggage early and Kathryn was wondering why Dawn-Marie needed all these clothes and belongings. Dawn-Marie's room was ready and Alison had asked Irene, Kathryn's personal assistant, to arrange Dawn-Marie's clothes in the bedroom next to Irene's, which used to be Sebastien's room. They were originally the servants' quarters, where Kathryn had once slept. When Sebastien had arrived last year, he was first put into this bedroom in the attic. If Dawn-Marie wants a different room so be it, but Kathryn thought it might be nice for her to be with girls of her own age.

In a few weeks the riding school would be up and running. Two girls were already booked to stay for a couple of months to learn to ride and other horsemanship skills. They had ten horses for the students and three stable hands came in every day from the village. Sebastien was there to manage and give lessons accordingly alongside two other riding instructors. One of them was Geoffrey Montgomery, a very experienced horseman, who had been racing and hunting all his life. Once a successful jockey now in his fifties and no longer able to compete professionally, he was looking for a more sedentary pace. He was staying in the cottage next to Dawson's until building works would start to convert them into the restaurants. The actual racecourse would not be built until the end of August once they had all the plans confirmed. Alexander had suggested they would bring in some revenue from the riding school first before they started to spend money on the racecourse. Sebastien had wanted to get cracking on the main project, but Kathryn had agreed with Alexander to delay the works until late August. It had only taken a couple of months to renovate the old stables. New boxes would be added in time, especially when they needed to expand, but for now it was a good way to save money. Sebastien had clashed with both of them about it, so it was a relief when a solution came for him to move out and have his independence. Ernest had been worried that perhaps Sebastien had been taking advantage of Kathryn's good nature and she had to agree with him. Also there would be many attractive girls staying at Dallington House and Kathryn thought perhaps Sebastien would concentrate better on his managerial skills without the distraction of living with the pretty students.

Everything was falling into place and Dawn-Marie was arriving any minute. Her skills and knowledge about horses and racing would be invaluable. It will be lovely to have her staying and able to repay the favour to the Fitch family for what they had done for her. Kathryn watched the automobile come to a slow stop. She saw Dawson open the door for her to get out. Kathryn was not quite expecting what she saw. She thought she would be seeing a girl full of youthful energy jump out, but from what Kathryn could see, this girl waited for Dawson to pick up some of her bags before she stepped out. Kathryn should have gone to the front door to greet her but she was transfixed. This girl, or a young woman no more than seventeen, that looked worldly beyond her years and was clothed in the finest of Hollywood fashions.

She looked more like an American movie star than a Texas horsewoman. Wearing a fitted, light grey, pinstripe skirt suit especially made by Hollywood costume designer Gwen Wakeling, white gloves and a cloche hat prettily sitting on her shiny black marcelled hair.

She puffed slowly on a cigarette as Dawson made two trips with her luggage to the front door, then she stamped out her cigarette, took his arm and carefully walked in her heels over the gravel to the door. Kathryn heard the bell, straightened the curtains and walked into the hallway to answer it. Dawn-Marie's lipstick was bright red with a little still left on her teeth that was the only thing that marred her incredible beauty. Kathryn supposed it was not surprising as Alison was pretty and her father Ned strikingly handsome. She really was quite stunning and sophisticated, her features almost doll like with her alabaster skin and brilliant blue eyes. 'So good to see you, Aunt Kathryn,' she said stretching out her gloved hand to Kathryn with a polite smile.

'I hope you had a good journey, Dawn-Marie,' replied Kathryn ignoring the hand and kissed her on the cheek.

'Just dreadful darling aunt, but you can just call me Dawn. Dawn-Marie is my stage name,' she replied as she sashayed into the front room past Kathryn.

Kathryn's eyebrows rose and then relaxed. Perhaps she could also drop the 'aunt' and call her Kathryn, she thought to herself. 'Please, just call me Kathryn,' she said finally. 'That is all right Auntie,' said Dawn, clearly oblivious to what Kathryn had just said. The girl was already getting under her skin; no wonder her mother had sent her over.

'Would you like some tea?' offered Kathryn motioning Dawn to follow her into the sitting room. Perhaps she had judged her too harshly. After all, Dawn had been travelling on the *Queen Mary* liner for a week in rough seas. The poor girl was clearly exhausted. 'Or would you prefer to rest? Travelling all this way must have been exhausting for you,' asked Kathryn sympathetically.

'Oh no, I have been in London for almost a week now!' she said looking around the house in awe. 'I cannot believe I am actually here. I told my agent that I was coming back to my ancestral home and he was very impressed.'

Kathryn could not help but notice the words "her home." 'Well, let us take your coat. Dawson would you mind?' said Kathryn nodding at the rather tired looking man.

'I would love a drink if that is possible, brandy or wine, whatever you have. And where is Sebastien? I cannot wait to see him,' she chatted away.

'He will be over later. He has moved into new lodgings on the estate and will be finishing work soon,' replied Kathryn, noticing Dawn's eye lighting up with the mention of Sebastien.

'Sebastien working? Interesting!' said Dawn walking gracefully over to the red armchair and plonking herself down on it in a rather unladylike fashion.

Kathryn could feel a headache coming on. It was going to be a long day, she thought. Perhaps she should have a glass of wine herself. She asked Dawson to pour them a glass of wine each. 'I have put you in with the other girls. They are here learning to ride for a couple of weeks,' said Kathryn, putting down her glass and going to the door. 'It has been a long day and my fi— Alexander has just left for New York so I have been quite busy. Perhaps we could all do with an early night,' suggested Kathryn, realising she had almost called Alexander her fiancé.

'I am actually rather hungry, is there anything to eat?' asked Dawn now yawning.

'Yes of course, Libby my cook, left some food in the kitchen, please let me show you.'

Dawn dutifully followed Kathryn down to the kitchens. 'It is an amazing kitchen, enormous,' said Dawn looking about her in awe.

'Well if you could imagine, there were at least twenty to thirty staff working down here and abouts at one time. I worked here when I was your age, I am sure your mother has told you.' As soon as she had said it, Kathryn regretted mentioning it because she could see a sneer on Dawn's face. Her nose seemed to tilt a little higher and then she smiled haughtily at Kathryn.

'Yes I know, and I do not suppose you come down here much now?' she asked politely.

'Not really,' replied Kathryn, looking around the kitchen, which now needed updating. How she remembered dear old Mrs Potts showing her around, twenty years ago, for the first time. 'How time flies, Dawn,' said Kathryn still reminiscing the old days.

'That is what Mother always says too.' Dawn looked curiously at Kathryn. Sitting down around the kitchen table sipping tea, after Dawn had eaten small mouthfuls of cold meats and vegetables, Kathryn approached the subject of horses.

'I do hope we can pick your brains about horse breeding. Sebastien tells me you are so knowledgeable,' she said looking at Dawn's pretty face.

'Oh, it is all quite straightforward and Father was perhaps hoping he could send a few horses over from our ranch in Texas and breed with the Dallington horses,' said Dawn, momentarily looking serious.

'Do you think that would be possible?' asked Kathryn, thinking how exciting that could be.

'Father also mentioned that the cottages are still ours, is that correct? I was hoping to stay there,' said Dawn.

'You know, I had quite forgotten,' said Kathryn paling. She did remember that Devlin had mentioned when the Fitchs sold Dallington Place to him, one of the cottages would still allowed to be used by the Fitchs or Dawn in particular. But owning it, she was not so sure, she would have to check.

'The cottages are being used for the time being I am afraid,' said Kathryn watching a crinkle in Dawn's brow appear.

'But Daddy said,' said Dawn almost making a wailing sound.

'Well, Dawn, we will have to see, I cannot just throw Dawson and Mr Montgomery out of the cottages,' said Kathryn trying to keep her temper.

'Oh I see, perhaps we can come to some arrangement?' asked Dawn. She had been really looking forward to staying in her own house.

'Well Dawn, I was going to invite you to lunch in the village tomorrow, to show you around, we can talk then. I really do need an early night I am afraid,' said Kathryn rather sternly as she stood up and smoothed down her skirt.

Dawn put down her tea cup, yawned and got up to follow Kathryn to her bedroom.

Kathryn sighed, as she reached for Bertram's fifth letter.

24th October 1928

Dear Kathryn,

I feel I am not adjusting to life here. Sometimes I want to be left alone and Jorie is always socialising with everyone. If it is not Father Michael and Parson George Elsby, working their way around the men at the ranch, blessing everyone even the horses and other animals. I feel I should be on my best behaviour, and most of the time I am not. Even Father Michael has taken me aside to ask if I was being a good husband to Jorie. Maybe the doctor had mentioned something to him, but they all seemed to know our business. The Stedfords were in trouble only last week when eight of their farm labourers went missing and two were caught fighting. One had been tarred and feathered and is now hospitalised. Father Michael was around here again yesterday, asking if I minded some of our workers, Roger or the others lending a hand on the Stedford's ranch. I cannot understand it really, it is not like they could not afford to employ some temporary workers, but Jorie says it is neighbourly. I cannot help but feel it would be more neighbourly if I could fly again. I shrugged, I have lost interest in the ranch. It's Jorie that loves running it, not me. At least Sebastien enjoys it here. Her sister is arriving tomorrow and I must admit I am looking forward to seeing her again.

Kathryn put down the letter for a moment and removed her spectacles. Rubbing her eyes, she laid back firmly on the four pillows she loved to have to support her comfortably so she could read in bed. It was Kathryn's one luxury she could not do without now. All those years sleeping in a little truckle bed in the servants' quarters were far removed from the huge bed with sumptuous cushions she had now. For the first time, she somehow related to Bertram. His feelings of loss and responsibility weighing on his shoulders. Jorie wanting to lean on him for support but it was something he could not give. Now Kathryn had responsibility of Dallington Place and at times she had felt the burden without Devlin to lean on, more so recently. She could read from his scribblings of poetry verses that he was in a dark place.

Bitter sweet the pill we have to swallow, the saccharine view from my shuttered room, he had written. He was feeling trapped and she felt sorry for him. By his accounts he wanted to be free, up in the clouds flying in his biplane, but people depended on him on the ground. So he was grounded. Had he felt trapped while engaged to her, she wondered. Kathryn thought of Alexander. Devlin never felt trapped, he was happy to be with her. Kathryn's eyes were now shutting. Her thoughts drifted to her happy marriage with Devlin and then another thought popped into her head. What was that business with Mr and Mrs Turoc? She would find out tomorrow.

Sun was streaming in through the windows. She could hear an automobile's engine on the driveway. It was Ernest, he had arrived home early. Kathryn looked at the ornate china clock on her bureau. Ten o'clock? She could not believe it! She rushed to the window and promptly opened it. It was boiling hot outside and the heat warmed her face. Smiling and waving, she tried to catch Ernest's attention. She heard a female voice and saw Dawn approach the automobile. Kathryn stopped waving to watch. Next minute Dawn was climbing into the seat next to Ernest and they were off down the drive again, past the fountain, disappearing in a mist of heat and gravel. Kathryn sighed annoyed Ernest had not come in to say hello. Just as she was lowering the window, she heard more footsteps on the drive. It was Sebastien. She grabbed her dressing gown and ran down the main staircase to the hallway. It was Dawson's day off today, she remembered, she went to open the front door herself.

'I have just come to see Dawn, but was that her leaving in the automobile?' asked Sebastien his face flushed from the heat wave that had suddenly descended on them after weeks of rain.

'Yes it was, and Ernest. Would you mind driving me into the village, maybe we can catch up with them and have lunch?' asked Kathryn now self-conscious she was not dressed. Her hair still fastened in clips at the side of her head, to keep her marcel wave in place. Sebastien was staring at her and she was suddenly aware she must look a mess. A smile spread over his lips.

'What are you smiling at?' she asked feeling cross and pulling her robe over around her neck. Sebastien moved closer to her and Kathryn flinched as he pulled a feather out of her hair. 'See only a feather, that is all,' he said almost laughing. Kathryn smiled back.

She could not help but like this young and handsome man, his charm undeniably obvious, his dark looks exotic yet intriguing. Kathryn's attitude softened towards him. 'There's breakfast downstairs, give me half an hour and we will set off,' she said now running upstairs.

Sebastien ran down the backstairs only to bump straight into Libby. 'Master Sebastien, you gave me quite the fright,' she said blushing and rushed over to the stove with her back to him, trying not to look him in the eye. 'There is toast, some eggs and bacon still in the oven.' Sebastien sat down below the stairs and ate his breakfast. He was the only one to do so. Everyone else would not have dreamt to have eaten there but to Sebastien, it felt like home, from when his mother would cook by the table in their little cottage in Mesves-sur-Loire. His mother would nervously stand by the windows waiting for Alphonse to come home or to keep an eye out for Bertram in case he was coming for a visit. She was a good cook as Alphonse demanded a high standard. 'I provide the money,' he would say, 'Berenice, the least you can do is to cook me a proper meal!' Berenice had taken a pride in her cooking just like Jorie did when she could. Sebastien had learnt a lot but still wanted to learn more.

'Libby, can you give me some cooking lessons?' he asked, biting into some bread covered with sticky marmalade.

'Of course master Sebastien,' she said turning around and wiping her hands on her apron. 'I think your cooking is fantastic. All those American dishes you cooked for us at the party,' Libby continued with a shy smile.

'I know, but I want to learn more, and some of the basics again. Some I have forgotten,' he said, taking a bite of crunchy bacon.

'Sebastien are you ready?' called out Kathryn from the door, she had been eavesdropping on their conversation. Reaching for the pot of coffee, Kathryn eyed him suspiciously.

'Ready, let us go, see you Libby!' he said holding the keys and running outside to start the automobile. It had stalled in the heat this morning and as Kathryn climbed in next to him, he nervously started it but it stalled again.

'Do you want me to fetch Dawson? I can see him pottering about in the garden,' she asked him, seeing him begin to sweat. The car started again and they were off. A slight breeze had picked up and the cool air calmed them down.

'Where do you think they would be?' asked Sebastien turning right out to the main road from the driveway of Dallington Place. 'Well it is nearly eleven o'clock. Maybe they will be having lunch soon, probably at Drummond's I would think. Let us try there, we could at least have a drink ourselves,' said Kathryn as she studied Sebastien's face. She could still see the young boy's features in his face from all those years ago but he was so very handsome now. His strong jaw well defined and dimples appeared in his cheeks when he smiled. 'You know Kathryn, it is nice to have some time alone with you,' he said taking his eye off the quiet country road for a moment and looking at the pretty lady beside him. Her green dress with white polka dots suited her so well. 'You should wear green more often, it suits you,' he said with a cheeky grin, sounding more French than American for a moment.

'You know Sebastien, you are an incorrigible charmer, you have all the women in Sussex in love with you!' laughed Kathryn, enjoying the flattery.

'I know, but what can I do?' he said chuckling, pretending not to know it.

'And how are you and Carlyon getting on, may I ask?' she asked primly with her white gloved hands resting neatly on her lap.

'Carlyon?' asked Sebastien. 'Why no, there is nothing between us, I have my sights on someone else!' he replied with a mischievous smile.

'You do? I hope it is not Roberta, she is promised to Ernest, do not forget,' she gave him a curious look, wondering who this woman of his affections were.

'Know one thing about me Kathryn, and that is I do not tread on anybody's toes!' he declared proudly.

'Well Sebastien, that may be true but you seem to flirt with everyone!' she laughed.

'I am French, what do you expect?' he said looking teasingly at Kathryn.

'Well, just remember not to tread on my Ernest's toes?' she continued, hoping that the two young men would not be getting into a wrangle over a woman.

'I have yours and Ernest's back do not forget that Kathryn,' said Sebastien, feeling proud to be part of the family.

Startled by his firm and comforting words, Kathryn dropped the subject. 'It is nice to be honest with you and get to know you a little more,' said Kathryn, briefly touching Sebastien's arm, as they pulled into the allotted parking space of Drummonds restaurant.

'I would like to think I could be honest with you Kathryn, and there is something I want to discuss with you,' he looked at her suddenly serious.

'Really?' Kathryn turned to look at Sebastien with interest. 'Yes I was waiting for Alexander to get back, but well, please do not think that I am not interested to manage the racetrack, I am, but I have also other interests,' he said now looking Kathryn directly in the eye and slipping off his driving gloves.

They entered the restaurant and found a table near a window. 'What Sebastien, do not tell me you have changed your mind, only after six months into this project?' asked Kathryn, shocked to hear this coming from Sebastien.

'No, no, it is just that in my spare time I want to study fine dining and perhaps once the racing and breeding business is underway after the first few years, you will let me run the restaurant side of things,' he said, cautiously looking at Kathryn for her reaction.

'I think it would be a fantastic idea, but if you were to oversee the catering side, would it give you enough time to manage the racecourse?' asked Kathryn.

'I do not know, Kathryn but it would be way into the future and meanwhile I can still study my cookery. It would only be a hobby to begin with,' he said.

'Should you not have told me this before, Sebastien?' said Kathryn, rather annoyed this was the first time for her to hear about such plans.

'I suppose I was not sure myself, but cooking for the family at Christmas brought back so many happy memories for me, and perhaps that is what I want to do in future,' said Sebastien again flashing his broad smile.

He evidently loves cooking, Kathryn thought. 'I can see that, you cooked so effortlessly Sebastien, and you clearly love it. Well, it is better we get things out in the open. You have given me something to think about,' said Kathryn smiling at him. 'As you know, I have been thinking of converting the cottages into restaurants but I have been led to believe that the Fitchs may still own them,' continued Kathryn. 'I was aware of this,' said Sebastien looking at Kathryn suddenly all serious.

'You were?' Kathryn looked surprised.

'Yes Dawn told me before I left Texas,' he continued, now regretting that he had mentioned it.

'I see,' Kathryn flinched.

'She said that her father still owned them and Devlin had the opportunity to buy Dallington Place on the condition that one of the cottages was still owned by the Fitch family. They wanted to keep them for Dawn,' he continued furtively.

'Well, Devlin did not discuss this with me, or perhaps I have forgotten, but we must find out for the sake of the business. Can you come up to the house this evening so we can go over some accounts? I wanted you to help me sort out another problem as well,' said Kathryn.

'Really, what is that?' Sebastien leaned back in his chair and looked at Kathryn with curiosity.

'It is just something I do not understand regarding some accounts from 1A Willow Tree Cottage. You have young eyes, I cannot find the reason why there have been some cheques issued to an old tenant,' said Kathryn, without wanting to reveal more.

'Of course I will. Do you want me to cook dinner tonight?' he asked, keen to impress Kathryn with his cooking skills and appease her.

'Thank you Sebastien, that would be marvellous. Oh and by the way, Dawn was not quite what I was expecting,' she gave Sebastien an amused look.

'Really?' said Sebastien, folding his arms across his chest and throwing his head back with laughter.

'It is just that she seems far too glamorous to be wanting to work hard in the stables or particularly interested in horses,' said Kathryn.

'Oh that is Dawn for you, she is all show but really, when she rides there is no one like her, you will see,' he said.

'That is them!' said Kathryn suddenly as she saw the young couple linking arms as they walked up to the steps of the restaurant. Kathryn knocked on the window and both Ernest and Dawn turned around startled. Ernest smiled the biggest smile at his mother when he realised it was her.

CHAPTER TWENTY-NINE
HOMECOMING OF ERNEST

21st JULY 1934

Kathryn had been completely overwhelmed with all her new duties and organising the new staff, so it had been a good choice to employ Irene to help her with the administration tasks. Although her main duties were to organise the new accounts of Dallington Races, Kathryn had asked her to locate some of Devlin's old files to check if there were any reference to the Turocs. Irene was starting this task on Monday but Kathryn decided to ask Sebastien to help her that Saturday night. He promised to bring over some files still stored at 1A Willow Tree Cottage, on his way over to cook for the evening. Kathryn was relieved that Ernest was back, and as his last year of school had finished, it was time to celebrate. He would be starting at Oxford in October and maybe she would not see him so much.

Sebastien had arrived later than he promised and frustratingly for Kathryn, she knew she would have to wait until the next day to sit down with Sebastien to go through the accounts. As Kathryn had just come back from the stables to oversee the last of the horses turned in for the night into their stables, she bumped into Geoffrey Montgomery. 'Evening Mrs McAlister,' he said tipping his cap.

'Evening Mr Montgomery, everything in order I hope?'

'Everything is fine with the horses, Ma'am, I just wanted to say that I am very impressed with Miss Stedford's riding,' he continued.

'You are? I am surprised, I had not thought she had ridden yet, since she only arrived two days ago,' said Kathryn surprised.

'Yes Ma'am, up with the larks this morning, but I have to say I did not quite agree with the riding methods that she proposed, so maybe we will have to sit down and discuss this,' continued Mr Montgomery little uncomfortably. He did not want to mention that Miss Stedford had marched in and tried to boss them about that morning.

'I hope she was not rude Mr Montgomery, I do apologise,' Kathryn looked at Mr Montgomery rather embarrassed. She respected the old jockey and did not want to lose his expertise.

'No Ma'am, just forthright I suppose, but the thing is she has her ideas and I have mine,' he said looking pensive. 'Then again, I was very impressed she even rode bareback!' he continued.

'Bareback, Mr Montgomery?' asked Kathryn looking horrified as she had a vision of Dawn riding in inappropriate clothing. 'I suppose side saddle is out of fashion these days!' said Kathryn now confused by what he meant.

'Bareback Ma'am is the American word for riding without a saddle,' explained Mr Montgomery, rather surprised how little Mrs McAlister knew about horses. 'He could not help but smile at Mrs McAlister's misunderstanding of the new American words.

'Oh I see I am relieved, I think!' said Kathryn putting her hand against her chest for a moment. Goodness, I am learning so much about the equestrian world, she thought. 'Let us all meet on Monday, say during lunch, when everything is a little quieter, and I will talk to Dawn,' suggested Kathryn.

Mr Montgomery tipped his hat at Kathryn and locked the stable gate behind them.

Dawson and Sebastien were unpacking some groceries from the automobile later than planned and Kathryn was feeling the frustration that it was already six o'clock. The guests were arriving at eight. She had invited Geraldine and William and of course, Roberta, who was back from her modelling job at Hardy Amies in London. She had also invited Nora and her husband John the Mayor and the vicar Sanderson and his wife. Not only was it for a social call, but also she wanted to ask him if he had known the Turocs well.

'Sorry Kathryn, we discovered a leak in 1A Willow Tree Cottage in the basement. We had a lot of mopping up to do and Dawson here was a star!' said Sebastien looking sheepish. Dawson looked exhausted and seemed to be limping.

'Are you all right Dawson?' asked Kathryn as she took hold of his arm for him to stop unpacking the car. 'It is alright Dawson you can go, I have Dawn and Libby here to help me,' said Kathryn shooting Sebastien a disapproving look. 'Oh Dawson before you go, I just wanted to ask you, did you know the Turocs at all?' asked Kathryn, as she turned back to Dawson.

'Who Ma'am?' asked Dawson confused and out of breath.

'Mr and Mrs Turoc and perhaps their daughter. Their name keeps coming up in the accounts from about ten years ago,' said Kathryn, hoping that he would remember something.

Dawson looked flustered for a moment and Kathryn was unsure if he looked uncomfortable with the question or just could not remember the name. 'I do not recall that name but I will see if I can remember, ask me later Ma'am,' he said, taking his handkerchief and wiping his forehead.

'Not to worry, you go and rest,' she said taking a box of carrots and onions from Sebastien. I was hoping we could have had tea together and go over a few things like I mentioned before but never mind, we will do that tomorrow. Do you really think you will have everything ready by eight when the guests arrive?' She looked at Sebastien, doubting that he was organised for the dinner.

'Sure thing Kathryn, no sweat!' he quipped with that broad smile of his.

'No sweat? I really do not know what you say half the time,' she said, puzzled by all these strange American sayings but relieved that he was so confident about the dinner. 'How many for supper?' he asked, as he offloaded the shopping from the automobile.

'There will be you and I, Ernest and Roberta, the Lovets, the vicar and his wife, the honourable Nora and John Parker, and of course Dawn,' Kathryn went through the guest list out loud.

'Eleven then, perfect. I am doing a stew. I know it is rather warm outside but I think there is rain in the air,' he said cheerfully.

'Perhaps I should invite Mr Montgomery, so that will be twelve of us,' stated Kathryn, shutting the boot of the automobile.

'Shame Alexander is not with us,' said Sebastien, wanting to see Kathryn's reaction.

'I know Sebastien, still let us carry on, he said he will telephone later tonight. Perhaps you could have Dawn set the table with Libby in the main dining room tonight,' She turned back to Sebastien, ignoring his comment about Alexander. She wondered why Sebastien would say such a thing.

With only half an hour to spare, Kathryn pinned her hair up. Her marcel wave bob was growing fast. She needed another trip to London to have it done, she thought. Slipping on her loose-fitting blue and black lace dress, she applied some red lipstick. She did not need rouge on her cheeks as she had been outside a lot more than usual and she had some colour to her face. Ernest was taking a nap, so she was sure to wake him to be the first one down to greet Roberta. She had already been down once to the kitchens and everything was going smoothly.

Sebastien was already dressed and knocked at her door to tell her everything was prepared. She grabbed her stole and quietly trod down the corridor to Ernest's room. About to knock and enter, she stopped as she could hear voices inside. She stopped and the door opened abruptly with a giggling Roberta shocked at seeing Kathryn standing there. 'Sorry Auntie Kathryn, I hope you do not mind, Sebastien told me Ernest was up here. Mummy and Daddy are in the sitting room,' she said struggling to hold her giggles.

'Good to see you Roberta,' said Kathryn as she kissed her on both cheeks. The girl was looking radiant although a little ruffled and Ernest's face was as red as a beetroot. 'I did not hear anyone arrive. How long have you been here?' asked Kathryn, surprised that no one had told her.

'Oh we arrived about half an hour ago, but we have been looking at the new stables. Just adorable and the horses are beautiful. Kathryn, I must have Dawn show me how to ride well,' Roberta managed to say.

'Ernest, will you please escort Roberta downstairs? I just hope the vicar has not arrived yet,' said Kathryn looking shocked when Roberta told her they had arrived at the same time.

'Goodness, I hope everyone has a drink in their hands, I do hope Nora has not arrived yet. And Ernest, please give your mother a kiss, you seem to be avoiding me,' said Kathryn giving her son an amused look.

She had a feeling that Roberta had sneaked into his room a while ago already.

'Sorry Mamma, I have just been catching up with friends,' he said blushing. Kathryn noticed the sparkling ruby and pearl ring prettily sitting on Roberta's finger. Thank goodness she thought, at least she has a ring on her finger.

Kathryn greeted Vicar Sanderson and his wife warmly and apologised she was late coming downstairs.

'Not at all Kathryn, we can see how busy you are these days. We have just had a tour around, very impressive!' said the vicar.

Kathryn was keen to ask him a question so she lowered her voice. 'May I ask you something, Vicar, in strictest privacy?' she nearly whispered.

'Of course you may, but perhaps after church tomorrow?' said the vicar.

'Yes of course,' said Kathryn rather embarrassed, knowing that she had not attended her usual Sunday prayer at St Dunstan's for two weeks because of all the early starts with the horses. With Alexander gone, there was far too much to do.

Wine flowed and everyone toasted Ernest for his success at school. He spent most of the evening tucked up by the fire with Roberta, much to the happiness of Geraldine. 'I hope they will get to see much more of each other now. Maybe Roberta can visit him at Oxford?' said Geraldine now rather tipsy from the red wine. Leaning in to Kathryn she whispered, 'When do you think they will marry?'

Kathryn smiled at her dear friend's keenness to get the young couple married. 'Oh Geraldine, stop it, let them enjoy themselves first. If it happens we can have a wedding here maybe when Ernest finishes Oxford?' she suggested.

'How romantic would that be,' said Geraldine musing about the wedding dress. 'She is making quite a pretty penny modelling for Hardy Amis fashion house you know!' nodded Geraldine proudly.

'You do not have to sell her to me, I am already sold because I adore Roberta. It is good she has made a good start in her career. And you do not think my Ernest is a good catch here at Dallington Place?' said Kathryn nudging playfully at her friend.

'Well, that is always a bonus!' giggled Geraldine. 'I cannot believe we have all come this far. You the grand lady, I would never have believed that all those years ago when we met at the job interview to be factory girls,' Geraldine looked at her friend, her eyes suddenly misting up.

'You did not see my potential then?' Kathryn teased her.

'Well Mr Devlin McAlister did, did he not?' said Geraldine with a wink.

'I suppose he did,' retorted Kathryn. She must have had a worried expression on her face that Geraldine, knowing her so well, noted immediately.

'What is wrong, you look a little stressed?' asked Geraldine.

'Well apart from being overworked you mean?' replied Kathryn, skilfully avoiding Geraldine's question.

'No that is not it, when have you not worked hard Kathryn. What is it? Something is clearly bothering you,' Geraldine looked at her friend now worried.

'Please do not say anything to William, well just yet anyway, I do not want you two to have secrets. I was up in the middle of the night going over some of Devlin's accounts, and I can see that he had been writing cheques for large amounts of money to a couple called Turoc,' uttered Kathryn.

'No wonder you look tired,' said Geraldine, giving her friend a kiss on her cheek. 'I do not know anyone of that name, do you Kathryn?' she continued.

'Well, apparently they worked at the factory for years, or at least he did and apparently they had a daughter. So evidently my mind has been ticking over, I just hope he was not having an affair.' Geraldine looked taken aback.

'Devlin, having an affair, do not be ridiculous Kathryn, I can see why after Bertram you would think like that, but Devlin, no, no, he loved you too much,' she said firmly.

'I know, I know and I hate thinking like this but what other explanation could there be?' Kathryn looked at Geraldine in desperation.

'I do not know, do you know anything about the daughter?' asked Geraldine, finishing her glass of wine in one gulp.

'I remember one Christmas party, Mrs Turoc, I think it was her, rushing off as it was said that her daughter was in the hospital but that is all I can recall and there is money gone after that from what I can see from the dates,' continued Kathryn.

'Well there you go then, maybe Devlin was just helping them because their daughter was ill?' Geraldine tried to rationalise.

'Maybe, but Devlin would have said something to me. Apparently in the books it has the Turocs listed for 1A Willow Tree Cottage. As far as I know, no one lived there after we moved out. I know that the estate manager stayed there for few months, but that is all. It does not make sense, but I will ask the vicar at church tomorrow, he will know more about the Turocs than I do,' said Kathryn, wanting answers.

'It does sound a mystery,' agreed Geraldine, 'but I am sure there is a simple explanation.'

Kathryn smiled at Geraldine with a sense of relief. She was so grateful to share her problem with her friend. 'I hope so, and also there was someone called Peter, but I do not recall that name either amongst those who worked for Devlin,' remembered Kathryn.

'There was an old Mr Robinson, I think his name was Peter. Do you not remember, he was the church warden years ago,' reminded Geraldine, slightly swaying now.

'Yes I do remember. Perhaps Devlin had made a donation to the church, he did do things like that sometimes without telling me, he knew I would be happy about that,' replied Kathryn, trying to convince herself.

'There you are then, I am sure it is something to do with the church,' said Geraldine reassuringly.

'Oh perhaps you are right Geraldine. Thank you, it must be to do with that. Anyway, I will know from the vicar tomorrow,' said Kathryn.

'Darling, I think we should go,' said William putting his arms lovingly around his wife's waist.

'I will walk you out to the automobile,' said Kathryn, taking Geraldine by her hand to steady her. 'You are lucky to have William,' whispered Kathryn, as she supported her tipsy friend outside.

'And you Alexander!' said Geraldine, clasping Kathryn's hand even tighter.

'I know but he is not here,' said Kathryn feeling tearful.

'Come on, he will be back soon, and we will all be together again. William promised to take him flying.'

Kissing Geraldine goodbye, she asked, as William started the engine, 'Do you think it is a good idea that Sebastien looks over the books with me tomorrow, to see if he can solve the mystery of these payments?'

Geraldine suddenly sobered and looked at her friend firmly. 'Certainly not,' she said, as she put on her coat.

'Really, why?' asked Kathryn looking alarmed.

'I do like him, really I do, but there is something about him I do not trust!' Geraldine gave her friend a cautionary look.

'Really, Geraldine you never said anything before?' said Kathryn surprised.

Geraldine had never shown a dislike or distrust before for Sebastien. 'Do not take any notice of me and stop fretting, but I do not know, he just reminds me of Bertram. You know what I thought of him,' said Geraldine looking serious.

'He does?' asked Kathryn surprised.

'Can you not see it, not his looks, of course, but the character is very Bertram,' continued Geraldine, remembering to be cautious as she knew how fond Kathryn was becoming of Sebastien.

'Well, he was not his biological son of course,' said Kathryn, her brow creasing.

'Something of Bertram rubbed off on him for sure! An arrogance perhaps almost as if he is invincible,' stated Geraldine holding on to the automobile's door, noticing Kathryn's pensive look, as she clumsily sank down next to William.

'Geraldine, you do say the most extraordinary things,' said Kathryn looking at her friend fondly. They really have come a long way the two of them, she thought. 'That is because I am drunk darling. Stop fretting, I am always very proud of you, clever girl!' she leaned towards Kathryn slightly banging her head to the side of the window. They sped away leaving Kathryn standing alone feeling vulnerable.

She wrapped her shawl around her, the gravel crunching under her shoes as she stood staring into the darkness. 'Penny for them?' said a familiar voice. She swung around and there was Sebastien behind her taking a drag out of his cigar. He pushed his foppish dark hair out of his eyes with the other hand. 'I heard my name mentioned, were you talking about me?' he asked with a mischievous grin on his face.

'No Sebastien, no one was talking about you. Why are you sneaking up on me like that in the dark?' asked Kathryn looking him straight in the eye.

'I am not sneaking,' he replied indignantly, his eyes darkening to a thunderous expression. 'I just came to check that you were all right. You looked tired tonight. I came out to ask you if you had enjoyed my cooking and that you were having an enjoyable evening, that is all,' he said, suddenly looking a little shy.

'Oh I am sorry Sebastien, I have not thanked you yet, do forgive me. The food was delicious and you have been a great help,' she said gratefully.

'I will always forgive you Kathryn,' he said and with that he turned and walked back to the house.

The vicar and Kathryn sat in the vestry after the service had finished. There was thunder and lightning over the South Downs that seemed to have been continuing for hours. Rain was pelting the roof of the church and Kathryn was pleased to be inside. She hoped the horses were all in their stables. Mr Montgomery and Sebastien had been up early running around in their waxed jackets to bring the horses in after their first ride of the day. 'How can I help you Kathryn,' asked the vicar sipping a small glass of sherry.

'Do you recall a family named Turoc?' asked Kathryn nervously.

'Yes I remember the Turocs, both dead now I am afraid, but they did have a daughter. Petra I think her name was, but I never met her,' replied the vicar, taking off his spectacles and curiously looking at Kathryn.

'Petra?' repeated Kathryn now realising her mistake, perhaps Peter in the books was actually Petra. 'That is a German name is it not?' she asked.

'Yes, in fact Mrs Turoc, Francesca, had been married to a German man and lived in Munich before the war. She met Lionel Turoc when she was nursing in Germany, if I remember correctly. He was in the merchant navy. She was a widow and Lionel brought her and Petra back to England. Petra was a teenager at the time and then a few years later she worked for the Red Cross in France during the war. I remember her training at the local hospital before then, or so the Turocs explained. I did hear that she had been killed in France, very sad for the Turocs. They never really spoke of her much after that, and as I said, they both passed away quite a few years ago,' explained the vicar.

'How sad,' said Kathryn, but still not really understanding why they had 1A Willow Tree Cottage as their address.

'Do you know where they lived in the village at the time?' asked Kathryn, now knowing perhaps she was asking the poor vicar too many questions.

'No, but they moved to, let me think,' he paused putting his glasses back on. 'I think they moved to Throgmorton Street in London after the war, that is it,' remembered the vicar.

'London? Could they have afforded that?' asked Kathryn surprised.

'Apparently Lionel came into some money, a rich relative had passed away and they moved to a rather comfortable house in the city of London,' he continued. Kathryn's cheeks started to burn. Rich relative, could this have been Devlin, she wondered.

Walking back in the drizzle, Kathryn could not help but worry. She could not understand why Devlin had not confided in her. She tried to brush away any concerns, she had a busy week ahead.

The new students were arriving for their six-week riding course later in the day and she had to work with Libby this afternoon to make up beds and to arrange extra food to be collected. She knew it was Sebastien's day off, but she needed extra help. Ernest was helping with mucking out the stables with Roberta. Walking passed Willow Tree Cottage, Kathryn could see Sebastien in the front garden sitting in a deck chair drinking a beer.

The skies had cleared now, and the sun was beginning to shine. Sebastien put down his newspaper when he saw her. 'Morning Sebastien,' she called out as she walked up the front path. 'Thank you so much for your help yesterday, I loved the food!'

Sebastien had now stood up and walked towards her. 'You are welcome, would you like something to drink?' he offered.

'No thank you, I am racing to get back to call Alexander and then to get cracking on the preparation for the new arrivals,' she said hurriedly.

'I was just reading one of Alexander's articles, in *New York Correspondent*. Look here!' Sebastien handed her the newspaper.

'Really, show me,' said Kathryn excitedly reading Alexander's article, an obituary for Marie Curie, the famous Polish physicist. Kathryn remembered Geraldine telling her about the mobile X-ray units that Marie Curie had set up during the Great War. She felt a swell of pride and could not wait for him to be home again. She and Sebastien walked back to Dallington Place, talking over the day's plans. Once the new girls had settled in, Kathryn asked Sebastien and Dawn to show them around the stables and then they would have a late supper together.

CHAPTER THIRTY
ALEXANDER: NEW YORK

30th July 1934

My dearest girl,
I know we only spoke last week but I feel I should put pen to paper. As I write, I am sitting in my apartment at the 1ˢᵗ Avenue in Upper East Side by the large bay windows. It is a beautiful sunny morning with clear blue skies. The Empire State Building is to my right and I can see right across the East River. I am sure the workers are already busy constructing the Triborough Bridge[4], that will finally connect the three loose ends: Manhattan, Queens and the Bronx. I have a rather exciting meeting next week to interview Robert Moses, the New York city planner known as the "master builder", a key figure in urban planning here in New York. He is also the mastermind behind the Triborough Bridge. He has even been compared to Baron Georges-Eugène Haussmann, who you might have heard of in Paris.

I have been extremely busy here in New York, and now I have given my notice to the newspaper in Paris, I will be leaving New York at the end of August to hand over my post in Paris to Charles Devilliars, a young and assertive journalist. It is good to let the young blood in and oldies like me out. Of course I will keep a hand in with New York, but stepping down I can probably get away with only being there three, four times a year. I am finally thinking of selling my apartment. I have been up most of the night thinking the pros and cons of selling it, but I have already had some interest so this maybe the best option. It would delay my return by a couple of weeks, but to soften this blow I thought perhaps we could have a couple of days in France in September? We could combine work with pleasure. It would get you away from all that building work at Dallington Place. It will be a surprise though, so no further details. I am sure you can hand over the reins (so to speak) to the youngsters and have a few days off. You must rest when you can, as I see how busy you are. When the new

---

[4] Triborough Bridge, now called the Robert F. Kennedy Bridge, opened in 1936.

students have gone then maybe you can put your feet up , just for a quick jaunt!

There has been a lot to report and I am receiving constant updates from Paris about some unrest and bad feeling about Adolf Hitler becoming the commander-in-chief of Germany.

I cannot believe I will be moving to England for good, considering I have lived most of my life in the Americas! I have even reflected on the fact that I could scoop you up and bring you back here for good. You would love New York with its fashionable ladies, restaurants and theatres on Broadway. I feel the Americas is safer than Europe at the moment, but it is just fear and nothing unfounded. And I do look forward to living permanently at Dallington Place, what man would not?

The heat here is unbearable! I miss the English rain, the beauty of the English countryside and your wonderful company.

Write soon, I will be back before you know it.

PS. Did you ask Dawn about her ownership of the cottages?

Your dearest,

Alexander

Kathryn folded his letter and placed it in the small side drawer of her bureau. She had just picked up her pen to write back to him, when there was a quiet knock on the door. It was Libby, announcing that lunch would be served in the main dining room. Kathryn had refused to have the bell rung, except for emergencies. She did not like to ring on anyone. Two of the students were already mingling with the family, clutching a glass of sherry. Sebastien was holding court, his arms gesturing around him, talking about his adventures in Texas. A young girl called Sabrina was listening attentively to his every word, her pretty head cocked to one side and nodding at the same time. Dawn was in conversation with Mr Montgomery and Ernest was standing with his arm resting on the fireplace locking eyes with Roberta, who had stayed over last night. Kathryn greeted everyone warmly and they followed her to the laden table ready for their Sunday roast. 'Sebastien, could you show the ladies to their seats please?' asked Kathryn, hoping that Ernest could sit in between them and keep them at bay from Sebastien's charms.

Sabrina was the youngest, only seventeen, from a rich banking family. She hoped to go into nursing, although her family were not very happy about it. They would have rather she meet a rich husband

and live the life of a country lady. 'Sabrina, Sebastien tells me you would like to go into nursing eventually?' asked Kathryn fixing her eyes at the pretty youngster.

'Yes Ma'am, I would like that very much, I am going to tour the local hospital sometime next week, to see if there are any courses starting in September,' said Sabrina shyly.

'You know Roberta's mother and I were in the First Aid Nursing Yeomanry in France during the war,' said Kathryn.

'It must have been a very exciting time for you, how brave you must have been,' said Sabrina full of admiration.

'Looking back, I suppose it was an exciting and worthwhile adventure but it was hard work, sometimes sad and depressing, other times exhilarating with a great sense of purpose,' explained Kathryn.

'That is what I want, a sense of purpose!' replied Sabrina, her eyes lighting up and beaming at Kathryn.

'Why would you want a sense of purpose?' questioned Dawn, now yawning.

'Because it makes life worthwhile, takes you out of yourself!' replied Sebastien, looking at Dawn in annoyance. She really is spoiled and shallow, he thought.

'Well said!' said Ernest.

'Well, all I know is you are born, you live, have as much fun as you can, and then you die!' said Dawn taking a mouthful of Yorkshire pudding, oblivious to the mockery.

'There is more to life than that Dawn,' said Mr Montgomery, hoping he had not spoken out of turn.

Dawn just shrugged and Kathryn turned to Mabel, the other student, more studious looking than Sabrina with thick tortoiseshell rimmed glasses. 'And Mabel, what would you like to do with the skills you will be learning here?'

'Actually, Mrs McAlister, I love all animals, so to work with them would be marvellous, but I also enjoy cooking,' she answered timidly.

Sebastien's ears pricked up. 'I can give you some cookery lessons if you like?' he suggested to Mabel.

'Perhaps Sebastien another time, the girls must have their riding lessons. Mr Montgomery, what is on the agenda for tomorrow?' asked Kathryn. 'Well, we will show the girls around the grounds in the morning, and then perhaps Dawn you could show the girls your skills in bareback riding and side saddle early afternoon?' he replied.

'I would love to and perhaps we can take a couple of the horses out for a little trek, Mr Montgomery?' she replied delighted.

'Absolutely Dawn, I will accompany you and the girls. We can take Blue, Jackie and Toby, the little piebald. I will ride Sybil and you could get on Reggie.

'All the same to me, Mr Montgomery!' said Dawn looking exhausted all of a sudden.

'Dawn, did you sleep well last night, was it too hot in the attic for you girls?' asked Kathryn, noticing that Dawn was looking tired.

'No, perfect thank you,' she replied, trying to smile as she listened, rather bored, at the family's happy banter.

'I hope the bees nest under the eaves is not causing you too much trouble, I must remind Dawson to look into it tomorrow,' said Kathryn. 'Well welcome to you all,' Kathryn announced standing at end of the table. 'Here is to Ernest, well done for finishing your time at school with aplomb and welcome to the new students, Mabel and Sabrina. I fear Josephine has been tired out already but we will welcome her soon. Good luck to all the tutors and instructors,' said Kathryn raising a glass to Dawn. 'Welcome Dawn, we are pleased to have our American friends over, please make yourself at home.' Dawn managed a little smile.

'Here, here,' toasted Sebastien drinking his wine very fast.

'Here is to Roberta, thank you for joining us this week before you venture back to London, have a wonderful summer to everyone!' Kathryn raised her glass again.

The following day, Kathryn caught Roberta's arm as they went for a walk in the late afternoon sunshine. 'Roberta, I hope you do not mind but I would like to accompany you back to London tomorrow morning. I have some business to attend to, maybe Ernest would like to come too,' she suggested, admiring Roberta's fashionable cream silk blouse that complimented her red hair. Kathryn felt self-conscious of her hair frizzing in the humid heat.

'I would love that Auntie Kathryn, I always feel lonely on my way back from Dallington Place,' said Roberta looking delighted.

'Good, good. Would nine o'clock be good for you? I will have Dawson drive us all to the station,' asked Kathryn, linking arms with her as they walked along.

'That would be perfect, I have a fitting at two o'clock so as long as I am in London by lunchtime,' said Roberta feeling relaxed in the company of Kathryn.

Mr Montgomery had left to check the horses with the students. Sebastien and Ernest had already managed to bring the croquet set out and were beginning to spread out the hoops on the lawn near the lime trees. Kathryn and Roberta walked passed them towards the wooden bench in the cool shade of the oak tree.

'You know,' started Kathryn, 'you must explain what you do with your modelling. I hear from Ernest that you make rather good money?' She could feel the coolness of the timber as she sat down on the bench.

'Well, it is not as glamorous as it sounds, but I am paid more than a shop girl or a clerk. I work for two English designers, Hardy Amies and Norman Hartnell. Most days we are being pinned into sample designs or trying them on to check that they have the right measurements. Pretty simple really. Last week at Norman Hartnell's new atelier in a mews house in Bruton Mews, I was standing in while an evening dress was being made for Elizabeth Taylor. Hartnell used to show his couture in Paris and Coco Chanel was a regular guest. I have one fashion show lined up for Madeleine Vionnet fashion house in Paris in the autumn,' explained Roberta excitedly.

'Oh, how lovely! I would love to see that,' said Kathryn putting her arm around Roberta. She was impressed that her goddaughter seemed to have made a great profession for herself.

'Well, if it is a definite assignment, I will see what I can do. Perhaps I can get you an invitation, but I cannot promise you anything yet,' said Roberta hugging her godmother.

'Goodness, do not go to any trouble on my behalf! But I would love to go,' replied Kathryn, imagining herself at the Vionnet show sitting next to the Parisian fashion crowd. She could also see herself having tea in The Salon de Thé at the Ritz designed by Coco Chanel.

'I am so happy for you and Ernest you know,' she continued. Roberta just smiled back at Kathryn. 'Shall we?' said Kathryn. The ladies got up to approach the croquet game that was in full swing. Dawn and some of the students now joining in after an afternoon of riding.

She checked the piece of paper again, the address she had been given was twenty-five Throgmorton street. Kathryn had taken a taxi from the Victoria station. She was standing outside where she felt the house should have been. Irritated it was beginning to rain. As she doubled back, she caught sight of a cobbled mews leading to a large, imposing, grey stone house. She balanced over the slippery cobbles and walked up the attractive black and white chequered steps. She was relieved when she saw the number twenty-five written in black ink on one of the stone pillars aside the large front door. She rang the doorbell. She waited a few minutes. No one answered. Giving up, she turned around to walk down the steps, she bumped into a lady running up the steps. 'I am terribly sorry,' said Kathryn looking into the lady's eyes. She was a similar age to Kathryn, about thirty-three or four but she looked tired and her hair was salt and pepper grey.

'If you are looking for Mrs Maine, she works at number thirty-nine,' said the woman in a rushed tone, clearly not in the mood for strangers at her door.

'I was looking for a Miss Petra Turoc, my name is Kathryn McAlister.'

The woman registered the name and stopped looking for her front door keys. She looked as if she recognised the name, it was written all over her face. Her lips pursed. 'What business would you be wanting with Miss Turoc?' she replied tartly.

'Oh, excuse me, I thought perhaps you were her, I do apologise,' said Kathryn, feeling foolish that perhaps she had come to the wrong door.

'I am Petra Turoc,' the woman's voice now softening, 'perhaps you had better come in, I know who you are,' she said turning the key. 'Please sit in there, I will fetch us a cup of tea.' She pointed to a sitting room on the left, the door wide open revealing a small waiting room, with blue papered walls covered by large tapestries. Two large armchairs facing each other, covered in scatter cushions of green and red silk, she beckoned Kathryn to sit down.

Eventually Petra walked back into the room carrying a large tray, which she placed on the narrow mahogany table between the two chairs. 'Sugar?' she asked, busying herself with pouring teas and not looking up at Kathryn.

'Yes please,' replied Kathryn watching this petite woman carefully take the sugar cubes and placing them daintily into the cups.

'Let us have the fire going, it's rather chilly in here,' she said now picking up the fireplace poker and stoking the ashes.

'I knew you would come one day, it was just a matter of time,' said Petra finally, after she got the fire started.

'Really?' asked Kathryn surprised. She instantly liked this woman, who seemed kinder and less abrupt than the woman who she had met on the steps outside. She had taken her hair down, her pins were neatly placed on the mantelpiece. Her extraordinarily long hair was now down her back in a long plait. She sat down and shook her hair out to let it loose. Kathryn watched mesmerised. Her clothes were unusual too. She was wearing a lime green silk scarf knotted tightly around her neck. The colour set off her bright turquoise eyes. She had taken off her tiny, thinly framed spectacles that made her seem matronly at first. Her long skirt revealed velvet, emerald green shoes, which she had changed into on entering the house. She was far from ordinary looking. She hoped there had been nothing romantic between her and Devlin. A stab of jealousy went through her as if she was looking at Berenice again. She sipped her tea and waited for Petra to sit down opposite her again. She was nervously biting the inside of her cheek but she stopped when Petra sat down.

Petra looking her squarely in the face, asked: 'How much do you want?' Kathryn nearly choked on her Earl Grey tea, spilling some of it on the saucer.

'Want?' Kathryn looked astounded, placing her cup and saucer down on the table as quietly as she could.

'The money. I presume Mr McAlister has sent you to redeem all the money my father squandered out of him,' said Petra now leaning comfortably back into the cushions. 'Now that my father is dead and cannot blackmail him anymore.' Kathryn could not believe what she was hearing.

'Blackmail, squandered? Oh dear, you really have me at a disadvantage!' said Kathryn her eyes filling with tears. The shock of what she was hearing was too much.

'Sorry, am I not making myself clear? You are Kathryn McAlister of Dallington Place, Mr Devlin McAlister's wife?' asked Petra now looking irritated.

Passing Kathryn a tissue from the box balanced on the edge of the table, she sat back firmly in the chair and waited for Kathryn to dry her eyes before she spoke again. 'Yes, Devlin was my husband,' said Kathryn, as she thankfully took a tissue and dabbed her eyes.

'Was? Oh my dear, I am terribly sorry I did not know he had passed away,' said Petra genuinely sorry. 'He was such a good man your husband.' Petra got up and pulled the long thick rope that was hanging by the door. 'Now let me see if Mrs Maine has returned, she may be able to fix us something stronger.'

A few moments later, an older plump lady entered into the room carrying another tray with a glass decanter, some scones and jam.

'Here you are dears,' she said in a motherly tone, trying not to notice that Kathryn was desperately trying to hold back her tears.

'Thank you Pearl,' said Petra, waiting for the woman to shut the door before she spoke again. 'Here, take this glass,' she said passing the whisky to Kathryn.

Kathryn took it gratefully feeling more composed. 'I am so sorry, I do not know what came over me. I think it was mainly the relief to hear that Devlin was not having an …. affair' Kathryn finally managed to say.

'With me, surely not? That would be impossible, men I am afraid are not my cup of tea! Also I have seen how they think on occasion. I am a psychoanalyst you see, no not my cup of tea at all,' she said now winking at Kathryn and passed her a plate with a scone and jam.

Kathryn sighed in relief, she could not help but smile back. 'You are a doctor?' she asked.

'Yes, a psychoanalyst now. I see many patients here in this room. Many I treat from the war, you know, soldiers with shell shock and patients with bad memories from the war. Women too,' replied Petra sipping her whisky.

Kathryn leaned back in the armchair and started to relax. 'I can see that you have a nice way about you,' she said, feeling her worries wash away with the effect of the whisky.

'Thank you, would you like another shot of whisky?' asked Petra, reaching for a decanter.

'No, thank you, you are kind but I just wanted to understand what had been going on. You see, I found your name in my husband's papers and cheques written to your family and the address of 1A Willow Tree Cottage being used,' said Kathryn calmly.

Petra poured another whisky for herself and got up to stoke the fire again. As she reached for a woollen wrap hanging over a back of a chair near the fire, Petra began the story.

'My parents lived in Munich in Germany together before the war. Father being English, never really enjoyed it but to appease my mother who was German, he agreed to live there a few more years until I was thirteen. One day he announced that we would be moving back to England, he had found employment in a factory in Sussex. We moved swiftly, hardly saying goodbye to anyone. Lionel was not my real father but my stepfather, however I loved him all the same… until one day he began to behave oddly. You know, forgetting things, being late for work and losing his temper. Nothing was said for a while and then

258

my parents had a quarrel about something and he hit my mother badly and she subsequently ended up in the hospital. I could not forgive him for that and our relationship was strained from then on.

I decided that I wanted to become a nurse and trained at the hospital. When the war began, I worked for the Red Cross and then travelled to France. I was away for three years and for some reason my father had spread rumours that I was missing presumed dead and later that I had been found in Germany. There was gossip that I had been a spy. My mother later told me that there were whispers that I was really working for the German army and had been shot by the French. Appalling I know and quite shocking, it was almost as if my father wanted me dead. When I eventually returned home, he was so shocked, he wanted me arrested, but my mother told him she would leave him if he did. He wanted nothing to do with me and I had nowhere to go. People from the village, who had thought they recognised me, were hostile towards me and apparently someone reported me to the police that night. So in a terrible state, my mother went over to Dallington Place to seek help from your husband. There was a party going on and she was invited in. Everyone was having the most marvellous time and there was my mother in such a state. Anyhow, my father had followed my mother to Dallington Place and also went to see your husband. My mother begged Mr McAlister to let me use one of the cottages until things had died down and my father had come to his senses.'

Petra took a sip of her whisky and Kathryn had a chance to say something. 'I think I remember your father and mother at the party,' she said intrigued, remembering back to that Christmas party.

Petra nodded. 'So I stayed at 1A Willow Tree Cottage for three months more or less out of sight, but my father had taken to blackmailing Mr McAlister, by saying he would let the authorities know he was hiding a German spy. Your husband gave my father money just to stop him harassing my mother and I. But it made it worse, as the more money he gave to my father, the more entrenched he became in this drama. And then one morning Mr McAlister came to the cottage and told me that the only way to stop my father from blackmailing was to have us all move to London, to leave Sussex and the trouble. After that father was just happy to have a large house in London bought for him by Mr McAlister and he never caused any trouble again.

People thought I had died in the war and my grief stricken parents had moved to London to stay with relatives.'

Kathryn had never anticipated the story about the payments to be so complicated. 'But why did he not say anything to me, Devlin I mean?' asked Kathryn looking at Petra. Her poor Devlin, she thought.

'He was probably trying to protect you. If he had been accused of any war crimes, then it would have reverberated on to you. You both could have been charged with espionage,' explained Petra.

'I can see that, he was always the protector of me but war crimes, my Devlin?' replied Kathryn in horror.

'Well, they were uncertain times and such things did happen, you know,' said Petra sympathetically.

Kathryn nodded, she understood how people could get the wrong idea, especially when Devlin was richer than most.

'Father went downhill quite quickly after that. He would become disorientated and got lost often. My mother and I would be up in the night running up and down the streets calling out for him. We found him going through old rubbish bins once like a homeless person. He was suffering from dementia, we later discovered. He did not live much longer after that episode. My mother passed away soon after him. So eventually I trained as a doctor because I wanted to help people with mental health illnesses.' Petra looked momentarily sorrowful and cast her eyes to her glass.

Kathryn thought about Bertram and Robert for a moment, Petra could have helped these men.

'So the house, this house is really yours, the deeds are in Mr McAlister's and my name,' Petra continued.

'I had no idea and I certainly do not want to take it away from you, it is your home,' said Kathryn, hoping that Petra would not have thought that was the reason why she had come to see her.

'Well, you can have it back one day, your family I mean. I do not have any descendants or family, only friends,' said Petra.

'Well I did not come here to talk about the house. I just wanted to find out who you were and what you were to my husband. And now I know. I really must not keep you any longer than necessary, you have been very kind to see me,' said Kathryn smiling warmly back at Petra.

'Well, if you or your family need a place to stay when you are in London, there is no need for a hotel, I have eight bedrooms,' said Petra sincerely. She really liked Kathryn, how elegantly and kindly she had handled the news.

'Thank you and the same goes to you, come to Dallington Place anytime you like. We have a new riding school and soon there will be a racecourse too,' said Kathryn, as she stood up and put on her jacket.

'How marvellous, I cannot refuse then, but I hope no one will recognise me,' replied Petra momentarily worried.

'We will cross that bridge when we come to it, but please come stay once we are really on our feet,' said Kathryn as she kissed Petra on her cheek and they walked to the door.

It was still raining outside and Petra handed her an umbrella. 'I will return this to you when I see you next. I have your address, I will write to you,' said Kathryn, walking out into the wet and cold air.

CHAPTER THIRTY-ONE
BERTRAM: TORNADO TEXAS

SEPTEMBER 1934

The weather had turned in the last few weeks. Kathryn had had great difficulties heating Dallington Place. There had been storms, a major one in the last twenty-four hours. Two large oak trees had fallen down not far from the house. She and Ernest had been up during the night attending to the horses, which had been spooked by the lightning. Dawson had been helping more with the horses during the day, assisting Mr Montgomery, while Dawn and Sebastien had gone for a few days break to Deauville in France. Alexander would be back the following day and she wanted them to wait for his return. Sebastien had already arranged a business meeting with a major horse trainer there, who would come over to Dallington Place to advise them on the continuation of the design of the racecourse. She was not very pleased with them, but there was nothing she could do. She understood they were young and wanted their freedom. Poor Dawson was out of his depth, not really taking to the horses, but assisted Mr Montgomery where he could. By five o'clock the old man was exhausted and Kathryn had sent him off to rest. Luckily all the students and guests had left a week earlier at the end of August so she did not have to cater for them.

'Mamma, do you think there is more to Sebastien and Dawn's getaway?' asked Ernest as he filled buckets with water for the horses.

'Why do you ask?' asked Kathryn looking puzzled as she gave some fresh hay to the horses as they walked around the stables.

'I do not know, it just seemed awfully sudden, this great meeting in Deauville, and I heard Dawn asking him what she should wear,' said Ernest brushing Toby, the piebald.

'You think they are courting?' asked Kathryn, putting down the rake, her eyebrows raised. 'I think they are, there's something more between them,' replied Ernest. He had noticed the way they looked at each other, a few longing glances over the dinner table.

'Perhaps you are right, I have been busy this last month. I suppose I have been thinking about you two, your wedding to Roberta next spring,' she patted Ernest on his shoulder lovingly.

Kathryn was proud of her sensible and even tempered son and pleased he had chosen Roberta as his bride.

'When is Alexander arriving tomorrow?' asked Ernest as he moved on to Reggie in his box to brush him.

'Later in the evening I do believe,' said Kathryn. 'I am going to London tomorrow to do some shopping and have my hair cut, as I did not have the time to have it done last week. I want to look suitable for Deauville. Roberta will be leaving at the same time. Could you drive us to the station at noon please? I think we should give Dawson a rest,' said Kathryn.

'That is fine by me, I was thinking of going to London to meet Roberta for dinner anyway so I will leave earlier and come with you both. May we stay at Alexander's club?' asked Ernest locking the stable door.

'I have a better idea; you could stay with Petra Turoc in Throgmorton Street. She has given an open invitation to anyone in the family to stay. I am sure she would welcome the company,' suggested Kathryn.

'Should I telephone her then?' asked Ernest, wondering who this Petra Turoc was.

'I will, do not worry. It will be fine and the area is fascinating. It is bustling with bankers and businessmen. Have a look at Drapers' Hall, where the bankers have their meetings. It used to belong to Thomas Cromwell, Earl of Essex,' replied Kathryn. 'Please make sure you are back by Wednesday as Alexander and I are travelling to Deauville for this meeting on Friday that Sebastien has set up for us. Hopefully he will be back to cover for us,' said Kathryn.

'Will do Mamma, do not worry,' replied Ernest. He wanted to prove that he could be trusted to take charge.

'Any problems while we are away, ask Mr Montgomery who can ask the farm workers to help out in a crisis. I only hope this rain stops, all we need is some more flooding!' stated Kathryn. She had enough problems to deal with, without the weather.

That night in bed, Kathryn could not sleep. The wind was howling and the hail stones were pounding on the windows. She could hear a gate opening and slamming, but prayed it was the garage door, not the gate to the stables. She turned on the bedside lamp, put on her reading spectacles and reached for Bertram's sixth letter. He had called it

Tornado Texas 1929.

Dearest Kathryn,

Only twice since I have been in Texas, have I wanted to return home. Today is the second time. We have spent the day in the basement as a monster tornado has approached us fast and without warning. Pedro alerted us to the black fog that has descended on us, threatening our lives. He went out to check on the barn and said he would be back, but has been missing for four hours. We cannot move out and we cannot see out. We are crouching down almost below the earth, waiting for this hell to dispel and move on. But it does not. We hear screams above us, and now as I hold on to Jorie's hand, there is a sudden eerie nothingness. She is crying, rocking back and forth, Sebastien with his hands over his ears laying at our feet. No one is brave at this moment. This is the third and the worst tornado that has passed over us in the last month and now I fear our luck has run out. Jorie is crying for Pedro and I cannot comfort her. My arms do not comfort her anymore. There is a divide between us now. If it was me that was missing I doubt she would be crying for me.

We wonder how the animals are doing, me biting my fingernails, tearing at the flesh. If we lose livestock, our livelihood is lost. We have been fighting back all this year, and I was beginning to think we were going to make it. But I can hear the wind tearing down what we have built up. This has been my life, up to now, I fight, but it gets torn down. Where we are now reminds me of the hellish pits of the trenches. Not knowing if we will get out alive this time. I think back to Robert, my friend, who disappeared from my grasp, so quickly and brutally. I hope that Pedro returns to us, I cannot bear another loss for Jorie.

By the fifth hour, Sebastien's smoky and anguished face looks upon us. The wind has died down and we must have fallen asleep. I open the shattered door, to fear the worst. There are dead chickens scattered around, feathers and blood by my feet. The chicken barn has taken a direct hit, but miraculously the house is almost untouched but for a few tiles on the roof. The stables and cattle shed appear to have come off unscathed too. I thank what and whomever I can. Only Pedro is still missing. As I walk out to the stables, a man approaches, his face etched with terror I have seen before, years before in France. It took me a while to realise it was Pedro. He is alive but his face, ripped and torn, blood trickling down, his legs buckling beneath him. I catch him before he falls. He is safe and so now is Jorie.

Kathryn repeated what Bertram had written. *'I catch him before he falls.'* This was the old Bertram that she remembered, a man with decency. Not a coward, the selfish man she witnessed in France. Putting the letter down, she soon fell asleep, the best sleep she had had in a long time.

Ernest had let her sleep in. When she woke up she remembered it was Sunday, and rushed to get dressed for church. Her mood was light. Alexander would be arriving soon. He had been delayed by two days because of the storm. All will be well when he returns, she thought to herself. The storm had passed with no ill effects, but no sooner had she arrived back at the house, Dawson greeted her at the door with a solemn look and a telegram. Not since the war had there been telegrams received at Dallington Place. Her first thoughts ran to Alexander. His postings could be dangerous. Feeling sick, she held on to the door a little longer as she passed through into the sitting room. She looked out to the orange lilies, which had managed to survive the storm last night, and were bobbing in the late morning wind and sunshine as she ripped open the telegram. She had not noticed the hallmark of America. Please let it not be Alexander, she said under her breath.

2nd September 1934

Dear Kathryn, the Stedmans returning to England. Tornado hits ranch. Please expect us. We are all safe. Love to Dawn. Alison

CHAPTER THIRTY-TWO
KATHRYN: DEAUVILLE

SEPTEMBER 1934

Heston aerodrome in Middlesex looked to Kathryn a rather bleak place. Feeling safe with Alexander, she still could not brush the nervousness away. It was early in the morning and she and Alexander along with five other passengers waited in line for their seats. She thought of the stories Bertram had written to her about his flying endeavours, meeting Alexander and flights with Jacobson and Le Sierre. 'Le Touquet, here we come!' said Alexander elated, gripping Kathryn's hand. Kathryn turned around to watch the stewardess in her neat uniform with the initials BANCO stamped on a little brooch. Alexander had informed her it stood for British Air Navigation Company. A new company, which had started in May that year. Kathryn hoped they knew what they were doing. She gripped the arm rest with her other hand as the aeroplane took off along the runway and then rose fast into the skies above England.

'What time did Sebastien say they would be back at Dallington Place?' Kathryn asked Alexander trying to distract herself. As the B494 aeroplane soared sharply to the left and it juddered slightly, Kathryn took a sharp intake of breath.

'Sebastien said around dinner time. He would oversee the horses,' Alexander smiled comfortingly at her as he let Kathryn grip his arm tighter.

'Good, good, and what time is our meeting tomorrow?' she asked, still trying to catch her breath.

'I will telephone Sebastien for all the details later, but I do not think it is until the afternoon. I thought I would take you out for lunch to a surprise rendezvous,' said Alexander relaxing with his gin and tonic.

Kathryn was sipping hers. She did not normally drink very much but she needed some Dutch courage. 'Sounds wonderful, I am going to try to relax on this trip. I know this is for work but I need a break too,' she reminded Alexander, snuggling up to him.

The plane was rather cool and the dark skies outside did not help the temperature. They had been given a blanket and Kathryn wrapped it around her shoulders. She hoped Le Touquet and Deauville would still be warm, even though it was September.

Kathryn was not disappointed. As soon as the aeroplane doors opened, they could feel the heat of the morning sun beat down on the runway's tarmac. She immediately felt happy and relaxed as they stepped into a taxi to take them to their destination, the Normandy Barrière hotel. 'This is where Coco Chanel often stays,' said Alexander as they pulled up outside the imposing hotel.

White shutters adorned the windows and Kathryn full of energy and verve, ran up the white marble stairs that led through to the revolving doors. 'Do you think we will see her?' she asked wishfully, taking one of her small bags from the porter who seemed uncomfortable to allow her to carry her own luggage.

'Let him carry it Kathryn, you are here to relax!' demanded Alexander as he caught up with her.

'Tomorrow we must work Alexander, I want to set up the meeting as soon as possible!' she said, eager to meet the French racing experts.

'I know, and I have it all under control. You should be thinking about what you would like to do today. Would you like me to book you a massage?' asked Alexander as he wrapped his arm around her waist.

'That would be lovely but it can wait. I would rather enjoy the scenery and the good weather. Thank goodness we left the rain behind in England,' said Kathryn, marvelling the picturesque views. 'Shall we go to the beach?' she said straining her neck to see the promenade in the distance.

'Sounds lovely, we can take a stroll down the Planches by the La Plage Fleurie,' said Alexander pointing to a walkway to the beach to the left of the hotel. He knew the area well and had been to Deauville many times as a child.

They wasted no time unpacking and as Kathryn flipped through her appointment book, she wondered if Dawn had read the telegram from her mother to say they were coming back to Dallington Place. She had left Libby and Irene in charge of domestic arrangements at home. As she arranged her clothes into the wardrobe, she hoped she could forget about work, concentrate on Deauville and enjoy some relaxing time with Alexander.

He poked his head through the half opened bathroom door to check to see if she had finished unpacking. 'Where are we going tomorrow, darling?' she asked.

'That is a surprise!' he said with a wink.

'Shall I change into my new trouser suit or wait?' she asked excitingly.

'What about your bathing costume?' he answered.

'I do not know about that, I will see what everyone else is wearing.' She kept her pearls on loosely around her neck and changed into her light striped blue blouse and linen pants.

As they walked down the Planches, the wooden decking slightly bounced as they made their way to the seafront. Sitting on the last bench by the beach, they sat eating an ice cream observing everyone around them. Kathryn looked at the fashionable women as some walked past, Alexander tipping his hat at each and every one of them. Two older ladies nodded back to him, the hems of their skirt long and rather prim, their hesitations to move with the times. Three young girls ran past wearing the latest in bathing costumes, raising even Kathryn's eyebrows. She did not think these costumes would be welcome back on Brighton beach quite yet. Three very attractive and wealthy looking ladies walked passed hurriedly chatting away in French, Kathryn thought they looked like Vogue models. Their clean white blouses drawn in closely on the hip, where their fashionable trousers, wide and flapping in the wind, skimmed their ankles. They too were wearing pearls and red lipstick. Kathryn reached for her pearls intently. She hoped she looked sophisticated enough. Another girl with her beau walked arm in arm giggling and snuggling up to him. Kathryn noticed the pretty scarf in pink and blue silk she was wearing draped over her blouse. It was crossed over her chest and the end of the scarf tucked fashionably into the waistband of her silk trousers. 'I like her outfit Alexander,' said Kathryn nodding at the woman as she finished her ice cream.

'The scarf is probably Chanel, trés chic,' he said kissing her on the cheek.

'I must learn French,' said Kathryn, 'then I will know what is going on,' looking lovingly at Alexander.

'Absolument,' said Alexander jovially pulling her to her feet. 'Let us find some lunch here and then this afternoon maybe we could go shopping,' he suggested as he put his arm around her.

'How lovely, a man that loves to shop!' she said kissing him on his cheek.

Over a lovely lunch of lobster fricassee and a bottle of champagne, they were watching the sailing boats bobbing along on the horizon. Kathryn admired the fashionable Deauville set with impeccable style. Men were stylish too, in their white linen suits and trilbies puffing away their expensive cigars.

After lunch they walked along rue Jean Mermoz towards the shops. Looking in Coco Chanel's[5] window, Kathryn gasped at the sumptuous clothes. She pulled Alexander by the hand into the shop, like a little child in a sweet shop. Kathryn decided to look at the shoes first downstairs.

'I have a telephone call to make. Let us meet back in the hotel in an hour,' said Alexander suddenly disappearing. Kathryn did not mind, her eyes were agog with all the beautiful things around her.

'Open it!' demanded Alexander as she lay next to him fully clothed on the bed. She had fallen asleep, and it was now almost dinner time.

'Where have you been, have I been asleep for a long time?' asked Kathryn slightly disorientated.

'Two hours, and yes I went back to the shop,' he replied with a mischievous smile.

'Alexander you did not, all that way for me?' she said.

'Nothing is too much for you my dearest, for goodness sake open it!'

She sat up and opened the Chanel white and black box with a ribbon on it. Inside was the most beautiful blouse she had ever seen. In the palest pink silk organza with a pretty rose at the shoulder. She held the delicate garment against her. She thought for a moment how lucky she was, and perhaps she had never been this happy. Underneath the tissue there was a scarf. The same one the chic lady at the beach had been wearing that she so admired. 'They are beautiful and you are spoiling me!' she said blushing.

'Wait until tomorrow and you know what it means to be spoilt!' he said with a mysterious look on his face.

'Have you been planning something?' she asked folding the blouse and scarf neatly back in the box.

---

[5] Coco Chanel opened a boutique in Deauville in 1913, where she introduced deluxe casual clothes suitable for leisure and sport.

'I have, but you have to wait. I spoke to Sebastien and Dawn. They have something to tell you, but do you want to hear it from me?' asked Alexander looking momentarily serious.

'What, is it something I want to hear?' Kathryn's heart skipped a beat.

'I do not know, but it is not terrible,' replied Alexander, not giving anything away. He enjoyed sometimes teasing Kathryn a little bit, seeing her cheeks blush.

'I think I can guess, did they buy some horses without our permission?' she asked.

'No, you are on the wrong track, so to speak,' said Alexander tentatively.

'What are you talking about, you are making me nervous, spit it out please,' she said now jumping out of the bed and sitting on the bedside chair.

'They married in France two days ago,' said Alexander with a nervous smile, not knowing how Kathryn might react. Kathryn's face fell.

'They eloped?' Kathryn did not hear the reply. Her mind raced. Did Sebastien really love Dawn? He had never said anything. 'Why and why out in France?' she finally managed to say.

'Maybe they thought you would not have approved,' said Alexander his eyes downcast. He had a feeling that she might not approve.

'And I do not. Dawn is too young and Sebastien is too flighty! What were they thinking? You do not think she is pregnant?' asked Kathryn, still finding it difficult to take in the unexpected news.

'No I do not,' said Alexander taking her hand. 'Seems to me a bit of a business deal. You know, Dawn's ownership of the cottages,' he looked at her paling face. Kathryn pursed her lips.

'Would he have stooped that low, a marriage of a convenience, a slice of Dallington Place?' she asked looking into Alexander's eyes for answers and reassurance. She did not get any. 'What will I say to her parents? Alison will be so furious with me,' she replied, already fretting that conversation with Dawn's mother.

'It is not your concern Kathryn; you have enough on your plate. Besides you always believe in living life to the fullest. Maybe they do love each other in their own way,' he said, trying to think positively of the situation.

'Do you really think so Alexander?' Kathryn looked at him, not believing any of it.

'Not really, but it is done, sealed and there we have it,' he said giving her hand a gentle rub.

'Oh well, it is done,' said Kathryn, moving back onto the bed feeling a headache coming on. 'At least my Ernest has more sense,' she sat up again. 'He does though, does he not?' giving Alexander a look of desperation.

Alexander sat down on the edge of the bed, lovingly tucking a strand of hair behind her ear. 'Yes of course darling, stop fussing and let us please enjoy our time here.'

The drive was much further than Alexander had anticipated. He had hired a driver only the previous evening, and this man had seemed to be knowledgeable of the Calvados region. But this morning he seemed rather vague and tired and had got lost three times already looking for the entrance of the thoroughbred breeding farm Haras de Meautry in Touques. 'We are now driving out of Touques!' shouted Alexander at poor Davide, who was perspiring profusely in the heat and with nerves.

'Where are we trying to get to?' demanded Kathryn who after four hours was losing her patience.

'Touques is that way,' Alexander shouted at him in French. The automobile swung around sharply. 'There, there, look at the sign post!' Alexander shouted.

The automobile came to an abrupt screeching halt and Kathryn's handbag fell off the seat. As she reached for it she had not noticed the wonderful gate at the front of the magnificent estate. Davide slammed the automobile door shut and walked over to the man guarding the gate. Alexander loosened his tie, feeling hot under his collar. It was seventy-five degrees in the shade and his heart was racing with impatience.

As Davide came back to his taxi, the guard disappeared inside and few minutes later he appeared again to wave them through. The automobile slowly edged its way over some large cobbles in the picturesque courtyard. She could see a large table with at least eight to ten chairs balancing rather precariously on the cobbles, beautifully set up and white lilies adorning the table.

Davide opened the door and Kathryn stepped out, careful to look where she was going as there were potholes on the courtyard. She could smell the horses and she saw the surrounding stables with horses neighing quietly. She had stopped to fasten one of the buttons on her new organza blouse that had slipped open and she failed to recognise the man approaching them. 'Buster! Pleased to make your acquaintance, Madame,' said the small man with a pretty brunette in tow. 'This is Mae my wife,' he said introducing the woman.

Kathryn looked up just in time to catch the lady's smile. 'Kathryn McAlister, owner of Dallington Races, may I introduce Mr Keaton?' said Alexander.

'Buster Keaton?' Kathryn whispered to Alexander but he did not hear her.

'Very pleased to have your acquaintance Miss McAlister, trés charmant!' said Mr Keaton with a broad smile, revealing perfectly white teeth.

All Kathryn could do was to stare open mouthed. Hollywood royalty, she was meeting Hollywood royalty!

'Come sit by me, I think Mr Rothschild should be with us shortly,' said Mae warmly. She patted the wicker chair with a blue velvet cushion next to hers. 'Just beautiful is it not Kathryn, you do not mind if I call you Kathryn?' Mae asked, looking at Kathryn with her emerald green eyes that her impeccably marcel waved dark brown hair framed so perfectly.

'No of course not, I am so happy to be here, it has been quite a journey,' replied Kathryn smiling warmly back at Mae. She could not help but admire this exquisite woman she now recognised as Buster's second wife. She had seen them in the social pages of magazines and newspapers. The gossip goes that she was Mr Keaton's nurse and they married after a whirlwind romance last year.

A rather tall and elegant man approached to pour some wine that was now rather heated on the table. Tutting, he called to a young stable boy to fetch a new bottle. The boy ran off very quickly. 'Do we drink this or do we wait?' asked Mae rather amused.

'Darling, I am sure it is fit for a king, and there is more where that comes from,' laughed Mr Keaton with his strong American accent. 'So how long are you staying?' he asked turning to Alexander.

'Oh just the day, we are staying in Deauville for a few days. Tomorrow we go back to Sussex, England,' replied Alexander, taking a swig of the wine. He could never tire of the real French wine, he thought.

'So is Sussex where you live Kathryn?' asked Mae, sipping her wine elegantly her little finger protruding upwards.

'Yes that is my home and where Dallington Place is,' replied Kathryn.

'Sounds wonderful, we must visit, Buster!' enthused Mae, looking at her husband.

'You are most welcome to visit, just let us get on our feet first,' said Alexander nodding approval at Kathryn.

'Of course you must, as long as you take us as we come. We are deep in the English countryside overlooking the view of the famous South Downs. It is beautiful especially in the morning when the mist descends over the nearby forests and hills,' said Kathryn joyfully, secretly getting excited about welcoming Hollywood stars at Dallington Place. How marvellous would that be for the Dallington Races, she thought.

'And when you are in Hollywood, please look us up,' said Mr Keaton.

'We would love that would we not, darling?' said Alexander his eyes twinkling.

'Yes that would be wonderful,' said Kathryn now feeling out of her depth. Her, the little girl from Dallington village, socialising with Hollywood film stars, she just could not believe it.

Mr Rothschild came thundering down the marble steps in front of them, his forehead glistening with sweat. 'My apologies, I have been test driving my new Cadillac with the new V-16 engine that Mr Keaton kindly shipped over for me from the Americas. If anyone would like to drive in it after lunch, please let my chauffeur know,' he announced.

Alexander nudged Kathryn enthusiastically at the prospect of taking a closer look at this automobile he had heard so much about.

'I presume you have all met. And where is my butler?' asked Mr Rothschild looking around for him, his face getting redder. Turning around again he spied the young stable boy racing over. He looked towards Kathryn. 'This must be the famous Kathryn McAlister?' he asked looking at Alexander.

'Kathryn, may I take great pleasure in introducing you to Eduard Alphonse James de Rothschild,' said Alexander. A man in his late sixties, distinguishably handsome with even features. Mr Rothschild shook her hand firmly, she liked the man immediately. She could sense he was a serious businessman.

'Now Mr Pillard, you have contacted the Société des Courses de Deauville?' he asked, turning back to Alexander, who nodded in agreement. 'Good, everything is straight forward and I will show you all around the stables. Is there is a horse you favour? I must show you Brantome, our champion, that is about to race at the Prix de l'Arc de Triomphe and tipped as the winner,' said Mr Rothschild.

'What fun!' Mae clapped her hands together in excitement.

'First let us eat. Here we have caviar with quails eggs, smoked salmon and cheeses from our vaults. Please help yourself!' Mr Rothschild said sitting down at the head of the table sipping his wine.

It was the most beautifully warm day and at two o'clock, two men rushed down the marble steps in front of them with a large cream canopy to shield them from the heat of the sun.

'Now Mae, tell me all about Buster, I want to hear all the Hollywood gossip, all that the papers do not tell us!' said Eduard casting Mae a curious look.

Mae giggled, he was clearly flirting with the petite brunette. 'Mr Rothschild, of course I cannot tell you the inside knowledge on my husband but he is a very good husband, never a dull moment!'

Everyone laughed and Kathryn was really enjoying herself. She could hardly believe she was in France and now sitting with a Hollywood actor and a Rothschild.

'And you Miss McAlister, when are you going to marry Alexander?' asked Mr Rothschild looking inquisitively at Alexander.

Kathryn had noticed both Mr Keaton and Mr Rothschild called her miss, she wondered why. Perhaps Alexander had not told them much about her yet. 'Well, we are unofficially engaged, but we thought we would wait a year. You see, my son is newly engaged and will marry early next year and my …' Kathryn thought for a moment what exactly her relationship to Sebastien was. She was about to mention Sebastien but thought better of it. The wine had been flowing and she became more open. 'You see, I am a widow and it is better we wait a year,' she continued.

'Oh, I am sorry I had no idea,' said Mae hoping Mr Rothschild's inquisitive questions were not upsetting her.

'No, no that is alright, my husband Devlin, he was a good husband and we were married for many happy years. He passed away a few years ago,' replied Kathryn with a sympathetic smile. She like Mae, they seemed to have an affinity with each other.

'You must have married very young, Kathryn.' said Buster politely, surprised that Kathryn was a widow. No wonder Alexander had been discreet about her, he thought.

Kathryn blushed. 'Well, I was engaged before I met Devlin but my fiancé, he was fighting in the war and ...' There was a sigh from Mae and Kathryn stopped in her tracks. She did not want to talk about Bertram.

'So Kathryn, is this your first visit to France and this region?' Buster hurried in to change the subject.

'Well, this is my first visit to Touques and Deauville but not my first visit to France. I was a nurse in France during the war,' she replied.

'Oh my goodness, how brave!' interrupted Mae, in awe of this woman's courage.

'Quite the gal, I should say,' said Buster impressed. 'You must visit me in Hollywood and give a talk to the committee I am on. The women at my club would love to hear your stories,' suggested Mae.

'Really? I am just a woman who did my bit for England really,' replied Kathryn blushing.

'Nonsense!' said Mr Rothschild, raising his glass to honour Kathryn. 'Here's to your return to France, and enjoy your day with us. May you return to us in the not too distance future... to Kathryn!' toasted Mr Rothschild.

'To Kathryn,' everyone raised their glasses.

'And not forgetting the Dallington Races!' added Alexander, reminding everyone of why they were there. It was always business first for Alexander.

As everyone put down their glasses, Mae dipped her head towards Kathryn in a conspiratorial whisper. 'Did your previous fiancé die on the fields of France, Kathryn?'

Kathryn took a deep breath. 'No actually he died in Texas, where he went to live on a ranch. He loved to fly you see, he was a pilot during the war. He loved his freedom,' said Kathryn suddenly feeling the sense of loss.

Mae nodded with sympathy, clasping Kathryn's hand. She understood.

CHAPTER THIRTY-THREE
BERTRAM: TURMOIL

'Get him indoors!' shouted the man to Jorie, who had found Bertram face down in a pool of his own blood, barely conscious outside a bar. He was holding Bertram up, his blood soaked face hanging to the side. A large cut above his left eye oozed blood.

'Sebastien!' cried Jorie hysterically, 'Go get Pedro and Grey!' Bertram had been fighting again late at night in the bar in town. Jorie had given Pedro and Bertram strict instructions to have their meeting with James Tives Tomlin, or Buck for short, a great horse breeder and rancher who was making a name for himself, and then return back to the ranch as quickly as possible. The horses he bred and raised were Quarter horses and Jorie was interested in changing over to Quarter horses for breeding and barrel racing.

It was a bad one. Bertram's breathing was stifled. He cried out for Jorie and then his head lolled to the side. 'Sebastien, hurry! Get the doctor too!' she shouted. 'Where is Pedro? Does anyone know?' she asked Grey, as he picked up Bertram's legs, sharing the weight as they lifted him up to the porch. Jorie ran inside to get a blanket and some cushions for his head.

'They have found Pedro in the barn, Ma'am,' said Roger undoing Bertram's neckerchief.

'What in the name of God have they been doing fighting in bars again?' she said.

Pedro was now sleeping off the drink. His left hand was badly cut and someone had tarred and feathered his fingers. They were stuck together, clamped and bloody. It was all a mess. Pedro's Mexican mother Jovita had been an activist in San Antonio working with Hispanic Workers' Movement union activist Emma Tenayuca. She had an affair with Jorie's father Douglas twenty years ago, and then moved on as soon as Pedro was born, leaving him behind at Doubletree's ranch. She made the occasional visit back to see her son, but her political and wayward views had left a mark on Pedro and he was always getting into fights with his own political views.

276

'Is Pedro all right?' asked Jorie, mopping Bertram's bloody brow and biting the inside of her lip in frustration at how long it was taking for the doctor to get there.

'Some racist guy was taunting him, calling him names and calling his mother a whore. Bertram was sticking up for him, that is all,' said Grey.

'How do you know?' asked Jorie confused.

'Pedro just explained before he passed out. Three men jumped them in the bar on Kail Street,' continued Grey now listening to Bertram's chest.

'So Pedro is all right, but look at my Bertram. It looks bad, Grey!' cried Jorie in a state of desperation. She could not lose Bertram, not like this.

Roger did not say anything but he did not have to. Having seen so many wounded old horses, he recognised that look and shallow breathing, as if the soul was ready to leave the body. Bertram was slipping away and not even the doctor could save him. Jorie put her head to his chest. Tears of many long years of frustration trickled down her cheeks.

Jorie sat opposite her brother in the outhouse, her head in her hands. His body crumpled and old before his years sprawled next to the wall. Jorie looked and winced at the state of his hand. His eyes opened for a moment and Jorie leaned over him. 'You have done it now, Pedro!' she cried cradling his head in her hands. 'The doctor is at the house, get up if you can, we have to sort out your hand.'

Pedro looked up to her dumbfounded. 'Christ Jorie, what happened, I do not remember a thing!' he said looking down at his mangled fingers.

Jorie was twelve when she watched Pedro being carried into the house as a baby. His dark skin and black hair made him so sweet and appealing. Jorie remembered her father's conversation with Pedro's mother. 'That is nonsense, you cannot drag a baby all over the country with your political movements. You are not doing that to my son, Jovita, leave him here with me.'

To Jorie's mother, Beulah, the boy did not exist. She called him 'it' and refused to talk to him. But Jorie and her sister Winnie took on the role of little mothers. They cooed and fussed over him, almost to the point of spoiling him. And he had quite the fiery temper that neither Jorie nor Winnie possessed. Always fighting and bending the rules at school, he was trouble from the start. When Pedro was fifteen, his mother returned to collect him. She was now in the Texas Farm Workers Union and she wanted him to enlist with her and fight for her cause. But Jorie's father had insisted he stayed with them to finish his education. As Jorie recalled the day's events, she now wished he had left with his mother. The last few years he had become a layabout and no matter what anybody said to him or tried to help him, he always reverted to the good for nothing he had become. Jorie loved him, but now her Bertram was dead. But she could not blame this troubled soul. It was no one's fault, Bertram was troublesome in his own way.

Pedro got to his feet, with his arm around Jorie's waist, they managed to walk back to the house, slowly but steadily. 'Get some lard!' she screamed at Sebastien who was sitting on the staircase, motionless in shock that his father had gone. His face was stained with tears and smudges of mud after mucking out the horses. He watched whilst Jorie and Roger brought Pedro in, his body lolling limp with pain. He was alive, Sebastien could see that. He did not want to move from the stairs. Why would he help, he thought, this man had caused Bertram's death. He wanted to walk right out there and then, just leave. He grabbed his coat, which was lying beside him. He ran out, catching the toe of his boot on the edge of the doorway. He fell forward but saving himself as he wobbled. He ran past the doctor, who called to him to come back, in vain. Sebastien ran to the stables, grabbed the tack and mounted Lupin. He dug his heels into the stallion's sides with such strength that it reared up and it tore off down the dusty trail, all the way to the Stedman ranch five miles away. Going at full speed past the horse and cart that Dawn was driving, Lupin finally stopped outside the ranch house, reared and knocked Sebastien off. He hit his head on the red soil just clear of Lupin's hoof and lost consciousness.

'Dawn I need to go back to France, I cannot stay in Texas anymore!' muttered Sebastien in thumping pain when he came around as Dawn helped him to sit up. He had nothing left in Texas and he wanted to go home. He felt desperate, he did not feel he belonged in Texas anymore now that Bertram was gone.

'You are not going anywhere until your concussion has worn off. You have to make peace with Jorie, you have not spoken for a while. Do not go without making things right with her,' pleaded Dawn.

'Bertram was the only reason I am at the ranch, but I do not want it anymore,' said Sebastien in turmoil.

'But you and Jorie are the ranch,' Dawn tried to reason with him.

'Jorie was not making Bertram happy anymore, I am angry with her for that. I want respect for him, damn it, he was my stepfather, even though he was difficult, I know,' said Sebastien. 'I am grieving for France, I need to go back. Perhaps you can come with me?' he continued, feeling the need for solidarity.

The doctor and Jorie worked on Pedro's injured hand throughout the night. Eventually clean enough and perhaps safe from infection they had bound it tightly in a bandage. Jorie had not noticed Sebastien had gone until Alison appeared at the front door. 'He is staying with us,' she had simply explained. He had a mild concussion from falling off the horse. But Jorie was numb. For her it had been such a great shock to lose Bertram perhaps she had seemed unfeeling. But there was nothing she could do. She had nothing left to give to anyone, not even the ranch anymore.

She took to her bed for what seemed like weeks. She did not even remember being at the funeral. A week had passed and she had not left her room. Alison came to visit to check on her. 'Have you heard from Sebastien?' Jorie asked, missing having him around.

Alison shook her head. 'Dawn said he was bound for New York and then perhaps back to France,' she said conscious not to upset her.

Jorie sat upright in her bed, having not eaten for four days. 'I am going to sell the ranch. Pedro is incapable of working now, my sister is too busy in New York and she never wanted it anyway. Now Sebastien and Bertram have gone too,' she said, tears running down her cheeks.

'I will help you but what do you want to do?' asked Alison her brow creasing with worry for her friend.

'Something worthwhile, something where I get a return and appreciation for my hard work,' Jorie cried out. She felt a sense of frustration and a sense of immense loss.

'Is there such a job?' asked Alison smiling at her friend.

'There may be,' said Jorie, knowing exactly what she was going to do.

JUNE 1930

The *Good Year* liner had been at sea for a week now. It was ten days before Sebastien was due to arrive in New York. He checked his pockets. He had some money for lodgings, maybe get some work as a cook to pay for his fare back to France. He had left Texas with a few goodbyes. Dawn said she would follow in a year or two, when she was old enough. Sebastien could not look Jorie in the eye. He had avoided her before he left so as not to say goodbye. How cold towards Bertram she had become. Fussing about her brother whilst his father's body lay still warm but dead upstairs. The pile of Bertram's letters neatly stacked next to his bunk bed. He had meticulously uncreased the corners after they had been stuffed inside his jacket pockets.

New York was not what Sebastien had hoped for. It had taken him nearly a week to find some work but it was only on a week to week basis and it was not going so well. If he could last out just one more week he would have saved enough for his fare back home to France. He was lodging on the 105th Street in[6] east Harlem, next to a burlesque club, in an eclectic area full of young white Americans, African-Americans of the Caribbean origin and other nationalities making a new life for themselves. The streets were full of artists and poets and the atmosphere was vibrant. The large, brown brick, apartment blocks were full of tenants, people spilling out to the streets, musicians sitting on the pavements playing their instruments. In the evenings the music echoed from the famous Cotton Club on 142nd Street. Sebastien recognised the pretty girl who lived across the hall, who he had seen standing outside the Minsky's Burlesque club handing out flyers. She had introduced herself as Holly and had explained that she was trying to make it as a Broadway actress. Over the next couple of weeks, they became firm friends and Holly introduced him to New York pastimes. One Sunday they went to watch a baseball game at the Yankee stadium in the Bronx. Sebastien sat mesmerised by the huge crowds, it was the first time he had seen a baseball game. After a payday, Sebastien treated Holly to tea at The Carlyle hotel and an evening with Esther Jones, "Baby Jones" at the Cotton Club, spending money he could ill afford. Sebastien was grateful to Holly having secured him a week's work in the theatre on some backstage setting. The pay was poor but if he ate next to nothing until Friday, he would have enough to get a liner back to France on Sunday.

Saturday morning, he set off to book his one-way ticket. Clutching the hundred and twenty dollars he had saved from his pay on the ranch and the three weeks work in New York, he had been told he would have enough. Hoping there was some space left in steerage,

---

[6] Harlem Renaissance was a cultural, social, and artistic explosion that took place in Harlem between the end of WWI and the middle of the 1930s. During this period Harlem was a cultural centre, drawing African-American writers, artists, musicians, photographers, poets and scholars.

he asked about the *MS Lafayette*, which was sailing to Le Havre on Sunday. 'How long is the journey?' asked Sebastien.

'Six days,' answered the ticket clerk at the harbour.

'Any room in the steerage?' asked Sebastien.

'Yup, we have a few fares left, that will be one hundred and fifty-nine dollars,' said the clerk nonchalantly without looking up. He didn't see Sebastien's face crumble. His mouth dry, he realised he may have to work another week in New York. 'It leaves at seven in the morning, would you like to book it?'

Just then he felt a tap on his shoulder. It was Holly. 'How did you know I was here?' Sebastien turned around in surprise. 'I followed you. I was wondering if you would not mind me going along with you to France. I have just got the sack. I have had enough of New York and besides I want to try my luck in Paris,' she said beaming her beautiful white teeth.

The clerk was now shuffling papers and aware that there was a line of people behind them, Sebastien stepped out of line.

'No Holly, I am going Le Havre in Normandy,' he said as he let other people in the line through.

'Can I get from Normandy to Paris?' asked Holly.

'I suppose, but listen, I am not here to be social, I cannot look after you. I have problems getting myself on board, I am short of thirty dollars,' said Sebastien, frustrated with his lack of money.

'You take me along as your wife, we can share a small cabin and I will stump up the rest,' she said now almost begging to come along. Sebastien sighed, he did not have a choice. He stepped back into the line behind a rather large man with his three children.

'Booking this time, Sir?' asked the clerk in a sarcastic tone.

'Yes, one-way ticket to Le Havre, third class, my wife and I will share a cabin,' said Sebastien.

'Mr and Mrs Comte-Wright,' Holly called out proudly.

'That will be two for one cabin, Sir, but let me check, we are almost full now. You are in luck, last cabin in third class is available,' he finally said.

Sebastien handed over his and Holly's savings, sealing their fate together on this trip.

Back at Sebastien's apartment, they sat on his old leather sofa, sipping mint julep, Holly's favourite drink that she had introduced to Sebastien. He could see Holly was sad. 'I really thought I would make it in New York, you know,' she said wistfully, with a few tears threatening to drop down her face.

'You could have tried Hollywood, you are a good looking girl Holly. I am sure motion pictures could have been a success for you,' said Sebastien trying to cheer her up.

'Well, I do not know anyone in Hollywood and I would have not wanted to be one of those chorus girls succumbing to the casting couch,' she said jutting out her chin defiantly.

'Do you know anyone in France?' asked Sebastien rather surprised.

'I know you, do I not?' said Holly fluttering her eyelashes.

'Holly, I cannot look after you. Besides I may never go to Paris and I may end up in England. I am not sure exactly what I am looking for,' said Sebastien becoming irritated.

'Well, I have spent my money. I do not even have the money for this week's rent,' she replied, desperation starting to rise in her.

'Holly why did you spend it on me then?' asked Sebastien rather mockingly.

'It was my only option, I do not want to starve in New York,' she said. Sebastien was beginning to worry this girl was trouble, but quite truthfully he did not have much option either. Besides she had helped him out with the rest of the fare.

'So why France and England? A Texas boy like you?' asked Holly with interest.

'It's a long story.'

Sebastien began to tell Holly his life's story of his early years in France and then moving to America. He told her about his stepfather, Bertram, an English soldier, who had stayed with him and his mother in Mesves-sur-Loire during the war. How he had sat by Bertram's feet and listened to him reciting poetry and tales of war. He told her about flights in the little biplane over the ranch in Texas and his reasons for coming to New York. He told her about Bertram's tragic death and the unrest in Texas with frequent lynchings and the tarring and feathering. How African-Americans were fleeing violence, some ending up in Harlem. Holly sat wide-eyed listening to his story. She could see how close he had been to his stepfather and sensed his loyalty to France. They stayed up all night talking. Holly put her head on his lap and fell asleep, secure in the knowledge that Sebastien would take care of her on the journey to France.

As they stood in the line early the next morning, Holly was beginning to have doubts. 'Keep talking to me Sebastien,' she said as they walked up the many metal steps to the liner.

'You want to know what it's like to fly?' said Sebastien. Holly just nodded as she turned for the last time to say her goodbyes to New York. *MS Lafayette* was a new liner with very sumptuous interiors even in third class. The Art Deco furniture with its vivid red carpets, blue chairs and sofas made Holly squeal with delight. 'I think I have made the right decision coming with you, Sebastien,' she said linking her arm through his. A mature gentleman with a handlebar moustache walked passed and tipped his hat at Holly. She flashed him a flirty smile back. 'The men are not bad either, I wonder if some are single,' she said looking back to the man.

By the third day, Sebastien felt he was almost alone again. Holly had befriended a gentleman, one Alfred Lovelace the third, a rich bonds broker. She was dining with him at six o'clock so he thought he would go to the upper deck to see if he could find her. Sure enough there she was waiting for Mr Lovelace, sipping her martini at the silver and white cocktail bar. She was wearing a silver lamé flapper dress her brown hair pinned at the side with a silver diamante clip. Her fingernails tapping impatiently. 'You know he wants me to live with him in Paris as soon as we arrive,' she whispered conspiratorially into Sebastien's ear.

'Holly, you hardly know him, is that wise?' asked Sebastien concerned yet filled with admiration for her audaciousness. 'And is he married?' he continued.

'No he is a widow,' she replied rather too triumphantly.

'How convenient!' laughed Sebastien. She was a chancer all right, good luck to her he thought.

'Ooh there he is, be nice Sebastien!' said Holly as she turned around to greet Mr Lovelace.

'We finally meet,' said Alfred the third extending his hand for Sebastien to shake. Looking self-assured and well-groomed with his dark hair waxed back, his moustache trimmed to perfection, wearing a burgundy velvet smoking jacket and a tight bowtie around his bulging neck. 'It is so nice to meet Holly's brother at long last.' Sebastien just stared back at Holly, who was now blushing and taking a long sip of her martini. 'You have a slight accent?' asked Mr Lovelace his eyebrows dancing above his eyes.

'I lived in France as a young boy, so I did not meet my half-sister, Holly, until I moved to Texas when I was ten,' replied Sebastien, now reluctantly joining in Holly's story.

'Where about in France?' asked Mr Lovelace. 'Mesves-sur-Loire, do you know it?' asked Sebastien, knowing the man probably did not.

'No no, I only know Paris mostly, a wonderful, wonderful city,' replied Mr Lovelace dragging on his cigar.

'Do you work there?' responded Sebastien, quickly trying to avoid questions about himself.

'No, no, I am retired and I live in the seventh arrondissement. I holiday in the Hamptons just outside New York. I have lived in Paris for twenty years on and off. Since my dearest wife Mildred passed away a few years ago, she was not too fond of travelling, I now travel to New York more frequently to visit relatives,' replied Mr Lovelace, feeling a sense of rivalry.

Sebastien raised his glass to the pair, giving Holly a disdainful look. 'Well, congratulations on finding each other!' said Sebastien feeling a tinge of jealousy. Maybe he should have asked her to join him in Mesves-sur-Loire.

'I have asked the delightful Holly to stay with me in Paris. What do you think, do I have your blessing?' asked Mr Lovelace, offering Sebastien a cigar.

'Of course,' said Sebastien patting the man on his back. Sebastien was not convinced this man believed that Holly was his sister at all.

When Holly finally managed to get back to the cabin the following day, she asked him why he was sulking. 'Are you jealous?' she asked.

'Not at all, what would I do with you anyway?' laughed Sebastien as not to let on that perhaps he had made a mistake by letting her go.

'Well, I think we should keep in touch?' she said.

'Keeping your options open are you?' said Sebastien in a cynical voice.

'Do not be like that Sebastien, I like you very much and you have been so kind to me,' said Holly taken aback by his unkind words.

'Well, as I said, I do not know how long I will be in France for, I may go to England. I will give you two addresses, my mother's in Mesves-sur-Loire and where I may go eventually in Sussex, in England,' said Sebastien, softening up. He knew Holly meant well and she had been great company during his lonely weeks in New York.

A silver Rolls Royce was waiting for Mr Lovelace and Holly. Parked neatly on the quay, waiting for the rich man and his mistress. 'Can we take you somewhere?' offered Mr Lovelace, as they prepared to leave, hoping that Sebastien would say no.

'I am going to catch a train to Mesves-sur-Loire, thank you for offering. Take care of my Holly,' said Sebastien shaking Mr Lovelace's hand.

Holly kissed Sebastien on his cheek, leaving a red lipstick mark. 'Take care brother. If we go to London, we will look you up,' she giggled her face lighting up.

'Like I said Holly, I probably will not go, I will be in France,' said Sebastien, feeling a twinge of regret. He had come to dislike goodbyes and he had grown very fond of Holly and her infectious laugh.

Holly shrugged and followed Mr Lovelace outside to the Rolls Royce. Sebastien watched as the chauffeur took her luggage and opened the door for her. He stood alone at the dock watching her pretty face pressed against the window disappearing into the distance. A sudden loss engulfed him, he tried to convince himself she was better off with this gentleman. He put her out of his mind for the time being.

CHAPTER THIRTY-FOUR
KATHRYN: FAMILY CHRISTMAS 1934

Four years had gone by since he left Texas and Sebastien had not left Mesves-sur-Loire. He had become lazy and unfulfilled. As soon as he had arrived, he found some work on a nearby farm that offered bed and board. He could not believe that the years had passed so quickly. He had left as a ten-year-old and now he was back as a grown man. He had looked for his mother but he had no luck finding her. There were rumours in the village that she had run off with an Australian soldier, not long after Bertram and Sebastien had left. He even looked for Alphonse, only to discover he had died from drink some years ago. He began to see a pretty local girl but lately she had become demanding and wanted to get married. Sebastien did not want to be tied down, not yet. It was time to move on. Taking the bunch of Bertram's letters, he tried to press them flat between the pages of a large book. It was impossible. He knew that they had been crumpled inside the pocket of his brown suede jacket all this time. He had not wanted to do anything with them, the memories were all too painful. He looked out of the window overlooking the poppy fields where he had sat with Bertram all those years ago. A sudden feeling of nostalgia took a hold of him and he felt resentful of Bertram taking him to Texas, away from his French roots. Bertram, Berenice and Alphonse gone, these letters by Bertram were his only tie to any family he had.

Lying back on his bed he thought of Holly for the first time in a long time. She would have gone to England, on a whim, she would have taken the opportunity to discover a new place. He slammed the book shut with the letters firmly inside and placed it in his suitcase. He would leave tomorrow, if it did not snow. Christmas time may be a good time to go to Sussex, he thought. He could come back to France if England was not full of promise. He hoped that the fantasies Bertram had filled his head with about Dallington Place would measure up. One letter had fallen out from the book, and as he retrieved it from the floor he couldn't help but read it. It was the chorus from the song

Yellow Rose of Texas[7], which Jorie had introduced to him and Bertram when they had first arrived in Santa Anna. Bertram had been very fond of it and he had called Jorie his yellow rose with her silky blonde hair. Reading it brought tears to Sebastien's eyes.

Chorus from the Yellow Rose of Texas:
When the Rio Grande is flowing, the starry skies are bright,
She walks along the river in the quiet summer night:
She thinks if I remember, when we parted long ago,
I promised to come back again, and not to leave her so.
Oh now I am going to find her, for my heart is full of woe,
And we will sing the bango gaily, and we will sing the song of yore,
And the Yellow Rose of Texas shall be mine forevermore.

CHRISTMAS 1934, DALLINGTON PLACE

'Dawn, I cannot believe you are a married woman!' Alison said hugging her daughter.

Kathryn exchanged looks with Ernest. 'Where is Sebastien?' asked Alison, noticing there was an uneasy atmosphere in the room.

'Oh Mamma,' said Dawn sitting down quickly and dabbing her eyes.

'What in God's name is the matter?' Alison asked paling suddenly.

'I am pregnant!' said Dawn between sobs.

'That is good news, is it not Kathryn?' said Alison after digesting the sudden information and turning to Kathryn.

'Yes, the baby will be born around the end of July, is that not right Dawn?' said Kathryn interrupting the sobs.

'Come, come we all get emotional,' said Alison not understanding why her daughter was so upset.

'I do not think I love him anymore, Mamma.' Dawn blurted out between her heaving and sobbing.

This song became popular among Confederate soldiers in the Texas Brigade during the American Civil War; upon taking command of the Army of Tennessee in July 1864, General John Bell Hood introduced it as a marching song. (Lanning, Michael Lee. *Civil War 100: The Stories Behind the Most Influential Battles, People and Events in the War between the States*. Sourcebooks, Incorporated 2006. ISBN 978-1-4022-1040-2 p 306)

'Can you go and find where Sebastien has gone, he needs to see Alison as soon as possible,' she said to her son, knowing she was asking too much of him.

Kathryn went to the door and ushered Ernest out. 'I think he went into the village, he will be back. Last minute Christmas shopping that is all,' said Ernest rather fed up with all the drama since Sebastien and Dawn eloped.

'Do not be silly child, you have known Sebastien since you were little, why all of a sudden do you not like him, you married him! Kathryn do you know what is going on?' asked Alison as Kathryn walked back in.

'I think they have been arguing a lot,' replied Kathryn under her breath.

'You are just adjusting to each other's ways that is all,' Alison said putting her arm around her daughter who had stopped crying for a moment.

'No Mamma, it is not that, he seems to look at every girl apart from me at Dallington Place. I do not think he loves me anymore!' said Dawn and started to sob again.

'I am sure that is not true Dawn and let us face it, you are hardly the easiest of wives I am sure,' said Alison, feeling it all becoming rather tiresome.

'Tell her Kathryn, tell her what Ernest and Sebastien were arguing about,' said Dawn now sobbing again into her handkerchief.

Alison looked to Kathryn. 'Well, Alison we do not know for sure, but Ernest caught him kissing one of the students in the stables,' said Kathryn. She felt the whole thing had been blown out of proportion.

Ernest came back into the room and poured himself a drink. 'Sebastien is back and has gone to change for dinner. He will be down in a while,' said Ernest rolling his eyes at Dawn who was still crying. 'Can we at least have some peace for Christmas, please Dawn,' Ernest said firmly.

'Did you see Sebastien kissing that girl, Ernest?' asked Alison, fixing her gaze on Ernest through her reading spectacles, which were perched imperiously on the tip of her nose.

'I did, but I do feel he did it out of revenge. Dawn, you have been in London so much and you did not tell him about the baby!' he said defensively. For once he understood why Sebastien might have behaved in that manner, he thought. He knew how immature Dawn could be.

'I only went to London to make him jealous,' she said pouting.

'It is not going to help matters if you keep making each other jealous. You were arguing last night and I heard you call him ugly,' Ernest said angrily. 'If those two do not stop keeping me up with their quarrels, I am moving out, Mamma!' shouted Ernest with a pained expression on his face.

'You will do no such thing, it will be Sebastien going, if anyone,' said Kathryn sinking down into her chair. This bickering was giving her a headache.

'You have to make peace with each other, for the baby's sake,' said Alison, looking harshly at her daughter.

Sebastien opened the door to find everyone huddled around Dawn and suddenly falling quiet as he entered the room. 'Dawn darling, I bought you an early Christmas present to say sorry, I really am sorry. Hello Lady Alison,' said Sebastien tentatively, approaching them and kissing Alison on the cheek. 'I hear you are rather too generous with your kisses Sebastien, this has to stop!' she casted a disdainful look at her son-in-law.

'Yes Lady Alison, I am terribly sorry, I love my wife very much,' replied Sebastien, bowing his head with remorse.

All Ernest could do was to watch the drama unfold, he above anyone knew they had married in haste. They were better as friends and now they cannot even get on. Dawn opened her present and asked her mother to help her with the bracelet's fastener. She gave Sebastien a feeble smile, and he went to pour himself a drink.

Christmas Day brought good news to Kathryn. She sat in the kitchen whilst Libby prepared two turkeys for the Christmas luncheon. Neither of them had slept much last night. It was not yet six o'clock and Kathryn sat listening to the wireless, whilst sifting through a large pile of post from the day before. Most were Christmas cards, but the last one she opened was a letter from Burwash in Sussex. It read:

18th December 1934
Dear Mrs McAlister,
Thank you very much for your correspondence. After much deliberation, I am pleased to inform you that Mr Rudyard Kipling will be thrilled to accept your invitation to open the Dallington Races in the spring.

Please let us know the exact date a few months ahead as Mr Kipling still enjoys to travel and would not want to miss this exciting time with you at Dallington Place.

Best of luck with the completion of the project and look forward to hearing from you in the New Year.

A merry Christmas to you and your family.

Yours sincerely,

Anne Rolling

Secretary of Mr Kipling

Kathryn clasped her hands together and let out a whoop of joy. 'What is it Ma'am, I hope it is good news?' asked Libby rather surprised by Kathryn's sudden enthusiasm. She had been out of sorts for a few days concerned about Sebastien and Dawn, and with the sudden news of Alexander having to depart for New York only days before Christmas. She really needed some good news.

'Yes, it is very good news Libby, I must telephone Irene immediately, she will be pleased. She was the one that suggested we have a very important person to open the Dallington Races. I thought it was a good idea to ask Mr Rudyard Kipling, a key figure in Sussex and a hero for doing so much charity work for the war effort. I really did not expect him to accept!' explained Kathryn looking overjoyed.

'How wonderful, I just love his books. I read them to my sons when they were little,' said Libby stirring some soup. 'May I ask, when Mr Pillard will be returning? I want to make sure I have enough food in the storage over the New Year,' she asked, knowing it was a sensitive subject.

'He will be returning on the 27th, I am so sorry to miss him here at Christmas,' replied Kathryn suddenly looking downhearted, contemplating how much she would have loved to share this wonderful news with Alexander.

'Well, the house is full, that is one consolation!' said Libby, straining the soup into a selection of jars to cool.

The house was full and having such a busy time looking after the Stedmans, Lord and Lady Fitch and everyone else, the horses and the work, Kathryn had not had much time to dwell on Alexander's absence. On Boxing Day, she and Geraldine walked around the stables after lunch and Kathryn explained to her what the next plans were for the cottages. Mr Montgomery tipped his hat at the ladies. 'The racecourse is nearly completed. The workers have had to stop due to the rain, but it should be finished by February,' explained Kathryn pointing to the nearest field, which looked like a muddy ditch to Geraldine. 'I will show you the plans when we go in for a hot chocolate,' said Kathryn now producing the letter from Rudyard Kipling's secretary.

'I am so proud of you Kathryn, everything you touch seems to turn to gold these days!' said Geraldine squeezing her friend's frozen fingers.

'Yes and no,' replied Kathryn contemplating the absence of Alexander. 'Pity I cannot keep hold of my men though,' she said with a wry smile.

'Nonsense! That man loves you without a doubt,' said Geraldine.

'Yes, but it always seems that when the going gets tough they disappear on me. As soon as Alexander heard that the Fitchs were coming to stay, he was off,' said Kathryn feeling disappointed.

'It was work related, was it not?' asked Geraldine concerned for her friend.

'Yes, of course and you know I do not blame him, the Fitchs knew Devlin so well. They make him feel uncomfortable. He is such a man of pride. He always likes to think he was first and only man at Dallington Place with me, silly I know,' replied Kathryn.

'Exactly, Alexander has his pride but Devlin would have swallowed his! Give the man some space, I think he has a lot to live up to here. He copes quite well I think,' said Geraldine, her chin resting on her palm, sympathising with Kathryn.

'You are right, as always my friend. Where is that lovely husband of yours?' asked Kathryn, changing the subject.

'He is in the smoking room with your errant son and Sebastien,' responded Geraldine. She knew full well her husband was again indulging in too much drink and a game of poker, which would see him out of pocket for the third night running.

'My errant son?' asked Kathryn bemused by what she meant.

'Your son that has been talking to Roberta about looking for work as a journalist in Paris or New York once he finishes his studies in English and literature at Oxford,' said Geraldine suddenly feeling uneasy, realising this was news to Kathryn.

'Has he spoken to you about it? I thought perhaps he was going to settle down here and run Dallington Place with me and Sebastien,' said Kathryn quietly.

'He is Bertram's son all right. But he has the best of Bertram's traits, so quite the dark horse. He has the wanderlust,' said Geraldine intrigued about this maturing young man. 'I know you like your adventures too but you are the most content at home at Dallington Place,' she continued.

'Thank goodness for that, someone has to be here to run the place!' said Kathryn, suddenly feeling the weight of running the business on her own.

'Have you heard from Alexander today?' asked Geraldine, hoping he would be home for Kathryn tomorrow once everyone had left.

'Yes, he is on his way back, stopping off in Paris tonight,' answered Kathryn, relieved that he was finally returning. 'He seems distressed, I only hope there is no more trouble brewing in Europe with Hitler. Alexander fears there could even be another war one day.'

Geraldine looked at her worried. 'Really?' she said.

'He knows his stuff, and he is often right, but I do not think I could go through another war Geraldine, could you?' asked Kathryn, looking overwhelmed by all the recent events.

'Kathryn, I think we should not talk about these things. Let us go and have another hot chocolate and you can show me the racecourse plans,' said Geraldine, linking her arm through Kathryn's, as they slowly walked back to the house.

'It looks like snow,' said Kathryn looking into the powdery clouds above.

'It is certainly cold enough!' answered Geraldine shivering, looking forward to sit by the warm fire. 'I think I may have a brandy with mine,' she said trying to lighten the mood. But both women were unusually quiet. The talk of war had depressed them.

Kathryn waved off the last automobile that disappeared down the driveway. Luckily snow had not settled and Alexander's flight was on time. Sir Nicholas was the last one to leave and his chauffeur came to take him back to Endelwise Manor. Norfolk was a long drive from Dallington Place, they should make it there before dark. Kathryn blew a kiss and called out, 'See you in the spring, Sir Nicholas!' as he wound his window up. Kathryn found Dawn in the stables, now too pregnant to ride, brushing her favourite horse Reggie. She looked miserable and exhausted with dark shadows under her eyes.

She looked up and half smiled at Kathryn. Putting down her brush she put her arms around Kathryn. 'So you think I should leave him?

Mamma said I can stay in Norfolk until the baby is born. She is worried about the baby and me,' said Dawn holding back tears.

'No Dawn, I think you should ride out the storm with us here. There is no point in running away. Besides, keeping busy will do you good and you wanted to marry Sebastien after all,' said Kathryn slightly irritated that Dawn was behaving like a spoilt little girl. 'Listen Dawn, after the war as you know, so many of our young men died fighting for our country. And now as you can imagine, there is quite a shortage of men for women to marry. You are so lucky to have Sebastien, as imperfect as he is,' she continued, now softening her tone. She did understand Dawn was emotional due to her pregnancy and feeling lack of sympathy from Sebastien.

Dawn sat down on the hay bale next to her horse and listened to what Kathryn had to say. Her back and feet were aching, she was feeling the weight of the baby now as it kicked. 'Many women have gone without marriage, you only have to look at all the spinsters in our parish. You know, after the war women were encouraged to marry men with war injuries, psychological problems and even blind men. Nothing is easy and nothing is perfect. The human race goes on. One has to make the best of everything and every day. Think of these poor men who suffered in the war. After all it is all about procreation,' she said looking at Dawn's belly.

'You sound so matter of fact, what about love and romance?' asked Dawn almost wailing in misery.

'Do not ask me about that Dawn, I am on my third romance and it is not perfect. Alexander is travelling much of the time. I miss him desperately but Dallington Place keeps me busy,' said Kathryn, trying to cover up her own emotions and loneliness.

'I think Sebastien is unfaithful to me, Kathryn,' said Dawn looking up with her doe eyes filled with sadness. She felt so alone with the pregnancy.

'Dawn, you do not know that for sure. Besides if you leave him, it leaves the field wide open for every Doris and Mary to go after him,' said Kathryn with a smile.

'Who?' asked Dawn wide eyed.

'No, I am just saying, there are so many unattached women that if you leave, there will be a stampede,' clarified Kathryn. They both started to laugh. Kathryn imagined as soon as they opened the gates of Dallington Races, all these pretty fillies would be chasing poor Sebastien around the racecourse. 'Also you want to be popular in the village. If talk got out that you are dissatisfied in your marriage, people will think that you are spoilt and ungrateful. Human nature does not change, Dawn. We have to keep appearances up,' said Kathryn pulling her shoulders back and straightening her posture.

'Do we?' asked Dawn naively. She could not care less what the people in the village thought.

'When two people of a privilege of sorts, combine their interests in a union of marriage, it allows a rise in status. Dawn, you are very lucky. As I said, many women have gone without marriage and I am all for equality in marriage. But being pregnant and newly married, it would seem foolhardy to leave now. And you know, only yesterday I was reading the local newspaper, some woman had put a notice for a husband. I kept it, I will show you. There is talk in the village that for some reason Sussex is an unpromising area to find a husband,' said Kathryn trying to get her point across.

'Perhaps we could put in a notice for Sebastien, offering to loan him out?' said Dawn with a mischievous smile. They laughed again.

'Besides you love him, do you not?' asked Kathryn.

'I do and I think I should give him a second chance,' responded Dawn looking relieved.

'I would if I were you Dawn, besides he is devastatingly handsome,' said Kathryn with a wink.

'True, he is not all that bad!' said Dawn cheering up.

CHAPTER THIRTY-FIVE
THE UNREST IN EUROPE

'It is just as I had predicted,' said Alexander holding up the *Times* newspaper to show the headlines. 'See, Adolf Hitler announces secret rearmament that has been going on since the late 1920s.'

Kathryn looked at the newspaper over Alexander's shoulder. 'What does this mean?' asked Kathryn almost too afraid to hear the answer.

'Nothing at the moment particularly, but he is not to be trusted.' Somehow Alexander did not sound convinced, Kathryn thought.

'We will not go to war again, will we? I could not go through another war!' she exclaimed, her voice laced with concern.

Alexander looked up from his newspaper and gave her a reassuring smile. 'Do not worry my dear, we have each other. Besides we have a lot of work to do here. I may have to travel to France in the next few days or so,' he continued.

'Do not dare miss the opening in May!' said Kathryn trying not to raise her voice.

'Kathryn, I would not miss it for the world but if there is a work matter, then I have to go. I will be back in time, please stop worrying,' said Alexander, putting his arm around her and kissing her cheek.

The last few months Kathryn had noticed a change in his mood. She hoped it was work related and that he was not becoming complacent about her. 'If you had married me in January, we could have had a honeymoon in France and I would not have to leave you again so soon,' said Alexander. There was a tone of resentment in his voice.

'Alexander, I told you I need time to get these races under way and then I can relax and think about the wedding,' she supressed her irritation by grabbing his hand to be close to him.

'But Ernest is getting married on the eve of the opening, why not us?' he asked gently, realising she was in a sensitive mood.

'That is exactly why, we cannot take his and Roberta's thunder. Do not forget we have both been married before, it's their time not ours,' said Kathryn trying to hide her hesitation to marry again.

'Really? Well, I am just the marrying kind, it makes me happy, but not this halfway house kind of status quo,' said Alexander feeling the growing frustration with the situation.

'Is that how you see us? I had no idea Alexander!' responded Kathryn looking unnerved.

'All right, maybe I am exaggerating a little, but I am not master in my own house, I feel like a guest. And when we open to the public, how will they perceive me, as your live in lover?' asked Alexander feeling his pride bruised.

Kathryn sunk into the bench. It was Sunday afternoon. The sun had just tried to make an appearance through the clouds and then a dismal grey cloud had covered it. At least the frost had gone from the early morning. Kathryn was on the lookout for the flowering new buds of the orange lilies that were the most familiar to her of Dallington Place. Maybe she should invite Vicar Sanderson around for dinner, discuss the matters with him, but she knew she did not feel ready to marry again. In fact, she enjoyed her freedom now and as long as Alexander was not away for longer than a couple of weeks at a time, she was content with that. But clearly he was not.

'Shall we go in? It is cold and I need to discuss some plans with Sebastien about the renovation of the first cottage,' said Kathryn suddenly sensing Alexander's disinterest in Dallington Races.

'Well, it is rather well then that I will be away for a while, out of your way,' Alexander stood up and put his hands defensively in his pockets.

'Alexander, please do not speak like this. We were so happy in France with all our plans in September and now you seem unhappy. What has changed between us?' asked Kathryn, as she stood up to walk back to the house.

'My dearest Kathryn, nothing has changed, my feelings certainly have not. But to be a real part in all this, I should be your husband. It's been a major decision for me to retire and if Dallington Place is to be my home, I need to play a larger role. You can understand that surely?' said Alexander, now looking into her eyes for a sign of commitment.

As they walked back to the house together, Kathryn was pensive. She wanted to agree with him and make their partnership official, but something was holding her back and she was not sure what it was. 'Can you give me until you return from France? I will make peace with myself, knowing I will no longer be Devlin's wife, but yours.'

Kathryn hoped to see a positive response from him, but he gave no assurance.

He just shrugged his shoulders and appeared preoccupied as he gave her a gentle kiss on the top of her head. 'I am going to read the papers in the study, you carry on with Sebastien,' said Alexander as he took off his overcoat and threw it over a back of a chair in the entrance hall.

'You do still love me Alexander?' she asked hanging up her coat on the stand.

'Of course I do, that is why I want to marry you, silly!' he said picking up a newspaper without looking at her and walking away towards the study.

'Good. I love you too,' she called after him, but she could not help but feel irritated by him. Gone was the cheerful, happy Alexander. He was beginning to resemble a rather grumpy bear roaming around the house and he had gone unusually quiet. Too quiet.

'Perhaps he misses his work, you know, it has been quite the transition for him. And not to have you on his side officially, maybe he feels insecure,' said Geraldine warming her hands by the fire. It was Monday morning and Alexander had gone into the village with Dawson to buy some new shoes for Paris. William had dropped off Geraldine for breakfast at Dallington Place in his new racing green MG. The ladies were sitting in the drawing room by the fire.

'But I am by his side, it is just that I am not ready to marry again, not just yet,' said Kathryn feeling rather aggravated having to explain herself again even to Geraldine.

'Maybe you do not love him enough,' said Geraldine, curiously studying Kathryn's face. She knew her friend only too well and did not believe this was just about her hesitation about marrying again.

'I love him enough Geraldine, but I cannot help feeling the shadow of my Devlin,' Kathryn hopelessly looked at Geraldine for advice.

'Alexander can sense that too Kathryn. I think you may finally have to let Devlin go,' said Geraldine, realising that perhaps she had been too severe on her friend who was still clearly enjoying her unmarried status.

'And you would if you loved someone?' asked Kathryn now becoming annoyed at her friend.

'Put it this way, what if there was someone else for you, I mean in the future, and you settled for something less?' said Geraldine, sensing that perhaps Alexander was not a big love for Kathryn.

'I am not settling, we get on so well. He is a great business partner and he is fun to be with. I feel safe with him,' replied Kathryn feeling uncomfortable voicing her reasons to be with him.

'Safe?' Geraldine looked at her stunned.

'Yes, safe,' Kathryn said indignantly plonking herself down opposite her friend.

'You were safe with Devlin, but Alexander is not Devlin. He is a different kettle of fish altogether,' said Geraldine.

'Well, he has to give me some more time. I want to marry him but I want to concentrate on work at least for the next four months. Nothing is going to change my mind,' said Kathryn determined.

'I do not think he will like it Kathryn, not one bit, if he comes back at all from France,' responded Geraldine rather too sharply.

'What makes you say such things?' Kathryn nearly choked on her tea. It had not even crossed her mind that Alexander might not return.

'Because I think he needs something to hold on to,' said Geraldine.

'My dear friend, have you lost your mind? He wants to marry me, he says he does,' said Kathryn trying to convince herself.

'But you say yourself you are not ready. Only time will tell, see what happens in the next few months,' suggested Geraldine wanting to steer the conversation away from Alexander.

'I think you have him all wrong,' said Kathryn almost sulking now.

'He is very black or white and nothing in between, and you Kathryn are a dreamer.' Geraldine immediately regretted what she had said.

Kathryn looked at Geraldine astounded. 'Thank you very much!' Kathryn spat back as if her friend had betrayed her.

'No, I mean in a good way, look what you have achieved here. But if Alexander feels he cannot fit in here, then maybe he is right,' said Geraldine pursing her lips.

'You mean if I am not Mrs Pillard, then he does not want to be here?' asked Kathryn.

'Precisely. And you are clearly hesitating at the moment and it hurts him. He is a man with a lot of pride and I think you are denting it,' continued Geraldine knowing Alexander would feel belittled.

'Good lord! If I gave it that much thought, I would not be able to get out of bed and work in the morning,' said Kathryn stoically.

'I am just saying. Anyway, let him go to France and you will know how you feel in a couple of months,' suggested Geraldine as she walked to the window. 'Shall we go for a walk to clear our minds?' she smiled at her friend.

The wind was beginning to howl outside and Kathryn remembered the poem Bertram had written about March at Dallington Place. It was late afternoon and Geraldine had left and now she felt very alone. She could hear Sebastien and Dawn squabbling in the hall. Ernest and Roberta had gone to see a show in London and Alexander was in his study not wanting to be disturbed. Maybe she should take some whisky to him and chat to him before he leaves for Paris in the morning, she thought. She did not knock and when she entered into the room, she could hear him laughing with someone on the telephone. She had not heard him laugh like that in months. He was startled and swung around when he saw her, putting the telephone receiver down immediately. And if she was not mistaken, he had shot her a look of deep annoyance. 'I did not mean to interrupt, I am sorry Alexander,' she said hurryingly.

'It is alright, it was only my editor and the line went, bad connection,' said Alexander shadily not meeting her eyes.

'It is the storm… I brought you some whisky,' she said placing the glass down firmly on the table in front of him and not looking at him. She knew something was not quite as it seemed.

CHAPTER THIRTY-SIX
THE RACES AND THE WEDDING

30th MAY 1935

Kathryn did not expect any more guests now until two o'clock as the wedding was at four. The Fitchs and the Stedmans had arrived the night before and they all had a lovely meal together prepared by Sebastien and the new chef, Monsieur Pascal, hired for the restaurant from Paris. Geraldine and William would be arriving with Roberta. Kathryn had made their rooms into luxurious suites especially for the wedding. Orange lilies adorned the house everywhere and pretty cream and pink roses decorated the house outside. Kathryn and Sebastien had worked tirelessly until late yesterday afternoon turning Dallington Place into a beautiful wedding venue. Sebastien and Dawson had hung the McAlister family crest in red, yellow and black by the front door. This was a wedding gift that Kathryn had not had time to put up yet. She felt it fitting to have it placed at this moment in the memory of Devlin and to celebrate the wedding of their son. The crosses on the crest signified "One who had conquered", referring to the Gallowglass warriors who returned to Ulster in Ireland from Scotland in the fourteen century. Kathryn knew how proud Devlin was of his Irish roots.

Kathryn felt she could sleep for a week as she sat at her desk in the study looking out to the ten tables beautifully set up on the front lawn for the wedding breakfast. A canopy had been put in place just in case of rain, although good weather was predicted. The preparations for the grand opening of Dallington Races had been completed only the day before. Sebastien had turned one of the cottages into a restaurant, and that was where Sebastien had spent most of the last two months. Kathryn had suggested it to be called Sebastien's. Monsieur Pascal was working alongside seven other cooks from the village. Six new horses had arrived a few days ago from Deauville and another stable block had been completed for visiting horses and their jockeys. The paddocks beautifully mowed and the old gates painted white, new turf on the racecourse and food and stalls from various businesses had arrived earlier that day. The press had also been lingering outside the gates and although Kathryn was not eager to send them away, she was aware that for the sake of Ernest and Roberta's privacy, they were kept back. Alexander had kept his word and although appearing emotionally distant, he had sent money telegrams regularly to the point of extreme generosity. Kathryn had not had to ask him to settle anything, she was able to have what she planned and everything had gone smoothly financially. She had missed him, but she had been working so hard like never before she had not had much time to be sad. Poor Dawson had been relegated to the house until the racing season was over, and then he could move back to his cottage. He did not grumble and seemed to enjoy the hustle and bustle of this new business venture.

Kathryn only thought of Alexander as she stepped into her grey silk dress, one that he had bought her during their last visit to London. A dark orange hat lay on the bed and as she picked it up she felt her loss at going to her son's wedding alone. Reminding herself she was not alone, Dawson had offered to escort her into the church, she realised how lucky she was.

Peeping out of her bedroom door, she saw Roberta standing at the top of the stairs in her wedding gown, calling to her mother to help her with the buttons. Ernest and Sebastien had gone into the village to have a drink, and she so wanted to talk to Ernest and even help Roberta herself, but it was not her place to do so. She could hear Geraldine calling up to her. She watched the two embrace, the two women who were so dear to her. She was not alone, she reminded herself, far from it. The first automobile pulled up outside and she could see Dawson smartly dressed, his shoes making a crunching sound on the gravel as he went to help the guests. Kathryn carefully positioned her hat, tucking stray curls underneath it and walked downstairs to welcome the guests for pre-wedding refreshments. By half three, the garden was clear of guests and they were already settled inside the church. Kathryn went upstairs to talk to Roberta. Geraldine was sitting on the bed, with tears in her eyes. Roberta looked so beautiful, her tiny waist accentuated in her Lachasse Collections wedding dress by Hardy Amis. The silk tulle hung just above her ankles and her bouquet of forget-me-nots lay on the dressing table. Kathryn stood smiling at the pair and then reached out for both of their hands. They all stood there silently for a moment until there was knock at the door. It was Sebastien asking Kathryn to come downstairs and talk to Ernest. William had arrived to collect Roberta, Geraldine and the bridesmaids in a cream and black Daimler with cream ribbons tied to the bonnet. He stood patiently smoking outside the open door waiting for his wife and daughter. Two young bridesmaids were sitting in the car looking pretty with midsummer silver garlands adorning their hair.

Kathryn shut the study door and drew the curtains so Ernest could not see Roberta before the ceremony. She walked over to her son who was sitting by the fireplace looking pensive. She sat on the arm of his chair and brushed some imaginary dust from his shoulder. 'Are you ready?' she asked him.

'As ready as I will ever be,' he replied with a broad smile. She knew that smile and it settled her. He looked relaxed and handsome. Both with calm tempers and cheerful dispositions, in her heart she knew this union was going to last.

She could still hear the music as she shuffled papers on her desk before turning out the lights. It was past midnight and she presumed most of the wedding guests had gone home. A man stood at the door, ajar enough for him to see her and when she approached him, thinking he was a lost wedding guest, she did not jump in surprise straight away.

'It is me, I got back an hour ago, the car broke down near Pepworth, but here I am,' said Alexander his voice tired with emotion, pleased to see Kathryn again.

'You made it back, I cannot believe it, Alexander! You made it back in time for the opening,' she said her voice croaky with exhaustion.

'I said I would, did I not?' She ran into his arms relieved he was there for her.

THE RACES 31ST MAY 1935

Kathryn woke up early on the morning of the races. She could tell the weather was going to be fine and feeling restless, she decided to go for an early stroll down to the racetrack. She stopped to sit for a quiet moment perched by the edge of the fountain. She put her hand in the cool water and looked up at the stone carved horse and rider. She remembered Lady Fitch telling her it was a replica of the Adelaide's Boer War Memorial monument in memory of South Australian soldiers who died in the Second Boer War. It had been commissioned by Lady Fitch's mother Clare Astell, an Australian who met and married Lord George Fitch in Adelaide. It was put in place to represent the union of the families, the Astells and the Fitchs at Dallington Place.

Now it suitably represented the union of the three families – McAlisters, Wrights and Lovets.

Everything seemed crystal clear and gorgeous. The band was playing on the stage while attractive people milled about and photographers flashed away with their cameras. The racehorses and their jockeys wearing vibrant racing silks representing Deauville, Sussex and Yorkshire walked around in the parade ring waiting for the first race to start. Racegoers were standing by the ring checking out their chosen horse's pedigree and racing history. Horses with their gleaming coats bristling in the heat and their nostrils flaring up all fired up ready to go. A pretty woman on the arm of a well-dressed man was gracefully sipping champagne and asking people if they knew where Sebastien Comte-Wright might be. 'In the restaurant most likely,' said a newspaper reporter, who had just interviewed him. 'It is called Sebastien's, you cannot miss it, next to Dallington Place, the main house,' the man corrected.

Rudyard Kipling had just cut the ribbon, announcing the opening of Dallington Races. There was a sea of photographers and Kathryn shielding her eyes, thanked and toasted him lifting her glass to the sky in triumph: 'Let the races begin,' she announced. Beaming as she held on to Alexander's arm as he led her down from the stand. 'Where is Pilot?' she asked looking around for the horse she hoped may win the first race.

'There, in the orange and lime racing colours of Dallington Place,' said Alexander passing his binoculars to Kathryn. 'You know Kathryn, I did not really realise how much I have missed Dallington Place until now. I have missed you so much and with or without marriage, I want to be with you,' said Alexander lovingly placing his arm around her waist. He understood that people thought them husband and wife anyway. Friends and strangers alike nodded to them with respect as they walked on by. Children were playing at the fairground in the far end of the paddock and racegoers hurried by to place their bets on the first race. Kathryn lovingly crooked her head onto his shoulder.

'You know, when I saw you again last night Alexander, I realised I had been stubborn and perhaps you are right, we should get married,' she said meaning every word of it.

'I would not rush you Kathryn, let us just enjoy these moments when we have them. I am not sure we can take anything for granted anymore,' replied Alexander. He knew these were unpredictable times and another war was inevitable. He was happy to be there with Kathryn at this moment.

'You think another war is feasible then?' she asked sipping her champagne, which he had just passed to her.

'I do,' he said now stopping to lean against the white fence. 'There is Pilot!' said Alexander pointing to the chestnut horse, his nostrils flaring as his groom was walking him around the ring, ready to win the race of his life.

'There you two lovebirds are,' said Sebastien striding up to them looking very handsome in his black suit and a waistcoat carrying their racing colours of orange and lime.

'Well done, you have Pilot's racing colours on!' exclaimed Kathryn with excitement.

'Look Kathryn,' said Sebastien as he took off his jacket and turned around to show the back of the waistcoat. It had the McAlister's family crest embossed on it. 'I thought the family crest would be a good idea to put in front of the menu too,' continued Sebastien, noticing Alexander wincing uncomfortably.

'Good luck!' said a gentleman with a pretty lady on his arm as they walked passed.

'My goodness, it is Sebastien, is it not?' said the lady in a strong American accent.

'Holly, is that you?' said Sebastien shocked to see Holly again.

'How wonderful to see you, we were looking for you!' exclaimed Holly, delighted to find her long lost friend. Her cousin, who was in London had found out that the Dallington Races were taking place and on a hunch Holly had decided to go.

'Good to see you again, Mr Lovelace. Let me introduce you to Kathryn McAlister and Alexander Pillard, the owners of Dallington Races,' said Sebastien turning to Mr Lovelace and shaking his hand.

'I am Mrs Lovelace now, Sebastien,' said Holly as she shook their hands.

'How do you know each other?' asked Kathryn, eyeing Holly with interest but keeping one eye on the proceedings in the paddock.

At that moment Kathryn wished she had been introduced as Mrs Pillard, as she looked back to this beautiful woman proudly showing off her diamond wedding ring to Sebastien. 'We met in New York, what nearly five years ago now, is it Sebastien?' said Holly turning to Sebastien.

'I dare say it is, and I am married too. My wife is expecting our first child and is resting up at the house,' Sebastien said proudly.

'How wonderful,' she said again, but Kathryn noticed she said this without any gaiety in her voice this time.

'They are off, Kathryn,' said Alexander leaning over the fence and keeping a keen eye on the race. Roars from the crowd went up as the horses made their way around the track. Hooves pounding and a voice commentating live over the tannoy. Kathryn watched in exhilaration, digging her fingers into Alexander's forearm as Pilot made his way down in the middle of the stampeding horses. Suddenly he appeared in third, then second, his gait reaching further and speeding up even faster. He was now coming close to Captain Morgan, reaching past just before the finishing line. Bon Chance from the Rothschild's Haras de Meautry farm came third. 'I do believe he is going to be placed!' said Alexander holding up the binoculars to Kathryn who was jumping up and down in anticipation. The two horses were now neck and neck as they came close to the final furlong. Bon Chance from the Rothschild's Haras de Meautry farm lingering in third place. Taking the binoculars back from Kathryn, who was now clutching at his arm like a child, he lifted them up again only to see Pilot win by a nose length, or so he thought. 'I do believe he has won it, but just wait, see what they say,' he said turning to red faced Kathryn.

A roar went up in the crowd. 'Pilot gets his first win. Well done to Mrs McAlister!' announced the commentator. Another roar went up in the crowd again. Kathryn had never felt so proud to have brought life back to the area. She watched the crowds chatting and bustling about placing their bets in a hurry. Elegant men and attractive women in their finery lounged about. She had also noticed some men standing proudly in their military uniforms with medals hanging from multi-coloured ribbons against the dark of the uniform. Kathryn's thoughts briefly shifted to Bertram and Robert.

'Well done Mrs McAlister, you really are good at this!'' congratulated Holly, beaming flirtatiously at Sebastien at the same time. Sebastien walked over to Kathryn and lifted her up in the air and placed her down again to kiss her on both cheeks. Kathryn giggled like a young girl. Coming around from the exhilarating win, Kathryn held on to the fence to catch her breath. Sebastien was already running off to get a glass of champagne for her. Holly let go of her husband's arm and asked Kathryn if she was alright.

'I think so, I feel a little flustered, as if I am walking on air. It's the adrenaline I think. There is only so much excitement I can take in a day,' she said touching Holly's arm. She was warming to this American woman with her fun manner. 'Would you like to join us back at the house after I have congratulated the jockey and received the prize? I could do with a cup of tea back in the quiet. Also you can meet Sebastien's wife,' suggested Kathryn.

'I would like that very much, thank you. I heard so much about Dallington Place when Sebastien and I were in New York,' replied Holly delighted to finally meet Kathryn.

'You must tell me all about your time in New York,' said Kathryn being passed a glass of champagne by Sebastien to savour the moment of success. They all clinked glasses together.

'Thank you Sebastien, now let us go up to the winner's enclosure. Holly, we will see you in say half an hour?' said Kathryn taking Alexander's arm again.

Holly smiled and she and her husband walked off to mingle with the fashionable crowd. 'I would love to meet Rudyard Kipling, darling...' she was heard saying as her smile grew wider with triumph. Sebastien overheard and he smiled to himself. Holly, ever the social climber, he thought.

Dawn was lying on the chaise longue in the drawing room. Alison was passing her daughter a cup of tea and fussing over her placing a cold cloth on her forehead. 'I cannot bear missing the races, but my ankles are so swollen. Should I at least try to make an appearance?' she asked her mother clearly anguished in her very pregnant state.

Alison could see Kathryn walking along to the front of the house, talking to a couple she did not recognise. Sebastien walked behind them and had stopped for a chat with Dawson. He was sunning himself in front of the house, sitting in his deckchair near the front door keeping guard so no unwanted visitors made their way to the main house. 'It looks as if they have come to us instead!' said Alison turning to her daughter.

They could hear chatter and laughter growing louder as they entered the drawing room. 'How are you feeling, Dawn?' asked Kathryn, her face looking radiant and still blushed with the excitement of the race.

'Not too well, I hope the baby is not coming early,' said Dawn giving Kathryn an agonised look.

'How are you my love?' asked Sebastien as he walked in to kiss his wife on her cheek.

Dawn gave her husband a frail smile. She noticed a couple she did not recognise. 'Oh let me introduce you my love, this is Mr and Mrs Lovelace,' said Sebastien rather awkwardly, knowing Dawn would be furious with him later for not warning her they would have visitors.

Dawn looked to Holly as she tried to hitch herself up on the chaise longue, not to feel as enormous as she probably looked. The young woman was extremely attractive, Dawn thought, and considerably younger than her husband.

'How has the racing gone?' asked Alison eager to hear of any excitement. '

'We won the first race, can you believe it!' said Kathryn triumphantly.

'Good ol' Pilot, I knew he would do it!' said Dawn cheering up.

'You are knowledgeable about horses?' asked Holly looking surprised at Dawn.

'Why yes, I was brought up in Texas on a ranch. Just because I look like a whale, does not mean I do not know anything!' she replied arrogantly, trying to put Holly in her place.

'Oh I am so sorry, I was not implying anything, it was just Sebastien had not told me...,' said Holly blushing. Sebastien looked awkwardly at Holly, who just shrugged.

Dawn shot her husband a suspicious look. How does he know Holly anyway, she wondered. 'How does my husband know you, Mrs Lovelace?' asked Dawn abruptly.

Kathryn was beginning to worry that Dawn was stressing herself. She moved over to the chaise longue and put her hand over Dawn's. 'Would you all like some homemade lemonade? I will ring for Dawson,' offered Kathryn trying to warm the sudden chill in the room.

'We go way back and I am Holly by the way,' said Holly offering a smile.

Dawn glared back at her, she did not like this Holly at all. The impertinence of her flirting with Sebastien while her husband stood by saying nothing to his flibbertigibbet wife.

'We met in New York darling, we lived in the same apartment block,' explained Sebastien, noticing his wife's annoyance. 'And then I sailed with Sebastien to Le Havre, where I met my wonderful Alfred, did I not darling?' Holly joined in as she snuggled up to her husband.

'Yes and she told me that Sebastien was her little brother, my mischievous wife,' said Alfred now chortling.

'Why the deceit?' asked Dawn crossly looking at neither of them for an answer.

'It was a joke, Dawn for goodness sake, where is your sense of humour these days?' said Sebastien irritated by his wife who had become so tiresome.

'Sorry, I have been cooped up here for weeks on end, I cannot ride my horses and I am swollen like an elephant!' said Dawn with tears in her eyes. She was so tired of her husband's intimidating behaviour.

'Dawn, would you like the doctor to check on you this evening? Kathryn, would that be all right? She does not look well,' asked Alison with a concerned look on her face.

'I am fine mother, I am just pregnant,' Dawn felt her mother was fussing too much. Sebastien muttered something under his breath, which made Holly smile.

Dawn looked as if she was about to burst into tears, but just at that moment, Dawson came in with a tray of lemonade.

'Dawson could you ring Dr Laraby for me please. See if he can see Dawn later this evening when most of the crowds have left. And can you make sure he has a pass to get in,' asked Kathryn.

'Yes Ma'am, will do, I was wondering if you were going to see the next race?' asked Dawson as he poured some lemonade in the glasses.

'Dawson, did you put a bet on?' asked Sebastien slyly.

'Yes, I am afraid I did,' responded Dawson rather awkwardly.

'Good for you,' said Kathryn smiling back at Dawson. 'Where is Alexander? Did he go and find out where Ernest and Roberta have got to? They are leaving at five o'clock, just before the last race,' said Kathryn feeling rather overwhelmed at the fast pace of the day.

Finishing her lemonade, she saw Alexander on the main lawn from the window. She made her excuses to leave and watch the next race. 'We must find Ernest and Roberta, Alexander. I must spend some time with them before they leave on honeymoon,' said Kathryn clutching Alexander's arm tightly. 'I am worried about Dawn and Sebastien. I am beginning to think they can no longer stand the sight of each other,' she continued with a lump in her throat.

'They will settle down once the baby arrives, I am sure,' said Alexander soothingly as he patted his fiancé's hand.

'I am not so sure. Sebastien just does not have the patience for anything that is not fun!' responded Kathryn, knowing full well that once the baby is here, matters between them could grow worse.

'Well, he just needs the responsibility of fatherhood, all in good time I feel. Look there are Geraldine and William, let us go and join them,' said Alexander gesturing at them standing by the grandstand.

'Have you seen Ernest, Geraldine?' asked Kathryn as they walked over, expecting them to be with Geraldine.

'Did you not see them? They must have passed you just now, they have gone up to the house to pack,' responded Geraldine looking over to the main lawn of Dallington Place shielding her eyes from the sun.

'We have just walked back from the house in fact,' said Kathryn surprised their paths haven't crossed.

'You literally just missed them,' added William watching the second race with great interest. He had bet quite a bit of money on Kathryn's horse called Geraldine's Run.

'You know Geraldine, I was wondering, do you mind coming back to the house to take a look at Dawn. She seems ever so swollen, I am hoping there is nothing serious going on,' pleaded Kathryn with a worried look.

'She cannot be in labour yet, can she? I thought she still had a few weeks to go,' Geraldine paused and stared at Kathryn in bewilderment.

'I do not like the look of her and you have always been a better nurse than me,' said Kathryn looking at Geraldine with a growing concern.

'No, not better, you were fabulous in the war Kathryn. I just have more years of experience but I do not have my medical bag with me,' answered Geraldine, as they turned to walk towards the house. A roar went up in the crowd. 'Got it! She placed, how marvellous,' cheered William, trying to attract his wife's attention. Geraldine smiled at him, 'William darling, I will meet you back here in half an hour. I have something to attend to with Kathryn,' she continued.

'Right you are dear, go and do your thing,' said William with a jovial wink, not realising the seriousness of the situation.

'I have some things and the doctor is coming later. It is just that I would like to check her over that is all. If we have to get her into the local hospital, it is better we give them some notice,' said Kathryn knowing how the hospital had so few staff at the moment.

'Look, there is Dawson, but he is coming from the house. I wonder why he is not watching the race, he had money on it you see,' said Kathryn casting a worried look at Geraldine. They both instantly knew something was wrong.

'Ma'am, I am sorry to trouble you but it is Mrs Comte-Wright. I think she maybe in labour,' red faced Dawson managed to utter between breaths having walked so fast.

'Is Sebastien with her?' asked Kathryn not waiting for an answer as she started to run towards the house with Geraldine in tow.

'Yes, and Lady Alison, the Lovelaces have left for home, apparently their house is nearby,' replied Dawson hurrying after Kathryn.

'Well done Dawson, and thank goodness Geraldine is with me. See if Dr Laraby can be called out immediately please. We will have to manage until then,' said Kathryn her face flustered with nerves.

'Maybe we can get her to the hospital. It is her first baby so maybe we have got some time,' suggested Geraldine as she caught up with Kathryn.

'Oh yes, good idea and Dawson, could you please have an automobile on standby just in case we need to get her to the hospital?' asked Kathryn, her heart pounding wondering where Libby and Irene were.

'Yes Ma'am,' replied Dawson breathless and perspiring from the heat and excitement.

Kathryn wondered if she was asking too much of him. 'And Dawson, when you see Alexander, can you tell him to pass on my goodbyes to everyone, to Mr Kipling especially, and say that we have an emergency,' said Kathryn.

'Yes of course Ma'am I will, I am sure Mr Pillard will see to it,' answered Dawson as he turned around and walked down towards the racecourse.

The ladies ran the half mile to the house, Kathryn in front. The sun had just set and it had started to rain. A few automobiles were leaving the site, having seen the rain come and people were starting to think about ending their day at the Dallington Races. 'I do not like that thunder cloud up above our heads, I hope it will not frighten the horses. Thank goodness only one race to go,' said Kathryn out of breath as they reached the front door.

Ernest was standing in the entrance, nervously running his hands through his hair. 'She is in a lot of pain. Roberta and Alison are with her but they do not know what to do,' said Sebastien rushing down the stairs all the colour drained from his face.

Geraldine touched his shoulder to comfort. 'It is alright, we are here. Let us just hope it is straightforward,' said Geraldine knowing her nursing skills would only get her so far. She was not a midwife and if there was a serious problem, well, she did not want to think about it. 'Kathryn, go to the kitchen and boil lots of water. I will send Roberta down to fetch it. Has Dr Laraby been called?' asked Geraldine, rolling up her sleeves and running up the stairs to the bathroom to wash her hands.

Sebastien had already poured himself a whisky in the drawing room. He knocked it back as Kathryn shouted from the kitchen asking him to give her a hand. Just as they were coming up the back stairs with two pails of hot water, Geraldine was coming down the main staircase. 'Alarm over,' she shouted.'

'No baby?' asked Dawson now coming through the front door with Dr Laraby.

'On the contrary, Dawson, we have a new life here at Dallington Place!' She beamed proudly hands on her hips as she stood on the last stair.

Kathryn let Sebastien go in first. 'You have a daughter, Sebastien,' she whispered.

'What shall we call her?' said Sebastien as he moved by the bed and kissed Dawn's cheek. He looked at this little baby with thick black hair and smiled to himself how alike she looked to him.

'Well it is up to you, but I know you liked June. We are still on the last day of May, so how about May-Lilian after the beautiful lilies that Kathryn so loves here at Dallington Place?' suggested Dawn with tears of joy and looking up to the proud father. She felt a closeness to Sebastien that she had not felt in a long time.

'May-Lilian, I love it, but I will call her Lilian,' said Sebastien proudly taking his daughter from Dawn, loving her fragile little body immediately. He did not want to let her go, only passing her to Kathryn when he had to.

'I think the baby will be his making,' said Kathryn sweetly kissing Dawn on her cheek and nodding at Sebastien. 'What a bonny baby girl, welcome to Dallington Place, May-Lilian,' Kathryn gently placed a kiss on her forehead before leaving the room so the new family could enjoy their new addition in private.

The bags were packed into the automobile already and Roberta climbed into the beautiful Daimler and sat next to Ernest to begin their honeymoon. Geraldine was dabbing her eyes and Kathryn put her arm around her friend and rested her head on her shoulder. 'They will be alright, will they not Kathryn?' Geraldine managed to say through her tears.

'Of course, you old softie, she is with my Ernest. Of course she will be all right!' Kathryn assured her friend with a hug.

'I know I am just overwhelmed with today and delivering the baby!' sobbed Geraldine. Both women looked emotionally drained but overjoyed.

'Oh, you make me the proudest friend Geraldine!' exclaimed Kathryn as she held her friend even tighter. '

'Oh be quiet,' said Geraldine wiping the last tear away. Roberta and Ernest had left later than planned due to the new arrival and darkness was beginning to fall. Rain had been falling in torrents. 'New beginnings Kathryn, new beginnings,' said Geraldine as she watched William talking to Mr Montgomery near the stables. He looked to their direction and walked up to the front lawn. 'Mr Montgomery thinks the river may burst its banks, we will have to move quickly to get the horses in for the night,' said William. 'Goodness, better to be safe than sorry. Geraldine, could you check on doctor Laraby and stay with Dawn and send the men down please?' said Kathryn as she started to walk towards the house to fetch raincoats for everyone.

Calling for Irene to come and help, she passed Libby in the hall. 'Where is Dawson, Libby?' asked Kathryn.

'He is resting in his cottage, Ma'am,' she replied.

'Could you make sure he oversees the last of the racegoers and to ask if there are any volunteers to help us at the stables? And has anyone seen Mr Pillard?' continued Kathryn as she picked up some raincoats.

'I think he is in the drawing room on the telephone, Ma'am,' answered Libby.

The horses had sensed the change in the atmosphere. They were snorting and nervously stamping their feet on the field. Kathryn walked Pilot into his box, while Mr Montgomery was walking in two others. 'Well done boy,' said Kathryn stroking the chestnut's shiny neck, pleased as punch at her horse's success. She was wondering why Alexander had not come to help. Ernest and Sebastien brought in the rest of the riding school horses, while some local jockeys were helping to put the Deauville racehorses into their boxes, just in time before the downfall. Captain Morgan was neighing restlessly in a corner of his box. Shutting the stable doors half an hour later, Kathryn thanked Mr

Montgomery and made her way back to the house with Ernest and Sebastien. She was fuming with anger that Alexander had failed to help out. What an earth is he busy with, she thought.

No one got a wink of sleep that night. The river did indeed swell up and some of the cottages on the further side of Dallington Place and even Willow Tree Cottage were all flooded. 'No casualties though, Ma'am,' said Dawson with a sigh of relief next morning.

'Thank the Lord for that Dawson, and we were so lucky to have had the day we did and the sun shining during the races,' said Kathryn realising how lucky they had been. 'Ma'am, is it alright if I have the day off today, I have to go and see my sister in Bexhill,' asked Dawson. The hard work and high emotions in the past few days had taken their toll on him and he was desperate for some rest.

'Of course Dawson, you have been an invaluable help. I will ask Irene to take over, you go and rest,' said Kathryn watching him move slowly and exhaustedly to the door.

He turned as he reached to open it. 'Oh Ma'am, I forgot someone handed in a brooch this morning. It must have belonged to one of the racegoers. What do I do with it?' he enquired.

'Oh I will sort it out, you go and relax,' said Kathryn walking towards him to take a closer look at the piece of jewellery. As she took it from him she felt her heart race. 'My goodness Dawson, it's my sweetheart brooch! I lost it years ago, how on earth has someone found it now? I thought I had lost it for good,' said Kathryn starring at its two hearts entwined, not believing she was holding it once again. The risen river must have washed it up to the land, she thought.

'That is marvellous, Ma'am,' he said as he walked out of the door. 'The river has brought it back to me,' muttered Kathryn under her breath. How wonderful, she thought as she pinned it back on her lapel and felt a completeness wash over her.

CHAPTER THIRTY-SEVEN
CHRISTMAS 1938

'And those that we hold most dear can whisper on, if love is not requited.'

A plate hit the wall and smashed into pieces. Kathryn sat in her study overhearing the argument between Sebastien and Dawn. Little Lilian sat by Kathryn's feet playing with one of her dolls. She was just about to go to calm the situation down between them when the telephone rang. 'Ma'am, it is Pearl on the telephone for you,' Dawson appeared at the door.

'Thank you Dawson, and you know I can answer the telephone from now on,' said Kathryn smiling warmly at the old man.

'Force of habit, Ma'am,' he returned her smile. The old man was looking more frail than ever, but refusing to retire.

Kathryn expected it to be from Petra's friend Pearl in London, who looked after the housekeeping when she or Ernest and Roberta stayed at Throgmorton Street in London. 'Pearl, how nice to hear from you. Did Ernest and Roberta arrive on time this morning?' There was a pause on the line. 'Hello?' Kathryn repeated.

An American voice spoke down the rather crackly line. 'Is this Kathryn McAlister I am speaking to?' said the voice.

'Yes this is she!' responded Kathryn confused for a moment.

'My name is Pearl Pillard. I just want to inform you that Alexander and I were married this morning in New York,' the American woman continued.

'What, who are you, there must be a mistake,' said Kathryn now feeling rather faint. She sat down holding on to the telephone receiver as she heard muffled voices down the line.

Then she heard Alexander's voice. 'Kathryn, I am sorry, there is no mistake, I am not coming back,' he said down the cracking line.

Kathryn could not believe what she was hearing. 'Alexander, what are you talking about? You only left here a week ago and who was that woman?' her mouth was dry and her heart racing.

'I am sorry Kathryn to do this to you, but I was not happy and I think I am better off here in New York with Pearl,' he said slowly. Kathryn could hear he was embarrassed.

'But I was happy Alexander. And what about the business, what about our life together here at Dallington Place?' Little Lilian was now trying to climb onto Kathryn's lap as she could see large tears pour down Kathryn's cheeks.

'I told you Kathryn, I am the marrying kind and you did not want to get married,' he continued.

'But you told me you did not mind, why so sudden, this is madness!' she nearly shouted with a rising panic.

'I know, I know, but Kathryn the war is coming you have to understand, and the business, well when the war comes...,' Alexander's voice faded away.

'What are you talking about, it is not definite,' a cold chill suddenly passed through Kathryn. She had not thought about the possibility of war for a while.

'Kathryn, you will see. I have to go, I wish you all the best but start to close the business down,' he said abruptly without further explanation.

'What, I cannot do that, it is our livelihood! Alexander you are not speaking any sense!' Kathryn now nearly screaming on the telephone.

'The line is breaking up. I will write to you. I will always love you...,' he managed to say and then the line went dead.

Kathryn sat in silence for a moment with Lilian holding her tightly around the neck. The door burst open and Sebastien marched over to pick up Lilian in his arms. 'She is going to ride whether you like it or not, you confounded woman!' Sebastien shouted at Dawn, who marched red faced into the room. Both of them utterly unaware of what devastation had taken place in Kathryn's life just that second ago. Still shouting at each other, Kathryn could not bear it any longer.

'Will you both be quiet for once in your selfish lives,' she suddenly screamed at them. Lilian started to cry. They both looked at her surprised, they had never heard Kathryn scream at them like that before. Then Dawn realised she had been crying.

'Kathryn, whatever is the matter?' Dawn asked now worried.

'Please fetch Geraldine for me, something awful has happened, I need her here right now!' sobbed Kathryn.

'Oh my goodness, is it Alexander?' asked Dawn shocked to see the state Kathryn was in. Kathryn could not talk, she could only nod.

'Thank you for staying with me these last few days Geraldine,' said Kathryn grateful to her friend for always being there for her.

'You are welcome and I am glad you are feeling relieved,' replied Geraldine.

'I think it was the shock at first,' said Kathryn as they walked towards the stables. 'You know, although he loved the business side of things, he was never at home here, I see that now. Perhaps I pushed a situation that should never have been,' said Kathryn as she entered Pilot's box.

'No, you cannot say that,' said Geraldine stroking the chestnut's beautiful mane, watching how Kathryn brushed the majestic racehorse.

'Easy boy!' said Kathryn as she stepped out and shut the door.

'He wants you all to himself,' laughed Geraldine watching Pilot's brown eyes look intently at Kathryn. 'You have to concentrate on the business and keep Dallington Races going,' said Geraldine firmly.

'Well, I told you what he said, the Third Reich in Germany has dominated Sudetenland area of Czechoslovakia. Alexander feels this is the beginning of the war. He is usually right,' replied Kathryn her eyes edged with grief.

'Well, that is a lousy excuse for him to disappear to New York and not come back,' said Geraldine disgruntled.

'I suppose it was now or never,' said Kathryn pragmatically, straightening her posture. She had come to terms with the fact that Alexander had found love with Pearl Le Sierre and maybe it had been her fault as much as his. Perhaps she had neglected him and his wishes.

The day was extremely breezy and although the lilies were beginning to bud, frost had set in and killed the first few seedlings. As they walked back to the house to warm up, Kathryn suggested they go and sit in the kitchen so she could look over the menus Sebastien had prepared for the week. They settled by the Aga as Kathryn prepared some Ovomaltine as it was Libby's day off. She perused the menus over the large oak table while sipping her hot drink. 'Geraldine, what do you think of Sebastien's turkey option, Pascal prefers goose?' asked Kathryn.

'Turkey is fitting for the Christmas time but is it not too soon before Christmas Day?' replied Geraldine.

'Let us go for Sebastien's suggestion, I prefer turkey,' said Kathryn making notes for the restaurant.

'And what about the money, was that a guilt thing or had Pearl put him up to it?' Kathryn asked as they warmed their hands with steaming mug of Ovomaltine. Soon after her last conversation with Alexander a letter had arrived with a cheque for twenty-thousand pounds to keep the business and house going. 'Was Pearl a rich widow? It would explain everything. She bought him from you,' said Geraldine.

'That is ridiculous!' said Kathryn furrows appearing at her brow.

'Not really, he wanted to stay in New York. He could not leave you without supporting his side of the business, it makes sense,' continued Geraldine wrapping her shawl tighter around her shoulders.

'But why her, Geraldine, I am sure there are plenty of rich widows in New York to take an eligible bachelor off my hands,' said Kathryn feeling a pang of jealousy.

'Yes, but she was an old girlfriend, was she not? Pierre Le Sierre's widow, maybe she had something on him,' pondered Geraldine staring at the menus.

'You do not think he would have succumbed to blackmail out of some honour thing?' said Kathryn paling and feeling the chill.

'A peaceful life in New York for twenty-thousand, why not? And anyway Kathryn, if you really had loved him as much as Bertram or Devlin, you would have married him,' she looked at her friend, knowing that if she really had loved Alexander, they would have married a long time ago.

'I know you are right, you knew all along,' said Kathryn feeling a sense of regret.

'I knew perhaps he was not the right man for you, especially when he brought that dancer to Dallington's Christmas party,' said Geraldine amused as she remembered that party.

'I know, just awful taste,' said Kathryn smiling at her friend's sense of humour.

'Could I really spend that money if it was Pearl's?' she continued.

'They are married now. It is his money to do what he will with it and if he wants to spend it on Dallington Place, that is up to him!' said Geraldine.

'Well, I will put it aside for a rainy day and when and if war comes,' said Kathryn momentarily looking serious.

MAY 1940

I have nothing to offer but blood, toil, tears and sweat.

(Sir Winston Leonard Spencer-Churchill announced to his cabinet on 13th May 1940)

2nd May 1940, outside Abbeville

Dearest Mamma,

Do not worry about us, we are surviving. Sebastien and I seem to have escaped trouble everywhere we go. We are the lorry drivers for the Rifle Companies of the Seventh Battalion of Royal Sussex Regiment. Do not worry Mamma, his driving skills have improved immensely, we are safe here I think. As I write today, we are on the road to Abbeville, in the Somme region of France. We have just had orders to not continue and to return back to the headquarters. Abbeville has been severely bombed, only the countryside where we are sitting now to have a break, shows signs of life with its marigolds and stinging nettles on the side of the road. They reminded me of Sussex and I am feeling a little homesick, but I am safe Mamma. We have just heard a train has been hit by German fighter pilots with our boys on board near Amiens. Many casualties, Mamma. I am lucky as I was meant to be on that train but I swapped with another soldier as an officer had asked us to be two in the lorry.

I know father was in this area all those years ago. I now recognise the landscape and style of houses he had talked to Sebastien about.

Tell Roberta I love her.

Your loving son,

Ernest

'I have not heard from Sebastien since he enlisted and was sent to France six months ago. I want a divorce from him Kathryn,' said Dawn sitting by the fire with Kathryn one evening.

'I cannot see the point of it, you are just angry with him. What good would it do at the moment? I hear from Ernest on a regular basis and I know they are in the same battalion, so I know Sebastien is safe as well,' said Kathryn calmly.

Dawn had become quite the lady and more mature since becoming a mother, she thought. 'I do not want to be associated with him anymore, I know he was having an affair with Holly Lovelace before he left,' Dawn continued with tears running down her cheeks.

'You cannot be certain of that dear,' said Kathryn reaching down to stoke the fire. It was an unseasonably cold day and Kathryn had asked Dawson to light the fire from early morning knowing the sitting room would be used constantly through the day.

'Everybody knows it. You are the only one who stands up for him, why do you take his side?' Dawn looked at her with those blue eyes clouded with misery with little wrinkles appearing at the side.

'I am not taking sides, it is just that this is not the time to divorce, a man needs to come home to someone from the war, someone who will stand by him,' said Kathryn firmly as she sat down on the edge of her chair.

'Well, maybe I will enlist, there, he can stay here and wait for me!' said Dawn with her eyes firing up with anger.

Suddenly Kathryn saw that old Dawn again, defiant and spoiled. 'Nonsense Dawn, you have to think of Lilian, your daughter,' Kathryn continued aghast at her selfishness.

'Why, when no one thinks of me!' Dawn cried out.

'Well, I think of you and I need you here. God knows, there are not many menfolk left to help around here. Please do not make this any harder, I feel I am at a breaking point knowing my Ernest and Sebastien are out on the French battlefields as we speak,' pleaded Kathryn. She could not bear to be alone in Dallington Place. A sudden feeling of desperation took over her, petrified that her men may not return.

A knock at the door interrupted them, it was Geraldine. 'Dawson let me in. Sorry I should have telephoned, I thought perhaps Roberta may need my support,' said Geraldine entering the room looking flustered.

'Roberta is out with Mr Montgomery feeding the horses, she wanted to keep busy. Thank goodness Mr Montgomery is still here to protect us. Did you know he was refused enlistment, however he has just volunteered as a member of the local defence, so I am hoping he will be here as much as he can,' said Kathryn looking sternly at Dawn, who quickly rose to her feet.

'I will join them. Can you keep an eye on Lilian please?' asked Dawn already walking to the door.

'As always,' responded Kathryn rather sharply. It was not just Dawn that was upsetting her, it was her fear of the war. Yet another war, she was petrified. 'Geraldine, I fear this is probably going to be the worst time of our lives?' said Kathryn looking at her friend, finding it difficult to accept that her two young men were at the war.

'Not quite,' said Geraldine reaching for her handbag for a handkerchief.

'Oh Geraldine, I am so sorry my dear, I did not mean... I mean I had not forgotten Robert either. I am so sorry, I am just upset I can hardly think straight,' said Kathryn feeling guilty she had been so insensitive about her brother. 'Mr Montgomery told me this morning that the government is selecting some manor houses in the area to be transformed into Italian prisoner of war camps. Could you imagine Dallington Place as a prisoner camp?' exclaimed Kathryn holding her face with her hands. Geraldine was too deep in her thoughts to even hear what she was saying.

An automobile pulled up outside and a door was slammed shut almost angrily. 'Is that them, are they back? I did not expect them so soon,' said Kathryn walking towards the window.

She saw a figure of a lady dressed in black. 'Are you expecting someone else?' asked Geraldine, pouring herself a cup of Earl Grey. The women could hear Dawson answer the door and then he knocked and entered the sitting room.

'There is a lady to see Sebastien but I explained she would need to talk to you, Ma'am. Her name is Mrs Marjorie Wright,' Dawson announced standing at the door. Kathryn sat frozen to her chair as Geraldine put her cup down splashing the tea on the tray.

REFERENCES:

The Lime Tree is a tree for lovers. In France and Switzerland, the lime is a symbol of fertility.

Limes were planted to celebrate different battles, which freed countries from the domination of others.

Orange Lilies were The Prince of Orange's own regiment in 1701. In 1701 the 35th Battalion (Royal Sussex) were nicknamed the 'Orange Lilies'. King William of Orange gave them special permission to wear the orange facing on their uniforms. The uniform bore the French Lilies of Gold. The 35th Battalion in the *Orange Lilies of Dallington Place* are a fictional battalion in the First World War.

Illustrations by Sir Muirhead Bone. Official British War Artist. (1876-1953)
